THE ANDERSONS

VOLUME ONE: ENTER AMELIA

The thief cometh not, but for to steal, and to kill, and to destroy:
I am come that they might have life, and that
they might have it more abundantly.
John 10:10

Paula Rae Wallace

Order this book online at www.trafford.com
or email orders@trafford.com

Most Trafford titles are also available at major online book retailers.

Printed in the United States of America.

ISBN: 978-1-4669-4791-7 (sc)
ISBN: 978-1-4669-4788-7 (hc)
ISBN: 978-1-4669-4787-0 (e)

Library of Congress Control Number: 2012912777

Trafford rev. 03/14/2014

 www.trafford.com

North America & international
toll-free: 1 888 232 4444 (USA & Canada)
fax: 812 355 4082

DEDICATION

This book is lovingly dedicated to my family for their endurance and longsuffering as I get caught up in writing and the world of my books. To my husband of thirty-five years, Richard Wallace, and my two children and their families, I love y'all.

Thank you, too, to friends and readers whose encouragement means more than they could ever guess!

And I praise the Lord for saving me and allowing me to serve Him with my life and through my books. May they bring honor and glory to Him!

CREDITS

Cover map provided courtesy of Arkansas Highway and Transportation Department.

Thank you to the people at <u>Enstrom</u> <u>Candies</u> in Grand Junction, Colorado, for my growing up memories of their almond toffee, and for giving me permission to name them in my books. (Mallory sends their delectable confections as business gifts!)

This book is entirely fictional, in characters and storyline!

Who's Who~

MALLORY ERIN O'SHAUGHNESSY ANDERSON: Born in Boston, but brought up in tiny Murfreesboro, Arkansas, Mallory O'Shaughnessy received Jesus as Savior as a seven-year old at Vacation Bible School. Soon, her doting father, Patrick, and her disconnected mother, Suzanne, made decisions for Christ, too. While seeming poor, Patrick's dealing in junk, tinkering with inventions, and hand-mining regional Diamonds, was creating a fortune! Overcome with grief at his death during her junior year of high school, Mallory's future would have seemed terrifying, but for her trust in the Lord. With the help of a guardian and his family to oversee her fortune and her education, she moved forward, enjoying travel, her studies, and taking ownership of *DiaMo Corporation*. Relocated to a Dallas Mansion, she tries to live by her Dad's last wishes and find God's will for her life. But David Anderson is always there, pulling impishly at her!

THE ANDERSONS: Pastor John Anderson, his wife Lana, and their five children; David, Tammi, Jeff, Janni, and Melody moved to Murfreesboro to pastor Faith Baptist Church when David was a second grader. David and Mallory became instant friends, and because of David's inviting Mallory to VBS, she fell in love with Jesus, and never looked back. And, she fell in love with David! David, tall, dark, handsome, smart, and hard-working, faces problems of coming of age in a pastor's home, while pulled by the lure of the world. After a few bobbles and a shaky start, can he get back on track? And be in God's will? And be the kind of man that Mallory would consent to marry?

DANIEL AND DIANA FAULKNER: Daniel Faulkner, a third-generation well-respected Geologist and his wife Diana, get acquainted with Patrick O'Shaughnessy when Patrick hires *GeoHy*, the Faulkner's firm, to assess Arkansas Diamonds' flow patterns. Aware of his critical heart ailment, and with the Christianity of the two men forming a bond, Patrick asks the couple to help oversee his daughter in the event of his death. After prayer, they consent, knowing it will be an added responsibility. But unaware of what a totally wild and thrilling ride it will be! As dangers threaten, can they get everything into place? With three children of their own, who don't know how to deal with an outsider, and then the births of three more children, their life is never dull.

ERIK BRANSOM: A seasoned FBI agent visits Murfreesboro, Arkansas to assess accusations against a local sheriff of questionable character who possibly has ties to organized crime. Overwhelmed by the scope of his job and rising crime and corruption in the US, he stops by to visit Pastor John Anderson in his small church office. A life-changing transaction takes place in the crusty man's life, as he receives Christ and a new viewpoint on everything. As he falls in love with and marries Suzanne O'Shaughnessy, his link to Mallory, the Andersons, and the Faulkners, becomes complete. He advises the families in their security concerns, especially, dealing with repeated threats to Mallory.

SHANNON, SHAY, AND, DELIA O'SHAUGHNESSY: At age seventeen, Mallory reunites with her two cousins and grandmother who live in Boston. Estranged from Delia when they left Catholicism, Mallory and her Daddy pray and pray for her to find the truth in the Bible. But it isn't until after Patrick's demise, that Shay and Delia arrive in Murfreesboro for the will, that they hear the Gospel and respond to its call. Shannon, the older of Mallory's two cousins, arrives in Murfreesboro for a far more sinister purpose; that of his criminal father and other mob figures. With ties to the conniving sheriff and hit man Merrill Adams, Shannon is headed for trouble. However, Erik Bransom and the Lord intervene in his life! Sadly, his father, Ryland, dies mysteriously in prison. To the family's regret they have no assurance of his ever receiving the Lord.

LILLY COWAN: An Israeli Diamond Council executive, she becomes involved with American Diamonds and the effect they could have on the carefully controlled market! She maneuvers in the shadowy spy world of protecting Israeli interests, while trying to ignore the other ugly things world espionage brings to light. When the small violin virtuoso, Cassandra Faulkner, captures her attention, she rushes to Tulsa to wrest the little girl into her control. That begins an interesting interplay between the brittle executive and the strong-willed little musician.

HERB AND LINDA CARLTON: Herb enters the narrative as a pawn shop owner in Hope, Arkansas. Erik Bransom seeks him out as a witness in an investigation, and unexplainably invites the man to join an excursion to Turkey. On the trip, Herb falls in love with Mallory's Aunt Linda, and Mallory and Diana become aware that he is the jewelry craftsman they need for their designs. Herb, his son and daughter-in-law, Merc and Nell, with their four sons take the leap to found *Carlton, Corporation*, while keeping the pawn business.

ROGER AND BETH SANDERS: Roger Sanders owns a mid-size chemical company, *Sander's Corporation* in Hope. At Patrick's demise, Roger rehires Suzanne, and she efficiently handles much of his load as executive assistant. Roger has accepted the Lord as a result of Patrick and Mallory's testimonies, and Beth followed suit. Their four children, Constance, Katrina, Emma, and Evan, are all saved and they're a close-knit family. Constance is married and has two little ones; Katrina has been in school in the Northwest; Emma and Mallory's cousin Shay are an item. Roger has been a huge boat racing and yachting enthusiast, but realizes it has taken a toll on his Christianity when he didn't think it could.

DARRELL HOPKINS AND JANICE COLLINS: Mallory's two primary security people.

TAD CRENSHAW: The foreman of the small alluvial Diamond operation on the banks of the Little Missouri River.

KERRY LARSON: Dallas-based corporate attorney retained by Patrick O'Shaughnessy to form his corporation and to assist Mallory through the terms of the will. Kerry falls in love with Tammi Anderson, and she with him. They face a long wait due to a marked age difference. Kerry is basically a good guy and Christian, but Tammi sometimes clouds his perception. His senior partners aren't impressed by her.

Blythe and Bryce Billingsley are wealthy, socialite twins from Florida, who lost their parents suddenly in a diving accident. Becoming aware of Mallory and her loss of her father, they make contact. Mallory's Christian testimony gets through to Blythe more quickly than to the hard-headed Bryce! Blythe falls in love with, and marries Samuel Carlton; while the rebellious Bryce talks Lisette Schliemann into running off with him. In spite of their disastrous start, the Lord continues to tenderly help Lisette!

TABLE OF CONTENTS

Chapter 1: *AMAZEMENT*

Twenty-one year old David Anderson leaned back against a tree trunk, surveying his wife of a week with wonder. She was a beauty, with sculpted features and porcelain skin. Coppery hair glinted in the sunlight. Tall and slender, she was both athletic and graceful. Her features challenged him impishly as she sat astride her bike. "Let's race back to the house."

He laughed, his deep brown eyes meeting her gaze. "Maybe later, once I've had some nourishment."

She shook her head wonderingly. She couldn't figure out how he ate what he did, and stayed hungry. She shoved down the kickstand, and dropped down next to him in the fragrant blanket of earth, leaves, and pine needles. "Nourishment won't help you beat me!"

He pulled her near, giving her a lingering kiss. "I'm sure you could beat me," he assented. "But we aren't racing! For the same reason I won't let you ride *Zakkar* much right now."

She beamed at the mention of her Arabian, a beautiful little mare, technically a Gray, silvery white and beautiful. His wedding gift to her!

"Well, I wasn't sick at all this morning. I think I've been fighting a stomach bug. And stop kissing me; I can't think when you do."

"We're on our honeymoon, so you should take a break from thinking anyway."

Mallory Erin O'Shaughnessy Anderson was something else! Fabulously wealthy and president of a couple of corporations, and on the boards of others; she retained her equilibrium, and her Christian testimony. But, she was a tough competitor!

1

From David's first day transferring into second grade at Murfreesboro Elementary, Mallory had been his friend-and rival! Her first words to him: "Hi, I'm Mallory, and I can beat you at anything!" They had weathered some peaks and valleys since that day.

He remembered inviting her to *Faith Baptist's* Vacation Bible School where his dad was the new pastor, not because he cared about her getting saved, but because he couldn't bear a summer of separation. But, she got saved the first night, and turned into the most steadfast Christian he had ever known: aside from his dad and mom.

He twisted the lid off a Thermos® and poured it full of milk, offering it to her. Then he gulped thirstily from the remainder. Baloney sandwiches, chips, and cookies; he gobbled his and finished what she couldn't manage of hers. He tilted her face up and gazed into deep hazel eyes, turned cool green reflecting the forest tones. "Okay, Mrs. Anderson, we are not racing! We're just out together for a nice ride. Trust me; you don't have to prove anything to me."

⊰ ⊱

Daniel Faulkner paused in the midst of a hectic morning at *GeoHy* to phone Diana. "Hi, any word?"

Diana laughed. "Nothing like coming straight to the point without formalities! I'm having a frustrating morning, although you forgot to ask."

He laughed in kind. "Sorry, Di! Things are crazier here than usual, so I'm calling on the run. What's frustrating about your morning? If the kids are disobeying, tell them I'll deal with them later."

"Well, that's only part of it; I'm trying to get some cooperation from the company that's doing the *'Fear Not' Sparrow Lamps.* We have stacks of backorders we can't fill, and this new character is a jerk to deal with. I guess he doesn't take women in business seriously. Of course, Zave and Nadia's fighting in the background doesn't lend to my aura of professionalism. We should get a Nanny to help with them some of the time-"

"Okay, Honey, I gotta go. We can talk later." He escaped. He was glad for his wife's thriving business, but the deal had always been that they would rear their own children. The word *Nanny* didn't sit well with him. He raced to the conference room to preside over a meeting with his head Geologists.

2

❧ ❧

Caramel Du Boise drove through the deep green *Arkansas* countryside. Before beginning her internship at Johns Hopkins, she was taking her first real vacation, ever. Her starting point was Pensacola, Florida, where she had purchased her first car. It was nothing fancy, but it was hers, and it was new and economical. Her first destination, Orlando, for *Disney*, and Mallory and David's wedding. From there, it was home to Arkansas for a visit with family. She amped up her music! Her mother and a cousin were meeting her in the resort town of Hot Springs: kind of a cool treat for all three of them. She was excited! God was good to her. When her cute ideas spring-boarded her toward her privately cherished dream, she had feared how it might affect family members. Surprisingly, they were proud of her; and rather than demanding that she support them, they were following her lead about pursuing worthwhile goals of their own. Not just amazing! Miraculous! She greeted her family members with tears and hugs.

With lunch finished, her cousin Denise started telling her about all that was happening in their small church in Glenwood. Then, suddenly, she was blasting David and Mallory, repeating the words of the Pastor, Graham Wilcox.

"What?" Caramel's voice was incredulous. "Girl, you know that's not true! You should have straightened him out!"

"Now, Hon, he's a man of God," her mother reproved.

"Yes'm, he is, but Mama, you know about David and Jeff, and Duke, and what all they're doing! You know how much we despaired of Duke!" Her eyes snapped indignantly. Her brother, Duke, had been in jail, and headed toward yet more serious trouble, until Agent Bransom helped him. Then, David took the chance of putting him to work. "And look at him! Look at scads of men who have turned their lives around since that property couldn't get approval as a camp for kids!"

"Yeah, but Anderson's real agenda is to bring these guys in for cheap labor-smacks of slavery to me-to turn what Mr. O'Shaughnessy designated as a kids' Bible Camp into a country show place for Mallory. Mr. O'Shaughnessy made sure Mallory had one mansion! How many does she need?"

Caramel frowned. "I don't know. Pretty sure she's got a big one going up in Heaven, too. If she gets ten mansions, it's none of our worry. I think

David's done back-flips and jumpin' through hoops to satisfy our preacher's demands, and honor Mr. O'Shaughnessy's wishes."

They changed the subject, moving on; just gossip to them, but it weighed on Caramel.

※ ※

Back on their bikes, David and Mallory rode deeper into the woods where it was cool and serene. It was fun; they hadn't ridden bikes together in years. "Well, we still have eight days of honeymoon time allotted to us." They paused to watch a stream, sparkling in the sunlight. "Do you want to go someplace else next week?"

Mallory rested on her handlebars. "Like where"?

He shrugged. "I'm not sure. I'm thinking if you keep having this sudden nausea, a flight might be miserable; that leaves us with someplace within driving distance. San Antonio is pretty cool, I think."

"Yeah, I've heard it's pretty romantic. I like being here, except, it's like you're still working some of the time."

"Well, I wanted the kitchen finished before the wedding, but the appliances got held up in freight. It's coming together, finally. I'm not working that hard; just yelling at people occasionally. Do you like it up here?"

Her eyes met his, glowing. "I love it up here!"

Let's go saddle up your horse and let you have a little ride. Then, you should take a nap. Maybe we can sneak a steak over at the *Daisy* Lodge later, without seeing anyone we know."

"Sounds like a great plan. Red Sox play later, too; don't forget."

To her amazement Jeff had already saddled *El Capitan*. She watched as David saddled *Zakkar*.

"Okay, now remember," he whispered as she swung herself up into the saddle, "you need to let her know who's boss." He handed her the reins and she felt the animal quiver.

"Whoa," David steadied the mare with a firm hand.

Tears of frustration filled Mallie's eyes. "I can do it. It's just–I spend my life proving to everyone that I'm the boss! I just want to be friends with her!"

He nodded understanding. "You're getting there; she isn't nearly as jittery as she was." He mounted *Cap'n*, leading *Zakkar* into the arena. After

4

a couple of times around, he returned the reins. They rode side by side, then, allowed the pace to quicken to a trot! Mallory felt elated!

⊰ ⊱

Erik Bransom checked his phone; his pastor, John Anderson. He smiled. Usually, he was thrilled to talk to him, but lately everyone was attempting to coax him to make the FBI look into where the honeymoon couple's destination. He had worked his way up the hierarchy, but evidently his friends gave him more credit than he deserved. The *Bureau* wasn't their personal detective agency.

He studied a report placed on his desk earlier; a report by a special task force looking into a rash of recent home-invasions in various cities across the country. He shook his head. Amazing! Suzanne's hunch seemed to be right-on! Most home-security-system companies were what they seemed to be: a way to help people safeguard their homes and possessions. But sadly, one had hit upon a scheme to stimulate business! Sad! It could give an entire industry a black eye, and lead to more regulations. He sighed. Another sad part of the scheme was that it targeted the poor and elderly. He couldn't figure out how people could operate that way and still sleep at night. And the home incursions; doing minimal property damage without taking anything, would be low on any DA's list to prosecute. But with the nationwide scope, a Federal DA would put an end to the racket. He doubted anyone would do any serious time, even if a link could be proven between a corporation's orchestrating such a plot, and the people carrying out the crimes in the neighborhoods.

His phone vibrated on his desk once more. Faulkner! He wished everyone would relax. He trusted David, but the others were getting on his nerves. Mallory was special.

⊰ ⊱

Kerry Larson placed a call to his father-in-law-to-be, Pastor John Anderson. Larson, with the law firm *Jacobson & Jacobson*, was Mallory's chief corporate counsel.

"Good afternoon, Pastor. I heard from my client, and they seem to be doing fine."

5

"Well, okay, where are they?" The tidbit of information was a teaser; not solid information.

"Well, I'm really not at liberty to say anything further. I thought that information might relieve your worries."

It didn't! It made the pastor wonder why Mallory needed to contact her attorney when she wasn't contacting anyone else Maybe they were concocting documents for David to sign, after the fact, since he hadn't signed pre-nuptials. He was agonized! As much as he loved his son, he questioned if he could ever be a match for Mallory!

⊰ ⊱

Mallory napped, then, watched part of a baseball game while she dressed for dinner. David brought her an apple, sliced and peeled.

"Ugh," she moaned. "We're on our way to eat." She took a nibble. "See, these are treats for horses."

He remembered a corporate meeting at Hal's lodge, over four years previously, and Mallory's affinity for Larson's Apples. "I thought you really liked apples," he apologized.

"Yeah, I did. Nothing seems too appealing right now."

Still, she didn't get sick again and the drive to *Daisy* and the dinner overlooking the lake were incredible. Diners gave the couple admiring glances, but they escaped without running into any acquaintances.

"It's a pretty night. Let's rent a boat and paddle around for a while; want to?" Her shining eyes made him want to. But as he studied the forest, lining one edge of the lake, he knew from a safety standpoint, it wasn't the best idea. Mallory's personal security personnel, usually in close proximity to her, had been left behind for honeymoon privacy. It doubled her new husband's anxiety for her safety. It was totally on him! Well, he relied on the Lord, but there was no sense in being foolish.

Week two was even better than week one; and the time flew by. They bicycled, rode horse back, and played pool. David began giving her archery lessons, and taught her some personal self-defense moves. The nausea recurred at sporadic times. They had attended church services from Hot Springs to Texarkana. Immensely proud of his new bride, David's plan had been to attend *Faith Baptist*. But then he had agreed with Mallory that two weeks away from other members of their group would be better. They all tended to be clingy.

On Saturday, while Mallory went to the stable to tell *Zakkar* good-bye, David issued orders to his foremen and gave warning to the men who were currently in the work camp.

The drive to Dallas was slow and agonizing, with Mallory's being the sickest yet. David was ready to pull into a hospital at Mt. Pleasant; she could dehydrate so easily. The gravity of being a husband, and being responsible for her well-being, was sinking in. Then, thankfully, the vomiting ceased as suddenly as it started and she fell asleep.

He carried her over the threshold of the Dallas mansion, ignoring the surprised fluttering of the household staff. "We didn't know you were coming~"

She gazed around her suite in disbelief as he placed her down on the bed. "What happened here?" Her snowy suite was remodeled! Seriously remodeled! "You did this?"

His eyes met hers guiltily. He couldn't tell from her tone if it was just a question, or an accusation. "Hey, I've been with you the whole time~"

She smiled weakly. "Oh, so I'm your alibi. Did you orchestrate the changes?"

"Unh, I confess to being in on it."

Tears escaped from the corners of her eyes, making him wish he hadn't touched the area. "Hey, we'll do whatever you want done. We should have run the drawings past you."

"No, I like it! You're really talented. I can't believe it; in two weeks."

"Well, two and a half actually, they were tearing out walls almost before you were down the drive on the way to Florida."

─ ⚞ ⚟ ─

Kerry Larson arrived at the *GeoHy* offices in Tulsa fifteen minutes ahead of the appointment on Monday morning.

"What kind of papers are we signing here?" Daniel's question was tense.

"Well, we might as well wait for David and Mallory to get here, and we can all go over it together. She's basically handing the Candy Store over to him."

Daniel gave him a sharp glance. That didn't sound good. He felt a moment of acute panic! One of the elevators dinged, and Diana stepped off; followed immediately by the ding of the other one, announcing the newlyweds! Diana embraced them both warmly, then stepped back, concerned, as she took in Mallory's pallor and dark circles. Daniel swung open the glass door to the office suite.

"Hey, welcome back!" He shook David's hand and placed a peck on Diana's cheek. "Kerry's here already, so we might as well get started." He ushered them to the conference room.

David was nervous, too. He wasn't sure what he was here to sign. And he was worried by Diana's reaction to Mallory's appearance. Office staff offered coffee, juices, and assorted pastries. Mallory helped herself liberally; and strangely, he had no appetite.

Diana grasped the import of the paperwork before Daniel finished perusing it. Her bright blue eyes met Mallory's. "You must trust him."

Daniel was pretty much speechless.

Mallory shrugged nonchalantly. "If I didn't, I wouldn't have married him."

The Faulkners were amazed by the wisdom of her words. And, they had been accused of railroading Mallory into the marriage. Like anyone could railroad Mallory into anything she didn't want to do. She had married David because she loved him and trusted him. If she trusted him with her heart and her life; why would she not trust him as a business equal?

And Daniel nearly sagged with relief. None of the new structure affected his and Diana's positions and shares, whatsoever. David was co-everything with Mallory. They worked on paperwork for him to sign on all the accounts and obtain corporate credit cards. Stationery would feature David's name at the top, as well as Mallory's: Now Mallory Anderson, rather than O'Shaughnessy.

With that finished, Daniel turned to Mallory. "I'm meeting with all the *Geologists* in the Bistro at noon. I've wanted to invite you in in an advisory capacity. Are you interested?"

She was, but she shot David a questioning glance.

"If you're still feeling okay, and you want to," he acquiesced. "I brought along plenty to keep me busy. Is this room going to be in use?" His question directed toward Faulkner.

"No, it's free. Make yourself at home. We'll send lunch up to you." He smiled at Diana. "You want to join us down there for a bite? How long did your mother agree to watch the kids?"

She put her best smile on him. "Do you have time to call this guy for me?"

He tried to disguise his aggravation. "Di, just go in my office, and take care of it. The kids aren't here to cry and fight in the background."

"Well, just a masculine voice~"

David stepped in. "Is it something I can handle? You go down and enjoy lunch while the kids are taken care of."

Diana hesitated, but Mallory nodded enthusiastically

"Just try to be nice; it's really important." Mallory stressed.

Diana gave him the number and name, briefly describing the nature of the problem.

He kissed Mallory, watching them depart, before making the call. He doodled a note to himself: **Be nice**. Mallory's instructions! He usually tried being nice, first. Must mean the guy he was about to contact, Ted Norton, was a total idiot, jerk, moron. He used his new password to access a file regarding *Breeng the Lite, Inc.* He scoffed at the corporation's name. Three words and two of them were seriously misspelled! He studied the file: orders placed and filled for the cute little *Sparrow* nursery lamps. The orders kept increasing from the company owned predominantly by Caramel, *Sparrow Nest Products, Inc.* Payments for the lamps were always prompt, to take advantage of the discount. He sat, hands steepled, studying the screen. He couldn't figure out why Diana or Mallory should have to repeat themselves to this guy. He googled the company, jotting down pertinent information. He was armed with names for moving up the chain of command. Still, he didn't rush to make the call. As an architect and builder, he had some dealings with lighting manufacturers. There was more than one fish in the sea. Even if another company charged a little more per unit, if they could keep up with delivery on orders, it would be worth changing over.

He helped himself to the three remaining Danishes. It would probably be best not to tackle a difficult call on an empty stomach. He punched in the number on the *GeoHy* line, and the guy declined to answer the call. 'Be Nice,' he doodled again, placing the call using his cell.

"Helloooo, Ted here!" came a jovial voice. "How can I shed light on your subject today?"

"Hey, there, Ted, how ya doin', man? Name's David Anderson and I wondered if your company would be interested in manufacturing for a rapidly expanding company."

"Sure Dave! What company did you say you're with?"

"I said, 'David! I'm an *Architect* and builder, and I'm interested in ordering volume on small fixtures in commercial properties."

Confused silence! Ted Norton was aggravated with himself for getting snagged. He should have known the 'unknown' caller, following his declining the *GeoHy* call, was a set-up!

"Hello, Ted, you still there? I didn't lose you, did I?" David's voice edged on mockery!

Ted came back with both barrels blazing, making uncalled for comments about David's marriage to his boss. Pretty crude! David wondered if the guy had used uncalled for remarks to either Diana or Mallory.

"Okay, if we can get back on track, yes, I am calling in regards to your delay in filling our orders."

"Well, Dave, you're wasting both of our time, because I've gone over everything several times with Mrs. Faulkner. That dame doesn't get it, evidently."

David scrawled, BE NICE!! Bigger. "Yeah, women"! He commiserated. "So, why don't you go over it for me, and I'll try to draw a picture for the girls they can grasp?"

"Well, they're such small potatoes to us! We've tried to help them along with those silly little gadgets~"

"Really, I looked your company up on-line, and it doesn't look like your business volume is that big. I think you need their 'gadget' business. You accept their payments, and then you don't pay your suppliers. Now you can't meet production. Maybe you should stop selling until you can produce the goods."

Silence!

"Look, we understand business and growing pains," David continued. "As our sales expand, so should your revenue. Our working together should be mutually beneficial. That's frankly why we've been more than a little surprised by your seeming indifference to our calls. Maybe I should ask to speak to Bill Johnson; is he available?"

David doodled more 'Be Nice' reminders while he 'held' to obnoxious background music.

"Bill Johnson has stepped away from his desk. Please leave a message at the sound of the tone."

David rolled his eyes at the empty room. Was it really necessary to hold for eight minutes to get that?" He disconnected, dialing *Breeng the Lite's* main number. His call was answered by recording, but he pressed the extension for the ladder rung above Johnson, Cal Eckridge.

"Good afternoon, this is Cal; how may I help you?"

"Hello, Mr. Eckridge, my name is David Anderson, and I'm calling in reference to our latest order with *Breeng the Lite* for some *Sparrow* lamps. We keep having our delivery date pushed forward, and we can't get to the basis of the problem. We need to supply our customers with the items they've ordered from us. Our company's reputation is on the line."

"Well, Anderson, we can relate to that. But we do have other customers, and we're trying to service everyone and their orders. We've requested a little patience."

"Well, yes, Sir, and you've gotten some. But the truth is, this is business, and if you can't deliver, we need to move on to someone who can. It's a simple concept, actually."

Cal Eckridge had been threatened before. "Someone like whom?"

David had done some quick homework, and he also knew of lighting fixture companies from his building experiences. He named off a short list.

"M-m-m-h-m-m," Eckridge's acknowledgment was thoughtful. "Have you contacted any of their sales departments yet?"

"No, I haven't. I thought this relationship might be salvageable"

"Well, I'm familiar with the 'Big Boys', so to speak. Let me tell you something, David, they play 'Hard Ball'!"

David wanted to laugh, but he restrained himself. "Meaning?"

"Look, I don't mind admitting we're a start-up company, and we were desperate to get a toe-hold in the industry. We bid low on the *Sparrow* lamps, figuring y'all would never move the ten thousand in your initial order. Now we go in the hole for every contract of yours we take, while we're receiving orders from other places we actually make money on. It's a simple concept, actually."

David laughed at the come-back with his line. "It's such a 'simple concept' that I'm pretty sure Mrs. Faulkner would have understood it–if anyone had bothered to explain it. I'm sorry, but I can't understand treating a customer that way."

"Well, we were over-committed with them, and we kept thinking they would just go away."

David circled his 'Be Nice' notations with hearts, before his laughter again eased the tension. "Well, you may get your wish, and we might go away. You said the 'Big Boys' play 'Hard Ball', which I assumed was a metaphorical warning that your major competitors will charge us a lot more for each unit. Would you be interested in revisiting our contract, and renegotiating a price that would be mutually beneficial to both of us? How soon can you be in contact about it?"

Cal's entire attitude seemed to shift. "We'll get right on it. We can have something definitive by, say, three?"

"Sounds good; eager to hear from you!" David disconnected, feeling like he had remained 'nice' and accomplished something.

He checked the time. Strictly nice timepiece! Mallory had barely been gone forty-five minutes. He worried about her, but at least Diana hadn't insisted on rushing her to the ER.

A delivery kid appeared with a huge deli-style sandwich, and he enjoyed it as he contacted various lighting manufacturers by e-mail. Even as he compared their sites, he was convinced that Cal's warning about how the 'Big Boys' played 'Hard Ball' wasn't empty talk.

He accessed another of Mallory's files, studying the price list of the various *Sparrow* products. The cute little lamp was inexpensive. If the supplier raised the price, they could raise their retail and still be fair and competitive.

Cal Eckridge shot an e-mail prior to his phone call. The new proposal was neat and complete. The jump in price per item was significant. He surveyed the pages thoughtfully. It looked good. The new price probably compared with the larger rival company prices. The obvious advantage of staying with *Breeng* was that they already had the piece in production.

"Cal, this looks okay. We should both garner some earnings now. If I okay the new price, can this order get into production yesterday?" David's voice cajoled.

"Can you okay the price? Don't you need to check with your wife or Mrs. Faulkner? But, the best I can do, because of the factory-run in progress now, is begin your production Monday. Ready to ship Thursday at close of business."

"Sounds good. Send me a confirmation e-mail." David ignored the comment questioning his authority.

He nodded thanks to a secretary who appeared with a couple of Dr. Peppers for him and composed a to-do list. One of his first tasks he set for himself was a visit to the Diamond dig site. Mallory had taken his suggestion to move Peterson up to head security for her entire company. Now, David needed to make sure that Diamond production didn't suffer because of the move. That task could best be undertaken when they were in residence at the Ranch. He planned tentatively to return to *Arkansas*

Thursday afternoon for a long week-end, and he could make the drive up to check on Tad Crenshaw and the gems. That meant he needed to find some Dallas-based jobs to do in the meanwhile.

He placed a call to *Carlton, Corporation*. Linda Carlton answered the call, her voice crisp.

"Good afternoon, Aunt Linda, this is your new nephew-by-marriage."

A stunned silence before she recovered her aplomb. "David! This is a surprise. What can I do for my favorite nephew-by-marriage? I guess you're home from your honeymoon. Everyone's been trying to figure out where y'all went? Is Mallie okay?"

"Yes, Ma'am, we're back, and Mallory's fine. The purpose for my call is that I hoped to come by tomorrow and see your set-up; maybe talk to Herb and Merc."

"Well, is that what Mallory wants you to do? You know, we own our company. And *DiaMal* contracts with us."

"Yes, Ma'am, I understand that. And because you are so crucial to our business, I wanted to tour it, and have a greater respect and understanding for what y'all do. Mallory's actually in a meeting up here in *Tulsa* with Faulkner and his *Geologists*. I'm kind of penciling in my own agenda for the week, and being on the same page with *Carlton* heads my list. If I could come about ten-thirty, then I could see the operation and we could all go to lunch together."

"With Mallory, too?" Linda Carlton's voice was hopeful.

"Well, I won't commit for her. She's been out of the office for three weeks, and she's backlogged."

"Okay, David, let me buzz in and ask the guys."

He waited. At least their background music was more tasteful.

⊰ ⊱

Diana met Daniel at the backdoor as he entered from the garage. "How was the meeting? Was Mallory okay?"

Daniel kissed her. "Yeah, she seemed to be. You know, the guys all looked at her askance when I introduced her. But she spent the first hour and a half without saying a word until she was sure she grasped what we were talking about. Then, her contributions spoke for themselves. She's a smart girl." He laughed. "Not as smart as you, though! David got a promise

13

of delivery on your lamps from your guy, but the price per unit went up appreciably."

"That's what I didn't want!"

He laughed at her consternation. "You don't always get what you want. David's negotiation was good, and within ten days, you'll be able to catch up on backorders. You'll take a little hit on them until you raise your prices in your catalog."

"We don't want to take a little hit."

He pulled her into his arms. "Your business has been amazing, and I think you've gotten a little spoiled by your successes. But, Honey, if you're in business over the long haul, there'll be some 'hits'. The guy wasn't disrespecting you for being a woman, or hearing kids in the background. You're the one who wouldn't listen to them about the price change. There are some inevitabilities we have to face in life~whether we like them or not."

Her wide blue eyes met his. "Oh!"

Chapter 2: ACTION

David arrived at *Carlton* five minutes early, and Linda greeted him warmly, offering him a cup of coffee. He declined, and Merc appeared to guide his tour.

"This is a secured facility," Merc opened. "If you noticed, we seem to blend in with blocks of run-of-the-mill warehouses, and nothing announces this is a jewelry production facility. We have state-of-the-art security for insurance purposes."

"Yeah, I appreciate the tour. I understand confidentiality. I have no intentions of doing anything to in any way jeopardize what you have going on here. I've heard about your safes within safes that protect your inventory of raw materials. I'm mostly interested in watching some of the magic the jewelers do, to turn little bits and pieces into finished pieces of exquisite jewelry."

Merc nodded. "Well, there's more to it than meets the eye." He sounded proud of himself, and David nodded his understanding. Surprisingly, Anderson wasn't interested in the quick tour, but lingered at each phase, asking the craftspeople probing questions.

"You're really interested in this?" Herb had joined them.

David laughed. "Yes, Sir, I can hardly believe it, myself. I think I could spend a week here without grasping the full extent of what you do, but I need to move along. Thank you for allowing me the tour. What about lunch?"

"Yeah, sure, we can do that. Me and Merc?"

"Definitely, if you can both get away! And Aunt Linda, too, if she can forward the phones. If you don't get tired of the Mezzanine cafe in our building, Mallory might join us for a few minutes."

"How can we be tired of where we've never been?" Herb grumbled.

Within a few minutes, they were seated at a table with soups and sandwiches ordered. Mallory appeared, scooting close to her new husband. "How did you lure Uncle Herb and Aunt Linda here?"

"I just invited them. They actually allowed me an extensive tour of the facility, and I'm impressed." He kissed her cheek. "Still having a good morning?"

Mallory frowned at Chicken Noodle soup, opting for hot tea and a pastry.

"Herb, I'm aware that you and Davis Hall have some animosity." David had tried to think of a smooth way to approach a delicate subject. But having come up with nothing, he plunged in."

Herb studied him levelly. "Why are you bringing that up?"

"Well, because they offer a course in jewelry-making, and I'd like to attempt it. If you know of another place locally, where I can enroll-"

"You want to be a jeweler?" Merc's voice echoed with amazement.

"I'm not sure I could ever attain to that level, but learning the basics would definitely broaden my knowledge base for working with Mallory." David looked Merc up and down, with his tattoos, leather jacket, and dew rag atop his shaven head. "You don't look much like a jeweler, yourself."

"You should study under Davis," Herb responded, following the round of laughter about his son. "It will be good basis- We thought you were a rancher," he interrupted himself.

❧ ❧

Gossip filtered down that David and Mallory, finished honeymooning, had signed important documents and were back working from the *Dallas* office. Suzanne felt a pang of envy that her sister had already seen Mallory, and her daughter had yet to be in touch with her. Erik, always the voice of reason, assured her there was no reason for her to worry. He was right. Mallory showed up for a board meeting at *Sanders, Corporation*. She had tried to beg her way out, with Roger Sanders, founder and Chairman of the chemical company, but he insisted upon her being present, if possible.

"Have you gotten any rest?" Suzanne's face was a study of concern. "You look exhausted!"

"I have, Mom. I'm doing fine."

16

"Where's David?"

Mallory smiled. "Well, Roger wants him on the board of directors, too; but not for tonight's meeting. So he dropped me off, and he's spending the evening with Shannon. We're doing great, Mom. Don't worry."

"I'm not worried, Mallie, but I'm taking you over to the infirmary." She noted the obstinacy on her daughter's face. "You can stretch out and nap while I finish getting everything ready for the meeting."

Mallory gave in. The nap sounded suddenly appealing, and although she wanted to do some catching up with her mom, she realized she would face a bevy of curious questions. She was asleep immediately.

The meeting featured a meal of roast chicken, stuffing, mashed potatoes and gravy, and dinner rolls.

She did a fair job on it, missing David to gobble up the remainder. The meeting came to order, and she listened attentively to the 'old business'. Then, the 'new business' addressed the new acquisition *Sanders, Corporation* was purchasing. Mallory was familiar with the various aspects of the purchase, and she struggled to stay awake.

One of the board members made a motion to offer a finder's fee to David, and it was seconded immediately.

Mallory raised her hand. "Maybe I should recuse myself," she volunteered.

Sanders agreed, and she left the meeting.

David was surprised when Mallory called him so quickly. "Hey, you okay?" His concern was immediate.

"I'm fine, but they addressed some issues that didn't pertain to me, so I've been cut loose. I can do some work in Mom's office until you get free, if you and Shannon are in the middle of anything."

"No, I'll be right out there. Sit tight where security has eyes on you until I arrive."

Pulling up, he sprang from his seat to open her door. "Where to, next"?

"Well, I'm ready to go home," she confessed sheepishly. "Do you want me to drive?"

"Do you know how?" He couldn't resist teasing. She had gotten her license, but then never had much opportunity to practice before her life had changed to one of being chauffeured by security people.

She tried to scowl, and he leaned across and kissed her. "Which home did you have in mind?"

"Wow! Such decisions! I was thinking *Dallas*, so I can get into the office before afternoon. But if we go to *the Ranch*, we can get to bed earlier. And, I can see *Zakkar*."

He nodded, putting the truck into gear. "I like Plan B. I've been thinking I need to check on the mining operation. It was my idea to move Dale Peterson, and I need to see you aren't being robbed blind because of it."

Her eyes shone. "Yeah, we can go up there, and then drive back to *Dallas* on the back roads."

"Um, I wasn't planning on taking you," he confessed.

"You're not sure it's safe?"

"I don't want to take any chances. You can sleep until you wake up, then have your devotions and get dressed. If I'm not already back by that time, you can work your phone. You should dump more on Lisette, anyway. She's a dynamo."

She nodded. "So are you going up there announced or unannounced? I don't want you walking into any trouble."

"Unannounced, but I'll be careful. I promise. Then, if we drive home, I may teach you to drive the interstate. There are things you need to know how to do, even if you never use them."

"But, if we don't drive home, we'll fly and save ourselves the tedious trip. We should leave this truck here and get you another one to use when we're in Dallas."

⊰ ⊱

Daniel helped *the Maestro* load left-over soup, bread, and pie, into his car, and watched him careen down the drive. Scary!

Back inside, he looked at the kids inquisitively. "Why are you not getting ready for bed?"

Jeremiah fought tears. "Won't Mallory still come on Tuesdays for lessons?"

"Yes, it wasn't the same at all," Alexandra chimed in.

Even Diana's countenance was woebegone.

"Look, I haven't asked David about it. Mallory had to be in *Hope*, tonight, for a board meeting at *Sanders*. Maybe we should all go in the family room for a family discussion."

He hated it when his whole family looked at him like he had seven horns with ten crowns on them.

He took his place in his La Z-boy™, and the kids perched on the edge of the sofa. Diana fought tears, not meeting his gaze.

"Okay, look, here's the deal. Our guardianship of Mallory ended when she married David. Now, I know y'all are really attached to her, but I think David plans to distance her from us a little. I think he wants to pull her back toward *Arkansas*. He knows I think the camp property isn't best from a security standpoint~" He paused, fighting his own tears as they all broke down. "You know, even just the geography's against us. The distance between Tulsa and Dallas was an obstacle. Now, they're learning to navigate between Arkansas and Dallas. That's a lot of distance, without trying to fit in trips up here. But we'll be okay. You know, we were the Faulkner family before she came into our lives~" He paused with a heavy sigh. "I know; I'm not buying it either."

"Let's take a trip to Arkansas!" Cassandra's voice sounded inspired and suddenly hopeful.

Diana jumped up. "I'll start getting things together!"

By ten P.M. they were on the road.

⊰ ⊱

"What made the board think of that?" Beth Sanders was shocked at Roger's recounting of the meeting. "Did you try to recommend a lower amount? I mean, after Mallory left, you could have carried on more discussion."

"Well, just because she was gone, didn't mean she wouldn't hear about every detail. The amount they agreed to is standard. It's just; it never occurred to me, so I wasn't as mentally prepared as I should have been. Consequently, you're blindsided by it, too."

"Do we have to give it all to him at once? Or can we leverage it out over time?" Her voice sounded hopeful.

"I don't know. If we structure it, then do we offer interest? I mean, Honey, it's worth it. We could have been paying someone to trawl for a deal like this, been out their fees, and never landed on such a deal! It's just that since it started coming together, we've gotten the dollar signs in our eyes. Paying a Finder's Fee is the only ethical thing to do, really. Beth, it isn't just the figure we get at closing; Honey, it should shoot our annual income to double what we've had. And, I might add, will also require extra work. I'm thinking of promoting Suzanne, but we're still in need of new staff, yesterday!"

"Well, you're going to keep most of the people on, in Houston; aren't you?"

"Well, *Gemhouse* has worked out that way for Mallory. If the people can switch their loyalties to us, we should be able to keep using them. I guess what's bothering both of us, is that David just married Mallory and all her money. Why should we give him ours? But, believe me, Bethy, David swung open a huge door of opportunity and possibility for *Sanders*. If it's as rosy as it seems, we may owe him a whole lot more!"

⇥ ⇤

Mallory was awake before David, and was she sick! Well, two good days! He urged her, still hugging the trash can, back into bed. She moaned weakly. "You should still do your plan. I'm eager for a first-hand report, too. I'll be okay."

He went out and did some chores, giving orders for the day to the foremen for the 'campers'. When he returned to the house, Mallory was on the balcony with her Bible. A beautiful summer day was emerging from the earlier wash of color; hot, but beautiful.

"I'm doing better. If I keep feeling okay, I'll make some hot tea in a little bit."

"Well, you have a little color back in your cheeks. I'll have my phone so you can call me if you change your mind."

She laughed. "I won't. Promise me you'll be careful." She was more concerned about the motorcycle than any peril related to the miners.

He led the bike from the garage, circling around to blow her a kiss, before heading toward his destination.

Wow, she loved him. After brewing a cup of hot tea, she pressed a lever for a ceiling fan and reclined the deck chair. The tea, lightly sugared, tasted good, and she found her place in her Bible.

The next thing she knew, the sound of vehicles awakened her.

⇥ ⇤

After a short night in a Ft. Smith, Arkansas hotel, the Faulkner family was back on the road. Daniel, in the lead SUV driven by security, traveled with Alexandra, Cassandra, and Xavier.

The other SUV carried Diana, Jeremiah, Nadia, and Ryan. Daniel spoke by HeyTell ap. "I'm feeling like this has been a fun and scenic little jaunt, but we should turn around and head home. I mean, they're newly-weds, and obviously, they want some privacy. We're crazy to sneak around the country-side, stalking them."

"Well, we can just check out the store. My mom and dad and Juliet told me it's real cute."

"What store?"

"Where they sell Alpaca products. I guess there's a snack bar. You can get ice cream. It's open to the public, and we're part of the public." Diana's voice sounded like it was settled.

"And what? We were just in the neighborhood?" Daniel thought it sounded improbable. He felt a certain degree of uncertainty. He ruefully told himself that if he'd known David was going to end up being his boss, he would have been nicer to him. He hated to express that sentiment to Diana, and especially not in front of the kids.

His voice came back. "It's a pretty far drive for ice cream!"

The kids in both vehicles laughed.

⊰ ⊱

Ivan Summers pretended to change a flat. An agent of the Arkansas Bureau of Investigation, his jurisdiction covered the western counties of the state. He was dressed carelessly, his face partially hidden by a ball cap. Cheap sunglasses replacing his normal Ray Bans, constituted the remainder of his 'under-cover' persona. With the car on the jack, he pretended to struggle against tight lug nuts as he eyed the target of his surveillance. His partner, Haslett, followed instructions to patrol occasionally, but as usual the eager-beaver was too conscientious. Annoyed, Summers was aware when the big, official, state vehicle rounded the bend and disappeared. He was mumbling under his breath when he was suddenly aware of a presence beside him.

"Forget about your tire: we'll give you a ride!"

The pressure against his ribs told him compliance was the only option.

‹⧖ ⧗›

Jeff Anderson was nervous. His older brother had ridden away a couple of hours previously, leaving him in charge of the crews, and Mallory's safety. No big deal! Just another day at the salt mines! Everything was usually quiet and peaceful to the point of being dull. But a truck had appeared with a 'delivery' from a lumber company/hardware store in one of the neighboring hamlets. Except that Jeff was pretty sure they hadn't placed an order. Now, he really felt spooked.

David had stopped doing business there several months before, because a new employee was freaky! Like, seriously creepsville! Jeff shuddered, remembering the smoldering hate emanating from the guy! If he wasn't some kind of gang member, he could start his own gang! He didn't fit the groove of easy-going, rural *Arkansas*. David didn't scare easily, but he had diverted their business to *Little Rock*. That had been for the best, because David had begun building special features into the Ranch house, and the larger lumber companies in *Little Rock* filled orders without so much curiosity and familiarity about the property being developed in the west-central part of the state. More anonymity for David and his projects!

So, what had brought the scary guy out to their doorstep? Jeff's refusing him entrance to the property had caused the smoldering expression to flare into open rage. Which, then the guy had made a feeble attempt at masking his fury; instead, trying to act friendly and conversational. "Well, where was David? Where was David's new wife? Was she with him?" The entire episode jangled alarm bells. So, the guy had left, but the palpable sense of dread lingered. Surely David would be back soon.

Jeff led his horse to the store's yard, saddling him where he could keep an eye on the road. A seemingly normal summer day, except that the usually deserted road was hopping with an array of weird vehicles. Either his imagination was over-stimulated by the unpleasant delivery attempt–or something big was going down! Something big! Something to do with the Diamonds? An attempt to grab Mallory? When she was entrusted to him? He called his brother's cell phone, but he was hardly surprised when there was no answer.

‹⧖ ⧗›

David had taken a short-cut to the site where the miners were working; his reason for riding the bike, besides the sheer fun of it. Then, maybe a tenth of a mile from his destination, he had been stopped short by a figure on the trail. David had kind of figured the idiot would jump out of the way as the bike bore down, but he stood his ground. David stopped short as a weapon sited him in. He stood frozen, surveying his adversary. And the gun!

"Shut off the bike! Dismount!" The orders were clipped. Slight accent? Maybe! David obeyed, saying nothing. The guy was shorter than David, toned and muscular. Not young; but he seemed like he could be a formidable adversary, even without his 'vaporizing' gun, or whatever it was!

A barely discernible motion with the weapon indicated David was to precede him along the trail. He did so surprised the guy didn't pat him down. The piercing eyes had probably already discerned that David carried no weapon more sinister than a mid-size pocket knife.

With the river in view, David took in the dig site interestedly. The miners seemed to be going about their business as usual. Maybe he was in the clutches of a good guy. Maybe Mallory had found this guy who was even meaner than Dale Peterson to act as watch dog for her mine. If so, she could have mentioned it. He didn't really think so, though. Not a civilian. The most astonishingly competent operative he had ever confronted. Israeli! A flash of insight!

An aged panel truck skidded to a stop in front of the car, and Summers was pushed into it. His gun and badge disappeared into hands that held them mockingly, before duct tape covered his eyes. Hands like vices held him while tape bound eyes, mouth, hands, and feet. Then, as if that hadn't rendered him helpless, a blow landed on his head. Futile struggles ceased altogether.

Mallory gazed through wooden slats of the balcony, taking in the newcomers. She was chagrined with herself for having fallen asleep. The SUVs looked like *GeoHy's*. Jeff dismounted, escorting the entire Faulkner family in the front door. Mallory couldn't imagine what a wreck she must look. She stepped to the banister overlooking the entryway and great room.

"Hi. Y'all make yourselves at home. I've been kind of lazy this morning, so I'm just starting to get ready. Give me about~"

"No, Mallory, you need to come down, right now!"

Jeff's tone startled her. "Where's David, Jeff?"

His young face was grim with the burden of responsibility. "I'm not sure. He hasn't answered his phone. I promised to look after you."

"Well, I need to go find him."

"Mallory!" Daniel's voice backed up Jeff's.

⇥ ⇤

Haslett stared blankly at the car on the jack across from the *Dierks* gas station. He couldn't figure out where his partner had disappeared. Surely, he wouldn't have entered the store. His disguise wasn't that good. He circled back through his tight route, trying to comprehend the incomprehensible!

⇥ ⇤

Adrenalin pumped through Trent Morrison's system, making his heart race and jump. Based in D.C., he was the head of all law enforcement in the National Forest System. With literally millions and millions of acres of national forests and grasslands within the fifty states and U.S. Territories, much of it remote, his responsibility was vast. Operations were going down simultaneously in eight other states, within all of the regional divisions.

He listened to the briefing, standing next to Bob Porter, his Regional Director for the Southeast.

An Army Lieutenant, Ward Atchison, team leader of a special force, presented the battle plan. This was the real thing, and everyone engaged in the joint operation wore body armor, and carried highly sophisticated weaponry.

The enemy? Members of brazen and sophisticated Mexican Drug Cartels! Audaciously operating from U.S. cities, as well as the remote areas!

But Arkansas? Yup! 'The Natural State' drew its nickname from its expanses of mountains and forests.

Porter's face was grim as the briefing ended~with no questions! Just set facial expressions. "Terri's mad at me for this. How's Sonia taking it?"

Morrison fastened gloves without meeting the other man's gaze. "I didn't ask her or go into detail about what we're doing. She thinks I've 'done my time' in the field, and that I should sit behind my desk in Washington, and wait to hear the outcome. If she were happy about my facing dangerous enemies on the front lines, I'd be worried."

"Well, you do have a way of putting things into perspective."

"Good. Looks like we're moving out"!

Trent gave fleeting thought to the Diamond miners along the banks of the *Little Missouri*. They should be out of harm's way. They mined on private lands.

Actually, the Lieutenant operated from a different mindset. Morrison's brain was long ingrained with his responsibility to government-held lands. Atchison was taking the war to every corner of the area, public or private. Like if these goons fled from federal lands to private, he should retreat and leave them alone? Oh no! They wouldn't be safe until they crossed back into Mexico! Which, Atchison was determined, was not going to happen! He had been sent here to clean house, and that was his intention!

⊰ ⊱

David was treated deferentially by Crenshaw and the miners. They already knew he was co-owner of the empire with Mallory. The 'serious' guy escorted him back to his bike, and he was on his way, eager to check on Mallory, and whether her sickness had subsided. He had downed a bottle of water on his ride in, then, at the mine site, had finished off a Dr. Pepper. Now, he wished he had snagged a bottle of *agua* for the ride back. The day was a scorcher! He paused, approaching a small stream. Nothing fit to drink! He wasn't that dumb! He doused his handkerchief, patting his face and neck with the coolness. Rocking back on his heels, he listened. The sudden silence was eerie. He wasn't a woodsman, or survivalist, or anything, but he spent as much time outside as possible. Something was wrong! The leaves seemed to have stopped their gentle rustle so they could hear better.

⊰ ⊱

Erik Bransom's day began with calamitous news, followed by more. He was having trouble concentrating, before. Aware of the war being waged in

25

the *Ouachitas* and *Ozarks*, he felt a sense of concern for anyone who might be working at the camp property. Even his pastor and family as far up as Murfreesboro. He felt fairly secure about Suzanne and the other employees of *Sanders, Corporation* in Hope. But then, he had been notified that Oscar Melville had been knifed to death at the maximum security, Federal Pen at Cañon City. Very strange! Before he could absorb that, news reached him of Ryland O'Shaughnessy's demise under similar circumstances. Surely couldn't be coincidental. But who would suddenly want both prisoners dead? And, of more import, how could they have accomplished it? His heart felt extra heavy for Delia and her two grandsons.

⊷ ⊶

Mallory's thoughts whirled. Jeff pressed a lever, and a gun cabinet appeared. Daniel chose a twenty gauge shot gun and high powered rifle, attaching an expensive scope, and checking the sites. Jeff armed himself similarly. Both men always carried side-arms. Mallory watched as they both dug into the ammo boxes. Her concern was still greater for David than for herself. A sudden racket enveloped her, clattering, swishing, and banging. Bright daylight disappeared as shutters automatically covered windows. They were basically within a fortress. Her phone buzzed in her robe pocket. A text from her husband. It meant he was still in one piece, with phone in his possession. Still, the tersely coded text did nothing to alleviate her concern.

"From David"! Her eyes were enormous. "'C e'. I need to call Erik."

"Well, that could mean anything! Including he didn't have a chance to finish." Daniel's words.

"No, C e means call Erik!" Mallory was sure of it. And David wouldn't want her to call the FBI Agent, unless he was in trouble.

Jeff led the way to a skillfully constructed *Panic Room*. Daniel had a quick chance to marvel at it. "Okay, Diana, Mallory, kids, in here."

Diana's face set resolutely. "Alexandra, you make certain you care for your brothers and sisters. Don't open until you're absolutely certain it's all clear. You all be absolutely quiet. Keep Ryan quiet." She selected similar weapons from the arsenal, taking a post adjacent to the *Panic Room*. Their two security personnel members posted themselves, one watching security monitors, and the other, where he could view both front and back exits on the main floor. Daniel and Jeff stole quietly to the second story.

-ᴴ ᴴ-

Ivan Summers moaned weakly behind the thick tape, trying to get comfortable; impossible in his bonds; and to ease his throbbing head. He could feel and smell the blood oozing from his scalp. The panel truck was still in motion, and he could discern voices, but not words. The rocking motion was unpleasant, but he didn't usually suffer from motion sickness. If he could vomit, it might degrade and slick up the tape across his mouth. If he didn't aspirate it and choke to death! The ride ended and the worst part of the journey began.

-ᴴ ᴴ-

David rose to his feet and moved from exposure along the trail into the denseness of the forest. Hot and dry, he was aware that every footfall left boot prints in the dust. He found a long, sturdy stick and scrambled the patterns, then stepped into the creek, walking upstream until he came to a spot where a birch tree jutted a branch above his head. Jumping with all his might he caught onto it. When it held his weight, he pulled himself up, crawling inward toward the trunk, making his way higher. Thankful for summer's thick foliage, he pulled a pouch from beneath his shirt and secreted it as far above his head as he could reach. Then, he sat astride the limb, considering his options. In the days of childhood, he and Mallory had been agile tree-climbers, so able to scamper up and down, and from one to the next, that Patrick O'Shaughnessy said they were like a couple of monkeys. Patrick's laughing eyes, quite a lot like Mallory's, delighting in teasing his pastor by saying the kids almost made him believe in Evolution. David felt a pang of worry for Mallory, breathing a prayer for protection. He surveyed the area surrounding him. His body, not used to climbing, and branches he wasn't sure could support his weight, were factors to consider. He berated himself for making such poor provision: no weapon, no water, and less importantly, no food. Well, he had only expected to be gone three hours, at the most.

He forced himself to think. Okay, moving up the creek didn't leave footprints, but it pretty much paralleled the major trail. He felt a vague premonition of what was transpiring around him: good guys versus bad guys. Whoever they were, it stood to reason that there were skilled trackers on both sides. A big blunderbuss like him, barging through the landscape, was probably leaving a trail visible from space. Moving from branch to branch, tree to tree, still seemed like the best option. First, he needed a weapon. He scrambled to the ground for the large stick he had used earlier; then, back on the comparative safety of his branch, he tried different ideas for attaching his opened knife to the end for use as a spear. That seemed useless, so he went to work whittling an end of the stick to a sharp point. Better idea! He whittled over his shirt spread before him, to catch the shavings. They might make good kindling later, if he needed to build a fire. His first Tarzan-like swing was successful, and he gained a foothold in the neighboring tree.

⊣ ⊢

Mallory knew Diana was an excellent markswoman, but she was still surprised Daniel and Jeff hadn't insisted she enter the *Panic Room*. Mallory thought numbly *Panic Room* was an appropriate term for the space. She gazed around her blankly. The space wasn't particularly large, but seemed remarkably efficient. Supplies of water, canned goods, and other food items with long shelf lives, lined the space. There were armaments, other survival supplies, and an emergency radio. A few books, games and jigsaw puzzles were the only forms of entertainment; no toys for occupying the little kids. She focused on Alexandra and Jeremiah, who seemed to be having some exchanges in sign language. Evidently, seeing food and snacks reminded Jeremiah he was hungry, and Alexandra felt it would be wiser to conserve on the food. Mallory hoped the situation would resolve itself before they ate their way through this many supplies. There wasn't any formula, or diapers, either. And, she was terrified for David!

⊣ ⊢

Lieutenant Atchison voiced a single command, and the unit responded immediately. Usually a team of eight, each man fulfilled his own responsibility. If the team's size was reduced by a man, the others knew how to take up the slack. And, they were one man short! Atchison's own intuition had crystallized when Richards voiced a similar concern. Trust in one another was an essential in such a tight squad and Manuel Gomez' actions had raised some red flags. He was now under guard with no communications allowed him. Hopefully, he hadn't already compromised the mission. It was still on go.

⊰ ⊱

On the second story, Jeff uncovered David's telescope, moving it so that he could scan approaches from the south. Daniel surveyed the north through the expensive scope. Traffic moved along the road without stopping or presenting any threat.

Daniel's call to Erik Bransom heightened their nervousness. Bransom was aware of the joint agency raid. The FBI was about the only agency not in play. DEA, Forestry, INS, and Army were combining to locate and destroy any drug operations being advanced in the remote areas. Crops, labs, distribution hubs, and hopefully arresting the felons without incident! Governor Bateman, without giving specifics to compromise the Federal operation, had local law enforcement agencies on alert. Ruthless thugs, fleeing before the onslaught, could possibly leave a trail of carnage. Innocent Arkansans! Erik's worry for Mallory doubled; and David's riding merrily through the crossfire didn't sound too good, either.

"Tell him," Jeff instructed, speaking while still giving his attention to the telescope, "that we've had strange vehicles along this rode, headed north, all morning. And now~" He swung the instrument on its tripod. "Now they're heading southward, riding lower. I think some of them are attempting to salvage what they can, of their product. No one around here seems to be trying to stop them."

Daniel stared at him. He was in favor of stopping them, but not right here. He relayed the message, and Erik disconnected immediately.

Correction! The FBI was in on it, too.

⊰ ⊱

Two divers entered the water of Lake Ouachita (The Navy wasn't the only branch of the Armed Services to boast of divers), and attached charges to the hull of an expensive pleasure craft. Regaining the rugged and secluded shore, they stashed the dive gear. Atchison spoke into the communications system. "Gentlemen, let's party." He watched the surface through high-powered glasses as the charges detonated. No dramatic explosion blowing the craft to kingdom come! Just a rapid rocking of the superstructure, surges of bubbles, and down she went! That took care of the gang command center. The other agencies advanced on their specified targets.

⚑ ⚐

David had reached a cliff face, perhaps fifty feet high. It provided some measure of protection from one direction. It featured a cave, maybe two-thirds of the way up, and he hesitated. Maybe he should stay put. He mocked himself silently. Maybe he should climb down, return to his bike, and go home. Probably this entire exercise was the result of a silly figment of his imagination.

His thoughts returned to his bride. She was lovely beyond description, and he loved the entire marriage-thing. He wasn't positive she was as charmed by it. She had gone into it, being pretty naïve. He sighed softly. To him, it seemed as though he had married a radiant girl, and the lights had gone out for her. He was pretty thrilled about a baby's possibly being on the way-if she was. She mostly acted shell-shocked, tolerant of him, but missing her solitude. Redoing her suite in her *Dallas* home, without mentioning it, seemed like a mistake, in retrospect.

Shots rang out, interrupting his reverie! With a start! Oh well, hey, he was ready with his sharp stick! Before he could forsake his nest, voices carried to him. He watched, senses straining, from the thick cover of leaves. A couple of guys were on the cliff top, dragging a third guy. He watched as they rigged ropes. From his vantage point, he was pretty sure that the one who seemed to be the leader was a guy he recognized as a lumber yard employee. The guy they were dragging was inert; David wasn't certain he was alive. With their ropes tied off, and the lumber-yard guy giving orders in Spanish, the other guy descended, guiding the dead guy toward the mouth of the cave. David's eyes were wide. Wow, a remote place to dispose of bodies! More shots rang out, and a drone soared above him. Terror gripped him. He was in close proximity to the bad guys if the drone was targeting them with a bomb, or something. It continued its course, moving out of his range of vision. The one guy emerged from the cave, climbing up by the rope. They really were dumping a body!

⚑ ⚐

Morrison, Porter, and other Forestry Service Law Enforcement officers watched from ambush as a convoy approached. He was amazed that these suspects hadn't just tried to make a break for safety and freedom! Well, they were terrified, for one thing! Terrified of drug Czars that didn't accept excuses for failure! These drugs were of far more consequence than their lives were. The rough county road narrowed here to a one-lane bridge, and nail strips were camouflaged beneath dust and gravel. When one vehicle's tires went flat, the following vehicles had few options for going around. Morrison was sure they'd try. He gripped the rifle and his bull horn.

⊰ ⊱

Summers felt as though he had been half-carried, half-dragged, for miles since the panel truck's stop. He thought he was conscious most of the time; he was aware of conversation in Spanish, picking up on an occasional familiar word, but not understanding their intentions regarding him! Not good! Of that, he was certain. He had a new respect for blind people–not that he knew any, or would ever have an opportunity to express his respect. But it was terrifying, being at someone's mercy, and not being able to see what was happening. Like swinging suspended from a rope, feeling like he was over an abyss. Maybe he hadn't been. That was the dread! Not being sure. He wondered vaguely if Haslett even had sense enough to look for him, or report in to the hierarchy. Surely, people were combing the woods for him. He thought he was in the woods; it smelled like it.

⊰ ⊱

Diana knelt, gripping the rifle, agonized at not knowing what was coming, or when. She worried about her children, mere yards from her, yet isolated within their cocoon. Surely Ryan was hungry. She knew, uncomfortably, that it was way past his nursing time. She heard no sounds, but doubted that by this time, they were heeding her orders to be silent. Xavier and Nadia didn't know the meaning of the word. The sound-proofing must be excellent.

⊰ ⊱

31

Daniel scoped the landscape broodingly. Because nothing had happened yet, was no reason for him to let down his guard. Still, he hoped and prayed none of the action would come their direction, and for David's safety. The 'War of Drugs' was a term he heard, practically every day, and yet he was shocked that it was here! Colliding with his world! This was only supposed to happen in other countries, or America's inner-cities! He was aware of the need for national revival, and asked the Lord for it every day. But this situation lent fresh urgency to the requests.

⌖ ⌖

David watched the other two men disappear above the cliff, still undecided what his course of action should be. If the guy in the cave were still alive, what could he do? He didn't have water, even for himself. The guy was probably dead; the cave presented difficult access; and more bad guys could venture this way at any time. Stillness settled around him. He dropped his stick and climbed down warily, making his way to the foot of the cliff. He picked up a few large stones, tying them in his shirt with the wood chips. He didn't want to carry heavy stones that would impede his climb, but they could be used to pelt intruders. And, he needed to hang onto his spear, at all costs. It looked like he could find enough finger and toe holds to make his way up to the yawning opening. The effort was demanding, and the rock face was scorching! Although he worked hard, and was fit and muscular, the physics of his big body had changed his ability to scamper up the surface like he once could have. At last, he rolled into the cave's mouth. Expecting to find a corpse, he jumped when the bound victim jerked and moaned. As if to heighten the drama, an agitated rattle sounded in the gloom. And, he hated snakes!

With nervous haste, he yanked his victim nearer the sunlight at the opening and began working at the tape covering the guy's eyes. Another warning from the unseen reptile made the hairs rise on the back of his neck! He was trying to be gentle about the tape, not ripping skin off with it.

"M-mm-p-hm-mm"

"Yeah, I'm working on it." Then sensing what the victim was attempting to communicate, he cut his hands free.

More rattling caused him to reach a hand toward his stick.

With hands freed, the man was able to sit up, pulling at the bonds on his face, terrifyingly aware that he was in imminent danger.

32

"Just pull your pants and boots off together!" David's voice was terse. "Summers, is that you?" His voice changed to shock as the tape came off the agent's face and he recognized him.

Summers struggled to comply with David's order. The kid was right. The tape was wound tightly several layers thick, but he could skinny out of the whole mess, now that his hands were free, hands that didn't seem to cooperate as they should. Well, circulation had been inhibited to the extremities for hours. The tape wound tightly about his boots hadn't restricted blood-flow to his feet, so that was at least a good thing.

David was ready to fling trousers and boots to the landscape below, when voices carried up to him once more. The same two men were back, this time down below. He couldn't decide if he preferred to face them, or the snake. A plan formulated in his mind, and he acted on it. He motioned Summers to one edge of the opening. Forcing his eyes to focus in the gloom of the interior, he made out the outline of the bloated reptile. One hard jab with his stick, and the agitated creature writhed gruesomely. He had it! Whatever that was worth! Summers cringed, flattening himself against the opposite wall, as David whirled and sent one mad snake down onto the men beginning their ascent.

Chapter 3: ANGUISH

Morrison fought raw emotion as he awaited the oncoming force. Members of the gang had sent a mocking photo of Ivan Summers, bound mercilessly, while some clown danced around mockingly, displaying his weapon and badge. Their cryptic message: that the ABI agent was going to die, but the pain he would endure first, was up to the joint force. Atchison had proceeded anyway, taking out communications. No more word since then. Doubtless that had shot the torment level up for their friend and colleague. "Lord, please help him," Trent pled.

The head vehicle appeared within range, and a tire blew. Crippled, it continued forward–another flat. It could make it on rims for a ways. Trent sent a shot across the hood, followed by his amplified voice. "You don't have a chance. Surrender now! Get out of the vehicles, hands up high; then get prone on the ground!" The response, a shot fired directly at his position.

He ducked instinctively. Then with a whining scream, a missile tore up the road, incinerating the first several vehicles, their cargo, and inhabitants. In rapid succession, a second one took out the remainder of the convoy. Trent looked back at Bob, shocked. "Wow! The Army doesn't mess around!" Even as his tone reflected his wonder, he felt a pang. One of the vehicles just taken out, a decrepit-looking panel truck, seemed like it could be the one visible in the picture of Summers. No one was alive to question.

With this battle over before it began, Morrison's group received new orders; to move south and help the FBI gather up the gangsters who had fled earlier.

Shocky, he addressed his friend. "That isn't even the *National Forest* down there."

Porter laughed ruefully, but without genuine mirth. "That's right! Not our jurisdiction or our job. Let's let someone else do it."

⊰ ⊱

The scenario in the *Panic Room* went from bad to worse as the day progressed. Ryan didn't have any extra diapers, and Nadia wouldn't use the strange toilet. Then, the smells affected Mallory, bringing back her vomiting. Then, finally, the messy, hungry baby could no longer be comforted at all, and he screamed! And he screamed! Alexandra, doing her best, finally abandoned her attempts at bravery, and the tears slid down her face. Maybe everyone out there was dead. Her Dad! Her Mom! Jeff! Everybody! She knew Mallory was scared about David! She tried to pray for everybody, but the racket! And the stench! And Mallory's being sick! Were all combining to make her stomach queasy!

Over three hours had passed as Daniel and Jeff manned their posts. Traffic along the county road had returned to normal; like deserted. Still, Erik had told them to stay holed up! And vigilant! The fortress ranch-house would be a real prize for the gang members to capture. The situation would be ideal for staving off forces of law and order. Plus, with their lucrative racket of kidnap for ransom, Mallory and the Faulkner family would be prizes!

Jeff tensed. Through the power of the telescope, he could see the tattoos on a heavily-armed gang member approaching on foot, just inside the alpaca pasture in front of the house. The herd responded with terror. Jeff gripped the deer rifle without releasing the telescope. Definitely, the guy was up to no good, here, but he wasn't sure what course of action to take. Shoot him from ambush? The interloper was trespassing, by being within the fence. Or go meet him head-on and ask him what he was doing? While he deliberated, the man grabbed a cria. Empress, the gentle little mother, went on the attack, trying to defend her young. To no avail! Both animals dropped, throats slit.

Strangling a sob, Jeff transferred to the rifle scope and squeezed off a shot.

Across the expanse of the master suite, Faulkner tensed, riveting his attention on anything unusual in his field of vision. He thought he detected movement down near the stable, but he didn't see anything to site in. Then, a rifle report came from the bunkhouse. Followed by silence!

꞊긱 ꞊긲

David watched, fascinated, as the two miscreants below him struggled with the serpent. He was fairly certain it had inflicted venomous bites on both. Seeing him above them, one of them fired at his position. Using his stick for leverage, he dislodged several large rocks, rolling them down onto the hapless men. He returned his attention to the Arkansas agent.

꞊긱 ꞊긲

A shaken Haslett continued cruising, berating himself for letting down his experienced partner. If Summers died because of him, he planned to resign. He scoffed at himself. He would probably lose his job before that could happen. He pounded the steering wheel in frustration. He thought miserably that he wished there was something he could do to redeem himself. He circled through a nearly-empty campground, taking note of the stragglers remaining. He tensed!

꞊긱 ꞊긲

Daniel and Jeff riveted their attention on the surrounding panorama. Jeff swiped angrily at tears, upset at the senseless attack on the alpaca. He had no idea how much trouble he might be in for shooting the intruder. And they didn't know if the two gunshot victims were the precursors for an all-out war, or if they were a couple of stragglers. They waited, tense.

꞊긱 ꞊긲

Katy Graves looked at her phone. An Arkansas number, but she didn't recognize it. Maybe it was Mallory calling from her new country home. "Hello, this is Katy," she answered.

"Katy, you don't know me. My name's Haslett, and I want to know what you know about what's going down with Agent Summers!"

"I'm not sure what you're talking about. He helped me keep my kids when I was in some trouble. Is he okay?"

"Yeah! What I hear is that you tried to call in a hit on him. I've never been sure why he helped you get off, or cared what happened to your kids."

Terrified, she broke the connection, refusing to answer again. He texted angrily:

"I can have you picked up for questioning."

Tears filled her eyes. She knew plenty! She hadn't been the one to set Summers up, but sadly, she knew who did! She was smarter than to divulge anything. She dropped her kids at her parents' house, telling them to mind Grandma and Grandpa, and disappeared!

⚶ ⚶

David was paralyzed with indecision. Summers was in bad shape. He couldn't leave him alone; he was so disoriented he could fall to his death. The head injury looked nasty, and the abject terror, of being blindfolded with a drop-off on one side and a snake on the other, had seemingly unhinged him.

"It's okay, Summers. Somebody'll come looking for us. They'll have water and can get you evacked!"

The words were intended to be comforting, but the truth was, that the felons seemed a lot more aware of the cave-site than any of the good guys. He thought longingly of Mallory. He was hours later than he had promised, with no rescue in sight. He sent up another prayer.

⚶ ⚶

Haslett wished the Feds had briefed him. His information was sketchy on the operation, and even about who the enemy was. If Summers were here, he at least possessed years of experience. He pulled into a space in the campground parking lot, and did some quick research on the computer. He had noticed a kid who looked familiar from wanted posters. But Haslett felt that if he could spot the large boat, his ID would be more conclusive. Very few cars; only one with a boat trailer! It was small.

He was scared. There was no one out here to back him up, and this angelic-looking, young kid was ruthless. Images tried to force their way in breaking his concentration of his wife and toddler son. No time to go there, or even call. He unfastened his holster and released the safety on his service revolver.

He approached a small knot of people. "Afternoon! Have y'all been aware of any kind of trouble in these parts?"

The suspect swiped at tears, seeming innocent and vulnerable, making the agent wonder if his identification was correct.

The grandmotherly woman responded. "Well, this is Johnny Johnson, and he fell into the lake. He can't find his parents, and we're going to drive him around to some of the other campgrounds. He figures his mom and dad are really worried about him. He nearly drowned."

'Right! Fallen in the lake?' Haslett nodded. Not the best alias he had ever heard. He wasn't sure how to proceed. The kid had already snowed the elderly foursome, but he could easily grab one of them for use as a hostage.

"I have him made as being someone else. Anson Bennett's his real name; his folks are dead; possibly he had something to do with their deaths." He whipped his weapon up. "On the ground! Now! Bennett!"

"No!" The young man appealed to the couple. "Anna, Jimmy. I don't know what he's talking about. Just help me find my mom." Big tears filled pleading blue eyes. "And my dad! You'll see they're both alive; I've never killed anyone."

Anna smiled. "See, you must be wrong-"

Haslett stepped closer, edging between his suspect and the innocent, imperiled people.

The kid's eyes shifted uneasily as he realized his advantage was slipping. Then, his gaze moved toward a new target; a large SUV pulling in. He broke and ran, figuring he could gain the vehicle before the agent could recover and pursue him.

It was obvious to Haslett what the kid's intentions were. To hijack the vehicle! Probably with kids still in their car seats! He decided, and the report from his weapon echoed in the afternoon stillness. The kid sprawled away.

Jimmy's eyes filled with revulsion. "You think that was necessary? To shoot an unarmed kid in the back? He told you you were wrong!"

His wife, Anna, was speechless, gazing from Haslett, to her husband, to the gunshot victim, and back. The other couple glared daggers at the agent. Haslett wasn't certain what to do; he would face an investigation, as soon as someone could get here to start one. He emailed the bureau in

Little Rock, began filling out a report, and took myriads of pictures. He had noted down the plates of the SUV before the father placed it into reverse, wheels spinning, to escape the danger.

The outspoken couple's name was Abbott; James and Anna Abbott, visiting from Kansas. The other couple was Virginia and Harold Pierce, locals.

Haslett waited for instructions, certain of one thing! He had taken the only course of action presented to him. Maybe he would lose his job. Who knew? Maybe face murder charges and go to jail. Maybe Bennett would have allowed the two couples to take him where he wanted to go, sticking with his story, letting them live. Haslett was certain the youthful felon wanted their car, and would have willingly killed for it. Why had he been running around this area, wet and alone? Where was his legendary boat? The kid was lethal. Martial arts skills, probably armed, but hadn't revealed his weapon, hoping to keep playing on the emotions of the two couples he had deceived. The kid was dead, and Haslett was alive to go home another day. He called his wife.

⊰ ⊱

David was worried. Hours had passed with no sign of anyone. The victims below lay totally silent. It was looking like spending the night in the hole. That thought didn't appeal to him. He wasn't sure Summers would last much longer. Surely he must be bleeding in his brain, causing pressure to build. And he needed fluids. David felt trapped. Climbing the rock face had been unwise, understatement there. The only incentive that had kept him going up, was that it was harder and more dangerous to back down. No way could he climb down. Upwards didn't seem much safer. "H-m-m-m." Idea! He crept to the edge; it seemed stable and, took in the lateral approaches. Something he hadn't considered before. Maybe he could inch sideways, one direction or the other, and find a different escape route.

"Mblemessn slplsne!" Unintelligible mumbling from Summers.

"I'm not leaving you. I'm checking something different for maybe getting us out." Even as he spoke, he was wary. He didn't want any more snake encounters. He flopped back down, gloomily. 'Not good'. The cliff face wasn't wide, but the cave was located nearly dead center. No ledges, toe holds, anything, for scrambling to the edges where there was vegetation and where the vertical drop eased into steep slopes.

⚔ ⚔

Lilly Cowan kept eyes and ears on news related to Diamonds. The scenario transpiring in distant Arkansas was of primary importance to her. She was amazed when missiles fired from a drone put a quick end to the gang bust! She thought Americans were usually totally impotent and inept at handling their border incursions. She was relieved to see some solid response in keeping with the gravity of the problem. But then, as the hours passed, and no one could figure out who gave the order to fire, or who could have overridden the controls, she was dazed. Bransom fussing around about it, seemed to think it might have been her! Of course, he never confided his suspicions to anyone else. She laughed. He gave her way too much credit. True, she did have some Israeli intelligence in her Diamond council office; but none of them could have carried out an operation like this one. She rose and paced stiffly, her limp more pronounced than ever. Could it have been God? She started to sneer at herself cynically, as she always had. It was an incredible thought, though. Maybe information still incoming, would bring greater clarity.

⚔ ⚔

Lieutenant Atchison showed up personally to initiate the investigation into Haslett's shooting. He was eager to get Morrison and Porter on-sight. In the Ouachita National Forest, as nearly as he could tell by the GPS coordinates, their jurisdiction. He was surprised the victim had survived his boat's rapid sinking. He shushed Haslett's attempts at relating the incident." Save your statement. Don't say anything in front of these witnesses. They're lucky to be alive; they should be thanking their lucky stars and you for stepping in."

Morrison and Porter made a cursory examination of the body, and quickly took statements from the witnesses. The Forestry Service law enforcement division had been keeping tabs on the kid with the huge boat for months. Trent listened gravely to Haslett's recounting of the incident.

"Do you think anyone's been trying to track down that SUV?" he finished.

Trent shook his head wonderingly. "I'm not sure. If that had been me and my family, I would have kept going until I was nearly out of gas, and forced to stop! We're pretty sure you saved some lives, and glad you didn't take any unnecessary risks with your own. Good eye, good judgment, good job."

"Did you take statements from the witnesses yet?"

Morrison's face hardened. "Yeah, they think you gunned down a sweet, innocent boy, for no good reason! As usual, appearances were misleading. You made a good call."

James Abbott strode up, as the body was bagged, and the agents prepared to leave. "That man's a menace! Why hasn't he forfeited his badge and weapon and been relieved of responsibilities?"

Bob Porter regarded him steadily. "Look, Mr. Abbott. We appreciate it when the public gets involved and tries to be good citizens, and we understand your concern, but what happens to the agent, as far as disciplinary measures, frankly isn't your business. We still have plenty to finish this evening, and we're always shorthanded. This is a good man, and the one in the bag isn't-er-wasn't."

"Well, I thought Americans were guaranteed to be presumed innocent until proven guilty, in a court of law!"

Porter nodded agreement. "Due process! And yet, we assume people have some level of guilt, or we would never make any arrests! If that kid had surrendered to the agent, he'd still be living and breathing, to present his case to a jury. You watch too much TV, and maybe so did Bennett, to assume law enforcement owe it to them to chase them down when they run. That boy presented an immediate threat to the family in the SUV! We've been watching him for months, and Haslett was aware of the threat he presented. He risked his life to wade in before any backup could arrive, because your lives were in danger."

Jimmy Abbott's eyes widened in shock! "Oh!"

⚒ ⚒

Daniel exchanged information with Erik Bransom. Erik had said it was safe to leave the Panic Room and ease up on their vigilance. He was surprised to hear of the two shootings on the ranch property.

"Well, I'll get someone up there to look into that. Don't let down your guard, totally, but get the kids out of the Panic Room. They're likely scared to death. Let me know if anything else goes down. No one's seen any sign of Summers or David, but they're organizing a search. Try to keep Mallory calm about it. Don't touch anything out at the shooting crime scenes."

Faulkner was unprepared for the scene that greeted him when Alexandra released the thick door to the Panic Room. "Tough time, huh?"

"We were scared everybody was dead! We didn't have any diapers-" Jeremiah's voice was charged with emotion.

"Okay, okay, y'all did just fine! Everything's okay now. Come on out. We'll get the kids cleaned up."

"Mallory's been sick. Is David back? "was Alexandra's response.

He wished she hadn't brought up the subject of David. "Okay, we'll get everything under control," he assured. "Jeff's getting some steaks started, and everyone will feel better after a chance to clean up and have a good meal."

Mallory looked all eyes in a pallid face, scurrying to the privacy of the master suite. Obviously, she wasn't fooled by his ignoring the question about David.

He let her go, devoting his attention to helping Diana with the babies. Clothing was discarded in exchange for fresh new things as the two youngest came, pink and dimpled from the bath. Nadia was exhausted, but Ryan continued to scream, refusing to nurse.

"Oh, are we a mad little boy?" Diana's cajoling was drowned by screams. "We have to get fluids into him." Her eyes were frightened as they met Daniel's."

Frightened and frustrated, himself, he lashed back. "I told you to go in with them!"

She looked startled. "But you knew I didn't?"

"Yeah! There wasn't time for me to argue with you. You could have been prepared to fight for them from the other side of the door!"

Stung, she focused on the baby. "Let's find you something yummy." She pushed past Daniel to find a bottle of water. "Here, Mommy's putting nice sugar in here." Still, the baby refused to take the bottle.

⇥ ⇤

From the master suite, Mallory could see the dead alpaca and the gunshot victim. She showered quickly, afraid of missing a call from her new husband. She struggled against panicking, and against vomiting. An empty stomach had caused wrenching dry heaves. Then, remembering, she sprang the little kitchen open and found a Sprite™. She paced, trying to pray, be patient! She started to phone Erik, then hesitated. He had more to do than reassure her. She didn't want to be lied to, anyway.

Then, Daniel yelled at her, ordering her, in no uncertain terms, to come down and eat. Jeff, left in charge of her by his big brother, told her she didn't have to follow Faulkner's orders. Evidently, the emotion-charged day had left everyone with their nerves on edge. She summoned a smile for Jeff. "The steaks smell good. I'm hungry."

When the prayer was finished, she opened softly with the little chorus:

> *Thank you, Lord, for saving my soul.*
> *Thank you, Lord, for making me whole.*

The others joined in, and the musical harmony was perfect. Everything else was sadly out-of-tune.

Mallory offered to calm the baby and get him to try the bottle.

"You had your chance all afternoon. Could you not tell he was getting in bad shape? We need to get him to the ER!" Her words were directed at Mallory, but Mallory sensed they were more for Daniel's sake! Which flashed her back to her childhood, being in the middle of the fights between her mom and dad.

"Mallory, tell your father it's time for dinner."
"Mallory, tell your mother I heard her."

Daniel and Diana never fought!

⚜ ⚜

Daylight faded, bringing mosquitoes out in hoards. David figured he was probably covered with ticks, too, after his jaunt through the woods, and tree-climbing.

He started to drag Summers against the far wall of the small opening, and the loopy guy took a swing at him.

"Cut it out, Summers. It looks like we're roommates for the night, whether we like it or not! I'm moving you where you won't pitch yourself down the cliff with all your struggling."

"Huh?"

"Never mind! Stay put back here away from the edge. In the morning, I'm going for help."

"The snake~"

"It's gone. Try to get some rest."

⊰ ⊱

Ryan finally exhausted himself, falling asleep. Daniel was relieved. The incessant crying had rattled him. "See, Honey, he needed a chance to calm down. When he wakes up, he'll be hungry; you can feed him~"

She wheeled on him! "When he wakes up? You mean~If! Tiny babies are extremely fragile. If you cared about anything but yourself~"

He stormed out! "She said he didn't care about anything but himself? That wasn't fair! He cared about the baby, but he still felt like they could be targets for any criminal stragglers! He loved his new son, loved all his kids, loved her when she wasn't being an id~!" He stopped himself. This wasn't accomplishing anything, just making everyone more upset after a totally unnerving day. He needed to walk around and calm down. The air was still hot, even as the sun sank lower, but he was oblivious. He saw cars and agents arriving, stretching crime scene tape and taking pictures. He walked to where he could see what they were doing, and for the first time, he could see the other victim lying where he had fallen. Evidently, he had been making a move on the horses in the stable. He wasn't sure, but he guessed Mallory's Arabian must have been the target. Someone in the bunkhouse had put a halt to that plan. He moved to the opposite end of the stable to check on the horses! And they were gone! Not all of them, but *Zakkar, El Capitan,* and Jeff's horse, *Sergeant*! He gaped at the empty stalls, numb! The saddles were gone, too! He raced back to the house. "Have any of you seen Jeff or Mallory since dinner?"

They all stared at him blankly! As usual!

⊰ ⊱

Morrison, Porter, and Haslett struggled through thick growth, pushing ahead grimly. No telling where the gang members disposed of Summers, but they hoped to find David Anderson alive. Still, he was a big, able-bodied guy who should have been home hours earlier. Pictures forced their

44

way into Morrison's mind, in spite of his attempts to focus on the situation at hand. Not even a month since the wedding in Orlando! He could still see his kids having a blast at the Disney parks, and then Maddy's being carried away by the romance of the wedding. Well, it had been a special event! The reason why they just had to find David before something happened to him! They had started at the deserted mining operation on the upper Little Missouri. No one there for them to talk to, but they knew David had made it there, and was on his return trip. They were looking for signs along the trail to track him by. They were trying to make as little noise as possible, in case there were still some isolated, stray gang members. Twilight deepened.

Atchison had been summoned to his base commander to answer questions about the missiles. Now, the explosive charges sinking the boat! That he had accomplished, according to orders. He was as shocked and jubilant as everyone else when the heavy stuff took out all the drug cartel members and their merchandise!

⊣ ⊢

"We aren't going to find him there," Mallory's insistent tones in response to Jeff's search grid. "That's where people have already been keeping an eye out for him. When he left the bike, he headed a different direction, avoiding the trail, on purpose. I know him, Jeff."

"And you think I don't?"

"Look, I don't want to fight with you. I hate fighting!" She pointed to the map. "Let's go here."

He shook his head. "Well, you're right about one thing. Nobody's been looking for him up there. You're talking about eight or ten miles through inhospitable terrain. It's almost dark. There are bears, among other things."

She nodded, stubborn and resolute. "Yep, that's why he'd go there."

"To be bear bait?"

She slapped her reins and clicked, leaving her brother-in-law little choice but to wheel in behind her. She gave her horse some slack, allowing her to pick her way forward as the trail steepened, growing more difficult. Crossing a creek, they watered their mounts, before continuing on. Far above, stars pricked through the ebony of the heavens, but there was no moonlight, and shadows were deep, dancing eerily as they rode.

"Mallory, this is crazy. We need to turn around before we get numbered among the missing ourselves. David ordered me to keep you safe, and this isn't the way to do it."

She turned, annoyed, making a shushing signal with her finger to her lips.

"The horses are making plenty of noise; it isn't like we're stealth." His words seemed lost on her as she continued along the route.

⊨ ⊨

The hour was late in Governor Bateman's Little Rock office. He was proud that it was an ABI agent who had taken out Anson Bennett! Ha! The Army elite unit, with their mysteriously fired heavy stuff, had failed to do what one lone, rookie, Arkansas agent had accomplished. The sad side was the loss of Summers. He was aware that Morrison, Porter, and Haslett were searching for David Anderson and the body of the missing agent. He gazed at a map of the area pulled up on a giant screen. He buzzed his aide who was putting in a late night with him. "Arrange for another search party to move out at first light." He moved toward the corridor, his thoughts on David and Mallory and their recent marriage. In his car, he tried to phone the young woman to assure her the state would redouble their efforts to find her husband. There was no answer.

Chapter 4: ANXIETY

"Okay, Daniel, I'm not waiting any longer. We're going to Murfreesboro to the ER." Diana's mind was made up, and she was ready to leave by the time he reentered.

"Do you have any idea where Mallory and Jeff could have gone riding? It's dark." His response had nothing to do with her words.

She pushed past him. "My assumption would be that she's looking for David. Are you coming with me? Do you want me to bring all the kids with me?"

"No; I'm coming. We can all go. Let's all ride together, and security can travel in front and back of us." He could tell she was still mad, and the kids all looked abjectly miserable. 'Well, she shouldn't have accused him of not caring about anybody.' His phone rang, and it was Erik with an update.

"Everything quiet up your direction now?" Erik's question, assuming that it was.

"Well, not exactly. Diana and the kids and I are on the way to the ER with the baby. He screamed all afternoon, and–she isn't sure he's okay. Then, Mallory and Jeff just disappeared with three horses. We think they struck out alone to search for David."

The silence on the other end seemed endless. "Well, none of that's good news for me. Keep me in the loop, Faulkner!" He disconnected.

⊰ ⊱

Mosquitoes were annoying. 'At least they aren't snakes,' David's attempt at comforting himself and maintaining mental balance. Occasionally, he

47

dozed a little, propped up against the back wall of the cave; but Summers continued to thrash and moan, and every other night-sound sent shivers through him, despite the hot, steamy air. He quoted a couple of verses from *Psalm 139; verses 17 & 18:*

> *How precious also are thy thoughts unto me, O God! how great is the sum of them!*

> *If I should count them, they are more in number than the sand; when I awake, I am still with thee.*

He felt comforted, falling asleep more soundly.

-⦾ ⦿-

The three men in the search party felt total discouragement. They had been the entire distance between the deserted Diamond dig-site, back to the alpaca ranch. It was like David had disappeared without leaving a single piece of evidence to track. Morrison had little phone battery left, phoning Bransom with the reserve.

"We're all the way back down to the ranch," he informed the agent. "We didn't see a sign of him. It's like he went into thin air. Can you phone Faulkner and have him let us in? We're pretty tired and hungry. Maybe we can crash there, and go out again at first light The Governor is sending a party out first thing, too."

"Yeah, that's a good thing. I'm real worried about David, though. If he's okay, he would have found his way to a house or campground, or something, to beg the use of a phone and contact Mallory. The Faulkners are all on the way to the ER at Murfreesboro; they're worried about their baby. I'll call Duke; he's in charge up there, when David and Jeff are both away. Jeff and Mallory rode off on their own search."

"What? Please tell me you're kidding. That's crazy! We didn't run into them. They rode off on what? ATV's"?

"No; horseback. Maybe y'all can get some food, rest up a bit, and try to figure which way they headed out from the stable. There are a few more horses there; maybe you can ride instead of searching on foot. I'm on my way up there."

Despite their exhaustion, they gazed wonderingly around at the creature comforts of the main ranch house. "Quite the place"! Morrison whispered to Porter.

"No kidding! Well, I guess if you're marrying a girl like Mallory, you better be sharp! Kid's done okay here!"

Duke found phone chargers, and they plugged in while they foraged in the fridge and pantry. Refreshed, they made their way to the stable where a couple of guys finished saddling the remaining horses. Bransom appeared, and they took off at a gallop, following the trail left earlier.

At least they're leaving a trail," Trent observed." David's bike left a trail, but when he separated from it, he didn't leave a boot-print! I wonder why Jeff and Mallory are going this way; you don't think they're trying to lose us, do you?"

"Nah; that would be stupid." Erik's assessment. "They're on a mission to find David. I'm sure they won't mind having help, as long as we don't try to stop them. I guess when everyone had scoured that other trail she figured she knew where he wasn't. This still leads up into the higher country. She's pretty smart."

≼ ≽

Mallory reined in, dropping to the ground, and pulling *Zakkar* off the trail. Jeff followed suit. "What are we doing?" his whisper echoed in the silence.

"I heard something." Her voice was barely audible. "Be quiet; just listen." She stroked her high-strung mare soothingly. "S-h-h-h." She checked her watch. Two-thirty! She sipped water.

"I didn't hear anything." Jeff mouthed the words, but she shook her head, disagreeing. She was certain someone was on the trail behind them; someone also mounted. She hoped it was Daniel and Erik. And that they wouldn't be too mad. She wasn't giving up before finding David!

She eased her pistol free, just in case it wasn't good guys to the rescue.

≼ ≽

David tried to shake off the stupor. His mouth was unbelievably dry. Bad thing; sleeping with his mouth gaping open, when he was already dying of

49

thirst. Something had awakened him, and he strained his ears, listening. Summers was completely still. Maybe he had finally died. He struggled to hold himself together; he should have tried to do more to get the guy to medical help. He was a big baby to sit here, frozen by terror. Then, he heard it again. Horses? The jingling of tack? Muffled conversation as the riding party drew nearer. His brain couldn't process. No one would be looking for them in the dead of night. Terror gripped him anew! It must be some of the gang members. Coming to check on Summers, be sure he was dead, maybe hide out and regroup. He felt for his stick. What a weapon!

"David! David!" Mallory's first audible words in hours; it startled Jeff and the others who had overtaken them. "David, where are you?"

David leaped up, to crack his head painfully on the ceiling of the cave. "Mallory?" It seemed as though his ears were playing cruel tricks on him. "Mallory?"

He heard the horses picking up pace, and a new terror struck him. "Mallory! Mallory! Stop! Whoa, *Zakkar*! Whoa, Girl, Easy! Stop!"

"David!" Her voice rose with jubilation, and she dug her heels into *Zakkar's* sides. She was nearly there. "Get up!" She couldn't figure out why her horse resisted her command, but then, everyone was yelling at her to stop. She gazed down into darkness as pieces of rock crumbled, tumbling to a stop far below.

"Mallory! There's a cliff!" David cringed in terror, expecting the worst; but when horse and rider didn't hurtle downward past him, he sighed in relief.

Evidently, the near disaster had shaken the entire search party because David could hear men's voices and sense that they were drawing Mallory and her mount back from the precipice.

Her voice was a wail. "I think he fell, and he's hurt. We need to do something!"

"Mallory, stay back from the edge," David instructed. "I'm okay. Summers is here; I think he's in a bad way. We're in a small cave about a third of the way down. Be careful. We've seen quite a few rattlers; and I don't mean MHS alumnus."

"David, this is Trent Morrison. We have some rope; we're looking for something sturdy to tie off to. We can lower some water and snack items, but we're waiting for rescue choppers. It's too dark for us to do much more from up here."

David received the water and food items gratefully. "There are a couple of guys down below. I'm pretty sure they're dead. A snake bit them, they shot at me, and I sent some rocks down on top of them."

"Well, maybe they should have all stayed home," was Bransom's assessment. "Evacking you and Summers are the first priorities."

David tried to trickle water between the swollen lips of the other man. "Easy, Summers! There's a search party, and choppers are coming. They're gonna get us out of here."

⊰ ⊱

Ryan's condition was serious, and emergency personnel grouped around the listless little form, starting an IV, encouraging him to suck from a bottle of liquid that would provide nourishment and restore his electrolyte balance. "If there's a war going on, they could alert emergency services," the charge nurse confided to Diana, when the baby rebounded, becoming alert and smiling, in spite of the restraint on his hand. "We could have been inundated with casualties."

Diana nodded, relieved that damages were minimal. Certainly the hours had been tense, and David's and Mallory's being 'missing' was still a concern.

⊰ ⊱

Sonia Morrison felt jittery. The hour was late in DC. All four kids were asleep, but she sat in Trent's office, trying to sense his lingering presence. Her Bible was open on his desk. Her thoughts wandered to him and his career. She could see his engaging smile, hear his laughter, feel the pressure of his hand on hers. By far the youngest man ever to fill his post, he brought a zeal to it; not content to sit in his Washington office and send others into battle! She scoffed softly into the deep silence.' When had National Forests ever been battlefields?' She had received a couple of updates throughout the course of the day. She could feel her husband's rage and grief over their friend, Ivan Summers. The news had saddened her, at the same time making her grateful that Trent was still okay. Then, after he had put in an unbelievably long and emotional day, he was spending the night searching for David and Mallory. In the exchanges, she had missed the point of why the young couple was missing, and why it had to be Trent leading another

51

charge into the unknown. A tear escaped. That was just Trent! The guy who always did more, and not less! One of the reasons he had appealed to her so strongly in the first place-well, that and his good looks. One of the reasons he had set himself apart in the DC rat race! She gazed around the room, taking in his model train displays, the framed and matted pictures of vintage railroads on the opposite wall, the large silk screen-print behind her of a yellow locomotive barreling into the space!

She had met Ivan Summers; he was likeable enough. She didn't know him as well as her husband did. He was divorced and had a daughter in college. Details were sketchy. She tried to pray. Hopefully David and Mallory were okay. She jumped when her phone vibrated in front of her.

"Trent?" Her voice revealed emotions held in check for twenty-four hours. "Trent, please tell me you're someplace safe!"

His voice righted her world. "I'm someplace safe. I'm at the Murfreesboro hospital-in the waiting room," he hastened to add. "All in one piece. When we found David, he had found Summers. David saved Summers' life, well if he pulls through. Summers! That is! He's in bad shape. David's fine; just dehydrated, mostly."

Frustrated, Sonia tried to make sense of the disjointed information. "So, David was with Ivan, and not with Mallory? Is Mallory still missing? Do you have to go back out again tonight?"

"No. I'm just waiting for an update on Summers. He was critical by the time we got a chopper on scene to evacuate him. The wind kicked up; it was unbelievable. Anyway, this was the closest trauma center; not exactly big city, state-of-the-art, but they started fluids, and when he's more stable they'll move him. I love you, Baby; try to get some sleep. Mallory's fine, everybody's fine. I'll fill in the details later. I'll be home tomorrow, well-"

"Unless, Summers needs you to stay with him. Is his daughter there?"

"Good question. In the craziness of the day, I'm not sure anyone was notified that he was missing. I'll get with his partner, and the ABI's getting on site now. I'll be home tomorrow if I possibly can."

"I hope so; we miss you when you're gone. But we understand. Trent, I'm proud of who you are and all you do."

⊰ ⊱

Mallory squeezed into the small curtained place where David lay on a gurney with an IV started.

"You're mad at me," she ventured.

"Okay, let's just say I assumed you were safe at the house. I guess I should be mad at Jeff! I've spent my life being mad at him for one thing or another! Mallory, I thought you were going to plummet~ I thought I was going to lose you."

Her chin trembled. "Well, I was worried about you, and it didn't seem like anyone cared. It's a good thing we came looking for you. Mr. Summers was running out of time! You saved his life!"

Another nurse entered, telling her to go back out. The next procedure in David's treatment was a tick inspection and removal. He had plucked off a couple in the cave, but there were others that had been digging in for several hours.

"Go home when the Faulkners leave. Get some sleep. I'll call my dad to come get me and take me home if I get released."

She didn't argue. Married less than a month; and this obedience/ submission bit was already starting to wear thin! She always thought that it sounded so easy.

The nurse looked like she had spent her life playing the role of Attila the Hun. And probably Attila was a whole lot nicer and gentler. David ignored the indignity; that was what hospitals specialized in. He felt weird. Like he was about to come unstrung after the hours of tension and indecision.

"Could I possibly get something to eat?" He had a hard time keeping the tremor from his voice.

"Kitchen's closed!"

A few minutes later Attila and the Huns filed out with their little pan of trophy ticks.

In the isolation of the little cubicle, he went to pieces.

⊰ ⊱

Diana took note of Mallory's general condition. Not good! Well, everyone had put in a tough day!

"I'm glad Ryan's okay." Mallory's voice was timid and woebegone.

"I know you are. I'm sorry for snapping at you when you offered to help with him. And, I should have given him to you. Baby's nervous systems and their mother's nerves sometimes play off of each other. The more frantic one gets, the more the other senses it, and responds in kind. You probably could have calmed him down. You can calm down, too. David's fine."

Mallory started to cry. "Yes, Ma'am; I know."

Diana's gaze met hers. "He's upset with you for the moment. He'll get over it."

"Being married isn't as easy as I thought it would be." The words blurted out, and she was immediately sorry for saying them.

"Well, life isn't ever easy. I don't know how people deal with it, who don't know the Lord. I mean, even children, have their own sets of problems. And they assume adults have it easy. Poor people assume people are problem-free who have money. Marriage is wonderful, but it isn't easy. It takes constant work and nurture, like a flower garden. Other women look at you, and you don't have to clean house, or do laundry. So, although, you don't have those chores associated with being married, there's still the problem created by two self-willed people who have promised God that they'll live together kindly and harmoniously until death."

"Well, I don't want to be self-willed. But, I don't want to be treated like a little kid without sense to get out of the rain, either."

Diana led the way to vending machines, and sent Mallory a questioning look.

"Um, peanut butter crackers," she decided. "I have a bottle of water."

Diana selected and they sat at a deserted table.

"Well, it may be a little awkward, with both of you feeling your way, establishing your own ground rules. But, you guys were friends to begin with. Today was a tough day! I can't imagine how worried you all were in the Panic Room with no updates, a hard place to appease small children. We'll definitely make some additions to the Panic Room in light of today's experience. David had it okay for grown-ups. The medical staff came out; do you want to go back in with him?"

"No, he told me to go home with you guys."

Diana grinned impishly. "Well, you should do what he wants, but we aren't leaving yet."

⊰ ⊱

David sobbed and shook uncontrollably, glad for privacy. He didn't seem able to pull himself together. He wiped tears on the sheet, leaving grimy smears. He guessed he was atrociously dirty.

"Are you okay? Should I call a nurse?" His dad had appeared suddenly.

He shook his head negatively, trying to accompany his answer with hand signals. That made the IV and tape hurt. He couldn't collect himself enough to talk.

"Well, you're quite the hero!" His dad's hearty voice!

More tears squeezed out, and he shook his head again. If Summers survived, it wouldn't be any thanks to him. He kept trying to straighten out the story about his ending up in the cave with Summers, but as usual, no one listened to him.

"I'm not, Dad!" he managed to gasp out. "I'm not." He lay back, trying to choke off the rasping sobs. The more he willed his body to stop trembling, the harder he shook.

"Have you eaten anything?"

David scoffed. "Kitchen's closed!"

"Those have to be the two most dismal words in the English language," John Anderson commiserated. "I brought some bread, peanut butter and jelly, chips, cherries, and Twinkies™. Why don't you start with Twinkies™ and milk? They always have milk if you ask for it." He returned with a tiny carton.

Encouragement from his dad and some food helped. "I'm going to go check on Summers. I'll send Mallory back in. Don't be mad at her and Jeff. They should have both stayed home, but it's a good thing they didn't."

David closed his eyes. He wasn't sure how or when he could retrieve the pouch secreted high in one of the trees, or how he could break the news to Mallory that he had deserted a small fortune of her Diamonds.

Chapter 5: ABILITY

Mallory beamed as she and David found their way to a table in the mezzanine café in her office building.

"Here, you sit; and I'll go get our order." He pulled her chair back. She looked some kind of gorgeous. She wore the most delicate blush of rosy pink. The sweater set of a fine-denier silk knit, topped a tweed skirt that repeated the rosy blush mingled with ivory. A double strand of large pearls clasped at the side with a sizeable faceted Morganite, encircled with Diamonds, and set in rose gold. Her porcelain skin blushed softly with the same tone, and her lips featured a pale gloss.

He returned, placing the food carefully. Her nausea was a strange thing! Fine one second, and then just a whiff of the wrong thing- "Still feeling okay?"

"Yes actually. It all smells and looks really good. I'm hungry." She nibbled at a deli ham sandwich before sipping tea.

"What's your jewel? Is that a pink Diamond?"

"Actually, it's a Morganite, sometimes called Kunzite. A geologist named Kunz 'discovered' it, or rediscovered it and named it after his multi-millionaire friend, J.P Morgan. Geology is confusing because there are overlapping terms. Anyway, it's the pink form of Beryl. Green Beryl are Emeralds, pale blue are Aquamarines, colorless are called Goshenite, and there's yellow Beryl, also called, 'yellow Beryl'."

He laughed. "So, a yellow colored gemstone, could be, what? A yellow Diamond, or a yellow Beryl?"

"Yes, or a yellow Sapphire, or a Citrine, or a Topaz. They all have different chemical compositions and different crystalline structures."

"You're right," he agreed. "It's all hard to sort out, but it's pretty interesting. I'm going for a haircut; then I have appointments with both the tailor and a shirt maker. Why don't you finish making the two calls you were planning, and then go home and rest for a couple of hours?"

She nodded. "That plan sounds good. Do you want to take Pastor and Mrs. Ellis out after church?"

He nodded thoughtfully. "It's a good idea, if you get some rest this afternoon and you still feel good." He didn't mention it, but his dad worried about the other pastor.

"Does your dad not like the Ellis's?" she questioned perceptively.

"I guess he's just afraid you'll forget about him," David laughed.

She nodded her head, bemused. "Your dad isn't an easy person to forget; besides, he's my father-in-law. He should know I won't forget him or Faith Baptist. But even if I did, God won't forget him."

David laughed; then turned serious. "You aren't eating much. Are you sure you feel okay?"

"Yeah, I feel really good. I guess I just forget. Maybe I have ADD or ADHD, or whatever it is."

"Hm-m-m. You can concentrate when you want to. Okay, focus here. You finish this half, and these chips, and I'll help you out with the rest."

⊰ ⊱

Katy faced Jason over a Denny's breakfast. "I can't tell what I know. Okay, Jason? I wish I didn't know what I know!"

"Well, Bennett's dead. Wasn't he the main one?"

Her eyes filled with tears. "There are always more. When one falls, there are others who step up and fill in the ranks. It hasn't been a year yet since I was involved. I mean, I wasn't an insider. I didn't give any orders. I just followed them, tried to keep my mouth shut, and my head down. Summers' partner seemed to think I made the call to Bill, my boss, and that he set up the fake robbery to take Summers out. That wasn't it. But, when he called me, what's his name? Haslett? It panicked me."

"Well, I don't want to jeopardize you or the kids, but it seems to me like you should tell the authorities what you know. Then, it won't do any good to kill you to keep you quiet."

She sighed. "No, then they just kill you for revenge and to scare everyone else. Then, there's taking the witness stand."

57

He shrugged. "Maybe not. Maybe you can tell the authorities some stuff, to implicate people they aren't aware of, new people to investigate. Then, as they investigate, they can bring charges based on information they gather. The book of Proverbs says that righteous people need to take a stand against unrighteous ones. Even in the Books of the Law, it says that people aren't supposed to look the other way, but report what they're aware of. If they don't, they're part and parcel with it."

"Well, I'm not as good of a person or Christian as you are, I guess." Her voice was frustrated. "If you don't want to marry me, you can change your mind!"

"Calm down, Katy. You know I want to marry you. I have since that first day you and Richy and Amy joined Chad and me for burgers. But I don't want to have a wife that runs away at every shadow passing by. It isn't the way to handle it."

⊰ ⊱

"Dad, can we go back to Arkansas on Saturday?" Jeremiah's voice was filled with hope and excitement. "I mean, the war's over, right? And we wouldn't have to be in the Panic Room again?"

Daniel laughed. "Well, I guess the joint task forces in all the different states were extremely effective. Law enforcement doesn't plan to let anything like that become so entrenched again. But, I'm not sure we should just invade David and Mallory's space again so soon. We don't want to wear out our welcome. Actually, I'm not positive we were that welcomed to begin with." A rueful laugh followed his answer.

"Maybe we could buy some property in the country and build our own cabin," Alexandra's suggestion.

"Yeah, Al, that's a great idea!" Cassandra sounded amazingly 'Continental'. "We can have a stable, and horses, and bicycles~"

"Okay, hold on. We have a nice home here! With a game room, media room, indoor and outdoor pools, tennis court." Daniel's words were a reminder of how much they all enjoyed.

Their response was the usual strange look.

⊰ ⊱

Bransom conversed with Trent Morrison. Ivan Summers was bouncing back physically. "Well, he really had it put to him psychologically, though," Bransom affirmed. "Can you imagine being bound, gagged, and blindfolded? That would be terrifying and disorienting. Then, his captors swung him in mid-air, telling him he was two hundred feet up. Then, they abandoned him between the drop-off of the cave and a rattle snake. He said he tried to lie real still, but that snake knew that he was there, a living, warm-blooded threat. The whole thing makes my blood boil; speaking of warm-blooded! I hope everybody stays serious about stamping out this kind of thing!"

"Wow, I didn't know the whole story. That makes me mad, too. I know I plan to keep everybody in Forestry on their toes. I'll release this information, though. It's important for Americans to realize that these gang members aren't just giving 'Mexican bow-ties' to their enemies (law enforcement) in Mexico. They're trying to spread their brand of terror to us, too. We're all praying for Summers. At least, I guess, this is serving to warm up his relationship with his daughter. I don't blame him for feeling like quitting right now. The amazing thing is that Haslett took down Bennett by himself. He knew how dangerous he was, and he didn't take any chances. How are David and Mallory?"

❄ ❄

When David returned home, Mallory was sound asleep. He tiptoed out and brewed a cup of coffee. He was pleased with his two appointments. In seven to ten days, he should have more sharp new clothes that fit. He made his way to his drafting table. He was working on a project that was nearly finished. He was poking the drawings into a tube when Jeff called.

"Hey, everything delivered? Does it look good? I can't wait to see how it looks."

His brother laughed. "You don't have to. I'm forwarding a whole bunch of pictures to you. Let me know if you want any changes. I can't believe I said that. I need to clean up and go eat at home before church. Mom's fried Chicken!"

David forgot about the images of his mom's cooking as the pictures started arriving. Since the pictures on his phone were miniscule, he opened his computer for a better look. Strictly nice!

When Mallory wakened, the familiar queasy feeling was back. She sat up, fighting against it. "Lord, I want to go tonight," she whispered. Making her way into the bathroom, she started to freshen her cosmetics. She smiled as her new husband's reflection appeared in the mirror. His arms encircled her as his eyes met hers in the reflection. She leaned back against him. "Do you want to call Pastor Ellis and invite them to go out?"

"M-m-m. You look a little pasty. Why don't we play it by ear for tonight? If we make it through the service and you still feel okay~"

"Do you mind going out with them?"

"Well, I spent my life around preachers; my dad and his friends and associates. I'm not sure I'm as enchanted with the scene as you are. I don't mind going if you want to. I'm planning on joining tonight."

"Will that hurt your dad's feelings?"

David laughed. "I hope not. The Bible says a man should leave his father and mother and cleave to his wife. That doesn't mean the husband doesn't have any say in the church they attend. But Calvary is a great church. It may be an adjustment for my dad. You want to stop for burgers on the way?"

"Unh! I don't think so. Why don't you find something here to hold you? And eat it where I don't have to see or smell it."

⊰ ⊱

Lilly's eyes narrowed. She puffed out a mouthful of smoke before grinding her cigarette out. It was her usual brand; she couldn't figure out what was the problem. They must be blending in fillers or something, charging more for an inferior product. Maybe a different brand would be better.

"What do you hear about Cassandra?"

She glanced up to address the question. This group wasn't one to engage in pleasantries; they must want Cassandra to come back! And soon! She shrugged noncommittally.

The director frowned at the inquirer. "I want a report about what happened in Arkansas. Why haven't you submitted your report yet, Ms. Cowan?"

Lilly swirled her wine glass, and set it back on the table without sipping. "I'm still gathering facts. As you are aware, Americans often operate, not letting the right hand know what the left is doing, so to speak. In the aftermath, the reports are confusing and contradictory. A

60

little leeway, please, Mr. Director, until the dust settles, and I can report on solid facts."

"Well, yes. I think we are all hearing the same stories. And surely arriving at factual information is essential. But, Ms. Cowan, if there is an entity capable of overriding command systems of U.S weaponry, it would be in our best interests to know it." His eyes drilled into her humorlessly, while his voice dripped sarcasm.

Lilly remembered Mallory's words that Christians didn't have to be pacifists, or pushovers. "Yes, I would assume that to be correct. Have you spoken with the Americans? Are they addressing the problem?" Her words were accompanied by her habitual shrug and arched brow.

"Americans never address their problems!"

"And we address their problems only as they affect us. The missile system won my war. Crazy drug lords growing marijuana, or coke, on top of Diamond deposits!" She smirked, waving her hands dramatically. "If they learn of the wealth there, they will return. What's to keep them from creating problems like the RUF has in Africa?"

"The American government"!

"Ah, then maybe the Americans do sometimes address their problems." She couldn't resist!

The meeting continued, mostly wild surmising. 'China? North Korea? Russia? Iran?'

"If any of those nations possess that capability, why would they use it to help the Americans route out drug operations?" Lilly's point was good. "If any of them could override the system, why not redirect the missiles to attack more strategic places in the U.S. than a spot in the road in a National Forest?"

"Well, a hacker, then?"

Lilly's laugh echoed in the large room. "I'll write my report based on that. It's as good as anything."

Lilly moved to her office, not turning on the lights, and sat in a dim circle of illumination from a corner street lamp. At last, a tear escaped, rolling to her chin. She wasn't the only one that logic was failing. Could it be? Did Jehovah, Himself, really intervene in the affairs of men? She was aware of inside information. U.S. military forces were not supposed to fight wars on American soil. Police agencies were responsible for law and order among the American populace. But the fact was that elite teams with weapons' systems were on site! Why? To flex threateningly? Their presence at various positions on U.S. soil was nearly a violation of U.S. law. Of course, America's definition of war and enemy combatants was coming under scrutiny; with foreigners infiltrating her borders for one criminal reason, or another. She lit another cigarette, and, disgusted with the quality, snuffed it back out. She didn't want to forsake her reasoning ability and goofily assess everything that transpired in her life as being, 'A miracle'! So, there were other drones, bearing similar missiles, at three other locations; locations with larger drug operations to be taken down. And the only ones that fired or, misfired, were the ones that helped Mallory's interests. And, by association, Lilly's and the Diamond industry's!

She answered a blinking secured line, listening without speaking. She cradled the receiver.

⚞ ⚟

"The kids want us to have a country home." Daniel's laughing words to his wife were met with her expressive blue eyes and a smile.

"That would be fun."

He wandered to his study. 'Well, of course, it would be fun.' He thought he was doing a pretty good job of providing for his family. How many people had what they did? It wasn't fair! Well, the kids didn't have a clue what they were talking about! He sighed. Evidently, Diana didn't either. He sank into his chair and activated his monitor. As usual, there were 'accounts payable' requiring his attention; nothing past due. He shook his head gloomily. There didn't seem to be any end in sight for David Anderson's spending. More furniture! And lots of it, judging by the total sale!

"I brought you a cup of coffee." Diana set her mug on the coffee table and handed him the other. "We were talking, and you just wandered off."

"Yeah, I thought you'd be on my side. Sometimes Dads and Moms are on the same side."

"About what"? Wide-eyed innocence! "Oh, about a second home in the country? Well, that's something to consider."

"Diana~" He couldn't believe what she was saying.

She smiled suddenly. "Well, I know we can't afford one. Humanly speaking, it would be impossible for us to keep what we have going on

62

here, and maintain another place, too. But, don't forget, that with God, all things are possible."

He frowned. "Well, He probably figures that at some point in time, we should decide to be happy with what He's given us."

She sipped thoughtfully. "Well, yes, that's why in Philippians, it says to bring our petitions with thanksgivings for what He has already done. It doesn't say not to make petitions."

"Thanks for the coffee. I'd better start getting ready for church." They were getting back to normal in their relationship following the stresses of the 'war' day, and he didn't want to argue now.

"Well, God is able to do exceeding abundantly above all we ask or think."

"Yes, Diana, and He already has! Maybe you should open your eyes and look at all of it!"

She was stung, and he tried to backpedal. "Look, Diana, you've never been one to lose a grip on reality before. Usually, it's me. Honey, we don't have the money David and Mallory have. If you plan to 'Keep up with the Andersons', I'm pretty sure I'm out of the race before it starts. The kids said we could build a 'cabin', but I can't see you in a humble little abode next to Mallory's palatial one."

She laughed. "Yes, plenty of creature comforts."

"We have that. You want to keep adding to our family, and it's what I want, too. But, there isn't room on this lot to build on again. I don't want to sell and move. Homes like this one don't find qualified buyers every day. We have security in place here; I like the location. To build bigger would demand being even farther from downtown and the office. Let's live our own lives and run our own race and keep from being driven by what other people are doing. Is that unreasonable?"

She smiled. "No, not at all"!

Back from church with the kids all down, they sat watching the news. "Has Mallory confided to you any worries she has about David's spending?" Daniel broached the subject cautiously.

"Mallory doesn't confide much; not about anything personal. I never tell her any of our family business, either. What's David blowing money on?"

"I didn't say, 'blowing money', I said 'spending money. He bought a whole ton more new furniture."

☙ ❧

Erik made a call that he had been postponing.

"Hello, Agent Bransom," Came Nick's voice. "I hope everything is well. Has something new developed about Jennifer?"

"Nah, I just thought I'd call and touch base with you about how Jennifer's doing. I don't have any developments to report. Cases always seem to drag out before they get to trial."

Nick stepped out of the gallery into a blistering, Arizona alley. "Maybe I should have called you. Now, I'm out in this baking heat, and Jennifer knows something's up. She hasn't wanted to report to you or the Bisbee police department, but different men from her past keep showing up here. I think it's deliberate harassment, and not coincidence."

"I should have called sooner. Don't die of heat stroke, but write down, with as much detail and description as you can, the events that have transpired. If anyone else bothers her, try to take pictures with your phone and forward them to me."

"Okay." Nick's voice was anguished. "Agent, she doesn't want to be that anymore."

"She never wanted to be that. If there are people from her past that aren't already implicated, they should have left it alone. I can't for the life of me, figure why they feel the need to inflict more torment. I plan to make them sorry they didn't quit while they were ahead."

☙ ❧

The meal with Pastor and Mrs. Ellis was a little strained. David had visited briefly with the pastor before the wedding and in the foyer at Calvary following services.

If Mallory noticed the strain, she gave no indication. And, she was eating! The restaurant nearest the church that stayed open until ten was a barbecue place. Surprisingly, the intense aroma of meat's smoking didn't start the sick feeling. David and the two guests ordered full dinners, while Mallory asked for a pulled pork sandwich without sauce, and a side of fried okra.

Finally, as they rose to depart, Mrs. Ellis addressed Mallory. "The duet y'all sang at your wedding was beautiful. Do you sing together often?"

"Well, we haven't." Mallory was always so honest and earnest.

"But we plan to" David slid into the conversation. "I'm not sure what you'll think of this, but we plan to split our time between Dallas and Arkansas. And travel with the Faulkner family when we're invited to do music at other churches with them. We want to be good members, and we think it's important to belong and be in our place. But, we can't agree to any jobs that don't allow for flexibility. Like, we can't work in junior church every week, but we can sub in occasionally. Mallory can't commit to being the church pianist, but she can play offertories from time to time, and accompany special numbers."

"Did you not think that was kind of awkward?" David questioned as they headed toward home.

She turned toward him, and her features were gorgeous in flashes of light from passing traffic, signs, and streetlamps. "I didn't think it was too bad. Since Daddy died, I've had to force myself from my comfort zone more times than I care to remember. We have so much, that it's up to us to go out of our way to be friendly. No one will approach us much, if they think we're stuck-up rich people."

⚜

Mid-afternoon on Friday found David and Mallory escaping Dallas along Interstate 30; evidently, everyone else had the same exit strategy. "We should have flown; we may still be sitting on the freeway Monday morning when it's time to be back." David's words were met by a nod of agreement. The problem was, where to fly into. The few small airports that were in close proximity at all, to the ranch, didn't have car rental kiosks on site. No easy way to get from point A to point B

"I guess that's what's meant by the word, 'rural'. If it's easy to get to, everyone will show up, and then it will be a city, too."

David laughed as he opened his computer. "Could you please tell your dog not to read over my shoulder?"

"Dinky, get back! This may be a long trip."

The Faulkners were on a road trip, too. "Dad, why did you sell off the *GeoHy* jet?" Jeremiah questioned.

"End of that era, I guess, Son. The family outgrew it; it was a lot to keep housed, insured, maintained, and staffed."

"Well, you're a pilot. Why did you get too chicken to fly?"

65

"Jeremiah"! Diana's voice was stern, and amazed. Alexandra was the one who usually got too mouthy.

"Well, sorry." The tone didn't sound genuinely apologetic.

"If you care to rephrase your question Son, I might answer you, and we can have a discussion."

"What's the use of your keeping up with your pilot's license, if you're too chicken to use it?"

"Daniel Jeremiah Faulkner the Third! That is entirely enough!"

"Okay, Honey, I can handle it." Daniel patted Diana's hand.

"You're right, Jer, I've gotten afraid to pilot us around. Flying is a skill, and I'm good enough to keep my license current. I like to think if we ever get in a situation where I have to fly, I'll be proficient enough to reach the nearest landing strip and make a safe landing. The best pilots, Son, are the ones who do it all the time; that do it until everything is second-nature to them. When we owned the Gulf Stream, I wasn't confident that we flew enough to keep Captain Williams on his toes."

"Can I learn to fly?"

"Unh, you're just now learning to ride a bike."

Alexandra snickered.

╡ ╞

The afternoon was beautiful, if hot. Dinky seemed to sense his new-found freedom, and went tearing up the drive, barking furiously. The alpaca regarded the newcomer, unimpressed, continuing their grazing. Every time David looked at the herd, he missed pretty little *Empress* making her way to him daintily, her new cria following her with more and more assurance. Jeff was still being investigated for shooting the trespasser, and the shot taken from the bunkhouse. It made David laugh. Well, Mallory's Arabian, *Zakkar*, he was fairly certain, was to have met the same fate as *Empress*. Many of the campers living in the bunkhouse were either, parolees, or on probation; consequently, they couldn't be in possession of fire arms. But law enforcement, investigating the incident, was stymied. The gun fired to protect the stable, was covered over with every ones' prints.

Mallory sat on a deck chair with a tall iced tea beside her. Although fans above her circulated the air, she felt pleasantly drowsy. Her mare in the pasture swished flies, seeking the shade. She wished she could ride, but David seemed to be reliving the events of the previous days, and was still

66

touchy about it. She wondered idly where he was. She succumbed to sleep, lulled by the faint clicking noises of the fans. The next thing she knew, car doors were slamming, and the Faulkners had arrived.

"Hi. I didn't know y'all were coming," she greeted.

Daniel paused from unloading children and gear. "David invited us. Did he forget to mention it to you?"

She laughed, reaching for Nadia. "He knew it would be fine with me. Maybe he was trying to surprise me. I'm not sure where he went."

As if on cue, he appeared, driving a go-cart. "Who wants to ride?"

The kids all went berserk! Laughing, he handed his helmet to Daniel. "I guess they all want a turn. Throttle! Brake!" he pointed out.

"Honey, you want to try?"

"Of course! I thought you'd never ask." Alexandra held Ryan while her mom and dad took a couple of spins around the loop. They all played and took turns until the long summer twilight succumbed to darkness and night sounds echoed in the soft air. Steaks, salad, and baked potatoes appeared from the chow hall, to be devoured, followed by chilled watermelon.

"We should bed the little ones down." Daniel tried again with the same announcement he had tried to make several times. He had asked David a couple of times, where he should unload their stuff and set up the pack 'n plays.

"Okay, if you want to break the party up so early," David capitulated. "Load up in your car and follow us."

Daniel and Diana exchanged confused glances, but there seemed to be no room for argument. By the time they had the kids buckled in, David and Mallory pulled in front of them in a golf cart. "Follow us."

"You've fixed them a place haven't you?" Mallory fought tears. "I never had any idea."

He kissed her hand. "Well, when you adopted them all, I figured I should get on board with you. I'm glad I did. They're pretty amazing."

He stopped the golf cart before it could set off motion sensors, bringing up the floodlights. He motioned for Daniel to proceed.

A few yards farther, and spotlights shot up, illuminating another beautiful log home. Faulkner jammed on the brakes, staring at Diana accusingly. "You knew! That's why you had so much faith, when I didn't have any!"

Her gaze met his as the water works started. "Daniel, I didn't have a clue! Oh! My~ Oh!"

"Yes!" Cassandra yelped. "Yes, the Lord did it! Look Xavier! Now you can play in the dirt a lot more!"

"Well, we don't know that it's for us. Maybe it's just for any guests~" Jeremiah's cautious assessment.

David slipped the keys into Mallory's hand and stepped back. Her hands fumbled with the key, but at last, one of the heavy ornate doors released. She flipped the light switch and gasped with wonder.

Chapter 6: ANTAGONISM

    Suzanne Bransom parked the rent car in a space designated, 'Visitor', and removed her handbag and brief case. The Houston heat, combined with the humidity, felt overpowering. She gazed dismally around the parking lot and shabby assortment of buildings. This task might prove even more formidable than she had anticipated. She wondered if Roger Sanders was aware of what he had purchased. Driven by the heat, she approached what appeared to be the main building where executive offices would be housed. Assuming her most pleasantly authoritative expression, she approached a scowling security officer.

    "Good morning. I'm Suzanne, Roger Sanders' assistant. He sent me to do some preliminaries~" The muscular man leered at her, stepping more into her space, rather than yielding to allow her to pass. "Don't think I've heard anyone expecting~was it, Suzanne? You can just move your~"

    Shaken, but trying to maintain her poise, she retreated to the car, and then to the hotel, where the manager let her into her suite early. She unpacked her Bible and carried it with her to the in-house café. Over coffee, she read one of her favorite passages. She enjoyed a leisurely breakfast while she weighed her options. She hated to report to Roger that she had failed to gain access to the property. She couldn't call Erik and rile him up; he couldn't always bring the FBI to the rescue.

    She tried not to call Mallory too often, especially now that her daughter was a newly-wed. But Mallory had business acumen, and her company had bought out another. That seemed like the best choice.

    "Hi, Mom, are you in Houston?" Mallory's upbeat voice made her feel better immediately. "How come Roger sent you in alone? Are you okay? Are the employees acting decent to you?"

Before her mother could respond, Mallory spoke again. "Where are you, Mom?" In response to the answer, "Good; stay there until help comes. David and I are already on the way to Love Field. We'll bring our security, and I'm calling Roger and telling him to send as much Sanders security as he can. I'll call Kerry, too. Well, I'll talk to Roger about what legal counsel he's using in Texas."

"Well, I could have called him. I don't want him to think I can't handle the job."

"I'll call him! He shouldn't have sent you into the 'Lions' den' alone! I'll go easy."

She bounded out to reception with David at her heels. "Marge, find us flights to Houston ASAP. We're heading toward Love because Southwest flights depart regularly. "Lisette, take care of everything I was going to. We'll probably be out tomorrow, too."

In the car, she gave David a pleading look. "Why don't you call Roger? I'm a little miffed right now."

He laughed. "Well, I kind of am, too, but I'll do my best. You want me to call Erik?"

She considered. "Roger first, and see what he says. I'm calling Daniel and Diana, and Shay and Grandmother." She met his questioning gaze. "This is going to be a mess."

⚔ ⚔

Dan Wells, the agent from the Phoenix office, sent agents back to Bisbee. None of them were supposed to care about Jennifer, per se, although it was hard not to. Keeping the art gallery under surveillance was totally legitimate, though, as Bransom's take was that more suspects in the case continued to show up. Dawson had suggested Erik travel to Arizona. He phoned him.

"Okay, Erik, I may regret telling you this. I should have just let you go to Arizona. Sanders sent your wife to do some preliminary set-up at the company he bought out."

"Suzanne had trouble? Is she all right? It sounded kind of shaky to me, but I didn't figure Roger'd send her if he anticipated trouble."

"I don't think he thought she would run into trouble. These situations can become volatile suddenly, as you well know. She retreated and didn't press the issue. She called Mallory, and Mallory's lining up security, and making sure the legal work's all correct. Sanders would have seen to that, but she wanted to make sure they were within legal parameters. Houston PD is on alert to the situation; I think it's under control. I didn't want to leave you totally in the dark."

"Yeah, thanks. Keep me in the loop."

⊰ ⊱

Suzanne returned to *Chandler Chemicals, Inc.,* accompanied by David and Mallory, the Faulkners, Delia and Shay, and their personal security personnel. A different *Chandler* employee attempted to block her access, and David stepped forward. "We represent the legal ownership of this company. You should step out of the way."

The guys eyes shifted warily and he backed off.

David stepped up to the main receptionist. "Order a fire drill."

"Huh?" She snapped her gum.

"A fire drill! You know! Have everyone evacuate the buildings?" He turned to the security guy. "Order a fire drill." The guy hesitated, not because he continued to be belligerent, but because he didn't know how.

"A chemical company and you don't practice routine fire drills?" He broke glass and pulled the fire alarm.

"That'll bring the fire department!"

David shrugged, "Probably a good thing!"

"Why did he do that?" Suzanne was perplexed as she stood in the melting heat, watching *Chandler* employees saunter out.

"Well, to get everyone out," her daughter responded. "Then security's going through the buildings to make sure there are no weapons. The employees will all reenter through a metal detector. It's a sad day when employees go on rampages, but you never know."

Suzanne nodded. Erik lamented to her about that, too.

The fire department captain approached. "Who's in charge here?"

"I guess I am," Suzanne admitted. "I'm from Hope, Arkansas, and my employer owns a chemical company there. *Sanders Chemicals* has just purchased this company. Believe me we'll work on emergency evacuations. Roger's a real stickler about safety."

He gazed at her for several seconds, assessing her and her words. "Okay, Ma'am, well here's the deal. Now that we're on scene, frankly this place looks like a dump. You can expect a visit from the fire marshal. Let your boss know he better not be in violation of local codes. Did he look this place over before he bought it?"

Suzanne patted her neck delicately with a hanky. "Well, pictures on line of the facility, and all the financial information."

Ten guys from *Sanders Corporation* security arrived, reporting to Suzanne. She sent them to join the weapons search as the last straggler came out.

David moved to the straggler. "If the emergency had been real, you would have died."

She stared back hostilely. "Did you break down our elevator? I've been waiting on it. I had to walk down two flights in these!"

David tried not to laugh at the six inch platforms. "You should have taken them off so you could hur-ry a little faster. Go line up with your department." He couldn't help being annoyed. People placing themselves at risk, was one thing. He felt sorry for emergency workers whose lives were placed at risk due to the foolishness of those they served.

Security issued an all-clear, and the management team entered first. David made a quick walk-through, and found an office for Suzanne to work from. They all immediately noticed the off-colored material that seemed to prevail throughout the entire building. Swimsuit calendars, magazines, posters. Diana started ripping it down and throwing magazines in a pile to be disposed of.

"I'm not sure you can get rid of people's personal things," Daniel cautioned.

"Well, they should keep their 'personal' stuff at home. This is Sanders' domain, and it's inappropriate in the workplace."

Everyone else joined her, and they were attacking it when the employees began coming in from the drill on hot asphalt.

"Hey, those are mine!" A guy was retrieving possessions from the growing trash pile.

"Get it then. Take it to your car; don't bring it back!" Daniel's voice was clipped.

"You know what?" Mallory's voice and everyone paid attention. "I need to call Sam and Niqui. Sam needs to go through all the computers and see what's on them."

"Good thinking, Mallory," Daniel agreed. "I'll give him a call."

Diana found the infirmary, and it was in appalling condition. "Is there a janitorial crew that works here?" she demanded.

David came to the rescue. "I haven't seen a janitor, but I found his closet. It's really well stocked." He displayed a full cart.

Diana laughed. "Well, it should be! It doesn't look like anyone ever uses the supplies."

He went straight to work with a scraper. The entire facility looked like a good place for a work crew to get excellent experience; he just wasn't sure all of his 'campers' would stay and work, with big-city temptations lurking so near. Public transportation was nearby. He shrugged. The guys didn't belong to him. If they chose to bolt, they had been given a chance. He felt kind of bad about the fire drill. It had seemed like a good idea. Now, it might just have served to heap fines on Sanders as the new owner. Well, buying out this company had been his idea. He wondered if it was too late for Sanders to back out. He rocked back on his heels, mopping sweat with his sleeve.

"It's already looking lots better," Diana encouraged.

He laughed.

Diana completed an inventory of the infirmary. The janitor supplies were in far better shape than the medical ones. She joined David in the cleaning detail; there wasn't anyone else to do it.

Daniel entered with a cardboard box of supplies. "Where do you want this, Hon-What are you doing?"

She straightened, wiping at her forehead with a latex-gloved hand. "Just take it back to the car for now. There isn't a clean surface to put stuff on."

David squatted, defeated, in the middle of the infirmary bathroom floor. He guessed no one was reporting to Sanders because they didn't want to rat him out; didn't want to admit this was a bad idea! He scrunched his way back a couple of steps, leaning against the wall, and pulled out his phone.

"Hey, David, we're almost there." Sanders' announcement came as a surprise.

"Uh, well, yea, yes, Sir. The pictures on line of this place looked better than it really is. Can you back out of the deal?"

Sanders laughed. "No, I can't do that. I do have someone who wants to acquire it from me already. Offering a fair chunk of change"!

"Are you going to accept?" The young man was silently thanking the Lord for providing an exit strategy.

"Well, that's a leading question. But, definitely not! The guy that's offering nearly double what I'm paying is Donovan Cline! Suzanne told me I have problems galore there. I'm glad you're on site. Can you address them for me?"

"I can start making some calls; but you need a plumber, an air conditioning company, a roofer, general clean-up and trash hauling, painters-for starts. Did Suzanne give you a heads-up that the fire marshal will probably do an inspection before the day's up, and I'm sure there will be fines? I've wondered about the wiring-"

"Okay, breathe. You found this opportunity, but you didn't coerce me to buy. This mess isn't your responsibility, and I didn't walk into it blindly. The costs you're blindsided by are just the costs of doing business to me. Yes, contact all these sub-contractors for me, and you act as the General Contractor. I'm giving you carte blanch to do whatever you consider necessary. Are you familiar with *Proverbs 14:4*? Roger quoted it.

> *Where no oxen are, the crib is clean: but much increase is by the strength of the ox.*

"Hey, who are you calling an ox?" David's tone sounded offended. "Just kidding, I get it."

Disconnecting, he jumped to his feet and made his way to a cubicle. Most of the *Chandler* employees were fiddling with computers and whispering in small groups. David figured they were trying to help one another clean up their electronics. He knew Suzanne was going through the personnel files.

"Hi, David Anderson," he extended his hand "What's your name?"

"Mitch Knowles. I'm a sales rep; or I have been. We all getting canned?"

"What, about the calendars and stuff? I'm not sure; I actually don't work for *Sanders Corporation*. Mr. Sanders is a good guy; he'll probably explain the new mind-set. Some of these people may quit since Sanders runs a tighter ship than this seems to be. Can I use your computer and phone? I need to contact some people about doing some work here."

He looked nervous.

"I'm not the computer guy. Do you think any of these people would be willing to get their hands dirty? I'll pay an extra fifteen dollars per hour for the remainder of the day to anyone willing to do general clean-up work."

The guy shrugged. "Hey, I can always use extra. Most of us aren't doing anything much; we're not sure what to do."

A decent crew assembled, and David started assigning jobs. "I can do this, David," Delia intervened. "You can make your calls. Roger said something about making the air conditioning a priority?"

"I think we can all say 'Amen' to that," he agreed. "Write your names and your hours. We have your records for withholdings. Mrs. O'Shaughnessy's in charge, if there are any questions. I'll come around and check on everything later."

David contacted an air conditioning company that could be on-site within the hour. A good thing. Mitch Knowles was leading the sales force in beginning clean-up in the sales offices. David's gaze traveled beyond them to traffic moving fast on a busy four lane. A strip mall on the other side seemed empty and advertised to be for sale or lease. Inspiration seized him, and he risked life and limb to get there to check it out. Freshly remodeled! He dialed the number for the agent handling the property. Hey, Sanders had told him to do whatever was necessary.

David shook hands with the realtor and eagerly filled out forms to qualify for leasing the property. The agent seemed more eager for a lessee than David was to acquire use of the facility. With utilities included in the rent, and electricity turned on, the air conditioners hummed to life.

With the tiniest break in traffic, he crossed back over. Beth and Roger Sanders were pulling up as he burst toward the front door. "I leased that little mall," he explained, pointing it out. "It's freshly remodeled and the air is cooling off fast. Mrs. Sanders and Suzanne might be more comfortable over there. I'm gonna get a bunch of guys to help load some desks and chairs up to take over."

Beth surveyed the scene, aghast. Roger was more prepared. The neat little property across the avenue seemed like an oasis in the wilderness. "Great idea! I'll drive Beth around and be right back to help."

Several desks and the best of the office chairs got loaded into the backs of a couple of SUV's. David handed a wad of cash to Knowles. "They're going to unload these. Why don't you go rent a truck? You know your way around better than any of us do." Back in Knowles' cubicle, he placed calls to several commercial remodeling contractors. He made appointments to meet three of them in the morning, who could bid the jobs, and he got references so he could do his homework before they arrived. He contacted plumbers, making similar arrangement. Roger tracked him down.

"It's a mess, like I told you," David greeted. "It's mostly the cosmetics, though. Neglect when management stopped caring. The structures seem sound enough. I thought we could relocate the third floor people across the street; (shall we name that the 'Annex'?) while we remodel that floor.

Roger nodded thoughtfully. Well, let's put the executive offices across there. It'll make a better impression on customers, and the sales force over there. Then we can move accounting down to second floor, and advertising and marketing to first."

"What about the infirmary? It's a disaster, and Mrs. Faulkner's trying to bring order from the chaos. She has Nell Carlton coming tomorrow, and they're going to begin drug testing and TB screening."

Sanders' face registered surprise. "That's a good idea. I hadn't thought of that. I guess we should make room in the Annex for that. What are you addressing next?"

"Someone about the parking lot; they can fill in the holes and re-oil it, repaint stripes, curbs, and fire lanes. A landscaping company to weed-eat and plant a few flowers? What are your thoughts? Phil and Risa are coming, and Risa said she'll paint a temporary sign. Houston doesn't seem too stringent on zoning, so maybe we can put up a sign."

Roger laughed. "The fire marshal gave me a courtesy call. Since I've just acquired this facility, I'm getting a chance to get the place to code. That's a miracle. Sharp eye, David, noticing that other property! I called the realtor back, and told him we're interested in purchasing it."

David shrugged. "That street's a problem, unless you can get permission to build a pedestrian bridge across it. I nearly got matered, and I'm a fast runner."

A delivery truck arrived with electronic components chosen by Sam, and Sam and Niqui pulled in almost immediately behind it. David explained the developing set-up, and Sam opted to set up Suzanne and the executive offices first. David had already made calls in regards to moving the phone system around, and including the Annex.

Mallory paused from going through personnel records to phone a deli. Within an hour, an assortment of sandwiches, chips, drinks, and cookies arrived. People wishing to continue with the clean-up efforts helped themselves and kept working. By eight thirty, as darkness descended without cooling the air by so much as a degree, they knotted up the jobs for the night. The Annex was up and running, housing the executive offices, the infirmary, and the sales staff. The third floor of the main building was empty, ready to be torn apart and redone. The second floor housed the break room with new vending machines, a new refrigerator and microwave, was scoured top to bottom, and furnished with new plastic tables and chairs. More inviting, if less than elegant! Accounting took up the remaining second story. The first story housed shipping and receiving, advertising and marketing, research and development. Again, with a heavy coating of grime removed until it could be totally redone.

At David's orders, Shay and Shannon appeared with tubs of ice cream and toppings for ice cream sundaes. Most of the *Chandler* employees hung around, and the icy relationship between the two companies seemed to melt away faster than the ice cream.

Chapter 7: ASSOCIATES

David stepped from the shower, feeling like a new man. "Well, that feels better. Today has to be the hottest I've ever been." He shrugged into the terry cloth robe provided in the suite.

Mallory nodded. "Yeah, and I thought Dallas and Orlando were hot! You accomplished a lot. Roger was impressed."

"Yeah, he said he's still happy with his deal, but I feel like I gave him a bum steer."

"Well, you didn't. Remind me never to make a major acquisition sight unseen, though." She laughed. "Roger said the other buildings are much better on the inside. Evidently *Chandler* was more interested in the actual chemical side of the business, than he was the business side. All the chemicals and equipment in the inventory are as represented. And, although the place looked like a train wreck, there are good accounts receivable and cash flow. Donovan Cline has been trying to talk Roger into flipping it. So, it must be a good deal."

She bent to retrieve his clothes from the bathroom floor.

"Whoa, no you don't." He snatched them and pulled the plastic dirty clothes bag from the hanger clip. He went through his jeans' pockets, and there was something Sanders had handed him. Busy, he hadn't checked it out. Now, he stared at it in amazement. "It's a check made out to me!" His voice was incredulous. "It must be a mistake."

She looked at it." Two hundred thousand; that's two percent! Standard finder's fee! It's about time." She kissed him on the cheek. "You earned it, and you don't owe it to him to clean his place up spic and span. Let's do what we can tomorrow, and go home Wednesday. We have our own business to tend to."

Jeff and the camp crew were on-site first thing, and David conducted the interviews with the remodeling contractors and plumbers. He sealed the bids and put them in Roger's box with the results of his reference checks, and went in search of Mallory.

He saw her before he entered the Annex, through the plate glass window of the office adjoining Suzanne's. Her back was to the window, and across the desk, David could see a good looking guy she was interviewing. He hadn't seen him before. She turned and noticed him. With a smile, she beckoned him to come in.

"Hey, David, meet Cade Holman. Cade, my husband, David Anderson"!

David stepped in and extended his hand, and the other guy rose with an answering gesture. David spoke the appropriate 'pleased to meet you' and returned his attention to Mallory. "I wondered if you could slip away for a bite of breakfast."

"Nearly finished; can you give fifteen more minutes? Cade has his M.S. in Organic Chemistry."

David tried to act interested. "Oh, yeah, doesn't that include Diamonds?"

"As a matter of fact! All of the Carbons and its compounds were living substances at one time. I don't usually notice jewelry, but your wife's is hard to miss."

"Yeah, I'll move along so you can finish up."

〜 ⚜ 〜

Jennifer finished dusting carefully around several of Risa's sculptures. Nick had left to run some errands, and before he was gone long, a man dressed in suit and tie entered. She eyed him warily. The suit didn't look as expensive as they usually wore, and the tie definitely seemed to be grimy polyester rather than silk. "May I show you something?"

"Just browsing."

She felt relief. He wasn't one of them. He moved to the other side of a tall divider, and she kept an eye on him in a mirror installed for that purpose. She thought he was an agent, although she hadn't met him before. She hoped Nick hadn't mentioned her problems to Agent Bransom.

The bell on the door jingled; she looked up again, and froze! This was one. It seemed as though they watched for Nick to leave the gallery;

although, a few times, they had accosted her when he was present. She wasn't sure which was worse.

"Good morning." Her voice was terse.

He approached her directly without indicating any interest in the art work. "Good morning, Veevee. Do you remember me? I've missed you."

Her face hardened and she shrugged indifferently. "Evidently, I'm not who you think I am. Wrong person! I don't remember you. I'm sure we've never met."

He sneered and reached a hand toward her. She stepped back defensively as the agent behind the divider appeared and two other agents burst through both the front and back doors.

"FBI! Place both hands behind your head and get on your knees."

"Hey, what did I do? I guess it's just mistaken identity. I thought this girl was someone else." He smiled disarmingly.

To Jennifer's surprise, they arrested him, read him his rights, and shoved him out the front entrance in handcuffs, past his shocked wife and kids.

⊣ ⊢

"Where can you get breakfast around here?" Mallory's question as they moved toward the rental car.

"That's a good question. I guess we should go to the freeway and up to the Cracker Barrel. This area's pretty devoid of appealing spots."

She nodded agreement. A lot of south Dallas is the same way. If developers would chance it, I think some of the chain restaurants would do okay. Don't you?"

He laughed at her serious countenance. "Wow, that's a huge social problem for me to address on an empty stomach. But, I don't know. Obviously these people that live around here don't have a lot of discretionary income for eating out." He turned a corner.

"Stop"!

He jammed on the brakes, figuring her command meant the sickness had hit her suddenly. She unlocked the door and hopped out, but she kept going. He locked the car and took off behind her.

"What are you doing? It's hot, and I'm hungry."

80

"Look, this is a gymnasium someone built. One of the *Chandler* people said they used to come here to work out or play pickup basketball. I wonder why it's closed."

He grasped her by the elbow, pulling her good-naturedly back toward the car. "Don't you ever get hungry?"

Her eyes shone, and she laughed. "Don't you ever get full? Pull around in front so I can write down a phone number."

He shifted. "Okay, but I don't think Sanders is interested in buying up every vacancy around. This is a couple of long blocks from his facility."

"Well, yeah, but it looks like everyone cuts across. I might want to buy it."

"Okay, you can call about it from Cracker Barrel."

⇥ ⇤

Agent Wells met the accused harasser, Carson Felton, in the interrogation room. The guy was good-looking, arrogant, and insolent.

"My attorneys? This has to be the most fraudulent arrest in U.S. history!"

Wells sat with his arms folded across his chest.

"Maybe you'd like to explain to me why your baboons cuffed me and paraded me in front of my family and half the town's population."

Wells barely blinked at the tirade. If he asked questions, they clammed up. He made no response, and the suspect continued. He knew the charges against him, and he was right; they were kind of flimsy.

"I'll be out of here in an hour, and you'll be sorry your ever saw me."

Wells kept his poker face in place in spite of the inner smile trying to escape. 'Threatening a Federal Agent'! If Felton got out of the harassment charge, he could arrest him again.

"My attorneys better get here soon!" He shifted, studying the tassels on expensive loafers. "Why was the FBI all staked out in that pitiful little art gallery? It's mostly hick western stuff."

Wells wrote a notation. 'What had brought an east-coast industrialist to Risa's art gallery in Bisbee, Arizona, if not to shop for her work? A lot of time and trouble just to come gig Jennifer'! His brow furrowed as he listened to the guy rave on. While they sat, other agents were delving into every area of the man's life. If he cared about his wife and kids so much, he didn't stay home with them. Like many wealthy, handsome guys, he seemed to have political aspirations. It was hard for Wells to keep from grinning like the Cheshire Cat.

Exasperated, Felton stretched and eased his cuff out of the way to view his watch.

Wells gave up his attempts at the façade and broke into a grin! He recognized the watch! And the birth mark on Felton's inner forearm. "Bingo! Jennifer!"

⊱ ⊰

The realtor met Mallory early afternoon, and they viewed the gymnasium together. "Wow, it has an awesome floor!" She ran her hand admiringly over the glossy hard wood. Why is it closed up?"

The realtor was unsure what to answer.

"The neighborhood"! She answered her own question. "But still, it's sad to have something this awesome with no one's being able to use it." She was trying to think of ways to make it work.

He nodded. "Yeah, there's just a lot of vandalism down here."

"Vandalism? That's all? I thought maybe there were gang wars over who got to play and when. It seems like the vandalism's as bad with it closed up, as it would be, to have it open." She made an offer on the spot. Probably more than if David had been with her, but she wanted it."

⊱ ⊰

Diana and Nell arranged the new infirmary, happy when fresh new mattresses arrived for the two beds. Nell phoned in an order for emergency meds and equipment while Diana contacted the Harris County health department. The drug tests would be performed by an independent lab, but the County would come and do the Tuberculosis testing.

Sam Whitmore was on-site, too, installing new systems in the Annex. That was most pressing. He would deal with the other issue later. Diana was delighted to see Niqui.

"Look at you," she laughed.

Her sister made a face. "Yeah, look at me. You never stuck out this far on your due-date. Think about how long I still have to go."

Diana hugged her. "I'm so happy for you. Are you happy?"

Niqui smiled. "That's a leading question. But for the most part, yes. Parker told me-"

Tears flooded Diana's eyes when her sister couldn't go on. "Yes that the entire village seems to have opened up to the gospel."

Niqui blotted at tears with her hand. "I still can't say I understand why God had to do it that way."

"Sometimes His ways are past finding out. Our minds are so finite, and we hurt. We try to keep trusting, but when things don't make sense to our rationales, it's hard."

Niqui smiled suddenly. "You're amazing!"

Roger stuck his head in. "Wow, this looks great! I didn't realize how tacky the infirmary at Sanders has gotten. Have you seen David?

"I think he went across the street to meet with all the division heads. He wants to draw up plans for the interior, and the department heads are going over how they think the space should be divided up."

Roger frowned. "I'm not sure why he didn't advise me of that. I think I should have some input."

"Be careful of traffic."

❧ ❧

Chandler employees, for the most part, were applying and interviewing to stay on in spite of the changes. Suzanne was finishing some preliminary interviews when Erik called.

"I miss you. What are you up to?" Her voice sounded sunny and normal.

"Miss you, too, Babe. I'm getting ready to check out the neck of the woods where they found David and Summers. The two bodies at the foot of the cliff have been removed, and they were some wicked dudes. Ironic the way they set up the snake to get Summers, and ended up being nailed by it, themselves. Does David seem okay?"

"Yeah, he seems great. He's a hard worker, and he knows a lot. He and Mallory seem to be an amazing team!"

"That's good. If I come to Houston later, will you have any time? Roger isn't planning to have you run everything there, indefinitely, is he?"

She laughed. "I hope not. I've heard a lot of different places referred to as 'The armpit of the earth'. But this is really it."

Erik laughed in response. "Yeah, I never cared much for Houston, either. There's hardly any zoning, so if something looks nice, it probably has a dumpy place next to it. It just seems seedy."

"Yeah, poor zoning is bad, but it's good, too. Roger and David are getting permits to pretty well do whatever they want. I want you to come, but I'm putting together a banquet at the hotel tonight for all the employees and applicants."

⚜ ⚜

Mallory sank woozily into a chair in the waiting room of her mother's makeshift office suite.

"Are you okay?" Suzanne's voice was anxious. "I think Diana's in the infirmary."

"Yeah, I just need to sit down a minute and cool off. I've been in the heat, and it zaps me. Are you still conducting interviews?"

"One more to go today, then I need to go to the hotel and check all the banquet arrangements. I'm a little nervous. This interview's with the guy who sent me packing Monday morning."

Mallory straightened, lifting her head from her hands to meet Suzanne's gaze

"Do you want to keep him on?" She seemed revitalized.

"Well, he was unpleasant, to say the least."

"Can I see his file?"

Suzanne's face set.

"Okay, brief me on his story. What is he? Ex-military? Ex-law enforcement?"

"I thought you got Dale Peterson back. Why do you need someone else that's mean?"

"I'm purchasing a gym a block or two away. It's suffered from vandalism. I want to keep it open and have security on site twenty-four/seven."

Suzanne relinquished the file. "Here you go. I'll see you at the hotel."

⚜ ⚜

David arrived at the hotel with barely time to clean up, as Mallory was moving toward the elevator. "I was going to check if Mom needs any help."

"Well, she has *Sanders* employees if she does, and restaurant staff, but suit yourself. I won't take long. You look gorgeous by the way." He gave an approving nod to the beige, lace suit.

The banquet room was inviting with fresh arrangements at each linen covered table, and the strains of a string quartet. The selections were light classical; Roger was conservative about pushing Gospel in his secular corporations. Everything seemed under control, so she sank down at a place setting to listen to the Faulkners' music.

Cade Holman appeared immediately and joined her without asking her permission.

"Mr. Holman, I'm glad you could make it. Would you like me to introduce you to some of the other chemists?"

He leaned in toward her. "No. I was just wondering if you've made a decision about me. And the job"!

"I told you. I'm not the one hiring. I was helping Mrs. Bransom with preliminary interviews. I passed the ap. along, and someone will call you for a second interview if it's warranted." She was trying to extricate herself.

"Well, what does that mean?"

"It means, I don't know if *Sanders* needs you and your skills. They very well may; you seem highly qualified. I think Mr. Sanders plans to hire *Chandler* people first. I don't know what he'll need when the dust settles. He has your application."

She escaped as he attempted to press the issue. Delia was pinching and pulling at tablecloths, and Mallory made a pretense of helping.

Her grandmother's eyes snapped mischievously. "Where's David?"

"He just got back, and he's showering and changing."

"Yeah, I'm right here." David's voice startled her. "What did Holman want?"

"To know if he's getting hired. I told him I don't know."

David frowned. "I heard you tell him that this morning. If he can grasp 'Organic Chemistry', surely he can understand that simple concept."

She turned to face him before speaking thoughtfully. "Yeah, he really seems to want and need a job. Roger's always looking for people that are 'On the ball'. Cade seems to be that, but his application is just kind of there with all the *Chandler* dead wood. I mentioned to mom and Roger both that there was a sharp guy. I hate to say anything more lest everyone jump to the same conclusion that you are. I'm not interested in anyone else, David."

He smiled suddenly before kissing her. She was right. The guy was something to go ga-ga over in the job market. She didn't want Sanders to 'Let a good one get away', but she couldn't exactly stand out as his cheerleader. He approached Sanders who sat whispering to his wife.

"Excuse me." He smiled apologetically at Mrs. Sanders.

Roger rose to shake his hand. "No problem, David. I appreciate all you're doing. I guess y'all are headed home tomorrow, but you really have things organized and under way."

"Yes, Sir, there's this guy who made application. He just graduated with a Masters in Organic Chemistry. He seems to be eager for a job here. Mallory did a preliminary interview. I didn't know if it would be appropriate to introduce him to you here~"

Roger made a sweeping gesture. "Lead on McDuff".

Laughing, David made his way to where Holman sat. "Roger, meet Cade Holman; Cade, Roger Sanders." David made the introduction and retreated to join Mallory.

"That was nice of you. Maybe you'll get another Finder's Fee. Look, there's Cat!" Mallory waved a low-key greeting, as Beth and Roger's daughter made her way to the head table. Roger made some welcoming statements; then suddenly asked David to bless the food.

A hum ensued as guests began passing rolls and adding dressing to their salads. Most were seated by departments, and knew each other, so the stiffness was dissipating quickly. Mallory extended her hand to the couple who had joined their table. "Mallory Anderson, my husband, David. You're Amos McKenzie, and your wife, Billie. *Chandler* employees call you Mack."

Mack's hard eyes drilled into her! A perfect sign!

She took two rolls, and pushed her salad toward David before continuing. "That was my mom that you barred from entering the property."

He shrugged and growled. "I didn't have any information about her pending visit. I'm not sure what I'm doing wasting my time here."

Mallory laughed. "Well, it's a nice, free dinner, and Billie wanted to come. I'm glad you're here~"

Her words were interrupted by Roger's appearance at her elbow. "Mallory, don't recruit my people at my banquet!"

She blushed guiltily, not sure how to respond.

"I scolded your mom for not having you and David at the head table."
The twinkle in Sanders' eyes belied the severity of his words. "You should
have been up there just so I could keep a better eye on you. I didn't know
you were trying to pirate my people."

"Well, I made an offer to buy this gymnasium, but it'll need supervision
twenty-four/seven~"

Roger nodded soberly. "Yeah, we need to talk. You're buying property
out from under me, too! You and David are amazing! I get such tunnel-
vision! David noticed the strip shopping center that was empty, and you
saw a boarded up gymnasium. They're both such logical additions to what's
going on here." He paused to introduce himself to the McKenzies. "Mrs.
Anderson won't need you, after all, because she's selling the gymnasium
to *Sanders-Chandler*. If you're interested in staying on in security here, I
have an interview time at nine-thirty in the morning."

⚔ ⚔

I won't leave you there alone again." Nick's voice was savage. "People have
no right!"

Jennifer's face was blotched and tear-stained. "I can't get away from
it."

Nick's hand covered hers. "Yes, you can. You have! You're free, and
the Devil's mad. And not only, are you free, but you're leading the search
for others. And, you're an example of an over comer. Steb and Christine's
entire *Save Our Children Foundation* is largely because of you."

She shook her head obstinately. "No; it's because of Missy."

"Well, Missy had been missing for a long time. They had given up until
your story came to light. Anyway, I'm sorry for mentioning the visits to
Agent Bransom, but he asked me. He wants to nail these guys, and they
deserve it! I guess it just amazes me the time and effort they're putting into
hassling you." He leaned forward, his eyes searching her expression. "The
one today~his watch and birth mark matched one of the paintings you did.
He was one of the insiders. He's going to prison."

She pulled her hand back. "You don't deserve this fight, Nick."

"I want the fight! It's a righteous cause. The criminal case~your
paintings are enough. Steb thinks we should sue, too. They stole from
you, Jennifer, and from other children like you. They owe you for the
humiliation and suffering. They should pay."

She scoffed, horrified at the thought.

"They're pillars of their societies! My word~against any of theirs?"

"Well, if they are the 'Pillars of Society', they're rotten to the core, and the society is, too. Anything resting on such pillars is doomed to fall."

"I don't want any of their money."

"Well, you worked, doing what they told you; and all you ever got for it was scorn heaped on you. You deserve to take them for every penny they have. You know some POW's forced to labor in concentration camps have been awarded settlements. It's something to consider."

⊰ ⊱

"You should eat more than a couple of rolls." David's concern when Mallory pushed her entrée his direction. She ate a third roll and attacked her dessert. Then, he finished that, too.

"Do you think she's okay?" His anxious question was directed at Diana as she tucked her cello and bow into the case.

"I think so. She needs to see a doctor soon."

"I made her an appointment for Thursday. She's dreading it, but she knows she has no choice but to go."

"Well, that's a relief." Diana's facial expression reinforced her words. "I'm not sure how you convinced her."

"I told her a doctor might let her ride *Zakkar* more. And also, that I don't plan to help deliver a baby!"

Daniel joined them. "Are you and Mallory flying out early in the morning?"

"Actually, we're driving," David responded. "She doesn't tense up as much about getting sick, knowing we have a bucket and we can stop if we have to. We can get a lot of work done on the way, and reach Dallas early enough to make church. Where are all your kids?"

"With my mom and dad," Daniel answered. "Diana's mom and dad are in Paraguay on a missionary trip. My mom loves the grandkids, but she's never tackled keeping up with all six of them. Alexandra and Jeremiah are supposed to be helping quite a bit."

David gave the usual instructions to 'have a safe flight', and looked around for Mallory. She was taking advantage of the break to greet Catrina Sanders. Okay, good deal, Holman seemed to be keeping his distance.

"Hey, David"!

David turned toward the greeting, surprised. "Erik," He extended his hand. "I didn't know you were coming down here. Did you get anything to eat?"

The agent laughed. "Yeah, I'm about to. They're bringing out a meal for me now. How are you? You doin' okay?"

David laughed. "Stayin' busy"!

Erik's gray eyes met his seriously, despite the younger man's attempt to laugh things off. "Busy enough to make it all go away?"

"I guess it'll take me some time, too, to work through it. I mean, I know I did what I had to. I wish Summers would quit all that stuff about me being a hero and saving his life. It isn't true. I wish it were. Sometime maybe, I can explain to you what really happened."

"No time like the present."

"Your food's out, Bransom. We'll be in Murfreesboro this weekend. Maybe I can collect my thoughts enough by then that we can talk."

"Write it out. I think our brides are looking for us."

Chapter 8: *ABOMINATIONS*

Daniel turned on his phone as they deplaned in Tulsa. He frowned at a missed call. An old classmate and colleague he hadn't heard from in a long time asking to get together for lunch.

He kissed Diana good bye. "I'll be home a little early so we can eat and get to church in plenty of time." Headed toward the office, he returned the call.

"'Ey, Professor 'Iggins"! He attempted to mimic Eliza Doolittle's cockney accent. "'Ow goes it with you? Can you meet me downtown at the Bistro in the Sullivan building? I just got back in town, and I'm limited for time."

"Why don't you ever visit the University?" Higgins tried to moderate his voice, but it irked him to meet Faulkner on his own turf.

Daniel tried to measure his response. "I don't know. I guess I'm just never that direction. As I remember, parking places were hard come by. I've been out of the office for two and a half days, and I need to get a lot done this afternoon. That's too far out of the way."

"Well, what makes you think it's easy for me to drive clear downtown?"

"Maybe another day would be better. Maybe Monday?"

"I have a full class load on Monday. I'll be downtown in thirty minutes. Speaking of parking, central Tulsa's pretty expensive."

"I'll get it validated for you. See ya soon."

⊰ ⊱

Mallory was sick early, but then, she felt better, even eating a little bit. Roger had asked her to withdraw her offer on the gymnasium, but she hadn't decided.

"I wanted to have you drive so you can get more experience." David kissed her as she slid into the back seat ahead of him. "But, you're right. If someone else drives, we can finish quite a few projects." He mentioned several items, and she nodded. They were in sync, even to the priorities in business.

"I think we can knot everything up for the week, even with the first part of it gone helping *Sanders*. If the doctor's on time with appointments tomorrow, we should be able to head toward the Ranch by noon Friday."

Mallory's eyes shone. "Yeah, Diana told me they're trying to do the same. They're still blown away by the cabin! Well, so am I. That was so nice of you! And I love ours! It's just beautiful! Are you happy?"

He was taken aback by her sudden, direct question. "Yes, I really am. I guess I should have told you last night. *DiaMo* has hosted great banquets and fabulous trips, but I always had to keep my distance. And when they ended, I wasn't really allowed to tell you good-bye! And I was never sure how long before I'd see you again. Or if you were starting to like someone! It was just stellar sitting next to you last night, being able to put my arm on the back of your chair, and whisper comments in your ear. And then, when the banquet was over, I didn't have to say good-bye. We could still be together."

She snuggled against him. "Yeah, that's how I felt too."

⋈

Professor David Higgins scowled as Faulkner appeared at the hostess' stand. The businessman was always dressed impeccably. Higgins summoned a smile as the guy approached, extending his hand.

Daniel sank into an opposite chair, taking note of the drink Higgins had nearly finished. "To what do I owe the honor? I hear you're a full professor. Congratulations!"

"Well, I'm surprised you have that much of a bead on what's happening at your alma mater."

Daniel shrugged. "I'm still on the mailing lists; keep up a little. Life goes on." He paused to order.

"You buying?" Higgins' voice continued to challenge.

"I'm not. Your invitation! Your treat! That's a social grace. They still don't teach etiquette with the sciences?"

"What's your problem, Faulkner?"

"Well, I didn't think I had one. I'm not sure why you suddenly want to be in my face, and I thought you had a chip on your shoulder to start with. I didn't lose anything on the Tulsa University Campus. Well, my self-respect. Look, reliving college days, and being all gung-ho for the sacred halls isn't anything I care about. I know we differ on that score! And on lots of others! I got saved and changed my ways."

"Well, so what about your kids? You planning to keep them in a vacuum tube forever?" He drained his drink and shook it toward the server for a resupply.

"You out trying to matriculate students? Mallory said you asked her about Jeremiah."

"Well, you know, your grandfather, and then your father, and then yourself~"

"Yeah, if Jer doesn't enroll, we'll break our streak. That's the least of my worries. You know, I've tried to explain to you before, that my values have changed. I don't want my kids to go there and be involved in campus life, and pledging fraternities and sororities."

"You don't want them to hear anything but your own narrow brand of knowledge."

"And that's your concern because? Enrollment down? And they sent you out to put the squeeze on the alums?"

"I can't believe you don't think you owe anything back! You've been successful because of what you got at TU! You should endow the University."

"Are you here officially? Or is that your opinion? Look, Higgins, I respect you. But what I do with my money and my children is frankly none of your business. Believe me, they aren't in a vacuum. I wish they were. Evolution confronts them with nearly every statement made by practically anyone. University life and the Fraternity, we both know what that's all about. It isn't what I want for my kids. I wish I could undo my own shenanigans."

"Hey, you remember?" A leering smile as Higgins named a name. "Man, she was some kind of dish! Crazy about you, too, man! You ever hear from her?"

Daniel felt his face redden, and he placed a fork full of salad into his mouth to keep from responding. This was a nightmare.

"Take Mallory O'Shaughnessy as an example. You should have encouraged her to attend a real school. She took on Phelps Hensley in some stupid article, and he's tearing her to pieces. She had secretaries and employees write the few papers she's credited with. For that girl to claim the degrees she is~what a farce! Good lookin' for sure, but hardly a Geologist! Or a Hydrologist! Hey, did you ever~?

Daniel chewed slowly and took another bite. He chewed, swallowed, and sipped water while Higgins grinned like an oaf.

"In case you haven't figured it out, cyber-world is here to stay. That means more and more education taking place outside of the traditional class room. It's increasing every day, being refined, having the problems ironed out. I think you teach some classes that way, if I'm not mistaken."

Higgins ignored the rationale of the response. "I mean, what's to stop cheating on a massive scale?"

Daniel took another bite. He had cheated plenty in the brick and ivy world of learning. No use admitting that and having Higgins go to work on rescinding his degrees.

"Look, Higgins, we both represent an esteemed organization. I believe it still has a place, but it's entering the world of cyber education, too. That works for a lot of people for a lot of different reasons. It's flexible, and it offers advantages, as well as disadvantages. Some people live on campus and attend classes in person who never get caught up in the party life. That person wasn't me. No telling how many kids have been ruined more than helped by institutions of higher education. I've told you before that I believe with all my heart that the 'Sciences' tout a false premise, and consequently forfeit the right to be called 'Sciences'. But I don't want to sit here and argue. Hey, we have a place in the country now! The kids love it! Well, it's great! So, I need to catch up on some work I'm behind on so we can head out Friday at noon."

Higgins stood to his feet. "You were going to get my parking validated?"

Daniel stared after him. His intention hadn't actually been to brag, so much as to change the subject. Well, at least it had sent the guy on his way. He requested his food be wrapped to go, and in his office, he forced himself to concentrate on the pressing tasks. Closing his computer, he placed a call to Tom Haynes.

The high school secretary had to go locate him, but then his voice came on the line. "Tom Haynes; what can I do for you, Faulkner?"

"Well, I just had a strange encounter at lunch with an Earth Sciences professor from Tulsa University. We were classmates, and partiers together, back in the day. I'm not sure what made him think of me, but he came with a real burr underneath his saddle. Well, he tried to get me to come have lunch on campus. He thinks I owe my money and my kids to a system that nearly ruined me."

"Yeah, I've been under fresh attack for trying to offer people a viable educational alternative. Let me guess, he rattled you by bringing Mallory and the validity of her degrees up."

"Yeah, everything he said rattled me, but that was the one I figured you'd know about."

"Well, in the equivalent of her sophomore studies, she wrote a paper. It was pretty knowledgeable. She began it by posing. 'Why do pseudo-intellectuals adhere so ferociously to a theory that has more holes in it that Sponge Bob©?' Then, she was quick to point out that she was never allowed to watch anything related to the cartoon in question; after which she presented really organized and thought-out problems with the tenets of evolution. Some guy with twenty degrees, who runs an Earth Sciences publication, took her to task about it! Slamming Mallory, Christian Schools, Home schooling, and everything else! I got involved in the fracas to begin with, because Mallory wasn't a Christian School or a Home Schooled student. Her dad and pastor helped her formulate her own conclusions, although the public system attempted to indoctrinate her from first grade. It amazed me how determined this guy was to 'get her'! His name's Phelps Hensley. She's a kid who wrote a letter to cyber-space. In my opinion, he lowered himself to duke it out with her. We proved she completed all her own work, and she has passed tests he formulated for her. She learned her stuff, and did great. He should have apologized, but he was still huffing and threatening. He went so far as to have linguistics experts check her writing style in high school with her current speech patterns to prove she didn't write her own papers. He only proved she did."

"Well, why wasn't I aware of any of this?"

"Um, I'm not sure. Looking back, I can see that the whole thing helped me. We had to refine the courses even more, so they could stand up to the critics."

Daniel finished the call and pulled the lid from his salad. That was a relief. A tempest that apparently had long-since passed. And he hadn't known about it in time to worry. He knew the name, Phelps Hensley, far better than Haynes did. Considered one of the most brilliant minds in the Discipline, he had been a full professor, authored textbooks, appeared on talk shows, lectured, and led field trips around the world to 'prove' all of his hypotheses. But Mallory was right! They were as full of holes as Sponge Bob©.

He made his way down to the car, lost in thought. David Higgins' words still rang in his ears; asking about one of the coeds from years earlier. Mentioning any of it still made him cringe and caused his face to burn with shame. He had established behavior patterns, wicked behavior patterns, that hadn't yielded their strangleholds on him easily. His mind traveled to bouts with a mysterious, virulent disease that had taken him twice to the yawning abyss of death! He had received the Lord after the first time, and married his beautiful nurse! But he hadn't yielded to the Lord until after Alexandra was born, and the disease hit him again. He allowed the tears to roll down his face and soak into his shirt collar. Guilt was the worst about his behavior after Diana had trusted him enough to marry him. She had lost a baby in the first trimester, and he had barely cared, still so intent on doing his own thing.

"Lord," he whispered. "I don't know why you loved me. I don't understand why you're so good to me; so kind! When You gave me Diana- And you've blessed *GeoHy* and entrusted us with Mallory! I have such a beautiful home! More than a man could dream of. And I thought it would be wicked to want another home, in the country, when we already have so much. But You poured that out to us, too! And then, You've provided us with a way to build onto the house, which we thought was impossible to do on our acreage. What's impossible with man is possible with You. Please let Your goodness lead me to repentance; help me to stay right until the end. Please keep blessing my kids, and making them willing to home school and go to Cyber-college!"

Shaking off the oppressive feelings, he pulled into the garage and entered the kitchen, whistling. No one was downstairs to welcome him. In his study, he pulled out his checkbook filling in the *Pay to the order of:* line, Honey Grove Baptist Church. Higgins had been partly right, he should put his money into what he believed in, and into the One responsible for his success. He made a notation on the check. Thanksgiving Offering!

⊰ ⊱

Pastor Ellis' secretary phoned Mallory, asking her to fill in on the piano. She committed, though the queasy feeling had come and gone all day.

"Don't commit for Sunday, though," David cautioned.

She nodded, sensing what he meant without his having to explain. She felt like they were the objects of a bidding war between Pastor Ellis and David's dad. It was nice to be wanted, but still-

Following the service, Kerry Larson invited them to go out. Then, a weird assortment of people accompanied them, so if Kerry had something on his mind, he wasn't free to discuss it.

"Max, I haven't seen you around much," Mallory exclaimed. "You've met David. Did you go away to school?"

"Nah, it's just that this church doesn't have many available women to date. I've been visiting around. When you and Callie first showed up, things seemed hopeful."

"Well, God will bring you the right partner in His timing, if you just go about your business of serving Him. You don't need a big pool to pick from, anyway."

"Well, you aren't limiting yourself to just one church," Max shot back.

She gave up and turned her attention to the menu.

⊰ ⊱

"You seem quiet. Did the professor meet you for lunch?"

Daniel laughed softly at his wife's guess. "He did. Well, he drank his lunch, and stuck me with his bar tab. I carried my food up to my office and picked at it through the afternoon. Just his usual round of opinions! 'I'm not a bona fide scientist; Mallory's degrees are phony. I should send my money and my kids to TU'. Hey, here's something I didn't know. Mallory composed an open letter a couple of years or so ago, stating that the Theory of Evolution is more full of holes than Sponge Bob©. Then she was careful to add a disclaimer that her dad never let her watch Sponge Bob©. I guess she sent out a well-researched document on the subject. I mean, I'm not sure who would have seen it, or cared; but then this big proponent of Evolution took her to task on it. It's created an amazing following on both sides of the issue. Hensley attacked the validity of her degrees, but Haynes made mincemeat of him on that score."

His laughter died away. "Seeing Higgins always leaves me feeling such shame. It's hard to shake off. Well, maybe I'm not supposed to shake it off. I guess I need the reminders. Do you remember the song that had the line, *Roll back the pages of memory now and then?*"

She nodded. "A great old song! We should find it and work it into our repertoire. We all need the right balance between becoming hardened by our past failures, and being pulled under with guilt."

      ⚏ ⚎

Carson Felton was arraigned and released on bond. The judge seemed sympathetic toward the felon. The Feds didn't care. The guy was guilty of the harassment, for sure; and his involvement with Dietrich's criminal enterprise was a pretty sure thing. Proving it was the difficulty.

Bransom's order: Patience. The guy was smooth in business and politics, but jumpy in the criminal realm. He had already implicated himself once, by seeking Jennifer out. He would make more mistakes, drawing the net around himself, and others who were involved.

Not certain how much he could trust Bisbee law enforcement he mentioned the situation to Steb Hanson. Usually, he didn't care for vigilantes, but Steb was good people. By the time Bransom received orders to stop the stakeouts at the art gallery Steb's guys were taking turns. It made Erik a little nervous. If someone got hurt~ something else to pray about!

      ⚏ ⚎

Sam Whitmore was on site, setting up a new computer and phone system. Roger called a meeting with the *Chandler* department heads. He addressed several issues that he was sure weren't the way he wanted them. Jacobson had referred him to a reliable corporate law firm in Houston; he needed his facts before he addressed work relationships and his new guidelines. He was within his rights, forbidding offensive materials on his property; that included lockers and cars in the company lot. Computers belonging to *Sanders-Chandler* were to have nothing installed but business related software. Email accounts, though personal, would be monitored for questionable content.

"When you're here, I'm buying your time and your productivity. I don't want your head in some other game!"

A hand shot up. "What about our breaks and lunch hours?"

"Good question." Roger kept his temper in check. "The plant in Hope has a cafeteria on-site-that offers excellent food," he added as faces registered contempt. "We're considering adding a cafeteria here. It's a pretty good drive from here to anything decent. If you can get a good meal, right here, and shorten your lunch breaks to thirty minutes, we might consider flex-time, allowing y'all to come in thirty minutes later, or leave half hour earlier. I'd like to believe some of you could actually occupy your minds with something worthwhile. If any of you are interested in furthering your studies, you can notify Suzanne."

᚛ ᚜

Daniel's return ride from church, in the company of his three eldest was quiet. Al was reading a book, Cass was listening to a violin concerto in her headset, and Jer was usually quiet. He tried to relax, although the unpleasant lunchtime meeting kept reinserting itself into his consciousness. His phone vibrated, and he pulled it free, expecting it to be Diana. It wasn't! He pressed decline and turned the device off. Cass didn't seem aware of his action, but Al and Jer did their look-exchanging thing.

"Okay, kids head up toward bed," he ordered as the garage door slid down behind the vehicles.

"Okay, Dad, we're the big kids; it's barely eight-thirty, and it's summer. We were planning to swim. Are you coming in with us?" Jeremiah's gaze seemed to penetrate his soul.

"Oh, yeah, well, help your mom with the little guys. I'm going to go return a call." He escaped to his office, heart pounding. Sinking into his desk chair, he switched his phone back on. His hands shook as he pushed the button to return the missed calls.

"You called me back," A woman's voice caressed the words. "I was beginning to wonder if you really care, after all."

He recovered his voice. "So, after seventeen years, you finally figured it out? What do you want? Why did you call?"

"David Higgins called me and said he ran into you on campus, and that my name came up."

Daniel could barely believe what he was hearing. Evidently, the professor had less affinity for the truth than he had credited him with. "Yeah, it wasn't on campus, and he's the one who brought your name up. I didn't. Look, you know I'm married, and I'm a Christian. I don't know what Higgins was up to, but I'm not trying to instigate anything." He was attempting to be firm, yet cautious. 'A woman spurned'-his inner voice warned.

"Daniel, wait. We had something!" The sultry voice was insistent.

He ran his hand through his hair. They hadn't really! He had played the role, and she had fallen for the oldest lines in the book. Which meant that he had been a crumb! And he knew that!

"Listen, Nanci; that was a long time ago. Time marches on."

"I still look good, though. At least, that's what I'm told. Let's just meet for a cup of coffee, and catch up. You can show me pictures of your family. I can come downtown?"

A furious banging at his door told him Xavier was attacking it with something that would mar the expensive wood. And then a furious banging began inside his head. Fear gripped him, and he bolted dizzily toward the half-bath, and vomited.

⚔ ⚔

"She's beautiful." Parker Prescott tilted his new little daughter toward Callie so she could get another look.

"She is. She looks like you. I'm tired."

Parker kissed her hand lightly. "Get some rest. You did good. Shall I send out word, or wait until you've rested a bit."

A tired smile, "Go ahead; start sending pictures. I know they're all eager for news."

⚔ ⚔

Mallory studied the pictures of the beautiful new-born. "H-m-m, Parker says they haven't named her yet because Callie's too tired. We need to have names picked out. I hope Callie's okay. I've had misgivings about her staying on the field, but Diana thought it should go okay. As long as everything's fairly routine! What amazes me is the way Donovan and Carmine have been about all this. I'm not sure if they either one have the Christian maturity to be this trusting in the Lord, or if they're both just kind of checked out on parenting."

David smiled. "They probably know you're worried enough for everybody. I'm glad you're seeing a doctor tomorrow and giving birth in a big-city hospital with all the emergency back-up systems. Not that I haven't been praying for everything to be smooth."

She nodded. The medical appointment loomed large in her mind. "I'm surprised Diana hasn't called me about this. She has so many brothers and sisters, but this is her first niece. She's been excited. Well, she's probably talking to Parker, or her mom and dad and the rest of the family."

"Well, you're family. Call her!"

She tried, but there was no answer.

⊰ ⊱

Ivan Summers returned to Daisy Lodge, and ordered a large sirloin, cooked medium with a salad and loaded baked potato. Two weeks since the end of his ordeal with the gang members, he was mending well, physically. The Bureau chief wanted him to take more comp time and visit the shrink. It had sounded firmer than a 'suggestion'. He cut into the steak, and mixed meat and potato together on the fork, enjoying the melded flavors. The sky-tints swirled, darkened, rearranged; mirrored with a rippled effect on the lake's surface. Lovely night. Someone dropped a dish, and he jumped a mile, grabbing automatically for his service revolver. It wasn't there, and he eased back sheepishly into the chair. His nerves were shot. Every time he fell asleep, he bolted back awake, hearing the chilling rattlers of a snake, or sensing himself swinging blindfolded and bound, above a deep drop. Maybe time would heal; it hadn't been that long. He paid for the barely-touched meal and made his way through the soft, dark night to his car.

⊰ ⊱

Diana handed Nadia off to Cassandra and Ryan to Alexandra. "Where's your dad?" her question to Jeremiah as she hurried to grab Xavier before he broke down the office door.

100

"He's in there, making a phone call. I thought he was going to swim with us," Jeremiah's answer. He didn't mention the fact that his dad's actions had struck him as out of the norm.

She grabbed her small son. "Xavier, stop that. Look, you're messing up the door." She carried him up the stairs, much against his will. It seemed a little odd that Daniel hadn't told him to stop.

"Cassandra, who was Daddy talking to?"

She shrugged, struggling with Nadia and her pajamas.

"Well, I'm kind of wondering the same thing." Alexandra's eyes were big as saucers. "It was kind of weird. And then he told the three of us to get ready for bed like we're five-year-olds."

A troubled expression crossed Diana's features as she made her way back down the stairs. Leaning her ear against the door, she tapped softly. She pushed the door ajar. "Daniel, Honey; are you okay?" She moved quickly to the bathroom, where he sprawled next to the toilet. Terrified eyes met hers. "I'm sick again, Diana. It's back!"

She couldn't decide what to do. She had nursed him twice before. Now, she stood terrified. Everything was different now. They had six children. "I'm calling an ambulance." She backed out, shut the door, and didn't return.

To 911, emergency, she spoke softly, stating the emergency as she assumed it to be. Possibility of a virulent and contagious disease! She didn't want the kids any more exposed than they already were. Or herself!

Of course, the emergency response vehicles couldn't find the address.

※ ※

"Something's wrong." Mallory's face was a study in anxiety. "Neither of them are answering their cells or the land line."

"I'm sure they're fine. If there was a problem, they'd let you know. They have such a big family, and they're all so hyped about Parker's baby, they probably just turned it all off so they could get some sleep. Which is what you need to do! I'll be up finishing a few drawings for Sanders. If I hear anything, I'll let you know." David kissed her and tucked her in.

※ ※

The nausea subsided, but Daniel's head continued to pound! Diana! Her frightened eyes danced before him, and she backed away, shutting the door between them. No! "No!" He shrieked!

The door pushed open and eerie apparitions in hazard suits stood above him. He tried to shrink away, but they buckled him, struggling to the gurney. "Diana; I want Diana."

They pushed him out to the ambulance through an empty house. Diana must have taken the kids and left him! "No! No!"

He fought against the ghostly figures. They were stronger than they looked. "Diana," he panted. "I have to go~my wife and kids~Diana! I have~to~find~Diana. No! No! A-A-H!"

"Calm down Buddy."

"His name's Daniel," one of them informed the other.

"Calm down, Daniel. We're nearly to the hospital. We'll find out what the problem is. Your wife's going to get your kids~"

"A-a-a-h! No! No! Diana! Diana! Hone-e-e-y!" He thrashed wildly, shutting out the voices trying to reason with him. They waited while the ER prepared for isolation, before wheeling him in where more suited-up medical personnel awaited him.

One of the EMT's gave their assessment. "Through the roof BP but no fever! The wife seemed to think he has a virulent infection; something he's fought off a couple of times before. Something he got in Africa! He had high fever then, and hemorrhaging. She was trying to get her children to the grandparents', and then she's on her way. I guess he vomited."

"Mr. Faulkner, Mr. Faulkner, Daniel, calm down! Your wife will be here soon. She's making sure the children are cared for, and then she'll have to suit up when she arrives."

He tried to calm down and focus on the distorted voice emanating from behind a window in the protective gear.

"That's better. Hold still while we start a line. Was there blood in your vomit?"

� ꅥ

Diana realized her panicked response wasn't the wisest. Her immediate thought was to isolate the rest of the family; now she realized the three oldest had been in close proximity to their dad all evening, especially in the drive home. Then, she had handed the babies off to them. She knew she shouldn't expose Daniel's parents by bringing them to the house. She dropped them unceremoniously without so much as a toothbrush. With emotions in turmoil, she donned the protective suit and rushed to Daniel's side.

Calm now, his brown eyes met hers, and he smiled sheepishly. "I guess my blood pressure shot up and made my head hurt. I don't have fever, at all. I-I guess I just panicked."

She stared at him blankly, not sure the comm. system in the head gear was working properly. She rocked dizzily and reprimanded herself. She was too professional to hit the floor. Still, when a chair slid behind her, she sank down gratefully. Hypertension, and no fever? She could hardly process the miraculous news. Well, such a spike in BP wasn't a good thing! She patted his hand. "I need to go call your parents and the kids."

The nurse stopped her. "We aren't stepping this down, quite yet. Just a precaution"!

She nodded. "I feel a little foolish-"

"Well, don't. Believe me, we'd rather be safe than sorry."

⊨ ⊨

Mallory viewed more pictures of Parker and Callie and Elizabeth Marie Prescott. "She's really beautiful; isn't she? Callie looks better, too. I was worried last night."

He laughed. "Yeah, told ya everything was fine."

She nodded acknowledgement. She was still concerned at not hearing anything from Diana. But, hey, they had her married off now. She should probably stay out of their hair.

He caught her and kissed her. "You weren't really that worried about the Faulkners. You just wanted to go up to Tulsa to get out of seeing the doctor."

"H-m-m, that's a thought. I should have insisted."

⊨ ⊨

"We're doing that much work on the ride back to the office?" Mallory noticed a carton of files in the back of the SUV as she slid in following her appointment.

"Uh, no, actually, on the way back to Arkansas. I thought we might as well go now, as wait for tomorrow. Lisette's knocking out a bunch of stuff this afternoon, and we can accomplish as much riding as we could by being in at the office. Unless, you just particularly want to go back," he added.

She laughed suddenly. "No way! Arkansas! Here we come!"

They stopped for fast food, and then she started to yawn. He pushed a pillow behind her. "Go ahead and sleep. If I have any questions, I'll make notes to ask you later."

He smiled as he saw her sneak another peak at the sonogram stored in her phone. Relieved by the medical visit and knowledgeable instructions, he felt revitalized to tackle the documents.

Rain was pelting down hard by the time they reached the state line. He sighed, not sure what the forecast predicted.

Mallory sat up, rubbing her hand that had fallen asleep. "I love summer rains. Everything was getting dry. Wow, it looks like you did a lot." She swiped beneath her eyes with manicured fingers, in case there were make-up smudges; then checked the sonogram again.

They stopped in Hope at *Sanders, Corporation* to drop the drawings off for Roger. "I'll be right back," David began.

"No, I want to go in and see my mom." Mallory was gathering her handbag and feeling for her shoes.

"Okay, Darrell, let us out under the porte-cochère, and go park. I'll call when we're ready to roll."

Suzanne showed them in to Roger's office immediately, and the executive opened the tube and spread the drawings eagerly on his conference table. He glanced up sharply. He wasn't sure what he expected, but the drawings were first class, signed and stamped with David as a licensed architect. "Wow! Wow! These are incredible."

David nodded modestly. "Yes, Sir, the problem is with the bridges across the street."

Roger's eyes met his.

David continued, "Well, when Mallory was in the motorized chair, she promised the Lord she wouldn't forget what it was like; all the obstacles. If we make the bridges with stairs, the handicapped can't use them; neither can kids on their bikes."

Roger nodded, considering the concerns of the young couple. The plant had never been fenced. For security reasons, he planned to change that. Kids going to and from school had always cut across the *Chandler* property. The original discussion had suggested two bridges across the frenetic traffic on the avenue; one for employees, and another beyond the *Chandler* plant, for people in the community.

"What do you recommend?"

David shrugged. "Petitioning for traffic lights and pedestrian cross-walks! Maybe if the city can't do it right now, they'll give us some kind of a permit to place them, ourselves. The cops should set up a speed trap there, anyway. I'm sure the city could use the revenue, and people need to slow down. I mean, it's hard to get in and out of the plant property in a car. Making a left-hand turn is akin to a suicide wish. And pedestrian bridges wouldn't address that issue at all."

Roger nodded. Good points. "Hey, thanks for introducing me to Cade Holman. People that sharp don't knock on my door every day."

David started to give Mallory credit for the discovery, but she had slipped out. "Mallory did the preliminary interview, and she was impressed with him. She knew you wanted to give *Chandler* people first shot, though."

Roger laughed ruefully. "Yeah, I'm not sure why."

"Because it's fair, and you're a good guy. They'll get in line."

"I hope. You think Mallory's going to sell me her gym?"

"That I'm not sure about. She's in love with the place. She's such a sports fanatic. I should go check on her."

He found her, and it was kind of sad. She was trying to show her mom the sonogram. And, Suzanne was just weird. He sighed. She cared; she just had the strangest knack for not showing it!"

Roger came through with brief case and the tubular portfolio in hand. "Beth's meeting me at McKenna's. Can y'all join us? I'm buying. Suzanne, how about you and Erik"?

⚔ ⚔

Admitted, and situated in a hospital bed, Daniel sighed wearily, leaning back against a hard pillow that crackled like it would break before it gave.

"I don't know whether to call home again, or not." Diana's expression was questioning.

"Nah, you told them I'm okay; it's a blood pressure issue. Hopefully, everyone's asleep." Tears started. "Di, Honey~"

Something in his tone alarmed her. "What? What's wrong? Who were you talking to? Did something happen to scare you?"

He looked tired; disheveled, and vulnerable. "Well, when I talked to David Higgins today, he brought up Nanci Nichols."

He sensed her stiffen.

"I told him again, that I'm saved now, ashamed of my past, trying to forget everything and keep moving forward." His eyes pled for understanding.

"Go on." Her tone was tense.

"Well, I was trying to forget the whole thing, but on the way home from church, she called me. Higgins had called her, told her we met for lunch. And he lied about where. Then he told her her name came up, leading her to believe I asked about her. Honey, I didn't. He brought her name up. Why would he stir up trouble for me?"

"And-and, you called her?"

"Yeah! Yes, I did. I'm not sure why. It scared me; her calling. I started thinking I shouldn't make her mad; the thing about a 'woman spurned'. Was she going to extort money? Was she going to sue?"

Diana folded her arms, regarding him coldly. "Right!" she scoffed softly. "You know, the kids aren't stupid. And neither am I!"

The aide came in, filled his water glass, and checked his vitals and IV. She demonstrated how to pull the chair out into a bed, pointed out sheets and blankets, and left, pulling the door closed.

"I'm not trying to sleep on that slab. I'm going home. I'll be back in the morning. They'll probably release you then." She grabbed her handbag and was gone.

⇥ ⇤

In the silent darkness, Daniel Faulkner took stock. It was dawning on him that the illness he dreaded wasn't back, and he would probably live to see another day. As he faced himself honestly, he didn't blame Diana for seeing through his stupid excuses and getting mad. Some of it was true. His feelings were a hodge-podge of fear; maybe fear mixed with a curiosity that shouldn't have caught hold of him. The Lord had caught him up short! Now, in the loneliness of the hospital room, he was profoundly glad. Glad he didn't have the illness again, glad for salvation, glad the BP spike hadn't caused him to stroke out. Tears eased out, and he trembled with exhaustion at the toll the past few hours had taken.

The door pushed open and the light flipped on. She was back, and spoiling for a fight.

He laughed through the shakes. "Yeah, I missed you, too."

"Oh! You are so impossible, Daniel Faulkner!" She flung herself across him.

Chapter 9: ASSETS

David passed Mallory the basket of rolls, and she turned up her nose. Lately, bread of any type had been her mainstay. It was okay with him. He was hungry.

After the blessing, Erik buttered a roll and set it aside. "What's this about, Sanders?" His voice was loaded with suspicion.

Roger laughed. "Just like an FBI Agent to see plots where there aren't any. I guess I should invite the two of you out more often."

"You wanting Suzanne to move to Houston?" Small talk wasn't Erik's long suit, and he came straight to his point.

Beth laughed. "That would probably take more than a steak."

They all ordered, and Roger threw his hands up in a gesture of surrender. "I guess I do have a little agenda I could use your help with. I don't want your wife to run the *Chandler* operation, so you can relax on that score. I had a little talk with your son-in-law, but I don't think he 'got it'."

Erik's steely eyes met his. "Well, you're the boss. Maybe you should make sure you express yourself clearly and succinctly. If Terry mistreats my daughter or granddaughter, I got a problem with 'im. I've been under the impression Charity got herself a pretty good guy. They both got saved, and Terry seems to have a real passion about serving the Lord."

"Yeah, but that's not what I'm paying him to do. In his spare time, I don't care what he does. I mean, I'm glad he hasn't filled my computer up with pornographic sites like the Houston people were doing. But, I don't think he should use my electronics and the time I'm paying him for, to study and promote Creationism."

"Well, that is a lot better," Beth's voice was bright.

Roger shook his head. Terry had missed his meaning, and evidently, so was Beth.

"Look, when it's Evolution or Creationism, I haven't decided." Roger's words were candid, and they brought frowns from most of the group. "I'm not a 'pure' scientist in the strict sense of the word. 'Pure' scientists are the ones who just want to understand for the sake of understanding. I'm an 'applied' scientist, which means I take the knowledge and understanding they get, and apply it in practical ways. Sorry to sound so heathen, but to make money. There, it's out on the table. To me, the argument of how everything got its start is immaterial. To my employees, I want it to be immaterial. I don't want my people who are sticklers for evolution to jam that on everyone else. If your son-in-law wants to prove Creationism, and preach it and prove it to everyone else, he should resign from *Sanders*. He knows the money won't be as good, though."

Mallory hotly disagreed about Creationism, but Roger knew that. As a business owner, she sympathized about any of his employees stealing time. She spoke up. "Erik's right, though, Roger. You're the boss. You need to crack down on everyone who isn't doing what they're supposed to do, when they're supposed to do it. It's really hard to stay on top of people and keep it fair, though. I don't think Erik should have to be the heavy for *Sanders, Corporation* stuff. It's a delicate thing being an in-law, and addressing your own family stuff."

The only thing she had ordered was a loaded baked potato, and she devoured it. "Can I have yours?" She bestowed her most winning smile on David, but his response was measured.

Suzanne laughed. "Here, you can have mine." She scooted it toward her daughter. "That's something I can still barely get down."

David and Mallory both got her meaning. "Yeah, we've eaten lots of taters in our time; haven't we, Mom? Usually they sound good to me, but only if they're really loaded up! Especially with tons of butter!" Her eyes sparkled as she loaded on extra.

Erik had really been hoping for an opportunity to speak with David and Mallory alone, but this seemed as close as he was going to get. He plunged in. "Summers' noggin's about healed up. He wants to get back to work, but he admits he's still pretty shell-shocked. Haslett's doing okay; the investigation of his shooting is about to close. Part of him knows he did what he had to do~"

David rocked back on his chair, raising both hands defensively. "Not exactly dinner conversation, Bransom."

Erik laughed. "I guess that answers my question about how you're doin'."

"I'm doing fine!" The tautness in David's voice belied his words. "I just don't want to talk about it!"

"You know, when we went back in daylight, we couldn't figure out how in the world you scaled that rock face up to the cave! Or why! It was a pretty death-defying stunt!"

"How's Jennifer doing?" Beth's voice changed the subject to try to break the tension.

Erik ignored the question. Mallory didn't seem to like the subject of Jennifer, and he felt he needed to pursue his line of questioning with David.

"Has he said much to you about it, Mallory?"

"Um, no, Sir, he's just still kind of mad at Jeff and me for looking for him."

"Well, that's another subject that interests me. How did you know where to look for him?"

"Well, there had been all kinds of activity along the lower water courses all day. I figured he got away from all of that, but had to go where he could still have water. Since I moved to Dallas and can't get home very often, I've spent a lot of time studying maps of the area. For where there might be concentrations of Diamonds. I don't think any of my maps and charts showed there was a cliff anywhere."

"Yeah," David interjected. "And I'm not mad, as much as rattled at what could have happened. I'm glad Summers is getting better. He'll be okay. I wasn't a hero; I didn't want to be a hero. I think if I could have gotten away, I would have left him there."

᚛ ᚜

A nurse wheeled Daniel to the hospital entrance where the *GeoHy* RV puttered softly.

He stood up. "Thank you for everything, Jan. Here's a little leaflet I'd like for you to look at if you get a minute." He pushed a Gospel tract into her hand, and she thanked him.

"Nice rig, Mr. Faulkner. It looks like you plan to take the doctor's orders about relaxing a little. Hopefully we won't see you back with a BP like that."

"Hopefully not"! His voice sounded extra fervent as he hopped aboard.

Diana boarded with a handful of instructions and an appointment card for a specialist. "Okay, Arkansas, here we come. Cassandra, are you riding with us?"

"I can, and help with the kids. I'd rather go with Grandma and Grandpa and Al and Jer."

Diana laughed. "Go ahead. I can manage. I hope we can make it with just one stop."

The convoy headed out, and she started distributing food.

He bit slowly into a peanut butter and jelly sandwich, and nodded, yes, to the chips.

"I guess the kids are mad at me, too," he observed.

Her innocent blue eyes met his. "Why? What did they say?

They didn't say anything. They didn't say if they were worried about me, or if they're glad I'm okay. Al and Jer didn't even get out of the car, and Cass didn't say a word."

"Well, you pretty nearly scared us all to death. I scared your parents, too. We're all glad you're okay."

⚅ ⚄

"Pull up close to the stable," David directed Darrell Hopkins. A steady rain continued to fall, and he knew Mallory was eager to see *Zakkar*. "Forget it," he changed his mind. "We're both in good shoes. We'll change and come back."

In a few minutes, they were changed and wheeling toward the stable in the golf cart.

"I love this place." Mallory's eyes were alight as she gazed around appreciatively.

"Yeah, kind of a dreary evening."

She clasped his arm and leaned her head against his shoulder. "I love it; all soft and misty, with the hard edges blended. I'm jealous of Jennifer that she's such an artist. I wish I could create a painting of how beautiful this place looks right now; the foreboding clouds and the warmth of the lights from all the windows."

He enjoyed her snuggling and kissed her hard. "You aren't mad at me, then? For dragging you here a day earlier than planned?"

She laughed. "No. Don't forget, the main thrust of *DiaMo* is actually centered here. Before, it raised lots of red flags when I came. And this whole operation needs a lot of your oversight. You are amazing what you've accomplished here. Roger really liked the plans you drew."

He pulled the cart up as close as possible, but they still had to wade in deep mud. "I need to have the guys lay a stone path out to here," he observed.

He smiled as Mallory made over her horse, checking on *El Capitan*, the other horses, and the stable. It wasn't cleaned as well as when he was around. He made his way back to Mallie's side, stroking the mare's face, too. "You ready to go in? You can ride her in the barn, the doctor said. Tomorrow and Saturday, too."

They kicked off soaked boots in the mud room and made their way to the great room, where Mallory flicked the plasma on. *Sox* were playing the *Yankees*, who had been in a two-game slump. She was hoping that would hold for another game.

David was doing his usual rummaging in the fridge. "You want anything?" His voice carried.

"No, I guess not." She smiled when he emerged with a can of Dr. Pepper™ and a half gallon container of strawberry ice cream.

"Want some?" His offer seemed sincere, so she allowed him to spoon her a few bites. Then motors and headlights materialized. David grinned. "Looks like the Faulkners are here."

The convoy went past. She was trying not to feel hurt that Diana hadn't taken her calls, or called her back.

"It's raining," David reminded her. "I'm sure they're all in their city slicker duds. They'll just pull into the garage so they can unload and stay dry. Let's take the golf cart over, and see if they're all okay."

"Well, evidently, they are. I guess they didn't care I was kind of worried. Let's just watch the game."

"No, we can DVR it. Come on." He held his hand toward her to help her up.

Lisette Billingsley cut smoothly through the water of Mallory's swimming pool. The evening air still registered in the upper nineties. Bryce watched her from a deck chair. She dove and swam underwater to get closer.

"Don't you dare splash me," He commanded petulantly.

She laughed, hoisting herself from the water to the edge. "Why not? Are you afraid you'll melt? How come you're so sour tonight?"

She shouldn't have asked. He went into a tirade about how Mallory's mansion was nothing compared to the one he grew up in, the pool was basically a puddle-blah, blah.

She eased back into the pool, allowing her tears to blend with the water. She kept trying, but this was hard. She turned over, propelling herself away from him, on her back.

"Mallory was nice to let us use this. If you don't want to swim, we could drive over to Arkansas."

"What for? This place is a dump, and Arkansas's worse!"

"You don't know that. You've never been there. We could have some fun if you'd just come down off it."

He studied his nails in the fading light. "Who was that hanging around at the office all afternoon?"

She swam near and rested her arms on the ledge; her face looking cute bathed in lights turning on by sensor. She laughed. "Oh, the kid in the suit and tennis shoes? He just got his Master's Degree in Chemistry, and he's trying to get hired at either *Sanders* or *Chandler*. He wanted to talk with David; I'm not sure why. And, I didn't know they had headed out for the country instead of coming back after Mallory's appointment." She frowned. "Why?"

"Did you think he was handsome?"

She laughed. "I guess. Like I mentioned, his ensemble struck me as a little nerdy. I guess he was cute; like squeaky-clean looking. He's a brainiac, Mensa geek, and I felt out of my league." She was pretty sure Bryce didn't care about her enough to be jealous; not that there was anything to be jealous of. At least, this was akin to a conversation rather than his habitual pouting.

"He was probably really hanging around to see Mallory."

Annoyance shot through Lisette. 'It figured. If Bryce was jealous, it would be over Mallory.' She somersaulted and swam furiously for several minutes. Emerging, she wiped tears in a thick towel. "I guess I'm ready to go home if you don't want to swim with me!" She pulled on a cover up and jammed pedicured feet into flip-flops.

⊰ ⊱

There was quite a bit of commotion as the Faulkners unloaded and started carrying in suitcases and belongings. David helped.

"My mom and dad are planning to stay in the RV; where can we hook up?" Daniel hated to impose more on David and Mallory's good graces, in view of the fabulous cabin; but after his mom and dad had risked their lives to help with the kids, he had hated to say, "See ya", and leave them behind.

"Well, hooking up's no problem. But we have a nice caretaker's cottage that no one lives in. They might have more room. I'll take them over later in the golf cart. I'll go park the bus somewhere that it won't sink any more in the mud." The large vehicle would have been heavy enough, but bullet proofing in the glass and some armor beneath the skin added to the gross weight. He backed it carefully into the shop, then, curious he leafed through hospital release papers before bolting back through the rain.

Back inside, he thought the vibes were definitely weird. He addressed Jerry and Patricia. "I'll load your suitcases in the cart, and we'll take them to where you'll be staying. You can look it all over, and then I'll bring you back, or you can go ahead and bunk down; whichever you want. We can still hook up the coach, too, if y'all prefer."

He situated them in the attractive space, and they stated exhaustion. They were ready to retire. "The kitchen here isn't fully stocked," he apologized. "In the morning, breakfast will be served over at the bunkhouse, and Daniel and Diana have lots of groceries. We'll make sure no one starves. When I get Mallory back home, I'll bring the golf cart back and park it here so y'all can get around." He grinned at the senior Faulkner. "I'm assuming you've had quite a bit of experience with golf carts."

"Yes he has, and so have I." Patricia Faulkner wasn't one to be overlooked.

⊰ ⊱

"What's that guy doing here?" Bryce's voice sounded extra-whiny as the garage door rose.

114

"I don't know." Lisette was as perplexed as he was. "Maybe he doesn't have any place to go. Maybe he was hoping David would loan him some money until he gets a job nailed down and starts getting paid."

Bryce stared at her, trying to grasp the concept of being broke. He always burned up his inheritance money before it came in semiannually, but there was always the assurance that there were millions at this disposal if he got too jammed up. "Why don't you get into dry stuff, and let's pack for a couple of days and go to Arkansas, like you were talking about?"

She nodded. She hadn't been home since before they had gotten married. "If he doesn't have a place to stay, do you mind if he stays here while we're gone?"

He grimaced. "Well, maybe he'll want to go with us. You know, if he's looking for Anderson."

"Okay. I'll hurry. You talk to him."

⊰ ⊱

"Ooh, looks like the rest of our ice cream melted," Mallory observed as she resumed the baseball game.

"Yeah, that's how it's best." He plopped down next to her, slurping at the soupy mess. She gave him a strange side-ways glance, and he set it back down. "You feeling sick again?"

"No, I'm~I guess~I'm just~tired~"

He pulled her into his arms. "Your mom; she's just~"

She patted at tears. "I know, but sometimes~"

He held her while she sobbed, at last, he spoke, "And then, Diana usually comes through for you like a trooper! And she was all distracted tonight." He cupped her chin with his fingers. "I like to look at it. Send it to my phone. I love you, Mallory. We'll be okay."

She nodded, grateful for his perception. "I can't figure out what I did to make her mad."

He scoffed softly. "I'm pretty sure you're not the one she's mad at. I think Daniel's in the doghouse. There was a clip full of paper work in the RV. Daniel took an ambulance ride to the hospital last night, but then got released this morning."

She sat up, wiping at her eyes. "You shouldn't have looked through their stuff. What did it say? What's wrong with him?"

"That's all I know. I felt bad about going through their stuff."

115

‑⊰ ⊱‑

Alexandra awakened, aware that rain still tapped against the windows. She sat up to stretch and bumped her head on the ceiling. Oh yeah, as the big sister, she was in the uppermost bunk of the *Girls'* bunkroom. She liked it. Aside from vacations, she had never shared her space with her little sisters. She and Cass had whispered and giggled until Nadia's sleepy little voice had grumbled that she was trying to get some sleep. She scaled down the ladder, grabbing her clothes from the previous day, and headed into the bathroom. Quick shower; then before she finished dressing, Cass banged on the door. She cracked it open. "What do you want?"

She needed a turn.

With hair and makeup finished, Alexandra stole into the quiet kitchen. Maybe if everyone got plenty of sleep, they'd all be in a better mood. She brewed a cup of hot chocolate and stepped onto the back porch with the mug and her Bible. She was supposed to have devotions each morning, but today her perfect world seemed to be caught in an earthquake. She sat, staring across the gray landscape, repeated in her stormy gray eyes. She inhaled sharply. "Okay! At least, Daddy isn't border-line dead! Or Mama! Or any of us!" The illness hadn't really come back! Just a bad scare! A BAD scare!! She trembled as tears tried to ruin her makeup.

She didn't open the Bible; she just sat hugging it, and pouring out her thoughts to God. She was aware of her family's stirring inside, but she wasn't ready to face it quite yet. Whatever was up, it didn't seem like normalcy could ever reign again.

When Mallory drew up in a golf cart, and invited her to go with her for breakfast in the bunkhouse, she was relieved.

"Should you say something to your mom or dad?" Mallory asked.

"No, they'll figure it out. It'll be fine."

Mallory pushed in the throttle and they headed down the drive.

Frowning, Daniel stepped out onto the back steps. He was fairly certain Alexandra didn't have permission to leave.

The wind had picked up, sending the rain into the cart, so Mallory decided to take a short-cut. Then, she and Alexandra both screamed in unison!

"Whoa!" Daniel yelped in panic. "What are you‑"

Down the slope near the bunkhouse, David was watching the same scenario unfold. The cart mired down quickly in the mud, leaving the girls in a precarious position on the hillside.

Frozen at first, David finally managed to spring into action! He made a step or two, before one of his boots landed in a hole. His feet stopped short, as his body continued the forward momentum. He sprawled face-first into the muck.

Closer, Daniel sprinted, and got his daughter to safety. He turned back, grasping the cart to steady it from going over until David could reach them.

David lifted Mallory free as she protested. "Oh, no! Look! You're getting me all muddy!"

He set her down "Right! I'm getting you all muddy!"

Daniel started yelling at her, "That's a golf cart! Not an ATV. You're supposed to keep it on the paths~"

David laughed. "Save it for later, Faulkner We're going to go clean up. Why don't y'all go check what's for breakfast? We'll join you as soon as we can."

Slogging back toward the cabin, Daniel surveyed his own muddy shoes and pant legs. "Where did you think you were going? Pretty sure no one gave you permission to take off." His ire concentrated on his first-born, and she gave him a strange wounded look. "Help mom load the little kids while I clean up a little."

⊰ ⊱

Roger and Beth sat visiting with their daughter while they finished breakfast at the Hope Country Club.

"David did all of that?" Catrina was amazed by the drawings and all of the notations. He had already contacted the city of Houston, submitting the requests for the signals and crosswalks, as well as other zoning issues and permits. Roger had looked at the bids for beginning the work, with David's check on the references and recommendations. The *Chandler* site was moving right along.

"You really need a good secretary next," Beth observed. She and Roger were both proud of Cat's accomplishments, graduating with honors, double majors in Chemistry and Business Administration. She was champing at the bit for the oversight of the new acquisition.

117

"Did I introduce you to that Organic Chemist the other night?" Roger's question was casual.

She grinned. "No! I would have been tongue-tied anyway. What's his story?"

Roger did a double-take, surprised at his daughter's blushing response. "His story is that he has an M.S. in Organic Chemistry. Seems sharp, and like a real nice kid. I just don't think I really need him. He's probably out of our price range, anyway. Remember, you have a payroll budget."

"Oh, yeah"

⚑ ⚐

"Are you mad at me?"

David looked at her and dissolved in laughter, the staccato cackle that erupted when he was really tickled.

"What's funny?" she demanded.

"You are! Sometimes, I'm afraid you've changed so much that you're not the old Mallory. But then, no, you really haven't changed at all."

"Meaning?"

"That you're still all about the Diamonds. Like you always were"!

"That isn't true!"

The staccato laugh again. "It absolutely is true! That's why you decided to go off-road and cut across there! So you could check the heads of all the little rivulets!"

She looked at him, nonplussed. "Well, I didn't want Alexandra to get soaked."

He shrugged. "Well, yeah, you always cared a lot about people, too. My same girl! My friend!"

⚑ ⚐

Bryce and Cade slept while Lisette drove. She hadn't minded, playing her music through earphones, enjoying the solitude. She wasn't sure how she was going to manage unloading Cade on David and Mallory! A ticklish situation, but he had agreed to Bryce's invitation eagerly. He was cute, a little on the bashful side. Mid-morning, she offered to treat for breakfast at Hal's.

118

"When do you think I'll get a chance to talk to David?" Cade's antsy insistence.

"Okay, look, I work for them. They get away on weekends, and I'm pretty sure they don't want me barging in. If we go to Hal's we may run into them, or at least Pastor and Lana."

"Pastor and Lana? Who's that? Is that the guy's name or his title?" The Chemist seemed uneasy.

"His title! His name's John Anderson; he's David's dad. He's the pastor of Faith Baptist, here in town; he has been since David and Mallory and I were all in second grade."

Cade shot Bryce a desperate look. "You up with that"?

"Well, I'm up with breakfast. With any luck, they won't even be there."

⊰ ⊱

Trent Morrison shared a large round top with Bob Porter, Ivan Summers, Mason Haslett, Lt. Ward Atchison, and Erik Bransom. They all knew the lieutenant was concerned about his army career.

"Okay, let's remember to keep our voices down," Erik cautioned. "Most of the world isn't even aware of what happened. If they knew, they'd want the Army to sacrifice an officer higher up the chain of command than you are. I mean, if lieutenants can fire those systems at will, we're in a world of trouble. Since the Pentagon doesn't want to admit it was a miracle, they could just leave the file open, and say they don't have all the data in. Obviously none of the rogue states could have done it, or they would have done something to hurt our image; not help us fight our criminal elements. I mean they could take one of the drones in Afghanistan and fire it into a Christian enclave; eliminate some Christians that way, and point the finger at the U.S. for killing innocent civilians while we tout the Geneva Convention for the rest of the world to abide by."

"Well, don't give them any ideas, Bransom. They're not as smart as you are."

Erik chuckled. "Exactly! That's why they couldn't fire those missiles! Mallory doesn't want you to get court-martialed, but if you do, she wants to hire you." Erik's countenance clouded. "Sadly, that usually means prison time, too. I mean, you're a hero! Fighting for our country! They shouldn't hang you out to dry."

119

The tough, muscular young man shrugged. "Guess that's the way it goes sometimes. Hey, if I'm out of the fight, you guys have to keep at it. You know, National Parks and Forests were set aside so Americans wouldn't destroy the beauty for their financial pursuits: mining, factories, logging, and agriculture. We can't even take a rock or pick a flower. But these foreign entities are coming up like they own the place, clearing land for their crops, and posing serious threats to anyone who strays innocently into their operations. That makes me hoppin' mad! I said hoppin' 'cause you guys are all Christians. If I get court-martialed, whenever I get out of prison, I'm gonna form my own army to fight for what we have here."

Porter was concerned about the informal meeting of joint agencies. Working for the Federal Government made him paranoid. The men in the group were right. There needed to be cooperation and coordination among the agencies. Usually, they were all too busy defining territories and competing. This threat was serious, though, sneaking en masse through the cracks! The good guys needed to show a united front! And there was no more time to waste.

⊰ ⊱

Cade ate hungrily, but while Lisette tried to enjoy a leisurely cup of coffee, his impatience mounted. "Look, why don't you just call David and tell him I have something urgent I need to talk to him about?"

"Urgent?" Lisette heard that a lot, working for Mallory. "What's the nature of this urgent matter?"

"I can't tell you. Look, what will they do if we just show up at their place?"

"I don't know, and I'm not going to find out. If we don't just see them around town today, they'll probably be at church tomorrow. Maybe you can catch him then."

"Church? Where's the church? Maybe I can flag them down at the corner. I am not going into a church. I'm an atheist." Color rose in Cade's cheeks.

"Well, then, what's the problem? If there isn't a God, then a church is just another building, and who cares? Right? I mean, if your mind's made up, you can sit for an hour without having your entire belief system torn down."

120

He was amazed by her quick logic. Yeah! He knew what he believed! No one would ever change his mind! It might even be interesting to see what the sadly misled little parish embraced. And he had to get David's input. "David doesn't really go for all that stuff, though; right?"

⊰ ⊱

David was mystified. Diana had ranted over Mardy's baked eggs, something Mrs. Prescott had sometimes made on the mission field when they could afford the expensive all-protein meal. She complimented Mardy on the use of Tarragon in the recipe. Mardy flushed with pleasure at Diana's kind words.

David wasn't sure what Tarragon was, but the stuff was great! Eggs baked with lots of cheddar, butter, milk, and salt and pepper. Alexandra helped crack a couple dozen more eggs into another large casserole.

"She can make one of the guys help her if she feels pressured," David offered.

"That's okay. I want to help." She grated cheese across the top at Mardy's direction. Milk! Butter! Seasonings! And into the oven it slid.

"Is Mallory coming?" Diana tried to force her usually sunny voice out as she asked the question.

"I thought she was. I left the golf cart for her." He met Daniel's haunted gaze. "She knows now to keep it on the paths."

Something was definitely amiss between the couple, and David was almost glad Mallory hadn't appeared. This kind of stuff really got to her.

"No harm done! At least it didn't roll with them." Daniel's detached voice.

"Well, no thanks to me!" David was self-conscious about his inglorious tumble. "It's a good thing you were closer. I mean, one second, I was on my feet doing great! And the next, I was flat on my face in the mud!"

Faulkner emitted a wry laugh. "Yeah, tell me about it."

David coaxed another huge helping from Mardy and refilled his mug with cocoa. Returning, he straddled the bench next to Faulkner. "What's wrong? If you don't mind my asking!"

"Like you said, One minute, everything's great, and you're riding the Zephyrs! And the next-" His eyes were anguished. "You're on your face in the mud! At least, figuratively speaking."

121

"You're, you're sick? But not with the Africa thing?" The thought was awful. He still hadn't accepted the death of Mallory's dad. Neither had she and now maybe this guy who had stepped into her heart? She couldn't lose him, too.

Diana rolled her eyes and acted like she was refocusing on the little ones.

"I guess it's none of my business. I'm gonna go check on Mallie."

"No, finish eating. I–I'm still trying to figure things out–it–all happened kind of fast! We got back in town from Houston Wednesday, and a Geologist that I went to school with–um–he asked me to meet him for lunch. That's–that's part of the problem. *The fear of man bringeth a snare.* I guess sometimes–I worry–about what people think. And I forget it's what God thinks of me; that matters." Tears escaped.

David listened sympathetically, realizing Faulkner wasn't really interested in talking to him; it was more that Diana was listening.

"I always worry what people think of me," David confessed. "It's pretty hard not to."

"Yeah, but he wanted me to come on campus. I should just know to steer clear of the whole thing. Well, anyway, he brought up the name of this woman that was–um–a romantic interest of mine–a long time ago."

"Yeah, you told us a little about stuff in Aspen. So, did she show up at the lunch?"

A wry chuckle! "No, I just argued with Higgins. He's against my being a Christian, against my not sacrificing my kids to a system I don't believe in. I don't know. I told him about the cabin; I don't know if I was being obnoxious, or just trying to change the subject. He got mad and left. Which, the whole thing was just–well I tried to shake it off. But then, when I was riding home from church with Al and Jer and Cass, she phoned me. It made me mad! I mean, you know–the kids. So, I just turned my phone off. But it kept making me madder. So, by the time we got home, I decided to call her back and tell her off and never to call me again."

"When did you start feeling sick?" Diana's question inserted itself.

"I'm trying to work out in my mind what I should have done. Um–I'm sorry, Diana. I love you so much, and the kids. But first she said that Higgins told her I met him for lunch on campus–which was a lie. I didn't have time for lunch at all, but I was trying to be nice to him–It's just all so confusing. I mean, I can whitewash everything to myself all day long, but I need to be–honest!" He choked on a sob. "Well, I don't care about going on campus because it brings back lots of stuff I'm~ashamed of. And they think I'm an idiot, and not a scholar in a class with them. See, it's all a jumble, and I can't sort it out."

"Well, you've had a lot of powerful medication. When it wears off~" Diana's tone, less about forty degrees of chill factor.

"It isn't the medicine. I didn't stop to pray, or anything! I just stormed into my office to make the call! Big man! I can handle this one! Maybe I shouldn't admit this, but the whole thing hooked me. Just that fast! No matter how much I love the Lord, and you, and my life." He was truly shaken by the scope of his failure. "Well. Higgins had told her that her name came up at lunch, making her think I asked about her. Well, he's the one who tries to bring up lots of old times to me. So, she was telling me she still looks good; that people tell her so. And I was jealous of whoever was telling her that. And I was curious about how she still looks, and what she'd think of me~She was saying she could meet me downtown for coffee and I could show her all our pictures. And I'm thinking~not that we can't meet at all! Just, that downtown wouldn't be good because I know so many people down there! And that's when the Lord hit me with the blinding headache and nausea! I~I thought the sickness was back and He was going to kill me for sure, this time!"

An awkward silence descended. David studied his empty plate, amazed a guy of Faulkner's stature could get set up like that by the devil, but hey, it was like Satan to target such a strong Christian testimony, such an amazing family. And, he knew how to go about it. Cunning! Merciless! His troubled gaze met the other man's. "I'm glad you didn't try to 'whitewash' it, to yourself, or any of us. I mean, you could have said nothing happened, and you did have everything under control."

Faulkner laughed through tears. "Yeah, except Diana's smarter than that, and she knows me too well."

⊰ ⊱

David was sprinting toward their home when his cell rang; Mallory.

"Hey, I'm sorry for getting delayed. I phoned Mr. Haynes, and then the call took longer than I figured. Is there still breakfast? I'm hungry now."

"Yeah, Mardy started another big pan full, and it was good. Baked eggs! I never heard of it. Diana said her mom used to make it sometimes.

123

I'm almost there. I'll drive you to prevent further mishaps." He laughed at his own humor.

She met him at the side door. "I'm not sure the breakfast sounds that good. Will there be anything else?"

He kissed her. "Toast or biscuits, coffees, espressos, hot chocolate, and juices".

She gazed around the dining hall. "I thought the Faulkners might be here." Her voice registered disappointment.

"Well, they were, but I think they went someplace so they could talk stuff out. Why were you talking to Mr. Haynes?"

"He's calling in some of the graduates so I can interview a few of them this afternoon."

Chapter 10: ADULATION

Alexandra noticed a thaw in whatever had transpired with her parents. She took charge of the other kids. "I have an idea. We brought all our instruments with us; maybe Pastor Anderson invited us to perform Sunday. Or, Daddy just wanted to be ready, in case. Since it's still raining, why don't we practice?" She pulled out some toys and crayons. "Zave, you and Nadia play nicely right here."

Diana sat on the edge of the bed in the master suite. "So, that's really what happened? What you told David?"

He stepped into the room, shutting the door. "Yeah, I hope he doesn't tell anyone else." His handsome features looked ravaged. "Of course, that's what happens when you're stupid. People find out. Look, Diana, I~"

"So~so, you haven't been seeing~her~"

"What? Seeing? No, Honey!" His eyes met hers, horrified. "And I don't want to. It was just that one moment~I shouldn't have called her back. I can't explain stuff to myself yet. Except, I could have gotten tripped up! Listen, Diana, I love you. I love the Lord; I love the life He's given us! Our kids! The businesses, our friends~great Christian friends~and their good regard! You know, it's true: *Proverbs 22:1*

> *A good name is rather to be chosen than great riches, and loving favor rather than silver and gold.*

As she regarded him steadily, her world tipped right-side-up to the strains of the kids' practicing, *It Takes a Storm*.

~≒ ⊨~

125

Mallory liked the breakfast, and then they headed toward town. David shot her a cute sideways glance. "I'm going through the list of last year's seniors in my mind. None of them struck me as being really promising."

She laughed. "I'm sure that's what most business people would have thought about us a few short years ago."

"Well, about me. You had it together." He gave her hand a light squeeze.

"I'm pretty sure not. But, you know, we both had potential. Because everybody does! When Diana told me to hire as many of the kids from our graduating class as I could, I thought she was just being too Christian-kind. I didn't know there was such a great method to her madness. But, it worked! Even Colt's coming along. And Lisette's a wonder. I was always so busy not liking her that I never noticed what Mr. Haynes saw in her. She made a business out of the cheerleading squad, the pep-club, booster club, and eventually the whole athletics department! A profitable business! She was smart and worked hard, neither of which I would have admitted to."

"Well, yeah; I'm not sure how you've overlooked her back-stabbing."

"Well, part of her grievance was really my fault. And after I fell on my face so bad-about Cy-that taught me to give people even more leeway. I wish she hadn't married Bryce. We should pray harder for him to get saved."

He shrugged. "Okay, so how do you 'pray harder'?"

"I don't know! Scream and beat your chest?"

"Well, the Bible tells us the Lord hears even our unvoiced requests, and that He isn't deaf. We both pray for him together and in our personal devotions. He has some responsibility."

"We could fast." She was really cute when she was so much in earnest.

"You mean like for an hour or two? I'm a growing boy, and you're carrying our baby. Like I said, he has some responsibility."

He looked at his watch. "We're a little early. Let's stop at Sonic and get drinks to take with us."

He beeped lightly. "Look who." He was surprised to see Lisette and Bryce, and more than a little chagrined to see Holman.

Mallory leaned forward. Suddenly this was a lot of fun. Buzzing Sonic like a teen-ager, sitting next to David in his pickup. "Hey, I know y'all. What's up? Cade, have you heard from Roger Sanders?"

Lisette laughed. "Oops, caught red-handed by the boss!"

"Oh, for not being in the office today? Well, when the cat's away~. But hey, you never take a day off."

"Cade wants to talk to David." Bryce's voice was mocking. "Maybe if he can get it out of the way, we can go back to civilization and not have to come to church in the morning."

David ignored him. "We're interviewing some of the kids over at the high school in just a few minutes. Why don't y'all come out to the Ranch about seven and we'll grill up some steaks? Bring your mom and dad, too, if you want, Lisette."

"Oh, thanks, anyway, David; they're on a cruise. I kind of knew they were going, but I didn't realize it was now."

David grinned mischievously. "Probably best! They can labor longer under the illusion that you got a good guy."

Bryce leaned forward, his face a study of sudden rage. "I'll have you know, you country bumpkin, that in Palm Beach, I'm considered a 'Prime Catch' by all the debutantes!"

David laughed. "No jokin'! I should send them a news update. Anyway, Lisette, come on out later. Bring Cade and your 'Catch of the day'! We'll grill you a steak or you can stick with your fish." He paid and tipped the car hop before backing away.

"Let me guess. You didn't think I was funny." His gaze met Mallory's, concerned, and she smiled.

"I thought it was hilarious. I mean, sad really, thinking about Mr. and Mrs. Schliemann. And Bryce is so arrogant I always want to stick a pin in him and deflate his ego. But we aren't kids on the playground anymore. He can do worse than 'run to the teacher', so to speak. He's already tried to make trouble with his lawsuits which are still pending."

⊰ ⊱

Surprisingly, quite a number of kids showed up on Friday afternoon in spite of the short notice, when they heard about David and Mallory's setting up interviews.

They divided up the applications, with David's interviewing the guys, and Mallory's taking the girls. He surveyed the paperwork before him grimly. If these guys wanted a job, they hadn't taken the time to put their best foot forward. Messy, scratched out, written over, incomplete! Then, as if that didn't bury them, he knew them all, too. True, he had left as a

127

student five years earlier, but these kids were the same age and in the same class as his brother, and he had dealt with them when he was a substitute teacher.

The responses to his questions were about what he had expected. Less than brilliant! He handed his stack back to Mallory, with all of his notations, proud of what a shrewd interviewer he was. She placed them in a file folder with hers and met Lisette in the polished foyer. "Get all their paperwork; W-4's, Driver's Licenses, you know the drill. Buy a couple of houses and line up a truck to haul all their stuff to Dallas. Set up training for first thing Monday morning. See you at seven."

"You're hiring everyone? I didn't think the ones I talked to were hirable." David's comment as he assisted her back into his pickup.

"They're all looking for jobs. Who are you to talk? You pick your people up from inner-city St. Louis."

He frowned thoughtfully. "Well, yeah, but they don't all work out."

"Exactly! But the ones who do are worth the risk of giving everyone a chance. And, have you found out, that the ones you initially assess as having lots of possibility, often don't; and the ones you wouldn't pin a hope on, really take off, and leave you with your mouth hanging open?"

He laughed, quoting her verse, *Ecclesiastes 11:6*

> *In the morning sow thy seed, and in the evening withhold not thine hand: for thou knowest not whether shall prosper, either this or that, or whether they both shall be alike good.*

᚛ ᚜

Lilly finalized some details and leaned back smugly into her chair. Very nice! Very nice, indeed! By and large, things were going much better for her. She checked emails, and wasn't surprised to see a lengthy one from Nick and Jennifer. As usual, it repeated their invitation to come visit in Arizona. This one included a song attachment, and she pressed 'play'. The mixed quartet singing *Hawaiian Wedding Song* at Mallory's wedding. She watched for a glimpse of Cassandra. Beautiful wedding! Her mind advanced to the war on drugs that had taken place in Arkansas, and the missiles firing. She grinned, more of a quick grimace. It was like the Lord Himself was fighting on behalf of Mallory, her friends, and the Diamonds!

┥ ┝

Herb straightened up stiffly, groaning, and massaging the small of his back. Merc looked up. "You know what, Dad? We should ask David to send in some of his carpentry people to make our work areas more ergonomically functional."

"Guess I'm just getting old." He sprinkled some pills into his hand.

Merc nodded. "Well, I guess I am, too, but there's no sense placing more strain on our bones and muscles and eyes than necessary."

"Well, this is a standard jeweler's workbench and stool." Herb surveyed his latest bejeweled endeavor lovingly.

"I know, Dad; the way it's always been. But why? Jewelers aren't standard. You're short, and I'm tall; so why should there be a 'standard' workbench? I'm getting things changed; it won't cost that much, and it will more than be worth it. That's beautiful." Merc looked over at the sparkling strand spilling from his father's hands. He lifted a prong pusher from his bench, adeptly folding prongs snugly over rich, purple-hued Almandine Garnets, to form Sterling Silver and burgundy Pansies. His work was taking shape, too.

"Well, I don't want any interruption to the work."

Merc nodded. "I know you don't, but, there's a third cabin nearly finished in Arkansas that will be available on a rotating basis. Nice autumn foliage will be turning, and duck hunting season."

┥ ┝

Daniel and Diana talked quietly for over an hour. With Ryan fed, he was down for a nap. They could hear the kids still playing music, and when Daniel crept out silently to check on the other two little ones, they were sleeping soundly. He pulled Diana into his arms, and she stiffened.

"What?"

She was still tearful. "I don't know," she managed. "Remember a few years back when Lilly did that mean trick on Trent Morrison?"

He nodded. "Yeah, what about it"?

"Well, Mallory immediately figured out Lilly was at the bottom of it. The facts were obvious. Trent hadn't been unfaithful to Sonia. I was aggravated at Sonia for not letting it go and forgiving him. Not that he was even guilty of anything! But, for over a year, she had assumed he was buying expensive presents for Mallory and getting mad at her for every penny she spent. It took a while for the truth to sink in for her. This has only been a couple of days for me, but they were miserable days. I've been in agony, thinking you were trying to decide whether to stay with us, or go with her. I wasn't going to beg you to stay~although~I didn't have a clue what we'd do~" The tears flowed as he watched helplessly.

"Well, I didn't know you were thinking that, and I haven't known what to say. Why did you just close the bathroom door on me when I was sick?"

She shrugged. "I don't know. I was thinking about containing an epidemic. If I were exposed with you, who would care for the kids? I didn't want to expose them, although, the three oldest had just ridden with you from church. Then, I had handed the babies off to them to get ready for bed. In other words, we all had already been equally contaminated. I couldn't think. Then, when I found out who you were talking to~" She paused. They had already been over that subject. "I couldn't even deal with it. I thought the ambulance had gotten lost, but it just took them extra time to engage the quarantine measures. I'm glad you're okay, although, we need to determine what made your BP spike that way."

"Yeah, are you ready to go out and talk to the kids?"

She nodded, stroking the baby's dark hair tenderly. "You tell them what you think they need to know."

"Hey kids! Family meeting!" He brewed a cup of coffee, and indicated for them to get milk or a soft drink as he opened a package of cookies. They sat tensely, glancing toward one another as they characteristically did. He sat, sliding his hands around the top of his mug, studying his fingers, seeking for a starting place.

"Okay~" His voice was barely audible. "Do y'all know where David and Mallory are? Maybe they should be in on this."

"They left over an hour ago in David's truck. Come on; stop stalling." Jeremiah's voice mimicked his tone when he was serious with them.

"Okay, well, I'm trying to think how to start. I met a guy for lunch that I shouldn't have. I'm not sure why I let him bully me into it."

Diana registered disgust.

"No, it started there. He was my friend before I got saved, and he's as unregenerate as ever. He wanted me to go back to the old turf, too, on campus. That's why we don't allow y'all to hang out with bad influences.

And it would have been a pretty good rule for me to follow, too. He was already guzzling alcohol by the time I joined him. That isn't what I want, and I wouldn't have wanted y'all to be around that. I thought I was big enough stuff, and I could resist and be a testimony."

"Did you have a glass of wine?" Cassandra's eyes were bigger than saucers.

"No, but I listened to him, and it was like listening to the devil in person, belittling me for my beliefs and the way your mom and I are rearing y'all. There was no reason for me to expose myself to grief like that. I had work that needed to be done, anyway. Well, he did what the devil does. He came at me with one tack, and when it didn't work, he changed courses. He brought up the name of one of my old girlfriends. Listen, y'all know I love Mom, right?"

Six eyes bored holes through him. "Well, I do." He shot Diana an anguished glance. "Your mother~" Tears came, forcing him to struggle harder to get the words out. "Your mother nursed me~when everyone else was afraid to get near me! Um~she told me about the Lord. Well~she thought I was going to die~I thought so, too~and that she was a beautiful~angel. Well, I didn't know anything about angels back then." He dunked one of the brittle store-bought cookies and took a bite, grinning at Diana. "Sale on Indulgences for cookie-dunking; this afternoon only!"

Hands reached slowly for the treats.

"So, the woman who called me on Wednesday night was a former girlfriend. If Dr. David Higgins were really my friend, he wouldn't have been trying to get my mind off of what I have with y'all and focused on someone like that. And he lied. He said I was on the TU Campus, and he made it sound to her like I was looking for her, and still interested. I haven't been. You know, Mom saved my life, not once, but twice from that fever! And she's shown me the way to know the Lord better and give my life to Him. The Lord's blessings and your mother's efforts have turned me into a man who appeals to women: someone caring, kind, and financially well-off. Well, when the other lady called me, and y'all were riding home with me, it was embarrassing, and it made me mad. So, when I got home, I was going to get to a private place and tell her off! Which is how I started off, but then, she suggested having just an 'innocent meeting'~My mind jumped on that, and the headache hit me! I know it was the Lord, and not a coincidence! And I'm relieved beyond measure that it stopped me before I landed in disaster! And landed y'all there, too! I wasn't unhappy with any of my circumstances, or giving consideration to going back~just that fast, when I didn't expect it, the attack came. I adore your mom and every one of you! I love the Lord for His gifts to me of y'all! For His gift of eternal life and all the benefits He loads on us daily."

Chapter 11: APTITUDE

"What do you need me to do?" Mallory felt like she should help David with the meal.

"Go up and close your eyes for about thirty minutes. I have this under control."

⊰ ⊱

Lisette sat at her mom's dining room table with her laptop. Running out of business hours, and she had several jobs to accomplish. It was a good thing for her that many of the tasks could be done at any time, thanks to twenty-four/seven business hours. She opened a realtor's site that had assisted her before in the Dallas market. Having already perused the listings, she had a short list. She introduced herself, certain her name wouldn't ring a bell at all. Still, he pretended to remember, and she stated her purpose succinctly.

He stammered. "Okay, so you want to buy a couple of houses, like this afternoon, and you're a company rep?"

She laughed. "Yes Sir, for *DiaMo, Corporation*. We have some new hires moving to the Metroplex, and we want to provide housing as quickly as possible."

"Well, okay, Mrs. Billingsley, but don't you need to make an appointment to see the properties?"

"No, Sir, I guess not. I'm offering the asking price, and I'd like to get the properties under contract. I looked them over on the web-site. If they require repairs or updates, we have crews that can do that. Of course, it's all pending surveys and inspections."

Part of his brain was telling him this was too good to be true; another agent must be playing a prank. Two houses! Right now! No price-haggling! But when the financial information began arriving, there was no question about the validity of the offers.

Bryce regarded his wife wonderingly from the arched doorway. "How do you know she'll like those?"

Lisette met his gaze. "She will. They fit the criteria."

"She didn't give you any criteria."

"Exactly"!

"She called the phone company and ordered new cell phones on the *DiaMo* account, before phoning Sam Whitmore."

"Hello, Sam, a couple of things. We need ten new laptops for *DiaMo*, some new hires. Also, we need you to coordinate the systems at David and Mallory's Arkansas property with *DiaMo's* Dallas office, and *GeoHy* in Tulsa."

"Whoa! You don't want much, do you?"

She laughed. "No, that's all. No step for a stepper, Sam. Can you come to Dallas on Tuesday and teach the system to the new people?" Let's say, right after lunch. Gives you time to sleep in."

"You're so thoughtful! Okay, one o'clock on Tuesday."

American Express to order corporate credit cards for the new people's expenses.

U-Haul! Hire a truck.

She slid several crisp papers into a file folder so she could report to Mallory, and found the guys in the den, watching a baseball game. "We should probably leave now; it'll take us a little while to get up there."

She drove as she contacted all the kids to inform them they were hired. "Okay, be in services at Faith Baptist Sunday morning, and we can coordinate getting everyone relocated to Dallas."

"How can you make them go to church?" Cade's tone sounded horrified.

"I can't. But they didn't argue. And they want the jobs. If they had asked for different arrangements, I would have agreed."

⊣ ⊢

David was arguing with his dad. "That's crazy, Dad. They're all right here, and their instruments are with them. If you invite them to do the music, and I email people, attendance will be up. And all the followers on the web-site love them and their music. Yeah, you told me Mildred's singing the special. Reschedule her; she's bad, and she's willing to sing any chance you give her."

He listened while his dad reiterated his same argument. He guessed his dad was still jealous at times, of the Faulkner's popularity.

"Okay, well can Mallory play the offertory?"

"No, Dad, not Sunday night. We're going home in the afternoon."

⊰ ⊱

He checked the table setting: linens and china on the screened in porch. With the cooling effect of the rain, they should be comfortable with the ceiling fans going. He phoned Daniel. "We're grilling steaks, and Bryce and Lisette are coming, and that new guy, Cade Holman that's trying to get on with Sanders. Do you guys want to join us? Bring your mom and dad. Eating at seven, but y'all can come down any time. Or the kids can."

As he disconnected his dad called him back. "I'm not sure what I was thinking about. Anyway, I reconsidered, and called Faulkner. They're on tap to handle all the special music in the morning service. I told him to be sure to have Mallory play a special."

Daniel and Diana appeared almost immediately. "Where's Mallory?" Diana's concerned voice.

"She's upstairs. I told her to rest, but I keep hearing her moving around. Go on up."

"Do you need any help?"

"No, Ma'am. Everything's under control. You won't bother her."

Diana mounted the steps and tapped gently. "David invited us to crash your dinner party, so here we are."

Mallory laughed in response. "I'm glad you did. Are you okay?"

"Perfect! Can I have a do-over on your sonogram?"

"Of course, it's real exciting to me!" Her voice sounded apologetic.

"Well, it is exciting! I still got as excited with Ryan's at number six, as I did with Alexandra's. I'm excited for you, too, if you are."

Mallory exhaled! "I am happy! I mean, I was so shocked at first that things happened so fast!" Her dazed tone lent veracity to her words. "If the

Lord piles blessings on me, who am I to say, 'I'm not ready.'?" She brought up the image for the thousandth time, and Diana watched it with her.

"I'm sorry I was unfocused on you the other night."

Mallory's turn to laugh! "I'm sorry I'm such a brat that I try to demand your attention all the time." She changed the subject. "David and I went to the high school this afternoon for interviews with more Murfreesboro High grads."

"Really? Anyone with any possibilities?"

Mallory hugged her knees. "Yes Ma'am, all of them! It happened kind of suddenly. Can you guys get free at all next week to come help with orientation?"

⊰ ⊱

Bryce, Lisette, and Cade gazed around them wonderingly. "They don't have it too bad, do they?"

Even Bryce was speechless. If it didn't compare with his family estate, he couldn't boast a country home. For a guy who tried not to be impressed with anything or anybody, he had to admit David had done all right with the place. And he couldn't believe what Lisette had accomplished in a couple of hours.

Cade was still impatient for a conversation with David alone, but his host was busy supervising the placing of food onto the table.

Mallory and Diana appeared, everyone assembled around the table, and David blessed the food.

"Are you going to show Mallory that folder?" Bryce whispered.

Lisette grinned. "Don't worry. She'll ask. Are you okay? You seem quiet."

He was; he just hadn't known Daniel Faulkner was going to be at the same meal. They had a turbulent history. "Our attorneys won't like this." His whisper carried.

"Well, ours won't care. He's only interested in getting married," Mallory's amused voice.

Diana laughed, but refrained from adding a comment, and the conversation turned to the church music they were planning. "Mallory, you need to play your medley for the offertory, and sing *I've Been Through Enough*."

136

Cade's tone was filled with wonder. "You play the piano and sing? And run a company? Is there anything you can't do?"

"Yeah, she can't drive a golf cart!" Alexandra's quick response!

Mallory blushed when everyone laughed.

"That's the kind of thing <u>my</u> sister always says," David mumbled.

"Yes, whatever were you thinking about?" Diana's puzzled question.

Bryce always enjoyed someone else's humiliation. "Why, what happened? There's nothing to driving a golf cart! How could you do it wrong?"

"I guess~uh~I just thought they had more traction." She was trying to laugh at herself.

"Yeah, I watched them load up and head down the road, and then suddenly, they were cutting straight down the hill through the mud!" Daniel's version of the story, omitting the part about David's falling on his face! "I got mud to my knees trying to keep them from rolling to the bottom, cart and all."

Bryce grinned smugly. "What? You were that hungry?"

"No, she was looking for Diamonds!" Cade's flash of insight. "Is it true that rain makes them easier to see? Are there any here?"

Mallory regarded him steadily. "I haven't seen any here. David found one a couple of years back, up on one of the trails. Sometimes when rain washes them off, you can see them if they're on the surface. There are variables." She let it go at that, not mentioning that the one David had found was the large sparkly one on her left ring finger. "Great meal! Anyone care for more steak?"

Dishes passed back and forth for second helpings.

A couple of the camp men surreptitiously removed plates, bringing coffee, peach cobbler, and home-made peach ice cream.

Mallory laid her napkin aside. "Well, I don't want to break up the party, but I need to touch base with Lisette."

David whispered to one of the servers, and they delivered coffee and desserts to the girls as Lisette spread her file open.

"Well, I guess this is as good a time as any for you to talk about whatever's on your mind. Excuse us, please." David rose with his dessert plate and iced tea, making his way into the kitchen. Cade followed.

"How did you get a girl like Mallory?" Cade's question burst forth as soon as they were out of earshot of the others. "Okay, back up, that didn't come out too good. See, there's this girl, but~well, my mom and dad told me to focus on studying~"

"So, you've never really been in the dating game?"

"No, not at all! And, I must be crazy! Well, how did you introduce yourself to Mallory?"

David sweetened his tea. "I didn't. She approached me first. I'm just a chick magnet." He chortled at his own humor.

"Okay, where were y'all, to get her to notice you?"

"I was the new kid in second grade, and at the first recess, she told me her name was Mallory and she could beat me at anything! Which, her words have pretty well borne themselves out. She's an amazing baseball player; she can outshoot me at the pistol range, and she's going to make quite a horsewoman. The girl you're interested in; uh, anyone I know?"

"Maybe, but I'm not sure you need to know. And you'll laugh."

"I will not!" David was injured.

"Yeah, you probably will. She's pretty much out of my league!"

David took a big bite, watching the Chemist as realization dawned.

"Catrina Sanders?! Are you kidding me? Good luck with that, man. I have a friend that's been crazy about Emma for almost five years, and Sanders won't give him a nod."

"Well, yeah, but she's a lot younger."

"So? You have a point there?"

※ ※

"Bransom"! Erik grabbed his extension, knocking a coffee cup from his desk. The ceramic exploded across the tile floor, splattering cold coffee everywhere. Trying to mask his aggravation, he continued. "How may I help you?"

"Yeah, Erik; Dawson, here! I wanted to give you a heads-up; agents just arrested Oberson. He's implicated pretty deeply, or we would have been afraid to make a move against him. You've done some good work."

"Yes, Sir, thank you for the call. I appreciate being kept in the loop." He disconnected. "Nah, I'll clean up my own mess." He shooed away a secretary and one of the new agents. He guessed it was gratifying about Oberson's arrest. It was just sad when one of America's elected officials wasn't a person of character and integrity. This just looked bad to Americans, and the rest of the world! Who did kids have to look up to?

He sopped up the coffee and swept up the broken mug, feeling no sense of victory at the arrest.

⊰ ⊱

Daniel and Diana were arguing again. Daniel had exuberantly explained that David's architectural drawings for the new addition were complete, signed and stamped, so that he could apply for a building permit, and get underway.

They were going back and forth about whether to pay the standard architectural fee.

Diana pointed out that they would need to refinance in order to build again, and that David's fee could be structured into the new loan. Refinancing would take advantage of lower interest rates, anyway.

"Well, he just gave the drawings to me. If the third story costs us a hundred thousand, five percent'll be five thousand dollars." Even as he argued, he knew she was right. "You're right; give me a chance to mull it over."

⊰ ⊱

Beth carried a tray into Roger's office, and he scooted some papers aside. "Wow, chocolate silk pie and coffee delivered to my desk. What's cooking in that brain of yours?"

"You wound me. This is what was cooking on the range-top, and then chilled for hours."

He sipped the coffee and slid a fork through the pie. "I smell chocolate! And a rat!" He laughed. "Well, that's what you think~when I try to do something nice for you."

She laughed, settling in across the desk and sampling her sugary white coffee. "Well, I did see an e-mail that the Faulkners and David and Mallory are doing music up at Faith Sunday morning."

He shook his fork. "Ah, the truth comes out! Finally! You know how strongly I believe in being faithful to our church and loyal to our pastor?"

She nodded. "Which, I'm glad you are. You've suggested that pastor invite the Faulkners to perform at our church, haven't you?"

139

He nodded. "Yeah, several times! Guess I haven't sold him on the idea. You know I've been a little hypocritical at times, though, insisting we be at our church! Unless I had a boat in a race"! He laughed at his own failure. "I don't want to make a habit of visiting around at other churches, but you want to go, don't you? I do, too. If I can work it out, I need to speak to David, Mallory, and Daniel and Diana. It will save me trips to Tulsa and Dallas. Thanks for the pie and coffee! You're the greatest!"

☙ ❧

"Sorry I ran out on y'all." David rejoined the Faulkners. "Holman's been wanting a word with me; I guess the reason he and Bryce and Lisette all drove over. I guess he wonders if I know whether Sanders plans to hire him. Wonder how the new Houston operation's coming together. Maybe Suzanne can give us an update Sunday." He changed the subject. "Listen, I picked out the furnishings and accessories for your place in a rush. We're finishing up a third cabin, and if you want to pick stuff more to your liking, we can switch things out. Also, a drapery guy's coming tomorrow to hang drapes for us. Do you want to pick drapes out from him and let him take measurements, or hire your own person? That won't be a problem, as long as Jeff and the security guys are aware.

"Well, we like everything." Diana wasn't sure what to say. "We just love it here. We can hardly believe it's true. With all the shutters and everything, I never considered additional window treatments."

"Once everything is totally finished, I'll have a legal agreement for us both to sign. The cabin's yours! The land it's situated on, isn't. Which makes a confusing scenario, but not insurmountable. We have the home, itself, insured, but not your contents. Maintenance and upkeep become your responsibility, but whoever you hire will have to pass muster with our security. We'll keep it cleaned weekly, unless you prefer for us not to enter in your absence. You're free to use the common areas, and we'll stable horses for you, at the going industry rate. You're responsible for your own trash; here's the county pick-up schedule. You can kind of lease the property out time-shared; again, subject to security issues, but you're the one who taught us what we know about that. Mallory bought me a newer, more powerful telescope. You're welcome to use my other one; it's a gift from my parents, so I don't want to get rid of it. If you think it will be in your way, we can put it in the third cabin."

⊰ ⊱

Mallory finished her talk with Lisette. "I wish I could tell you to take the week end off." Her voice was apologetic. "Seriously, I hope these kids all work out. I need an assistant for my assistant. You do so much; I know you need help."

Lisette smiled, putting her entire body language into it. "That's okay. I love setting up training. Who should be in the sessions besides the new people?"

"Let's say everyone. We all need updates and reminders. Things tend to get a little loose and sloppy. When are you heading back to Dallas?"

"Not until Sunday afternoon. I'm getting the new hires squared away for their move after church. Hopefully, Bryce and Cade will be in church, too. Cade claims he's an atheist, but I think your music has him intrigued in spite of himself."

⊰ ⊱

The rain stopped and the clouds parted. "Maybe we can actually see the stars, tonight," David noted to Mallory as she rejoined the group.

"Hope so," was her response.

"Whoa, you guys have some awesome looking telescopes." Cade's comment, ignoring Lisette's attempts to leave. He plunged in animatedly about a planet somewhere, or a moon of a planet, that might have water, and consequently might be able to sustain life.

Mallory's gaze met his. "Well, life as we know it on Earth requires water and the correct atmosphere and temperatures, all in conjunction. If alien life-forms exist, we can't really be sure that water would be as central to their existence as it is to ours. Anyway, on Earth, we not only have water, we have a Water System. It's vast, amazing, and functional; and it includes weather systems, ocean currents, and gravity. Very vast and complex! So that, not only do we have water, but we have a world-wide delivery system. And a miraculous way to cleanse and renew itself! And besides being functional in design, it's also incredibly beautiful! Exquisite balance of form and function"!

"I guess I better not miss my ride." He escaped the logic, and the fact that not everyone was afraid to take him on.

⊰ ⊱

Lisette attacked the job of setting up the staff orientation. She was glad that Mallory saw the need for refreshing every ones' memories. She sent out a company-wide email, ending it with, "No excuses! Just be at the Dallas Grand Kempinski at nine on Monday morning, per David and Mallory's orders."

Then, she called the catering and events department of the said hotel, to be informed that the personnel she needed wouldn't be available until Monday. She called the General Manager, and she was in business! Of course! It would cost! Mallory liked to be conservative with money, and Lisette had considered conducting the necessary meetings in-house. Even with the other penthouse suite of offices, there wasn't a large enough meeting room for the sessions. And food would need to be catered in, anyway. She took a deep breath and plunged ahead.

⊰ ⊱

Mallory was awake by six, but David was already up and gone. She poured some Sprite and moved to the balcony to read her Bible. She loved the space, her gaze moving lingeringly from the pastures where Alpaca grazed, to a crew that was putting in more trees and flowers. No sight of David, though. She concentrated on the passage; then prayed through her journal. With her stomach feeling steadier, she moved down to check the stock in the pantry. Maybe not! She sat down at the Baby Grand in the great hall, and ran her fingers lovingly over the keys. Wow! Nice! She went through her offertory, then played a few other pieces. Then, a song came to mind that David, Tammi, and she had sung together when they were in middle school. She wasn't sure what made her think of it; maybe her words to Cade Holman the previous evening. It was a song they had learned from a children's album that posed questions, and then answered them, *It's a Miracle!*

David appeared suddenly. "What made you think of that one?"

"I'm not sure. I always liked it, though. I wonder if that CD's still available. I liked, *It's Bubbling*, too. What do you think about us singing a duet Sunday morning?"

"I'll be right back." He poured a tankard of milk. "Mardy made this amazing coffee cake for breakfast this morning. I brought you some since you've had a sweet tooth, as much as anything."

"Oh~my dreams have come true!" She surveyed the gooey, cinnamony treat bursting with pecans. Taking a bite, she played the intro to the song. "You want the questions, or the answers?"

"M-m-m, you're the better singer. Why don't you ask the questions?"

She nodded agreement. "Do you have a duck call?"

He looked perplexed. "That's not one of the questions."

"I know, but on the original, they put in that funny squawk; remember?"

He rummaged in a drawer of the gun case. "Voila!"

They sounded cute together.

⊰ ⊱

Lisette was nervous. Costs and tips were piling up at the hotel, and Mallory hadn't actually authorized things. Then, people from out of town had started phoning her to ask if rooms were reserved, in house. She sat, staring at her mom's 'Depression Glassware'. This thing was snowballing out of her control "What have I done, Lord?" she moaned. Another call; Roger Sanders! "Good morning, this is Lisette; how may I help you?"

"Hello, Lisette, listen, I just got wind of Mallory's new hires and the training sessions. I'd really like to get my key people in on the sessions. That's a big hotel; surely they can handle a hundred more people or so."

"Um, yes Sir, maybe so. I can call back and ask." Her thoughts churned. "They still have vacant rooms; how many do you need reserved?"

"Oh, wow. I hadn't considered that. Don't reserve us any rooms. I'll have Suzanne put our people in lower priced accommodations, and we'll rent a couple of coaches to get back and forth to the sessions." He ended the call.

Lisette fought panic. Mallory was incredible, always gracious when people pulled these things on her. 'Yes, a few more? No problem.' But that was when the decision was hers. She called the hotel back; maybe they couldn't accommodate a larger crowd. No such luck. She tried to force it to the back of her mind as she contacted the people who would bring sessions, working out the schedule, filling the time slots. Her phone interrupted her. Suzanne!

143

"Hello, Suzanne, I'm sorry. I should have called you back. The food service said they can handle the extra guests."

"Yes, I called the hotel, myself. I couldn't find enough economy rooms that were conveniently located with one another and the Grand Kempinski. With hiring coaches, and having our people strewn all over Dallas, it wasn't working. So, everyone's staying at the Grand. Between your crowd and ours, the rate came down significantly, giving everyone a nicer experience. Listen, Roger wants our companies to spring for the whole thing!"

Lisette stifled a gasp. "Well, y'all can work that out with Mallory." As she disconnected, the tears she had fought all day, sprang up. "Thank You, Lord; I don't understand why You still help me."

⚞ ⚟

Mallory watched the stable from her second story window. Daniel and Diana and the kids were watching David and Jeff, and a couple of other guys saddle several horses. David saddled *Cap'n* as Jeff finished *Zakkar*. Her eyes sparkled. Riding around the barn was better than not riding, at all. She was pretty sure the Faulkner's were going to do a trail ride. She watched as Daniel and Diana, with Ryan and Nadia, rode her direction on the golf cart. She skipped down the stairs to meet them, all smiles.

"Hey, Mallory," Daniel greeted. "We're ready to head out. Do you want to watch the kids here, or at our cabin?"

She was sure she was staring at them stupidly. She shrugged, fighting for composure.

"Our cabin," Diana decided. "Their cribs and toys are there. It should be a lot easier. Are you ready?"

Daniel hopped out of the cart. "I'll meet you at the stable when you get them settled." He kissed Diana, and Mallory climbed in numbly.

"I'll drive!" Diana's voice still teasing about the earlier fiasco!

⚞ ⚟

David wheeled *Cap'n* around when they reached the far fence line of the Dorman property.

"Oh, let's not go back, yet, "Diana wheedled. She was an excellent rider, with *Zakkar* firmly under control. "Let's go into the forest a ways."

144

"Just a little farther?" Daniel joined the plea.

"Well, I don't know. It's probably nearly a mile over to the gate, and rattle snakes have been bad this summer," David's voice of reason.

Diana smiled her most winsome smile. "She's like riding a dream."

David was aggravated. "Okay then, we need to step it up." He turned back toward the entrance to the acreage at a trot, and Diana galloped past him.

"Diana!" At least Faulkner was mad at the stunt, too.

She reined in and pulled the horse about. "He said we need to step it up."

⊰ ⊱

Ryan and Nadia were both naughty. Ryan wouldn't take a bottle, or stop crying, and Nadia deliberately disobeyed everything she said. They must be sensing her emotional turmoil, and mirroring it. Then, there was a diaper that didn't help her chronic nausea any. And while she dealt with that, Nadia redid the kitchen and herself with a squirty ketchup bottle. Mallory placed Ryan in his crib, screaming, and told Nadia to 'time out' in a chair while she scrubbed at the mess. With that finished, she threw Nadia's clothes into the washer. An hour had passed. Surely two hours would be the limit for the horseback ride.

Miraculously, both children fell asleep. She settled into a deep sofa to check emails on her phone, and saw the one about training sessions at the Grand Kempinski. 'Yikes! Lisette!' She rose and paced. It was probably best. But still, all the increased expenses and payroll for the new employees~

Then, a worse diaper than the first one, and Nadia used that opportunity to give herself a haircut akin to a Mohawk!

⊰ ⊱

David was seeing a new side of Diana Faulkner, who seemed determined to keep going and never relinquish *Zakkar*. He knew Daniel had a better sense of the situation, but since he was still kind of in trouble, he hesitated to cross her. So, they kept going, and going, and going.

"Honey, Xavier needs a break. You know, none of us are going to be able to move tomorrow. I'm already feeling saddle-sore."

"You know, the trouble with using the bushes is that some of them are Poison Ivy. Ticks are a major problem, too," David cautioned. "Not to mention Lilly has eyes everywhere."

Diana's face clouded. "We should probably head back then."

So, they turned around, and they rode, and they rode, and they rode. Finally, they reached the gate, and David swung down to open it and secure it again behind them."

"I'm gonna give her her head, and relieve Mallory of the kids." She gigged *Zakkar* in the ribs and surged forward.

"Honey, no!"

If she heard him, she didn't give any indication.

"Relieve Mallory of the kids~" David echoed. "I thought you were leaving them with your folks."

"Well, we were going to, but I didn't know they'd gone golfing."

⊣ ⊢

Mallory was worried that something must be wrong, before Diana finally thundered up to the cabin and reined in. She stepped onto the porch, carrying Ryan, and holding Nadia's hand firmly.

Diana swung down, frowning. "What happened to her hair? Were you watching her at all?"

Mallory's gaze took in her lathered, quivering mare. This might be a good time to just walk away. "I'll tell you later." Fighting tears, she reached the sanctuary of her master bedroom. A bout of sickness hit her, and when she straightened up, she made her way to the balcony. A bunch of guys were tending to the horses, cooling them down, watering them, but she didn't see David. 'So much for my getting to ride! Even in the barn!' Tears spilled out. And it looked like *Zakkar* was limping!

Chapter 12: ATTITUDE

David swung a hammer with all his might! A few more blows, and then he sank dejectedly onto the concrete of the workhouse. He twiddled his hair idly, gazing at the blocks of the far wall sullenly. His phone buzzed: a message from Faulkner that they were all cleaning up and going for dinner at Hal's. Then, they were going to the church at seven-thirty to practice. No invitation to join them for dinner. That was fine with him; he was a little out of sorts, anyway. He dreaded facing Mallory.

"Wow, Lord, all I want to do is make her happy! And it's like the whole world's stacked against me." He spread a tarp, and let rip with a couple of cans of paint. If it ran, he'd sand it out later and be more careful with the second coat. So, this project was supposed to be a wonderful surprise for her, too! Now, it didn't seem like that much; it still wasn't finished; and he hadn't yet thought of anything to say about her ride's not working out. "That Diana had acted like a brat all day?" No, he couldn't try to blame anyone. Dejected, he headed for the house.

"Hey Mallory?" No answer. "Mallie, are you in here?" He bounded up the stairs; no sign of her. From the balcony, he watched Jeff emerge from the stable.

"Is Mallory down there?" David's question as his younger brother got closer.

"Yeah, she's cryin'. What're ya gonna do?" Jeff's eyes were enormous.

"I don't have a clue. Any suggestions?"

"Maybe you should call Dad."

David's brows drew together. "Okay, Bro, that's a good suggestion of what not to do. He and mom have been married for years, and he still doesn't know."

꿔 ꮶ

Lilly patted at her hair in the ladies' room at Ben Gurion International Airport, and applied lipstick, rubbing her lips together to distribute it evenly. Ugh. Mallory always looked so cute doing that. She patted powder, then smacked at wrinkles in her skirt. She looked like she had already endured the flight that was actually still ahead of her. Never mind about all that! She had always been more about brains than beauty, anyway. She looked over a glossy schedule before tucking it carefully back into place. Passport check! She queued up for security.

꿔 ꮶ

"That's perfect, Cousin!" Nick had approached Jennifer as she touched the canvas to be sure the oils were all completely dry.

She jumped. "Maybe since we're married, you should stop calling me, 'Cousin'. Someone might get the wrong idea."

He laughed. "I will, if you want me to."

She smiled back. "You know I'm a pushover for you, don't you? Do you really think it looks okay? When David talked me into this, I didn't know I had to be there at the presentation. It makes my nerves really jittery."

"You packed and ready?" Nick's voice was always tender and patient.

"Except I can't get the suitcase closed. I always made fun of people who took so much stuff everywhere they went. I guess I was jealous, really, because I didn't have much."

He dealt with the stuffed suitcase and loaded it into the pickup behind the bench seat. Jennifer planned to hold her artwork in her lap until they reached Tucson, where Steb was meeting them. The picture would travel with him and Christine and Misty in his RV, while Nick and Jennifer flew.

꿔 ꮶ

Mallory grew aware of David's standing at the door of the stable watching her helplessly. Struggling for a measure of self-control, she turned to face him. "You~are~invited to a~pity~party!" She tried to force a smile through her tears. "I'm not sure~when I turned~so~bratty, about getting~my own-way. I mean, look at what-I have! Including you!" She spread her hand in an expansive gesture, taking in the stable with its contents, to the acreage and other buildings beyond.

"Mallory," he propelled himself toward her, and she was in his arms. "Honestly, I planned to let you ride today if it was the only thing I got done. It's my fault things went so haywire, though."

She laughed. "What kind of wire is 'Haywire'?"

He laughed, too. "I have no idea. Too bad the hardware store's closing, or we could get some and check it out. I planned to just ride around the circumference of the two properties; that would have been a pretty good ride. But, we would have been back in time for you to ride for at least an hour."

She rested against him as her breathing evened out. "Well, I know the Faulkners aren't coming next weekend. It's twice as far for them as it is for us. So, I wanted them to get to ride. I just wasn't thinking about her riding *Zakkar*, and that I'd be babysitting. That was a calamity. Nadia gave herself a Mohawk, and Diana was seriously mad at me. I never liked being an only child, but I'm seriously considering it, for this one."

David laughed. "See? Didn't I always try to tell you?" His mouth covered hers, and he relished the kiss and embrace.

⚜ ⚜

Diana wouldn't be quiet about Mallory and Nadia's hair, after which she began a tirade about the baby's developing a bad diaper rash. "Mallory should have given him a bath."

Jeremiah listened pensively before finally responding. "Well, Mom, if Nadia got in that much trouble while Mallory changed a diaper, how could she do a bath too? She was down at the stable later, crying really hard."

"Why should she cry? She's got everything! I mean, she wanted David, and now she's got him-"

"Keep your voice down," Daniel admonished as he took in the crowded dining room. "Look, Di, you're mad at me! I get that! I guess you're justified, but take it out on me, and not everyone else."

"Look! At her HAIR"! Blue eyes snapped.

"Shhh! We see it. It'll grow. A lot of kids do that. Honey, you've lost perspective."

"It's a miracle she didn't put her eye out! I trusted Mallory-"

Daniel lifted one of the remaining hair strands. "Hey, Nod, why'd you cut your hair?" Time to blame the real culprit!

Her eyes widened in alarm.

"Where did she get scissors? Who left scissors out?" His gaze traveled to Al, then Jer, and finally to Cassandra.

"Maybe I did!" Cassandra's guilty admission. "I used them to cut a couple of broken hairs off my bow. I thought I put them back."

"You did. I got them back out to clip a coupon." Diana's embarrassed confession. "But I left them on the counter top, and she can't reach up there~"

"Unless she climbed," Daniel finished. "Nadia, were you climbing, again? You know better~you're not supposed to climb. You climbed up to get the scissors?"

"Hunh-unh; the ketchup! I got in trouble with Mallory."

"Ketchup?" he questioned blankly. "You got ketchup and made a mess for Mallory?"

"I left that out on the counter," Jeremiah confessed.

Nadia started to cry as Daniel swooped her up. "We'll be back."

⚜ ⚜

Cleaned up, and in the pickup, David looked at Mallory apologetically. "Do you mind Sonic?"

"No. As a matter of fact, it sounds good." She polished off a banana split and ordered a large chocolate malt before they left. Not to be outdone, David laughingly ordered a malt too. Laughing like guilty school kids, they walked arm in arm into the church auditorium for the rehearsal.

Daniel glanced up. "Hey, y'all ready to hit it? Mallory, Nadia has something she wants to say you. Go ahead, Nod."

Silence! And when Daniel strode purposefully toward the toddler, she ran. It didn't take him long to catch her. "Hopefully, this won't take long. Y'all go ahead and start though. Honey, take over."

Diana started to cry. "I'm sorry, Mallory. I don't know what~" her words dissolved into sobs.

Mallory fought her own tears. "Hey, I'm the one who should apologize. I mean, it's a wonder that she didn't fall with the scissors, or something. I don't know how you keep up with what they're all doing. I'm thinking of having an only child." She forced a laugh.

150

Diana laughed, too. "Either that, or they have to obey. I don't know why I got mad at you instead of Nadia. She said she got ketchup?"

"Yeah, I tried to wipe it all up, but the wall's kind of stained. I'm sorry."

⊰ ⊱

The morning was hot and sultry, with barely a leaf stirring. Still, there was an excited buzz in the air as people assembled at Faith Baptist. The Sanders arrived in two vehicles, and Roger sprinted to help Faulkner unload kids, baby stuff, and musical instruments. "Are y'all doing lunch at Hal's after church? It's actually the best choice between here and Texarkana. I'd like to buy lunch and make you and Diana a proposal."

Daniel paused. "We'll see."

Roger knew what that meant. It depended on whether John Anderson preached a long sermon or not. The special music's cutting into the time frame, could very well mean a later dismissal. The crowd continued to assemble. The normal summertime crowd, plus the Faulkners and Sanders; followed by the Billingsleys, Cade Holman, and the new hires. Other visitors and quite a group of men from the camp completed the crowd. The air conditioning labored to keep up.

As Sunday School ended, the Faulkner kids joined their parents, ready to begin. They performed an interlude as people transitioned and found seats. David opened with prayer, and then Diana started to sing, accompanied by the piano and Cassandra's violin.

When I first fell in love with Jesus,
And I gave Him all my heart~

As she finished the first stanza, Mallory's thoughts had already traveled back to the day when she had first fallen in love with Jesus. She had given Him her heart; now she prayed that she would never take it back; that she would always stay faithful~no matter what. She fought tears.

Daniel and the kids joined in, singing in a round:

I keep falling in love with Him over, and over, and over, and over,
again.

I keep falling in love with Him over, and over, and over and over again~

The second selection was, "Remind Me", and Daniel seemed to be having a hard time holding it together. By the time they did "It Takes a Storm", tears soaked the chin rest of his violin.

There was a break for announcements, some prayer requests, a plea about the offering, another prayer, and then Mallory moved to the piano bench for the offertory. But rather than playing her medley, David joined her, leaning across the baby grand toward her. Her voice carried:

"What drives the stars without making a sound?"

The song posed a couple more questions, and David answered them:

I know! It's miracle!

It was a cute kids' song, asking about some of the wonders of creation, each time being answered with the miraculousness of it all. The audience laughed when David blew the duck call. The song was amazingly light-hearted, yet deeply profound.

Mallory's voice trembled slightly with emotion:

But God knows my name, and He cares about me!

Her tone conveyed the wonder and conviction she felt, and she joined David in the final refrain of:

I know-oh; I Know-Oh; I KNOW-OH!-It mu-u-ust, be a miracle!

Completed with a discordant plink-plunk!

Pastor Anderson approached the pulpit. "Thank you all for that music." He sopped at crocodile tears. Well, they've handed me a beautiful package, so I'm just gonna tie a bow around it. It's hot in here.

"Well the first song, about falling in love with Jesus. It took me back to the day I met the Lord and fell in love, and gave Him my heart. I could tell by some of your responses that y'all were taking the same mental and spiritual journey." A few nods and hushed 'amens', and he continued. "Then, we mean well, but we get flying pretty high, maybe get proud and puffed up. I know I have, often. And we need the Lord to remind us, remind us to stay in love with Him, remind us of the pit He drew us from. And He does lead us through mountains and valleys; it does take a few storms in life, to keep us where we need to be, teach us what we need to learn. And God is a miracle-working God, from before the creation, to the smallest needs of our lives. He does know our names! He does care about us! He cared so much for me that He sent His only begotten Son, Jesus, to die on the cross. He suffered for my sins. And when I first understood about Him doing that for me~well, I fell in love with Him! And I gave Him all my heart! If you've never done that, I wish you'd do it right now! I live with regret about some of the decisions I've made! But I've never regretted the moment I decided for Him. You never will, either. Please make your way forward as the music begins. Lana wasn't ready to play for the invitation, and Mallory was caught off-guard. And then, Cassandra's violin resonated with the familiar strains of "What a Friend We Have in Jesus".

Cade Holman bolted for the altar~with Bryce at his heels!

⊣ ⊢

"Did Diana say anything to you about lunch?" David freed Mallory's hand long enough to shift, and jockey his truck from its space.

"No, not a word! Let's stop at Hope for some McDonalds. I'd like a chance to rest before time to leave for church, anyway. Hal's is always busy and slow on Sunday afternoons."

He clasped her hand again as he nodded assent. "McDonalds, here we come. Wow! That was amazing about Billingsley and Holman."

"Yeah, no kidding! Your dad was right about its being hot in there. He did a good job, tying the songs together and giving the Gospel leading into the invitation. Was I supposed to play for the invitation?"

"Who knows? He doesn't always have things worked out in advance. It worked great with Cass, anyway." He tromped the accelerator to pass an RV towing a boat that resembled the *Queen Mary*. "I wonder if he plays with that thing in his bathtub during the week. It'd fit there about as well as in any of the lakes around here."

She laughed; then grew quiet.

⊰ ⊱

Roger made the mistake of laughing at Nadia's hair. Then could tell he had touched a nerve. Everybody's kids did stuff like that at one time or another. He wasn't sure why Daniel and Diana thought it was so important to come across as 'perfect' all the time.

With their orders placed, Roger leaned in. "Listen, the board of *Sanders-Chandler* has voted unanimously to ask the two of you to serve on our board. I mean, I can't even guess how busy y'all stay, but-

"Well, my term is expiring at *Phelps/Hagar*. Let us pray about it, but we're really honored by the invitation. When do you need an answer?" Daniel was dumbfounded by the sudden invitation.

"We would kind of like to know by the time the orientation ends Tuesday night."

⊰ ⊱

Jeff felt the strain of being in charge in his big brother's absence. He managed getting the campers back and getting Mardy moving in the chow hall. He knew he should exercise *Zakkar*. There were just so many demands on his time. Besides, Mrs. Faulkner had exercised her hard enough the day before to last a month. "Billy, go make sure the horses have plenty of feed and water. Especially water; with this heat! Go! Now! It's at least half hour 'til chow."

⊰ ⊱

Traffic was heavy. "You might as well head toward the church, and forget a stop at the house," Mallory suggested. "I wish I had more experience driving the freeway so you could have a break."

He grinned. "I'm good. You were quiet, but did you actually sleep?"

"No, I guess I just have a lot on my mind." She sighed, and he glanced at her, concerned.

"About the new hires, working out their compensation packages, getting them situated; and the nuts and bolts of the staff training. I mean, I've really stuck Lisette with the whole thing."

154

"Well, it's real cool Sanders decided to get in on it. He sent your mom and a couple of other employees to help out, and he's picking up the tab."

No response.

"Mallory? Hey, Baby, did you hear me?"

"Hunh? I'm sorry. What were you saying? I was kinda out to lunch there." She bit her lower lip to control the trembling.

"Did the McFlurry and the French fries settle okay?"

"Oh, yeah, it was good."

⊰ ⊱

Mallory slid into the air conditioned comfort of the SUV, and she looked extra-stunning for the upcoming sessions. She wore a grayed-aqua, raw silk, short-sleeved, suit, with matching leather shoes and bag in the exact hue. White gold jewelry glittering with Diamonds circled her throat and wrist. Her makeup and hair were superb. She smiled dazzlingly at David. He wore a new custom made sport coat and slacks with a white oxford shirt. Dressed up for him. She had hoped he would shave; now Daniel would be annoyed with her for not making it happen.

"Have you eaten anything?" His solicitousness in that department was wearing on her.

"Not yet. We're going for breakfast."

"Well, yes, but when you get there, you'll hit the ground running, and you won't eat a bite all day."

She gazed at her manicured hands resting in her lap. She was trying to be upbeat and happy, like she didn't have a care in the world, but a deep dread sucked at the edges of her spirit, seeking to pull her under. Maybe everything was okay. She met his gaze, and he noted her pallor for the first time.

"I promise I'll sit down and eat. Daniel and Diana will be there, and you and Lisette, and my mom, and Roger's other people."

"Yeah, well I'm holding you to it. Be sure to tell me everything you need me to do. Are you sure you're okay? Maybe we should get you back to the doctor."

"He said wait a month, and it hasn't been a week. I-I'm okay."

He let it ride. If something was wrong, hopefully Diana would notice.

True to her word, she stuffed down some of the attractive breakfast that evidently appealed to everyone else. David got a call, and she nearly jumped out of her skin. Okay, not yet~

Roger declared breakfast over and gave a ten minute break before the first session. There hadn't been a blessing before the meal, and Pastor Anderson wasn't anywhere to be seen.

Diana moved to join her, asking, "Did you ask David to shave?"

"No, I'm not his mom. Where's Pastor Anderson? Are you guys going to do any music like you usually do? If Pastor couldn't make it, one of the men could have prayed over the meal." It seemed as though everything was out of sync. Daniel always had his Bible with him, and always referred to it in his sessions. She wondered idly if the format was different because of Roger Sanders. He had asked to join their training; not change it.

The first session was a disaster! Mostly, because it wasn't really a 'session' at all! It was surprise drug testing for everyone! Meaning, people sat and grumbled while they waited for everyone to take turns in the little room. David's call to his dad proved that the Andersons weren't aware of the meetings.

Mallory passed a note to Daniel. "Get a piano rolled in, and sing. This is awful."

He looked shocked. The kids had gone home to Tulsa with his parents, and they didn't have the instruments. Mallory's expression didn't welcome any argument.

"What are you doing, Faulkner?" Roger Sanders seemed resentful, but Mallory's glare spurred Daniel on with the mission. Staff scrambled with the sudden request for the piano. Mallory played the introduction for 'You Can Have a Song at Night', but then she could barely make her voice come out. With another song completed, she took over the microphone.

"Okay, I think we're about finished with this process. My apologies! We are going to break again, and then we'll have the session on appropriate business attire, followed by some work ethics pointers from my husband. Then, Erik Bransom will give us some instruction about both corporate and personal security. Immediately after lunch, we will go over Confidential Disclosure Agreements, and all of my new hires will sign one, as well as W-4's and other pertinent paperwork. The last afternoon session for today will be Daniel Faulkner, and our business philosophy. Okay, back in your places in fifteen minutes."

She saw David scowl at his phone, and make his way from the meeting room. She followed him.

⚔ ⚔

Jeff could hardly believe what he was seeing. He swiped the back of his hand across his eyes and looked again. It couldn't be. He needed to call David! Panic gripped him, followed by indecision. Instead of calling his brother, he called the local veterinarian.

"You're sure?" he questioned the grim-faced vet.

"Well, I don't have a way to x-ray her on site here. I know a doc in Louisville who specializes in Arabians. He doesn't come cheap. Whose horse is this? Have you contacted the owner, so they know the situation and can authorize treatment?"

Jeff forced his voice to sound steadier than he felt. "Not yet. I was hoping I could tell them something encouraging."

"Well, she may be fixable; may take more than one surgery. She'll never be like she was. You might still be able to breed her; I'm not sure."

"Okay, I'll go make the call. You can get a cold soft drink or lunch over at the store if you'd like." He walked away and called his dad.

⚔ ⚔

"What? Dad, if this is some kind of bad joke~" David could barely process the disastrous news. "Why didn't he call me himself? Well, why didn't he notice before this? Well, was she okay yesterday?" To his consternation, Mallory was moving toward him. "I'll call you back." He disconnected, trapped, unsure what to say.

"We'll have to put her down," came Mallory's barely audible voice. "Was that Jeff? It isn't his fault. It isn't anyone's fault, David. It's one of those things."

He stared at her, barely comprehending. It couldn't be happening. "But~"

Her tears came. "She was so beautiful! Such a perfect gift! I love you for getting her for me."

He was anguished. "Well, you ended up paying for your own gift! Some gift!"

157

Her voice was soft. "David, that's not true. What we have, is ours. We bought her, and she-she did something really special for me, that I needed. This isn't easy, but I can't bear her ever being just a shadow of what she was, and enduring painful surgeries. I thought about insuring that expensive violin, the minute I bought it, but it never dawned on me with *Zakkar*. We can't afford to pour more money into her. We aren't horse ranchers, Arabian breeders."

He nodded, knowing she was right. The Alpaca were easy, practically raising themselves. Everything they were doing dovetailed and complimented the whole.

"When did you know?" He was amazed by the fact that she already knew.

"She stumbled when Jeff and I were searching for you that night, and I was afraid I noticed a slight limp after that. But then Saturday afternoon, I couldn't deny it to myself any longer. But, we had to get into town and work on the music. We didn't have time to wait for a vet to come. I guess if someone needs to be blamed, it's me."

"Well, maybe if you'd said something sooner-"

She cried harder, and he realized that would have been hard for her to do, with his being so overwrought about the entire cave episode, Summers; his being mad at her for conducting her own search.

He put his arm around her, and drew her close. "Hey, look at me. Come on. Look here. You done good! Bad grammar, I know. I'm pretty sure you saved Summers' life. I need to call Jeff. You want to talk to him, too?"

☙ ❧

By the end of the fifteen minute break, she was behind the microphone, gracious and smiling. "Okay, Todd and Luke, can you please pass these catalogs out to everyone?" She addressed a couple of the recent graduates, and they responded.

"Okay, at *GeoHy*, *DiaMal*, and *DiaMo*, we have stringent dress rules. Because of that, we provide one set of coordinates to each new hire, and offer a fifty percent discount from our catalog items thereafter. Of course, you don't have to wear our lines as long as you adhere to our guidelines."

She was aware of some grumbling. That was okay. Some of this would be kind of a shock until people grew accustomed to it. She continued.

Usually, Diana did this part, but she and Daniel hadn't seemed to be as 'into it' as they ordinarily were. She discussed hygiene, mentioning health insurance, as well as dental; neat haircuts and styles, without extremes. Clean groomed hands, good shoe shines, and well-pressed clothing. She tackled facial hair, in spite of David's shaggy look. 'Facial hair might be permitted, provided that it was neat and groomed.'

"We-ell," Waylon Mayer's drawl, as he spoke out of turn from the floor! "What about David?"

Mallory turned backwards to regard David thoughtfully, before turning her attention back to the inquiring mind that wanted to know.

"Okay, he's the company president, and not totally your concern; besides which," she continued impishly, "he uses that persona to procure staplers for all of us! All office supplies should be requisitioned from Marge, except if you need a stapler see David. He scares little old ladies into turning theirs over to him! Any other questions"?

Most of the employees didn't get it, but the muckety-mucks who had been in the first class cabin of an El Al flight en route to Israel couldn't help chuckling.

⊰ ⊱

"Look at the choices," A new girl complained as she turned catalog pages. "Do you not hate looking like your grandmother?" Her disdain was turned, unwisely, upon Mallory.

She simply laughed easily. "I'd be thrilled to look like my grandmother. She's the last word in style and elegance. And, you can order the skirts in varying lengths, from mid-knee, to whatever. The design of the skirts includes ease, so that they don't pull up when you sit down. They're comfortable and easy to wear."

After another brief break, David took the floor for the final morning session. Opening his attaché case, he removed a couple of things and his Bible, placing them carefully on the podium. "Let's pray together." He bowed his head, and asked the Lord to bless his words.

It created a bit of disturbance, both between the new graduates and a few of the *Sanders-Chandler* employees who were totally unaccustomed to the practice.

David just stood, waiting for quiet to prevail, rubbing his chin, relaxed. "Okay. Now that I've jacked a couple of staplers, I should shave. I brought two razors with me."

The crowd, watched, perplexed, while he held them up. "I hate to shave." With that, he had the guys on his page, that he had lost with the prayer. "But I hate to look like a tacky rebel that scares people, too." A scattering of laughter and smiles! "Ladies and Gentlemen," he donned his theatrical persona. "In my right hand is the trusty electric razor given to me by my dad when I was about fourteen! He gave it to me, because he had finally bought a new one, because he'd had this forever and it was worn out!"

By this time, most of the guys were with him a hundred percent, laughing sympathetically, and wincing at the thought.

"So, shaving has always been an ordeal for me! And, I assumed for everyone! It always took at least thirty minutes, and it hurt. I mean, I shaved before my wedding, and it took me forty minutes to get the bleeding stopped so I wouldn't ruin my shirt and tux. Well, many mornings, I'd choose. Am I gonna shave this morning, or have my devotions? With Daniel Faulkner and my dad, shaving's a big thing, and they can tell if I don't do it-and give me dirty looks accordingly."

The guys among the recent grads were all attention. "Yeah"!

"So, I hate to admit this, but I usually shaved and promised the Lord I'd get to my Bible reading and prayer time later. Because man looks on the outward appearance, and I wanted especially those two guys to be pleased with me." He struggled for composure. "Then, one morning, it was like the Lord tapped me on the shoulder, and quoted the remainder of that verse to me:

But the Lord looketh on the heart.

He turned and winked at Mallory. "I wanted to marry Mallory, and I figured if Mr. Faulkner and my dad approved, it couldn't hurt my cause. But it was like the Lord was saying, 'I look on your heart, and I see a man who doesn't make time for Me'. Having a clean-shaven face wouldn't win that kind of a girl, if I was a carnal kind of a guy. So, my talk has two parts: addressing the importance of both the inner and outer man, and also-back to the object lesson of my two razors." He held up the other one.

"When we came back to Dallas after our honeymoon~" He blushed until cheers and whistles subsided. "We had turned Mallory's suite into a master suite for both of us, and someone, I guessed, Mrs. Faulkner had put in supplies for me of the toiletries and stuff I usually use. And, a sharp, new, state-of-the-art! Drum roll! Razor! Let me read you a verse. It's a good verse. My dad has preached on it several times, and I knew it was true!"

Ecclesiastes 10:10 If the iron be blunt, and he do not whet the edge, then must he put to more strength: but wisdom is profitable to direct.

"It basically says that if a man doesn't stop and take time to sharpen an axe, he has to put more strength and labor into the job. I've been amazed at the difference a sharp, new electric razor makes. What do you have in your world, that if you'd stop and think, you could sharpen and refine to do a better job? What course can you take? What tools could you get to make you as great and efficient as possible? When I talk to you about the work ethic we expect here, it means working hard, working smart, as well as possibly working long. Another example; I was doing some work in my office at the ranch, and Mallory took one look at it and laughed. Slow printer the size of a Sherman tank, old laptop, slow and full of viruses and what-not. I mean, I was being frugal, I guess. But I was proof of the old adage. 'Penny-wise and pound-foolish' What money I was saving on not upgrading, I was wasting in time, because, sometimes, 'Time is money'. The point I'm making illustrates why we have the clothing and grooming guidelines we have. Because we all need to appear as sharp as we possibly can. We encourage everyone, including ourselves, to continue more formal education. It's fine to look sharp in a shirt and tie; but then, not to know what the Dow Jones Industrial Average is, or the Closing Bell, is ludicrous. The inside and the outside! But, there's even yet another realm to the inner man than his mentality; there's his spirituality. Or the woman! Outer appearance should reflect your confidence that you're a worthwhile person. Your worth isn't based on your body. We tend to take good care of our bodies; eating right, maybe working out, taking vitamins, and going to the doctor. But our bodies aren't who we are; they're where we live. We have a soul and spirit that define who we are. The body will die, but the soul will live on eternally. That's why we should take better care of it. All of this is why we're against pornography and other habits that steal our valuable thoughts and creativity. Do I spend extra time thinking of how to close a deal with Mr. X of N. Corporation? Or do I give myself to trying to make the next opportunity to view things I shouldn't? Do I try to think of nice things to make my wife happy? Or do I try to get her off my back, so I can engage in things she won't approve of?

Some people were hanging their heads, others were staring him down belligerently. 'He was a kid! A newly wed! What did he know?'

"That's another important part of work ethic. When I'm at work, I'm focused. If I'm clearing brush, I mark it off in my mind, how much I can do in an hour, by noon. Then, I ask how can I do it faster? Better? Mr. Faulkner taught me to use the people around me, even if it makes them mad. They may grumble that they're out in the heat, clearing brush, and I'm in my office ordering groceries. I have to prioritize the most important jobs, and allocate people and resources accordingly. I'm trying to train the lady who cooks, to keep a running grocery order as supplies run low. Eventually, she should be able to do the order. When you're at work, you should give your best. We who are born again Christians know the verse in Galatians that tells us to do whatever work is at hand, heartily, as unto the Lord. By the same token, you should give your full focus, thoughts, and energies to your wife and kids when you get off work. Live life checked in! Engaged! Work on purpose! And then play on purpose! Serve the Lord on purpose! Don't just slump in the pew because your wife nags you to go. Be there because you're the man, and it's what you want! Smile! Shake hands! Give your name! Sing the songs! Get into life, or it'll pass you by!"

Chapter 13: *ALTITUDE*

Tuesday morning the profusion of foods actually looked good to Mallory. Early, of course, she chose a yogurt, a banana, and a pastry with milk. Finding the food supervisor, she asked where the piano had disappeared. Evidently, it ordinarily provided entertainment in the lobby bar. David helped roll it back in. He looked amazing in a navy silk suit with pale blue French cuff shirt and navy and blue striped tie. Clean shaven with no razor rash.

Mallory slid onto the piano bench and began playing as people arrived, buzzing and bustling with activity. She studied body language as music flowed beneath her fingers. Quite a few people were more dressed up, although, they didn't have to be. For the most part, they seemed happier and more energized. She thought David's talk the previous afternoon had been amazing. To live life on purpose, and enjoy it! Tears filled her eyes, but they weren't the grieving she had planned to give herself to. They were tears of joy and thanksgiving! That she had gotten her voice back, her eyesight, her hands and feet! That she was born again and a child of the King! That she was married to David, and they had a baby on the way! That they could hold a meeting in such elegant surroundings! With such a profusion of food! That she had all the Faulkners in her life, and other friends and associates. She was amazed when Lilly Cowan entered. People she hadn't met before, but knew who they were, the Hansons. Then Nick and Jennifer appeared. Her eyes sought for Lisette, to arrange for the new attendees. David winked at her as he made his way to greet the newcomers, and make certain the staff accommodated the growing crowd.

Daniel, Diana, and the three oldest kids appeared, getting their instruments ready. This was more like it! They seemed to be more themselves! Albeit still moving gingerly due to being extremely saddle-sore.

She had played an assortment of love songs before moving into sacred. Just before time to start, her hands swept into *Wise Men Still Seek Him*. Unable to resist, Cassandra joined in on her violin. Then at an encouraging nod from Mallory, David and Daniel and Diana joined her in singing the lyrics.

Though fools have said, in their heart, 'There is no God'-
Wise men still seek Him, today.

As the harmony died away, Mallory moved to the podium and the microphone.

"The first thing I did this morning was read my Bible. It's the source of all wisdom. If you knew how ill-equipped I am, to lead a couple of companies, you would be glad I have this Well to come to." She smiled. "Good morning. My pastor's here this morning-well, one of my pastors, and my father-in-law. He is going to pray before the sessions begin."

John Anderson's rich voice filled the room, seeming to still even those who resented mixing 'religion' into business.

"That song," Mallory continued, "*Wise Men Still Seek Him* is a real favorite of mine. I know the thrust of its meaning, is that 'wise men' of this age seek Jesus as certainly as the 'Wise Men' of Jesus' day did when they saw the star in the east. I like to think of the 'today' of the lyrics, not as just meaning this present time period, but literally, today. And every day! That's why I have Christmas every day! Because, He is the reason for the Season, and I don't just drag Him out for a couple of weeks around December twenty-fifth. Every day is Christmas Day for me, because He daily loads me with benefits. I shouldn't feel more joy from Thanksgiving through January first, than I do the rest of the year. He is my Joy. I don't need drugs or alcohol for temporary happiness, because when I'm filled with the Spirit, I'm filled with joy. It just overflows, and puts a song in my heart that's the real thing. Ideas and inspiration flow, and I can't wait to share them with Diana-" She paused, blushing. "Well, with David, now." Her voice quavered. "From the day he moved to Murfreesboro, I couldn't wait to share everything with him. He was my very best friend. But then, at the beginning of my junior year, my dad kind of tried to slow me down.

And then, I wasn't sure David still wanted to be my friend. And I was supposed to really keep my distance! So, then, the Lord sent Diana, for me to share with, and be excited. Anyway, when your conscience is clear with the Lord, and you let Him be in charge, He infuses you with life and ideas. My life is fun, and my work is immensely gratifying to me, because He has me plugged in where my gifts and abilities have equipped me to be. We want for all of you to know the same joy and sense of purpose! A thrill at what you do; not work-shifts to be endured! And since every day is Christmas day, I brought some presents."

David pushed back an accordion divider to join an adjacent meeting room, and there sat both jewelry divisions.

Herb Carlton rose, lifting the most elegant package any of them had ever seen, and made his way to where Diana sat. "A gift commissioned for you from Mallory," he announced soberly. "Mallory was truly correct about the brilliance of ideas given by the Holy Spirit. When you have opened this, there is much more surprise to the gift!"

Diana shot a guilty glance at Mallory, who simply beamed happily.

"The wrapping is so gorgeous~"

"Yeah, yeah! Rip and tear! Rip and tear! Since the little kids aren't here, do you want me to help you?" Daniel's eyes were alight with suspense and amusement. "We all want to know what's in it!"

Diana's hands trembled as guilty thoughts bombarded her. She couldn't remember now, why she had treated Mallory's precious gift of friendship so carelessly. The gift was heavy, larger than a jewelry box. She opened the velvet lined box and gasped with wonder! "Oh! Mallory"! She lifted the contents carefully as Lisette moved in for the photo moment. "Oh, Mallory, that's absolutely exquisite!"

And it was! A rock crystal perfume bottle, to make the Topkapi Treasures blush envious green! The rock crystal, faceted to represent a large Diamond, fit into a stand of bejeweled gold. Ribbons of gold set with precious stones and pearls enwrapped it, and a vial of Diana's favorite, Parisian fragrance nestled into the recess calibrated to receive it. The gift was lavish!

Daniel stared at it blankly. It was absolutely priceless! The value of the gold and gemstones, combined with Herb's investment of himself, the international acclaim he was garnering! He cried.

Diana was overwhelmed! She rose and took her friend in her arms. "Thank you, Mallory. I love you."

Mallory beamed through tears? "You like it?" She turned her attention to Herb. "Herb, you outdid yourself! And that's saying a lot. I'm intrigued. What did you mean, about there being more to the gift?"

Herb turned and indicated a couple of gentlemen she didn't know. "These gentlemen are with *Melton-Vanderhoff, Intl.*, a large conglomerate; their cosmetics and perfumes division, to be specific. They manufacture Mrs. Faulkner's favorite fragrance."

Mallory waited for further elaboration. "Well, many perfume makers create special bottles, that a patron buys once; and refills are available. Well, Mallory, remember, you told me to check with the company for the availability of such, but they've never done refillable bottles. And you said, 'If they don't, we'll just pour the fragrance in and make a stopper that's an applicator'."

Mallory nodded, remembering. She needed Herb to move his story along, because the crowd, having not received anything yet, was growing restless with the narrative.

"Well, my inquiry was passed along to William Pennington, who was horrified at the fragrance's quality being compromised by exposing it to air and other contaminants. Well, everything escalated, and they want *Carlton* to create ten similar bottles for launches in New York, LA, London, Paris, Rome, Tokyo, Hong Kong, Kuala Lumpur, and Sydney. Our bottles will be on display under armed guard for the promotion, and auctioned later. The consumers will be able to purchase lovely, mass-produced replicas, refillable. These two gentlemen are here to work out details of the deal a little later on."

Daniel Faulkner and Lilly Cowan were the only two to catch the significance of the jeweler's words. Millions!

Daniel stood and teasingly got the mic away from Mallory. "While we are in the process of making presentations, we have one for you!"

She tried not to be annoyed. She actually had a script she planned to stick to, with time constraints. And, as was often the case with people who were givers, she sometimes had a hard time being on the receiving end.

He laughed again. "Would you relax? You just said you have Christmas every day, and we're trying to give you a gift-"

"M-m-m, guess ya got me," she admitted.

David seemed to be 'in on it' because he had hurried to the back of the meeting room and was moving forward with a package of his own.

"Well, Mallory, this was David's idea, but the rest of us liked it. We know you keep a picture of your father on your nightstand, but we wanted to honor his memory corporately with a portrait of him as founder of *DiaMo, Corporation*."

As David set the portrait on an easel, and removed the black velvet covering, many members of the group stood to their feet, applauding; Mallory's hands flew to her mouth as tears sprang to her eyes. "Oh! That's amazing! He looks like he's ready to say something. It's perfect!"

Daniel's eyes met Diana's. They were always stymied about what to get the girl they thought 'had everything'. Mallory had been right about David. They had a long history of friendship and understanding of what made the other, tick.

"David suggested it, and then we wondered why we never thought of it, ourselves. So he called Nick, and Nick persuaded Jennifer to paint it. She's been a little reticent of being present at the unveiling," Daniel's voice continuing.

Mallory nodded understanding. "I won't ask her to come up here if she doesn't want to, but she and Nick are both talented artists, as is Risa Perkins. In our group, we try to be supportive of one another. Of course, most of you know Nick, as the cutup, Hawaiian guitarist." She turned her attention toward David. "You have the perfect place in mind for this, don't you?" Even as she spoke, she had a better idea. One that she would get busy on immediately!

"Thank you everybody! Thank you, especially, Jennifer! I can't draw stick men, so it's amazing to me how you did that. I love you."

Break time again, and then Daniel took the podium, Bible in hand. "Good morning. My session today is on business ethics. I know some of you already feel offended about my standing up here with a Bible, and wondering if I intend to force some weird religion on you. Well, first of all, let me give you the definition of the word, *Ethics*. According to the Encarta ® World English Dictionary © and Microsoft Corporation, some synonyms for the word are: morals, beliefs, moral code, moral principles, moral values, integrity, conscience, principles. The same source gives two definitions: 1) study of morality's effect on conduct: the study of moral standards and how they affect conduct. And 2) code of morality: a system of moral principles governing the appropriate conduct for a person or group.

My question to you is, who determines the standards? Society?" He scoffed softly. "Well, plenty of people are trying to establish a code of their own. The United States Supreme Court took the Bible out of the public school systems, trying to erase an absolute standard. I think that decision alone, has placed our entire nation on a massive decline. TV doesn't set our standards of dress and deportment, and the World-system doesn't set our behavioral standards at the companies represented here. We believe that the Bible is a fair standard, and it's absolute. When it says not to steal, it doesn't mean, 'unless you can sneak it by and increase our earnings. In which case, it's fine'. Sadly, many 'good' people accept the same low standard, without giving it any thought of their own. At our companies, we set a higher standard. We demand it of ourselves, and we demand it of you. So, it's only fair to communicate our expectations. I'll begin with theft. Most of you know the concrete meaning of the word. If someone grabs my wife's perfume bottle and takes off with it, obviously, that's stealing. We also consider things theft that may be more nebulous. An example is, and I'll use the example of pornography found on company computers, not to point anyone out, but to make a point. A solitaire game, while more benign, is still an indication of theft. No one pays you to sit at a desk and play a game. You not only owe the company your time, when you're on the payroll, you owe them your best! You owe yourself, to always give your best! In a sloppy, slothful world, this may come as a shock! I don't want to pay good money to a gal who sits at a desk snapping gum and filing her fingernails, who answers the phone like she's been interrupted while doing something profound! Personal phone calls, longer breaks and lunches than permitted, taking off early, coming in late, not prioritizing work properly and allocating responsibly! You get my meaning. If your pay gets shorted by so much as a dollar, you'll squeal. But all of us in management here, have paid full salaries to those of you who accomplish little, abuse sick leave and personal days, and tear down productivity and morale when you are on premise. And, speaking of 'On Premise', we lease large office suites to provide nice work areas. No, you can't stay home in your robe and bunny slippers and work by remote.

Lying! A lie is an intent to deceive. Let's say, Alexandra tells Diana she's going to the store, and then I ask Diana where Alexandra went, and she tells me 'she went to the store'. If Alexandra actually went to a friend's house instead of the store, then she lied to Diana, but Diana didn't lie when she gave me misinformation. She didn't try to deceive me. She told me what she believed to be true. Don't lie, for yourself or anyone else. You say, 'Well, I don't want to get anyone fired', so you sign off on their hours, or you fail to report what you should, enabling people around you to do wrong. You are not the one to cost someone their job! They are! Erik Bransom is an FBI agent, and it always amazes him when felons blame law enforcement personnel for putting them in jail. When they break laws, they put THEMSELVES in jail! They start on a course of action with inevitable results. This 'good ole boy and gal club' mentality is what has turned American business into a muddle of mediocrity. Well, not even as good as mediocre! Substandard! We get an F!

I guess I'll give a history lesson here. At the end of the nineteenth century, as the 'Industrial Age' took hold of society, there was an historical shift of demographics in the western world. Farmers left agriculture at massive rates, and booming industries were snapping them up to work in factories! Factories provided 'consumer goods' as never before, and an emerging middle class was able to own some of the coveted mass-produced items. The industrialists were making unheard of fortunes! Sadly, by often abusing the work force they desperately needed! Most of you are familiar with the child labor laws passed during this time. While I agree that children shouldn't be abused and misused by society, at the same time I'm not sure our children should be exempt from work, as some of them seem to think they are. Well, to give these overworked, underpaid people some counter-leverage, they formed labor unions. But, by trying to counteract greed, the unions succumbed to greed, themselves, making demands, which, combined with Federal regulations, eventually drove companies to explore foreign labor markets. Don't get bored. This is important, or I wouldn't be going over it with you now. Texas is a non-union state, and there's no state income tax. I'm saying this to give you a quick course in economics. As company owners, we have taken some risks, and really invested ourselves into creating viable businesses. Because of that, we make more money than you will. When my secretary locks her desk, she turns *GeoHy* off in her mind until she returns at eight o'clock the next morning. I eat, breathe, and sleep it—or lose sleep over it, as the case may be." He laughed, but didn't get much response. "We want to be ethical toward every one of you, and that's why we ask the same in return. Your pay packages, although I understand why y'all want more, are fair and equitable with your educational levels and areas of responsibility. When you consider your benefit packages, times a hundred or so (the other people on the payroll) you might get a sense of why we sometimes can't sleep at night. If you're nervous about your upcoming house payment, take it times thousands, and that's what's on our minds. Don't get me wrong. We all love our lives! But, we don't sweat how we're going to pay you, just because we like you and want to help you out. We need what you can bring to the table! We want Personal Excellence from every one of you. We demand it of you. If you want to advance with any of us, that's the avenue. We don't reward seniority. As a matter of fact, if you don't work, you won't get a chance to gain seniority! We don't give raises to who's been here the longest, but to who's working the hardest and making a difference to the bottom line. Any questions?"

Mallory cringed when Waylon Mayer raised his hand. "Question, Waylon?"

"Yeah, what did he mean by 'Bottom Line'?"

❧ ☙

During the break, people surrounded her, inundating her with questions, or just making small talk. The same with David. Usually, they welcomed the interaction, but she needed to know.

Finally, as everyone reassembled for the next session, she whispered. "Did the text come?"

His response was a tormented shrug.

❧ ☙

Jeff Anderson was struggling. David and Mallory had given him specific instructions to have the local veterinarian, Dr. Del Stabler, euthanize *Zakkar*, and then send David a text to say it was over. And, Doctor Stabler said he had left a message on the specialist's phone, not to come the remainder of the way. Already on a flight from Louisville, Kentucky, to Little Rock, he should have gotten the message upon landing, spent the night at a nearby hotel, and returned home as quickly as possible. But to Jeff's consternation, Dr. Harold Kingsley had followed his own counsel, renting a car, and appearing to render his services, anyway. Unbelievable! David and Mallory didn't want to pour more money into their ill-fated Arabian.

170

"They've already decided to put her down," he tried to explain. "That's why they said they'd pay for your round trip air fare and a night in a Little Rock hotel."

"Where's the horse?" Kingsley basically tried to stride past Jeff toward the stable, despite his words.

Jeff was mad. The guy evidently was determined to exact a professional fee. "Look, there's no sense in you seeing her. David and Mallory, the owners, don't want her to suffer any more, since she can't recover."

"Well, we won't know she can't recover, until I've examined her~"

"Look, Mallory and her dad were sports enthusiasts, and her dad followed, well, he wasn't a gambler, but he followed the race horses. Mallory knew last week she was going to end up having to put her down."

The specialist, who made the largest percentage of his livelihood from racehorse breeders, sneered scornfully. "Oh, and that makes her an expert? Now, I'll need to do some x-rays, and give her a couple of injections. If the injury is operable, as I suspect it is, the nearest surgical theater would be Little Rock. Although, if I could get her to my facility~"

"No! Traveling will just cause her more pain and suffering! No one's authorizing you to create any more expense!"

Kingsley pushed his way into the stable and introduced himself to Stabler.

The local doctor glanced at Jeff apologetically and addressed the newcomer, "Oh wow, there must be some kind of mix-up here. I left you a message not to come ahead."

Actually, it was Kingsley who had jumped off the starting line by deciding to come before actually being bidden. And then had still come on, after being informed his services weren't needed. Stabler tried to hold his ground. "My assistant's coming within the hour, and we'll take care of the euthanization. Your opinion's a moot point. The owners have given their authorization~"

Kingsley had edged forward, and could finally see the quivering animal. "My, my, she's a little beauty!" He was frankly amazed at her quality. He tried to size up Stabler's integrity. He smiled ingratiatingly at Jeff and the local vet. "Look, just let me have her. She's a gorgeous animal, and I should get some living tissue samples. Who are you calling, Son?"

Jeff held up his hand.

~ ~

Erik liked Steb Hanson fairly well. Both men held the same core values. Sometimes, Steb's recklessness about defending his values, made the cautious FBI agent nervous. Well, Steb's recent, on-going argument with Mallory, for one thing. Steb was zealous about his *SOC Foundation*! And, certainly, someone needed to be. And Faith Baptist in Murfreesboro, Honey Grove Baptist in Tulsa, and Calvary Baptist in Dallas, with many thousands of other conservative organizations world-wide, linked to the *SOC* site. And Mallory was more than sympathetic to the cause. But, when Hanson had requested that Mallory link her business sites to his foundation, she had answered with a firm 'No'.

Bransom agreed with her. Customers for her goods didn't have to be Christians, conservatives, anti-gay, anti-abortion, premillenialists, or anything. If they had the buying power, the goods were for sale. Why should she alienate any of her clientele? He remembered years before, when Pepsi ® had made an issue of being sympathetic to the gay caucus. That had brought a huge boycott from the grass-roots conservatives. That was before he was saved, and he had never been an investor. But, at the time, he had thought that if he held stock in the company, he would have been ticked about losing money on an issue having nothing to do with soft drinks. Pepsi should stick to controlling as much of the soft drinks market as possible, without polarizing their consumers needlessly. Pastors needed to address sin issues in peoples' lives; that was their job.

So, Hanson had stuck around at the Grand Kempinski long enough to watch the portrait's being presented to Mallory. Then, he had lit out like he was on fire! Just up the toll way to the Addison airport to rent a plane! The flight plan he filed was for a small, rural Arkansas airport. Bransom placed a call to Ivan Summers.

"Hey, Summers? Ya back in the saddle yet?"

A laugh that made the Arkansas guy sound more like himself. "Not if you have a job for me to do. I don't work for you. Remember?"

"Yeah, yeah! But I have a feeling something's going on at the Ranch. David and Mallory are trying to act normal and upbeat, but there's something~" He cleared his throat. "That Arizona fella lit out of here, and I was trying to tail him, but he cheated and rented a plane. His flight plan takes him right to your neck of the woods. I thought you probably have nothin' better to do than bein' eyes and ears for me. Don't go in without Haslett, and I don't think Hanson's trouble. He may be walkin' into some."

⊣ ⊢

Gift time! Security people entered with boxes of gifts. Enstrom Candies, chic brief cases, Mont Blanc pens, leather-bound Bibles, and two hardbound books: <u>See</u> <u>You</u> <u>at</u> <u>the</u> <u>Top</u> by Zig Ziglar, and the <u>The</u> <u>One</u> <u>Minute</u> <u>Millionaire</u> by Mark Victor Hansen and Robert G. Allen. A video of <u>The</u> <u>Bethlehem</u> <u>Star</u> completed the gift giving.

Diana conducted a session on 'Talents, Gifts, and Finding Your Niche', followed by a break for lunch. Mallory tried to hide her anxiety. 'How hard could it be to put a horse to sleep and send a text?'

While the crowd was preoccupied with lunch, David led her to the parking garage, where they gained the isolation of the SUV. "I guess, I need to call, and find out what's going on." He pulled his phone free as it buzzed. Jeff!

"Put it on 'Conference'." Mallory's features were a study in anxiety as she spoke.

Reluctantly, he complied.

"Jeff, what's going on? We thought we'd hear before this." David didn't try to disguise his frustration.

"Well, yeah, there's a new wrinkle. The equestrian vet from Louisville came on anyway, and he wants to take some tissue first. Do you guys have a problem with that? He's pretty much of a determined guy."

Mallory started shaking. "Tissue samples? Why? She doesn't have a disease, or anything. What? Is he going to clone her? No! No tissue samples!"

David pulled Mallory closer as he spoke. "Okay, that's your answer, Jeff. No! Tell him to leave."

"I have. Uh, he doesn't listen. Maybe we should give him what he wants so we can put her down, and he'll go on his way."

Mallory grabbed for the phone, but David moved it to his other ear, out of her reach.

"Let me talk to him!"

There was a cacophony of angry voices, seemingly interminable, as David tried to make sense of what was happening. "Jeff! Jeff, Je-what's going on?" His gaze met Mallory's, helplessly. She listened too. At last, a gunshot made them both jump, and Mallory screamed involuntarily.

"Finally, Jeff's shaken voice, "Okay, Hanson showed up, and she's-uh-gone. It's over. I'll call ya later."

Mallory buried her face in David's shoulder and sobbed.

⊰ ⊱

Lisette looked around as Sam appeared; it was nearly time for the first afternoon session, and Mallory was a stickler for the schedule. Worried, she found Darrell Hopkins. "Do you have a heads-up where David and Mallory might be? It's not like her to disappear, especially with its being time for a session."

"H-m-m, David got the keys from me; they were going to the car to make a call." He pulled out his phone, punching in David's speed dial number.

"Hey, Darrell, we're ready to go. Come drive us. Tell Lisette to keep the afternoon on track."

Mallory shook her head negatively, but he disregarded. "No, we're going home, so you don't have to hold yourself together. I can find out from Jeff what's happening. The employees want to talk to us on breaks, which is a good thing. But for today, it's too much."

Her eyes met his. He was serious about going home. Relieved, she sagged against him.

⊰ ⊱

Erik was shocked by Ivan Summers' report. "So Hansen went to the ranch to kill Mallory's horse? And he shot it, over Jeff's protests?"

"No." Summers attempted to lend clarity, as he understood it. "There were two different vets there; one was the local guy who was supposed to put the horse down; she was injured. The other one was insisting on getting tissue samples. Well, David and Mallory had said 'no' to the tissue deal, and they had told that high dollar specialist guy to go home when he first landed in Little Rock. Well, then Hansen showed up, like you said he was going to. He went livid about the Louisville doctor trying to harvest tissue. Why is that a big deal, either way?"

"I don't know. That mare was a valuable horse. Maybe they can start little test tube horsies, and implant them into any number of old nags. Reduce the risk of delivery for champion mares? I don't know; just a guess.

174

That would give Hansen cause to be upset. He breeds his horses correctly, takes the risks-" Even as Bransom spoke, he was filled with renewed awe at the scams and schemes people could come up with. Wow, not only were human organs valuable, but pieces of full bred Arabians, as well. His heart felt heavy for David and Mallory and their loss.

⊰ ⊱

Mallory kept dabbing her tears away. "I'm not sure which is best. Now, I don't have to go on like nothing's wrong; but at the sessions, at least part of my attention was diverted from feeling sa-a-ad."

David simply held her. It seemed too soon for him to croon, 'There, there, we'll get another one'. Well, the price tag, for one thing. "Maybe you can get a nap," he suggested. "Actually, we're behind on a couple of contracts. I can read them to you later. And, there's a Red Sox game."

She nodded. "Yeah, those are pretty good ideas. I wish I had asked the doctor about my batting cage. It's usually pretty therapeutic."

"That's probably not a good idea. Why don't you ever want to swim?"

"I don't know. Since I nearly drowned those two times, it makes me gag, even just to get swimming pool water in my mouth. I'll kick around a little in the hot tub while you swim."

He led her up to their suite, and pulled her shoes off. "Please try to rest. I'm going to make a couple of calls, and check on a job. Then, we can swim and order pizza when the baseball game comes on. Maybe I can get some more details from Jeff. I can't figure out what Hansen's problem was."

Mallory actually slept until her phone notified her of an email from Lisette. True to form, it was informative about the afternoon sessions, filled with fancy tech and frills. It was complete. Lisette was amazing.

⊰ ⊱

Daniel packed his attaché case, and smiled tiredly at Diana. "You need help carrying your gift? You can trust me. It's strange for Mallory to leave early; she usually supervises these sessions more carefully than this."

"Yeah, maybe it's just the nausea and queasy feelings. She and David both acted jumpy, though, I thought."

Daniel's gaze met his wife's serious blue eyes. She had amazing powers of observation.

"Well, let's go check in at the Westin. We can eat dinner, and call them later. Maybe they'll join us for coffees."

She usually loved staying in a suite at the high end hotel adjoining the Dallas Galleria, but her concern for their three youngest was foremost on her mind.

"They'll be okay. You deserve a break; not that worrying about Mallory gives you a real break. My mom and dad can handle it. It'll make them appreciate you even more." He clasped her hand. "I don't tell you often enough how much I appreciate you. You're an amazing, amazing lady, to do what you do, and keep it all balanced and going."

⚒ ⚒

David checked out the 'Sports Bar' room of their gracious home. Stocked with soft drinks, ice cream, and other ball-park snacks, it was cuter than if it fulfilled its originally intended purpose. He spoke to the crew finishing up, highly satisfied. "I think it looks great! Hope she likes it. Okay, get the old furniture loaded before she comes down."

"That don't look like no 'old furniture' to me," one of them grumbled. "It don't look like it's ever been sat on. You selling it, or what?"

"I'm not sure. If the Faulkners build on to their house, they might be able to use it. Or I can put it in the third cabin. I just liked the dark green better. What do you think? Does it look arranged okay?"

The other man chuckled. "Well, I'm a Braves fan, or I'd like it a lot."

The conversion of the space was delightful. On the large, unbroken wall glowed a silk, screen print of Fenway Park, from the pitcher's mound toward home plate, with stadium and fans in the background. Deep green, leather love seats opposed each other across an awesome coffee table created from an old piece of scoreboard atop legs fashioned from baseball bats. A couple of stadium seats removed from Fenway flanked an end of the table. The bar was refaced with matching deep green leather, and new stools created from baseball bats completed it. Spacious recliners, again of the same rich leather, faced the big screen.

He sprawled into one of the chairs as the crew departed, and pulled out his phone. This would be easier from his laptop, but Mallory was more

176

likely to get wind of his plan that way. He finished his plot, and dropped his phone into his pocket, just in time.

❧ ☙

Erik disconnected from his conversation with Steb Hanson. They had spoken at length about Erik's concerns. He rubbed his hands up and down over his face, and refilled his mug. Suzanne sat at her computer, continuing to iron out details at the *Chandler* facility. His conclusion was that most doctors were good people, trying to be leaders in their country clubs, while juggling altruism and helping the plight of society. He could see why pressure might cause even a professional person to stray onto a wrong path. Darius Warrington came to mind; just do an illegal procedure occasionally. It didn't hurt the old bank balance, while it saved someone's life! (Not concerning himself with details like who might have lost theirs). The same with the legitimate industry of Home Security! Most of it was what it seemed. With the exception of a rogue that decided to terrorize neighborhoods into believing they needed security systems they couldn't afford. Or putting in burglar bars that trapped them in infernos if houses caught fire! Now, here were these high dollar veterinarians, most of them, good people, helping the population care for their pets and livestock. But, evidently a few couldn't resist the temptation to make a few fast bucks by underhanded schemes. In answer to Bransom's questions, Steb had admitted that his stallions weren't always where his staff or security kept them under constant surveillance. Black market horse breeding? But what about papers? He paced, then, placed a call to Faulkner.

❧ ☙

"Have you talked to Lilly? How come she's here?" Daniel and Diana and the three big kids were enjoying a meal at Pappadeaux.

"Well, yes I talked to her. I think she's here because of Mallory, but Mallory~" Cassandra's voice foundered. "Do you think she's happy? Married to David, I mean? I always thought that should make her very happy."

Diana rested her fork. "I believe she is. I mean, it's an adjustment. They have a baby on the way, so she hasn't felt well some of the time."

"But Lilly hasn't talked to you, about going back with her; has she?" Daniel could hardly bear the thought; one of the reasons he had tried to steer clear of Lilly.

Cassandra sighed. "No, she knows when I am not ready."

Jeremiah fought tears that wanted to free themselves. "Well, I don't think Mallory's happy. I wish she wasn't married! I hope *Zakkar* didn't really get killed!"

"What are you talking about?" Alexandra's tone could be sarcastic. "You always try to be such a drama king!"

Daniel's phone buzzed. Erik Bransom. "Hey, Erik, everything okay?"

"Yeah, why do you always answer your phone that way? Am I always a harbinger of bad news? I just wondered if David and Mallory are with y'all and how she's holding up about her horse."

⚔ ⚔

"I'm hungry. I hope the pizza doesn't take too long to get here." David's usual drumbeat as he toweled off and put on dry things. "Just wear your robe," he suggested as he noticed she was redressing. "Come on. Relax. It's getting late; nobody should be dropping in."

"You're right. It's strange that Daniel and Diana haven't come and stayed here. I mean, they stayed at the Kempinski last night. I hope they didn't go back to Tulsa. I'm kind of counting on Diana to help me aclimate my new people in the morning. I mean, help us acclimate our new people. She does all these cute little aptitude tests and quizzes, to figure out where to start people. And she tells the high points of <u>See</u> <u>You</u> <u>at</u> <u>the</u> <u>Top</u>: that your **Attitude**, more than your **Aptitude**, determines your **Altitude**. I need her to do that before Mr. Haynes shows up to line up their academic work. Like, I'm thinking about Deborah Rodriguez helping with our accounts with the Rivera's in Spain. Carlos and Calista are both fluent in English, but they're often unavailable, leaving other family members to work the phones."

David nodded agreement. "Pizza's here. You coming?"

"Let's just watch the game up here. It's more comfortable." She plumped pillows.

"No, it's pretty comfy downstairs; and the TV's bigger."

"Okay," she acquiesced.

"Don't go in there til I get the pizza paid for."

That was kind of weird, but she stepped out of the sight-line of the door as he took care of the transaction. He juggled pizza boxes with his right hand while he laced the fingers of his left with hers. "Okay, come on." He pulled her into the remodeled space and flipped the light switch.

She took it in, wide-eyed, as he waited nervously for her response. "I love it! It actually feels like being there!" And, she really did. It was just such an emotional roller coaster! She threw herself into his arms. "This is amazing!" She settled into one of the recliners in time for the first pitch. "This furniture's more comfortable, too."

Chapter 14: ACCUMULATION

Mallory and David were the first ones to enter the *DiaMo* suite on Wednesday morning. "Is that where my dad's portrait is going to hang?" She indicated an empty wall near the public elevator.

"Is that where you want it?" David liked to tease her by answering a question with a question, a tactic he had learned from his dad to avoid answering direct questions.

She smiled sweetly. "Yes, it is, and I want one of us, to hang just inside here. See, what do you think?"

He shrugged. "If that's what you want, we can get Lisette to take our picture when she gets here, and I can forward it to Nick."

"Yeah, I haven't heard from Diana. I hope she's coming. If she does, she's the best photographer of any of us."

⊰ ⊱

Kerry Larson looked up from the documents spread before him. "Herb, this looks like a good deal to me. Amazing, actually!" He returned his attention to the numbers. "So, Mallory just commissioned you to make the jeweled bottle for Diana, and it turned into a sweet deal like this?"

Kerry was a Christian, and had been for a long time. He knew the many Scripture passages in both Old and New Testaments that promised God would always bless and give back to generous people. He was forced to admit that it certainly proved itself true time and time again in Mallory's life.

The master craftsman nodded slowly. "Yes, that is correct. I contacted the subsidiary of *Melton-Vanderhoff, Intl.* that manufactures their fragrances. They were in the middle of a brainstorming session for new promotion. Not only, they commission me for more bottles, but they compensate Mallory for idea."

Kerry shrugged. "Yes, but it's not exactly a new idea. The bottles at Topkapi are centuries old. Usually, you'd have to sue a company like *Melton*, and prove they infringed on intellectual property."

Herb shrugged. "Yes, the book of Ecclesiastes, in chapter one, I believe, states that:

There is no new thing under the sun.

I guess God had readied their hearts to idea of exquisitely decorated decanters. William Pennington, the director of this project, had recently traveled to Israel, where his tour included viewing my work on display there." He removed his glasses and cleaned them fastidiously, before dabbing at his eyes. He cleared his throat. "Mr. Pennington was familiar with both my name and the quality of my work, before he ever spoke a word with me." He chuckled tremulously. "How many times does Mallory go over this with me?"

"Well, I think you and Mallory both need to get ink on the line before they change their minds. I'll see if she can come down right away. She'll probably have David sign with her. I guess the adage is true that, *The rich get richer~*"

⊰ ⊱

Diana appeared at eight on the dot, to help get Mallory's new hires fit into positions. The problem was that Mallory had composed herself about *Zakkar*, and Diana had showed up, tearful from a sleepless night after hearing about it.

Mallory dissolved into tears again, too. "I didn't even want you to find out yet. You already said you weren't coming to the Ranch this week end, and I figured another week~" She blotted at her mascara. "It isn't your fault. It has nothing to do with you. It's one of those things. Look, I don't think God was punishing me for loving her too much. But~I was loving her too much! When I was here, I couldn't concentrate on what I needed to, and when we were there, I was annoyed that David couldn't help me with her every second. I was even mad about the baby. It's real sad, but most of the time I'm okay. It helps if I stay busy." She blew her nose. "I'm excited about these new kids. I thought you were nuts when you told me to hire everyone that applied from my graduating class. But you were so right about them." She paused to frown at her phone. "I wonder what Kerry needs this early. He isn't even waiting for Marge to activate the office phones."

Diana watched as her friend's countenance changed from annoyance, to questioning, to wonder, and finally to delight. Tears sprang up, tears of joy, as Mallory hugged her exuberantly. "Can you start everybody? Something unbelievable has come up, and I need to go to Kerry's office to sign some papers. Where did David go?"

She found him in the other suite where he was busily fixing his own office space. He caught her before she could go any farther. "What's up?' he questioned curiously. She was positively alight!"

She laughed triumphantly. "You're about to find out. We need to go sign some papers in Kerry's office!"

She planted a jubilant kiss on him and he laughed. "Well, okay~"

⚔ ⚔

Rhonna Abbott, Damon Benton, Heather Clark, Todd Daly, Waylon Mayer, Deborah Rodriguez, Anna Stevenson, and Luke Torrance circled the conference table, puzzling over the W-4's and other paper work.

David had tried to teach the group this very thing when he substituted in Business Math the preceding year. "Okay, when you agreed to come to work here, you moved and left home. Your folks are no longer supporting you; you've joined the ranks of the self-supporting. You are now claiming yourselves as one exemption. Your parents are dropping you as dependents. Bad news for them, in a way. Except, hopefully, they reared you to join the ranks of the self-sufficient. Sign and date it; make sure you follow the instructions, and turn it in right away."

Waylon, slouching disrespectfully, shoved his to the middle. A couple of others followed suit.

Heather texted her dad to ask if it was okay, and Rhonna carefully read both sides of the entire form, located a pair of scissors, and cut the paper on the dotted line. The top part, which said to retain for your own records, she slid into the front of her notebook.

David sat grinning. Who knew how insightful this simple exercise could prove to be? A would-be leader, leading people the wrong way; a cautious girl; a conscientious girl!

Diana moved in with a stack of five-page tests and a stop watch. The kids all exchanged nervous glances as Diana cheerily voiced some instructions. "Okay," she repeated herself. "Make sure you read over the entire test before beginning. You'll have twenty minutes~ beginning~Now!"

She punched in the stem, and Waylon and crew started with the space that said, 'Name': David could barely keep a straight face, except they reminded him so much of himself in the recent past. Waylon, who had sped ahead to fill in name and date, was now waiting for Anna to finish a difficult problem, so he could copy. Rhonna, her face a study in anxiety, scanned onto page four, aware the others were working madly.

Luke, bogged down on the fourth arduous equation, spoke out; "Man, there is no way~"

Tears of relief sparkled in Rhonna's dark eyes as she laid her pencil next to the unmarked exam.

An exasperated Waylon told her, "Look, at least give it a try. Don't give up that easy."

"Stop! Put your pens down." Diana could hardly keep a straight face as frenzied kids tried to keep working.

"This is nuts," Damon muttered as he complied.

"Okay, short break while I evaluate the results," Mallory announced.

She figured they were pretty much complaining and carrying on amongst themselves as they refilled plates and drinks.

"I'd laugh at them with you, except they remind me of me," David confessed.

"It's already so enlightening," Lisette added. "I mean, just following the simple instructions, like, not talking." She blushed, "Of course, I always talked when I wasn't supposed to."

The kids reassembled as Diana handed out blank sheets of paper. "Okay, on a more relaxed note, 'Thinking and Dreaming Time'. If you were freed from your 'I can't's', what would you do? Where would you go? What would you be? Try to remove the ceiling and let yourselves soar."

They all stared at her like she was turning green.

Rhonna raised her hand hesitantly. "Can we talk now?" she questioned when Mallory nodded at her.

"M-m-m, I'm not sure you need to. Your dream should be what beats in your own heart, not latching on to what someone else says that may 'sound good' Just give it some thought." Mallory had always like Rhonna. A lively black girl, she had always worn her hair in an array of pigtails secured with vivid barrettes. Now a more grown-up version of herself, without the barrettes!

Tears welled up. "I don't know. Take Caramel. She dreamed, but she didn't tell nobody; 'cause she was afeared they'd laugh."

"Rhonna, this isn't Murfreesboro. Talk right! I mean, correctly. And we aren't going to laugh. We don't even have to see what you write down."

"Then, how will you know if we did the assignment?" Waylon always tried to figure an angle.

Mallory sipped her coffee, and smiled. "Well, remember how Mr. Haynes always told us, that if we cheated, or took short-cuts, we mostly cheated and short-changed ourselves?"

"Yeah, I'm glad I graduated and got rid of that guy." Waylon snickered and snorted at his own hilarity, glancing around for support from the others. Finding himself isolated, he returned his gaze to Mallory with a smug grin.

Mallory's turn for smugness! "Well, actually, Waylon, you aren't rid of him. He'll be here mid-afternoon to find out what your academic goals are and get your courses lined up for your Bachelors' programs."

"Well, I don't really plan on bein' a bachelor for long. I'm lookin' ta find me a woman!"

Mallory scrambled away to do something in the kitchen, leaving Diana, Lisette, and David trying to maintain straight faces.

Mallory slid back into her seat. "Okay, have any of you written anything? We actually need to get some major decisions nailed down in a short amount of time. We aren't giving you some silly busy work. We gave you books the other day; have any of you looked at either one?"

Bent heads were her response.

"Was there an assignment?" Heather's voice sounded desperate.

"Okay. Y'all aren't high school kids any more. We're trying to turn you into thinking people." Mallory's voice was patient. "When we gave you the books, we hoped you'd be interested enough in who we are and how we operate, to at least look at them. With your college curriculum, you will have required 'Assignments'; but we want you to start thinking beyond doing assignments and getting by with the minimum." She excused herself back to the kitchen, and David noticed she was cooking something that smelled good.

"Look, I can't decide on anything this major this quick without talking to my parents." Heather's face set obstinately.

David crossed his arms. "Well, y'all have known you were getting ready to graduate and move on. Mr. Haynes has been pushing you, since at least your junior year. You've all had lots of time to think, and there's been a guidance counselor. Look at it this way. All knowledge is valuable, and you can't learn the wrong discipline or body of knowledge. Halfway through my Architectural studies, I had a panic attack. 'Is this what I want to do? And do it forever?' Mallory told me in no uncertain terms, to finish. So, I am a licensed Architect, which I enjoy to no end! But I'm not only an Architect! I do lots of other things, and my formal studies are ongoing. So are hers!"

"Well, can we just work and put off going to college for a couple of years?" Damon hadn't said much up to this point. "I'm not real sure I'm college material. My dad said that being a college grad's just a crock and it won't help you get a job. Lots of people are unemployed who have degrees."

Mallory had returned with a sizzling steak on a platter. "But, you're employed, and you're employed by a company providing you with this opportunity most people will never get. Mrs. Faulkner's going to fill the dry board up with courses of study and careers to give you some ideas. Maybe you can pick something that will mesh with your dreams and goals you didn't write down. Because your minds have been working on the 'assignment', whether you've committed anything to paper, or not!"

Diana began writing, Sciences-oriented careers, mostly.

"You can include some of the Arts," Mallory suggested.

"I'm not doin' it." Waylon slung his pen rattling to the center of the table. "It all starts with more English. I hate English! I've hated it for ten years. I got my high school diploma; that's good enough. I'm done here."

Rhonna turned toward him; large, expressive, dark eyes filling with tears. "Will you shut up? You don't have to mess things up for the rest of us. This 'Dream Paper'? I haven't put a word. Here's why! A week ago, I was hoping to get hired to carhop at Sonic. That was my dream, and the best I could come up with. That's how a lot of us Murfreesboro kids are. I never dreamed of bein' in Dallas and workin' for a company. I mean, I'm not real sure what it is I'm gonna be doin'. I'm already way up the dream ladder by bein' here. College scares me, too. It's gonna be harder than takin' English."

David's curiosity got the best of him. "What's with the steak?"

"Well, not much," Mallory answered. "Can you swallow it for us?"

He did a double-take. "How can I do that? Are you saying I have a big mouth?"

She smiled. "No, I'm saying, unless you want to choke on it, you'd better swallow it one bite at a time."

He nodded, lifting a knife and fork. "Ah! An object lesson! Very good! These guys are feeling overwhelmed about taking on four years of college in one day; which is akin to swallowing the steak, rather than taking manageable bites."

She nodded. "Exactly"! She turned her attention earnestly to the group of kids. "We all love the Bible." She indicated David, Diana, Lisette, and herself, "Because it's a wonderful Book full of wisdom and knowledge! We believe that all true Knowledge interrelates with It seamlessly. The book of Proverbs tells us we should seek for Wisdom and Knowledge, not shirk from it. See, the steak was very appealing and palatable, until David was suddenly overwhelmed with the size and impossibility of it! Learning should be palatable, too, and enjoyable."

David rested the utensils. "Wow! That's a big steak!"

"Seventy-two ounces"! Sometimes, we can break big jobs into small tasks, and get them done. Sometimes~"

She disappeared and came back with a stack of plates and flatware. "~we have to ask for help."

David couldn't help being amazed by her as he sliced pieces off to pass around. "Waylon, could you help me with this big job?"

The young man laughed, "Gladly"!

"You know, we're hiring you because we have a big job we can't do by ourselves." Mallory continued as David passed pieces of the prime steak around the table. "You'll all find that you need help, too. Don't be afraid to ask. You have so many friends that have already helped you along in life. One of those is Mr. Haynes. Think about your parents; they can help you do a better job here. If I chew you out, don't have your moms help you by calling me to remind me you're only seventeen, or whatever. But, you can have your parents help you in other ways. Well, for one, wearing our designs and making them part of their lifestyle. Or ask your parents to hand out your business cards. That way, as they promote you, they also promote us. You have a history of helping one another. I don't mean cheating; not that any of you would ever-have-done-that! Waylon, you're more than capable of learning English, and you need to get it down, because we require that everyone learn a foreign language. When you study conjugations of French verbs, it's by equating them to their English counterparts. If you can't conjugate verbs in English, you'll really be lost. But if you're struggling with something that is someone else's strong point, ask them for help. It's the same with work projects. We talk about *Synergy*, a concept that's made pretty clear in one of the two books none of you have started on. It's what we're about. I don't want to spoil the suspense, so you can read it for yourselves."

During lunch break, delivery men appeared with a crated baby grand piano. David indicated where to place it, in his spacious office, relieved when it fit through the doorway. Mallory watched as the crate fell away, revealing the beautiful instrument. Within an hour, a professional arrived to tune it. It looked gorgeous, lending the huge space a gracious aura.

Inspired, Diana summoned the newest workers around the beautiful instrument. Her fingers danced through an introduction, and she motioned the kids to sing with her as she began: one of Mallory's favorite songs from Disney's <u>Cinderella.</u>

And because these daft and dewy-eyed dopes
Keep building up impossible hopes,
Impossible, things are happening every day!

Mallory laughed. It exemplified the hopes and dreams they were trying to pull from the kids. "Let's sing it again. Come on; everybody sing."

So, the guys were less 'into it', but the girls knew the lyrics, joining shyly except for Rhonna, who couldn't resist swaying back and forth before adding her own counter melody that went to the stratosphere!

Diana turned from the keyboard to gaze at the girl wide-eyed!

Rhonna clapped both hands over her mouth. "I'm sorry, Ma'am; I get too loud and carried away!"

"No, you don't! Have you studied voice?"

"Oh, no Ma'am! My family's real poor. I wanted to study piano." She gazed at her blank sheet. "Maybe I can write that on my page here. I begged and cried for piano lessons. Miz Mallory; I was always jealous you got to learn it. I used to tell my daddy, 'the O'Shaughnessy's house is worse than ours. They're poorer than us, and she gets lessons'."

Diana laughed. "You have such a beautiful voice that learning piano might only be a distraction. Your placement, control, phrasing! All sublime! Such a gift! You know, God gave it to you. He's the One Who has given all of us everything we have. The Bible teaches that to whom much is given, much shall also be required."

"So, you're sayin' I should sing Gospel? I know some Gospel songs, but we haven't ever gone to church much."

Diana's gaze traveled from face to face, resting on Rhonna. "No, that isn't what I'm saying, exactly. I'm not talking about going to church or limiting a repertoire to Sacred music. I'm saying that we all need a time when we realize that God sent His Son, Jesus, to Calvary to pay our sin penalty; and we receive His free gift of Salvation. Then, because we are grateful for His redemption, we should surrender ourselves to Him. My husband and one of my daughters are world-class violinists."

"Oh, Yes'm, at church Sunday!" Rhonna's features were mobile and expressive. "I liked that."

Diana nodded. "The classical world condemns Daniel for performing Christian music, when he's gifted for the complexities of Classical music. Cassandra is pursuing a Classical career, and our Christian friends tend to think that's worldly, and she should forget it. The truth is, Cassandra, at age almost ten, is a strong and vibrant Christian, and God is using her testimony and her talent to reach a segment of His population for Him. If you accept Him, and surrender yourself, your talents and abilities, your dreams and goals, it's truly amazing what He will do."

"So, Slime, is that what happened to you?" Waylon's voice, although huskier than normal!

"It's Mrs. Billingsley to you, and yes, Mr. Haynes and Tommy led me to the Lord one day after school. It's the best decision I ever made."

"You know," David interjected, "getting saved is so simple that a child can understand it and receive Him, although adults often miss it because they try to make it more complex. You just say a simple prayer, asking Him to be your personal Savior. No pressure from us. It's your decision. We recommend it, though."

A hush descended as decisions were made.

Diana's fingers rippled the keys. "Okay, let's sing it again."

By now, the guys were singing as well.

And because these daft and dewy-eyed dopes {dewy-eyed dopes}
Keep building up impossible hopes {impossible hopes}

Damon's ad libing in an incredibly deep bass sent everyone into gales of laughter. Still, Diana was enchanted. "Okay, that's good; that's cute. Damon, add that part! Come in even stronger! And then, Rhonna, go up on your high part at the end. The rest of you, harmonize like you were."

Mallory's gaze met David's across the piano. It was like the prayer moment and the singing together had melded all of them into a cohesive unit.

Tom Haynes appeared, and his job went incredibly smoothly. With academic courses settled, he went on his way.

Mallory suddenly felt exhausted. "Okay, that wraps up today. You are all the greatest. See you in the morning at eight sharp. We have church tonight; we attend Calvary Baptist. The service starts at seven. You're welcomed to attend, but not required. In the morning, we'll be meeting with each of you individually, to define your jobs and areas of responsibility."

"So, we're all still in?" Waylon's voice was tense.

Mallory nodded, laughing. "Yes Sir! We look forward to working with all of you."

Chapter 15:   AGREEMENTS

Ecclesiastes 5:4-6 When thou vowest a vow unto God, defer not to pay it; for he hath no pleasure in fools: pay that which thou hast vowed.

Better it is that thou shouldest not vow, than that thou shouldest vow and not pay.

Suffer not thy mouth to cause they flesh to sin; neither say thou before the angel, that it was an error: wherefore should God be angry with thy voice, and destroy the work of thine hands?

A couple of the new hires appeared at church, and even more delightful to Mallory, was the fact that Bryce and Cade appeared with Lisette. Both men were dressed up beyond their norm, but it was their countenances that made a truly dramatic difference.

"Why don't you want Blythe to know?" Mallory questioned.

"Okay, it isn't that I don't want her to find out," Bryce responded evenly.

Mallory was amazed at his tone. She had never heard his voice when he wasn't both defiant and sarcastic.

"I don't want people to go around saying I got saved. I want them to see for themselves. I'm not ashamed, if that's what you thought."

"Well, yes, "David entered the discussion, "That's a good thing. The first step of obedience to the Lord, though, is public baptism. I mean, how soon are you planning on being around all your family and friends, so they can figure it out? Jesus gave an example that the way to testify to the world is to 'follow Him in baptism'. I know you think your plan's a good one. But we can never improve on His! Trust me; I've tried."

"M-m-m, I'll have to think on that one," Bryce hesitated.

Mallory was nervous when David didn't let it go at that. "Well, I don't know what you need to think about. Delayed obedience is actually disobedience. It's impossible to grow in the Lord when you resist doing His revealed will. It'll get harder, not easier, by delaying."

"Yeah, come on, Man, let's go for it." Cade's voice. "I mean, if Jesus really <u>died</u> for **me**-then He actually isn't asking that much in return-you know?"

"Okay, then, it's settled." David clapped Cade on the back. "Let's go find Pastor Ellis. I'll introduce y'all and make sure the baptismal's ready and everything."

"Mr. Anderson?" Damon's voice was so timid David wasn't sure he had heard his name. He turned.

"Can we come too?" Heather stood diffidently behind her classmate.

"Yeah, sure! Come on!"

Mallory and Lisette watched joyfully as David led the little flock of fledgling Christians away.

"I don't deserve for Bryce to have gotten saved," Lisette confessed as she fought tears.

Mallory hugged her. "None of us deserve all the gracious, kind favors He bestows. I'm happy for you."

David reappeared, all smiles. "They're all going to be baptized at the beginning, before people get dismissed to classes and AWANA. That's good; less chance for them to get more nervous, too."

The Faulkners slid in next to them as the prelude ended and the baptismal waters stirred.

An emotional pastor announced that four new converts were obeying the Lord in baptism.

"What a miracle," Diana breathed softly. "I'm glad we didn't miss it."

Mallory nodded as Lisette snapped pictures. It was amazing, for sure; and she was really proud of David.

"Your dad would be so proud of you," she whispered.

He smiled. 'Maybe so, but more than likely, his dad would be miffed at him for not setting it up to transpire at Faith'.

⚞ ⚟

Jennifer winced at the picture of David and Mallory. "I don't want to do it, Nick. Why don't you?"

He was surprised by her response. Their financial situation was moving upward, but another portrait commissioned by *DiaMo* would be helpful.

"Well, I'm not really a bona fide artist, here. Certainly not a portraitist! And you have such a gift~"

"Come on, Nick, what's a bona fide artist? All I ever did artistically was fix make up." Her strident tone was a shock.

Wounded, he struck back! "Is this still about that Cyrus-character?"

"No, it isn't! It isn't about anything but that I don't want to be told what to paint! And when to have it ready by! I guess, although, I'm not a bona fide artist, I may have a little artistic temperament. Maybe Risa could do it."

"Maybe so, but the two portraits will have more continuity, more flow, if they're painted by the same artist. I'm not sure David and Mallory want their faces to look like some impressionistic Picasso interpretation."

His opinion of Risa's portraiture struck her funny; his intention. She laughed~and then burst into tears.

⚞ ⚟

Mallory looked gorgeous! She always did. Today, she wore an elegant, glowy, ivory raw silk suit. The ivory silk shell was tone-on-tone in a barely discernible jig saw puzzle pattern. A gold necklace gleamed at her throat~a puzzle, some of the pieces etched with various fragments that comprised a life: Family, Friends, Career, Hobbies, Organizations. The 'missing' piece, engraved with the name, *Jesus*, set with Diamonds, perched next to a void.

She greeted the employees cordially as they arrived. Everyone was actually a little early. She thought they were disappointed not to have breakfast waiting for them again.

"Okay, the first order of business for today is everyone's completing a CDA; Confidential Disclosure Agreement. All the information you become privy to is to be held in strictest confidence. It's a quite intricate document, and we're serious about it."

192

Waylon snorted derisively, and she frowned at him. David had flown our super-early for Houston to check on progress at the *Chandler* property. He had told her not to put up with any baloney from any of these kids, particularly Waylon. Like he needed to tell her!

Rhonna had inclined her head ever so slightly at her fellow classmate, rolled her eyes, and pursed her lips in her characteristic disapproval. "You gonna ruin this fer everbody."

Mallory smiled. "Well, maybe we should talk about that. I know you're referencing your experience with MHS and Mr. Haynes. He often did punish an entire class for the antics of one person. Or, one wild senior class could make it so that there were no more senior trips ever."

They nodded.

"I always thought that was unfair. When I was a kid! Rhonna, you won't get fired from *DiaMo* and *DiaMal*, based on Waylon's behavior. We like to think each person succeeds or fails, totally by his own actions. But, life isn't always fair. My cousin is an example I can think of right now. He has liked this girl for a long time, but her dad is on the war path against him, not for anything he's done. But, because the guy's oldest daughter's husband has turned into a jerk. I know," she agreed with their murmuring. "Another example is of a 'Home Security Company' that did some really bad things to try to scare people into installing their systems. Well, they're causing more regulations and government over sight that adds to the burden for an entire industry. All of that adds to costs to consumers who already have a hard time making ends meet. Now, Waylon, did you have a problem with signing this document?"

He ran his hands back and forth through his hair, leaving it standing on end, and depositing creepy stuff on the conference table. "I just can't figure out what's the big secret deal. Are we manufacturing military stuff?" He smirked around at the others.

Mallory surveyed the group thoughtfully. "You know, most Americans talk too much. I'm going to read a couple of verses that address the problem. Again, not trying to force religion down anyone's throat, but giving practical information that will contribute to your success here, and in all areas of your life, if you'll embrace it.

Proverbs 13:3 He that keepeth his mouth keepeth his life: but he that openeth wide his lips shall have destruction.

And

Proverbs 17:28 Even a fool, when he holdeth his peace, is counted wise: and he that shutteth his lips is esteemed a man of understanding.

Waylon, your questions and concerns are pretty valid, and I think the others are probably wondering the same things. You could be a little more respectful in the way you present them. We all need to be respectful and kind to one another, if we want to accomplish all we need to. No, we don't supply the military, but American business is extremely important. Waylon!" Her tone and countenance warned. "I'm not sure who has made main stream America cynical and scornful, but it's as important for American business to be strong and viable, as it is for the military. We create jobs and products, and help strengthen stability. In third world countries, where young people have no jobs and little hope, as well as nothing to occupy their time and their minds~they're given to unrest. Our products are important. Mankind has clothed and adorned himself since the Creation. We work hard to be creative and innovative, and capture a large share of our market; and what we come up with would be valuable to our competitors. You know, there are stories on the news, all the time that paint American business people as the bad guys of the whole world. I'm not saying that all of their behavior has always been stellar. Again, it's a few 'bad apples' hurting the entire barrel. But don't hang your heads about being part of something great! You'll be learning some business etiquette, also, which includes discretion in both conversation and behavior. You know, I'm a Christian, and I've read the Bible all the way through every year for more than five years. I'm not bragging; I'm saying that the Bible speaks of trade and commerce, from practically the beginning. Most of the business text books and all the self-help stuff is based on its truths. The Bible doesn't condemn accumulating goods on Earth. But, they will all pass away eventually~or we will!" She chuckled. "That's why it's important to do right and be honest; not making haste to be rich by empty schemes. Only the treasure we lay up in Heaven will last forever. And, we should make certain we're going to Heaven by accepting Jesus."

"Okay, is everyone hungry? We told you yesterday that breakfast's being provided here isn't an ever day thing. Lisette's going to give you some things and instructions about them. Make sure you pay attention and remember what all she says. Taking notes is a pretty good idea. After that, you can all go down and lunch in the café here, remembering that the *DiaMo* reputation is important to me. After lunch, the guys are going to the Ranch in Arkansas for some further training and placement. Diana, Lisette, and I will be meeting with you girls individually. I have some calls to make."

Lisette breezed in, cheery and effervescent in a bright lime lineny-look dress sparkled with Lime Quartz and pearl jewelry. Ivory high heeled sandals and clutch bag finished the look. "Okay, I have a laptop, a phone, and an expense account credit card for each of you this session, and I'll be going over all of it in detail."

Mallory took note of the awed expressions before making her way to her office. She had barely begun reading a long contract when Marge buzzed her.

"Yes, Marge?"

"It's Nick, on line one." None of them ever attempted Nick's Hawaiian last name. "He's looking for David; says it's urgent. He tried his cell."

"Okay, I'll talk to him. Thanks, Marge." She punched the button.

"Hi, Nick. This is Mallory. David went to Houston this morning. I'm not sure why you couldn't reach him on his cell. I can call *Sanders Corporation* and see if they can locate him, and have him be in touch–"

"No, no, hey, Cousin, maybe you can help better anyway. I got that picture from David, of you and him, to paint a portrait from? I thought Jennifer would be tickled. She felt like she did just an awful job on your daddy's; well, I thought it was perfect, and you and David wanting her to do another–I thought it would prove to her that her work's high quality. But she said she didn't want to do another one; I kinda tried to tease her a little, into doing it–well, she went to pieces! She threw a bunch of stuff and locked herself in the bathroom; and she's still crying."

Mallory breathed a prayer. "Okay, well, ask her if she'll talk to me."

Mallory's eyes filled with tears as she listened to muffled conversation in the background. There was no reason for Jennifer to agree to talk.

"Hello, Mallory! This is Jennifer. Nick said you want to talk to me. I doubt that, though, because he made the call! Did he not?"

"Hi, Jennifer, Yes, he did. He was hoping to talk to David, but he's in Houston. Just tell me what happened about the portrait to make you upset."

"Why do I owe you to tell you that?"

Mallory laughed. "Oh, so you don't even know! I get that! Sometimes things just set me off; and a lot of times I can't come up with any rationale for why. If you don't want to do it, we're easy. And there's certainly no 'rush order' on it. Come on; don't let it upset you. It isn't worth it. Nick's worried now. We love what you did with my Dad's, and I figure David pressured you to get it done? He was trying to keep me from being crazy about putting down *Zakkar*."

Jennifer was taken aback by the candor. "I guess you are correct. I can't give a good reason~to Nick or you."

Mallory's voice was emotional. "Well, think about it. For all those years, your life wasn't your own; your time wasn't your own! You had to do what was expected of you! All the time! And now~for the most part~you and Nick are free spirits. I guess you aren't ready to enter into any form of control and demands on you. I can see that. Yeah, your painting, everything you do right now, should be for you. You deserve that."

"Well, I should be willing to help out. I just don't know~" She was sobbing again.

"Listen, Jen, you do help out. And Nick knew when he married you that you needed to stay free. You're healing, Jen. Don't be hard on yourself."

⚔ ⚔

Waylon found himself shoveling the stable. He was dripping sweat, and huge flies tormented him. He paused to wipe sweat with his forearm. One of the camp men named Davis worked with him. Neither was given to much conversation, focused on the task at hand. A bell donged and Davis rested his shovel. "That means 'Chow'. We just have a couple of stalls left to do; we can finish them after we eat."

They joined a line of other men to 'wash up' and clean boots. Then a meal of tamales and tortillas was followed by icy watermelon.

"Jeff, we're almost done," Davis informed his supervisor.

"Good deal. Then you can have some rec time til lights out." Jeff moved along, filling his own plate.

Waylon bunked atop Luke. With fear instilled by the CDA, Waylon was afraid to start a conversation. Luke seemed as beat as he was anyway. He stretched stiffening muscles, surveying the ceiling as his thoughts wandered tiredly. Funny to be taking orders from Jeff Anderson! Jeff was his same age, would have been among this graduating class, except Jeff had opted

196

for finishing high school in Home Studies under Mr. Haynes' supervision. Now, Jeff was far along on a college degree, and he was an important right hand man for David and this operation. Waylon castigated himself. He had decided to enjoy the entire 'high school years' experience, especially playing sports. He sighed softly. Most of the seasons, he had ridden the bench, academically disqualified. In his free time, unencumbered by the mundane business of studying, he had gotten into a few brushes with the law. With his poor academics and police record, he figured he was pretty lucky to be here shoveling out horse stalls. Jeff had explained to him that he might have difficulty being 'bonded' to handle money, a tough time getting a hand gun license, and problems academically with tackling college courses when he lacked some of the fundamentals taught in high school. He thought of his options; none! That didn't take long. So, he needed to stay and try his hardest until they fired him.

⊰ ⊱

Rhonna squealed with delight when Diana displayed her first *DiaMal* business attire.

"Oh my, I never had anything that beautiful before." She was a little nervous being under the tutelage of Ms. Faulkner, rather than Mallory or Lisette, whom she knew better.

Diana smiled. She thought the clothing had turned out well. She had tried to suggest that the girl didn't have to choose black. Oh well. It was cute and youthful enough, and should transition from the hot Dallas summer into the hot Dallas autumn: a solid black, short sleeved, fitted jacket; a solid skirt, flared ever so slightly; a pleated skirt; a solid, and a capped sleeve top, creating two different styles of two piece dresses. Then, unable to resist, she had added a coordinating ensemble: Black and ivory batik print, in a linen look. Three new pair of dressy shoes: black, high heeled platform pumps, black high heeled sandals trimmed in ivory and ivory heels with a broad strip across the vamp. Three handbags coordinated with the shoes. A wide silver necklace supported carved onyx elephants, and a heavy silver ring, bangle bracelets, and preposterous hoop earrings finished her look.

"Oh, my, my! This is too pretty for me, Ma'am. Is it comin' outta my pay? I told my daddy and mama I'd try to help them out. And I don't even know what my job's gonna be, or if I can do it!"

"No, remember the first day when Mallory explained to you what the dress standard is? And that we would help everyone get started with some basics? Why don't you change into the print skirt and top, and we'll go get your hair and nails done."

～ ～

Mallory surveyed Deborah Rodriguez across her wide desk. "Okay, Deborah, one of the many things about you piquing our interest, is that you're fluent in Spanish."

The girl's face fell, and Mallory picked up on it immediately. She laughed. "Okay, let me finish, and then I'll gladly listen to you about what interests you, and what you hoped to do at our companies. We have a Spanish family in Seville, the Riveras that we work closely with for a large percentage of our leather goods. Carlos and Calista both understand and speak American English, and we can communicate with them fairly easily. The parents and aunts and uncles who help in the business are a different story. The kids are all studying English, but conversationally, they have a ways to come. As soon as we can get a passport expedited for you, we would like you to accompany the Faulkner family to Spain for a couple of weeks. We assume the Spanish language will be a little different, as well as the culture. We would like for you to finish reading three books before you depart. The two we already distributed and this one on business etiquette. It has an appendix at the end that gives some different cultural do's and don't's. And, a crash course in leathers and leather goods! Now, what were you thinking?"

"Well, I thought I might learn to make jewelry~But, your plans sound better. I'm not sure if my parents will let me~"

Mallory leaned forward. "They may have a problem with your being so young and going so far with people they don't know. Okay~so you're the baby of your family, right? Do you think your mother might be free to accompany you? We can get to work on her passport right away, too~"

"She has passport, for visiting family in Honduras. She has dreamed of seeing Spain, but such a trip. She has no money~"

"I understand that, Deborah, and I don't have any extra to burn. But remember what we said about making all of your parents our allies and satellites? I think your mother will be worth more to our company image with the Reviras than the cost of another person on the trip. We'll need to get her some clothes and spiff up her image. Will that offend her?"

"I don't know. She is mommy. She never cared for all of that! We never had money for such unnecessary~"

Mallory's brows drew together. "Well, we think those things are necessary; at least important! Get her to come back with you Monday. Explain the trip, and that we want her to accompany you. We would like to provide her with some outfits for the trip. And, you'll have a chance at the jewelry course. Let me warn you; it's a lot harder than it looks. Here are your first two outfits. Ordinarily, you can order what you prefer, but Diana already took liberty to get clothing underway for you for the Spain trip. You can trust her; I seldom choose anything for myself."

Deborah gasped in amazement! Brilliant colors sizzled in dazzling array! Mallory was a little amazed at the display, herself. Evidently Diana had stepped out of her conservative tastes to embrace colors of a Spanish Fiesta; but there wasn't a tinge of hokiness! Radiant yellow, turquoise, orange, hot pink, purple, and lime coordinated, drawn together by consistency of fabric textures, line, and proportion. It all looked fun. The accessory items were perfect, drawing the pieces into a chic whole.

Mallory laughed delightedly. "Now, time for hairstyle, cosmetics, and nails and pedicure. Lisette's taking both you and Heather. Have you ever had your hair cut?"

"No. I like it long; and so do my father and brothers."

"Well, that's up to you. If you tell them, they can leave most of your length, and just add in a little shape and style. Your hair is very beautiful. Just consult with a stylist, and if you still don't want it trimmed at all, just say so."

⊰ ⊱

Diana watched transfixed as a more polished little Rhonna emerged. She had opted for French manicure and pedicure that featured her naturally strong nails. She kept surveying them with wonder while the stylist worked on her hair.

The salon was owned by, and catered to, 'people of color', or whatever. Rhonna was thrilled. Her hair was taking a cute shape; corn rows with extensions. People coming and going to the popular establishment took notice of Diana. She didn't seem to notice, or be particularly nervous.

Rhonna didn't know the story of the Missionary's daughter who had been born and brought up in central Africa; that black people were mostly her world, with the exception of her large family.

"You look positively gorgeous," Diana complimented as a cosmetic consultant applied flawless, tasteful make up, demonstrating the techniques.

"M-m-m, what are they dollin' you all up for?" The salon owner's curiosity was aroused. "You a working girl?"

"Yes Ma'am. I got a job at this big company, and a week ago I was hopin' to get on as a carhop at a drive in. I'm not sure what I'll be doing, though."

The motherly woman grew more suspicious. "How old are you?"

Rhonna straightened up importantly. "Almost eighteen"!

"They trafficking drugs? They make you look all high class so you don't have people getting' suspicious? You know, you need to be careful. Where's your mama?"

Rhonna's smile lit her face. "Yes, Ma'am, I been knowin' David and Mallory since we were all school kids together in Arkansas. They train us for the jobs we'll be working at; and we're taking college courses, too. The Andersons are real upstandin' Christian people. David's dad's the pastor of a church in our town. I'm going up to Tulsa tomorrow with Mr. and Mrs. Faulkner, to do a singin' tryout."

"Well, do you have to leave with her? We can help you if-"

"Thank you for bein' so nice. I really like my hair and makeup. They're not makin' me do noth-anything bad."

The girl was terrified when she heard the bottom line for all the beauty processes.

"Put it on your corporate credit card," Diana instructed. "Remember Lisette's going over all of your allowable expenses earlier? It's money well-spent! You were adorable anyway! But you're positively stunning!" She turned her attention to the owner. "Thank you for your expertise. It's all perfect."

The business woman glowered! Until-Diana explained to the girl about tipping and figuring the proper amounts for everyone.

"Thank you. And I hope your tryout works out okay."

※ ※

Dinky met Mallory enthusiastically. She missed David, gazing at her phone to make sure she hadn't missed a call from him. Nothing! She wasn't sure if she should call him or not. She was still trying to transition from 'Girls don't call boys' to being married and needing to hear his voice. It was a little odd that she hadn't heard from him, and then his not answering his cell for Nick. She stretched out on the chaise lounge to review the <u>One Minute Millionaire</u>. Lisette had actually made her aware of the book, and now it was a book she recommended and referred to often. She didn't realize she had fallen asleep until her phone made her jerk to reality.

"Hey, how was your day?" she answered.

"Actually, great! Things are going smooth and progressing right along. Roger's really pleased. He was impressed to no end with our employee training sessions."

"He was? I thought it was the roughest and worst we've ever done. Well, Daniel and Diana were so not themselves."

"Yeah, well, neither were you, with your anxiety about *Zakkar*. Sometimes when we feel we've done our worst, God can use it the most. How was your day? I heard Waylon ran his mouth again."

"Is that why he's been shoveling out the stable?"

His deep baritone laugh! "Well, partly, and the fact that it needed it. I figure it might make him not complain when he has to start learning textiles terminology, and next season's color forecast."

She laughed in turn. "To answer your question, my day was busy but good. I fell asleep when I got home. We got a lot done. Rhonna's going to audition for someone Daniel knows in the Tulsa musical scheme. That's tomorrow. Diana got her all spiffed up and sent me a picture. Lisette was taking Heather and Deborah for beauty treatments, also. She went over all the details with them about their phones, laptops, and expense accounts. I'm trying not to miss you too much."

"M-m-m, I just miss you. No use pretending otherwise. Have you eaten today?"

"Uh~"

"Mallory! Come on. I have a flight out in a couple of hours, but that'll make it late by the time I get home. At least eat a can of soup and some crackers. Promise! Right now"!

"Okay, I'm going; I'm going. Like I said, I was busy all day, and I fell asleep almost the minute I got home."

⚜ ⚜

Roger walked through the Chandler facility, taking note of improvements to the property. It already looked two whole worlds better as he approached. David was in favor of replacing the asphalt parking lot with concrete, eventually. For the time being though, it had been filled in, rolled smooth, and resurfaced with fresh blacktop. It was freshly painted with parking spaces, handicap designations, fire lanes, and arrows indicating traffic flow. Nice iron fencing enclosed everything, and security cameras (real and dummy) loomed at intervals. Sod, hedges, and flowers perked it up amazingly.

Every time David requested draws to pay for materials or pay a subcontractor, he acted apologetic. Roger was convinced that he was getting a 'lot of BANG for his bucks'.

He rang the young man's cell phone. "Hey, I guess I just missed you," he began when David answered. "I can't begin to tell you how serendipitous I feel that you were in the right place at the right time to really give this place a thorough facelift. I know I've already mentioned this, a couple of times, but I'm really pumped, and so are all my people, since we joined your training. Some of it, I didn't know! And seriously, I've kind of felt like I knew it all."

"Well, there's no questioning your expertise in business," David responded. "Mallory thinks it's good to sharpen the axe heads often."

⚜ ⚜

Mallory tried to concentrate on the matters at hand. The trainees needed help and direction. Lisette was capable, but Mallory wanted them to be loyal and connected to her, so she was trying to really invest herself into each one. At the back of her mind nagged *Zakkar*. Friday, and she figured David probably planned to get them off early to head toward the Ranch. It always required his oversight, and she loved it-but! It just seemed a little quick to pull in past the stable, knowing there was an empty stall- Her heart felt raw.

⚜ ⚜

Waylon felt comfortable paired with Davis. They had mowed and finished some weed-eating, and it was lunchtime.

He accepted a bologna sandwich, stack of chips, and tall glass of milk eagerly, following his partner to a long table. Davis glowered. "I don't reckon we need to buddy up no more. You're a fair worker, but take off!"

Waylon disregarded his words, crawling across the long bench, to face the other man. "What's your problem, Davis? How did you come to be here?"

"Like you care! Why don't you go 'lunch' with them other white, management boys?"

Waylon laughed. "Uh, because I don't think I'm a white 'management' boy. If I ever had a chance, I think I blew it by running my dumb mouth. You from around here"?

"Nah, Man, I'm from Detroit!" He rose and made a point of moving to a solitary corner.

Waylon bit his sandwich hungrily, finishing it before he attacked the chips, polishing the milk off last. The way he had always eaten; one thing at a time. He still felt hungry, but he saw others returning to their places dejectedly. Must not be any seconds. He was surprised. These men all worked hard! Mostly for board and room! He rose, leaving his tray on the table, and approached Mardy.

"These guys work this hard, physically, and just get one sandwich? Is that David and Mallory's orders?"

Fear crossed her coarse features. "Please, don't say nothin' to no one! This is the first week I've been left to do the grocery orderin', and I bunged it all up! I was supposed ta keep track of what we run out of, and order all that. I didn't think nothin' about what we was nearly out of. I never been real smart."

He smiled suddenly. "Me neither. Trust me, I feel your pain. My name's Waylon; what's yours?"

She stared at his outstretched hand. "I'm Mardy Thomas. Uh-pleased ta meet ya. I'm real sorry I can't make no more sandwiches." She grasped his hand and forgot to stop shaking it.

Waylon tried not to recoil at her name. He was just shocked. Her son, Martin, had always been a huge bully at MHS.

He recovered and whispered conspiratorially. "I think I'm about to have to go back to work helping Davis. Last night, we earned some recreation time. If I earn more free time tonight, maybe I can do something to help you out. I'm not sure what. My dad and mom live fairly close, maybe I can get them to sneak in some groceries."

"What are ya'll whispering about, Mayer?" Jeff's voice made him jump. "Mardy, what's up with the short rations? These guys all work hard, and they're hungry!"

Waylon jumped in. "That's what we were talking about. This week was her first time ordering groceries. She knew what she was out of, but didn't think about other stuff that was running low. Next time, she will. I told her I'd help her with it, if I earn rec time again tonight."

Jeff's gaze studied them both. "Okay, help her with it now! Davis can work alone if that's how he wants it. Help her make the list, then let me know when it's ready. I'll go with you to town; you need to sign a couple of forms at the bank, and we can pick up what we need to get us through until the truck delivers next Tuesday. It's more expensive to pay retail, and we have the headache of loading and unloading it all ourselves. It's okay, Mardy. You're doing okay. I forgot a lot of things when I did it, as you well know. From now on, you complete the order, and then Mr. Mayer will look everything over before we place the order. Two heads are better than one." He strode away.

"Thank you for your help, Mr. Mayer, Sir." the woman's face was a study in relief.

Waylon shrugged, "Yeah, sure; no problem. I didn't do anything."

Her tired gaze met his. "Yes, Sir, you did! Would you like some cake? I done ordered too much of that!"

He laughed. "Get it cut into servings, then. Is there plenty of milk? Maybe cake and milk will-"

"Hey, y'all don't leave yet!" His voice halted the disgruntled exodus from the hall. "There's no more chips and sandwiches, but everyone gets two pieces of cake, and another milk!"

Cheers erupted! He wasn't sure what Jeff would say, but Jeff wasn't around.

Chapter 16: *ADULTHOOD*

Mallory was excited as the jet lifted smoothly from the tarmac at DFW and banked westward, en route to L.A. Rather than facing a weekend at the Ranch without *Zakkar*, David had arranged a week-end in Los Angeles, to watch the Red Sox play the Angels. Now, she slept against him as the engines droned soothingly in the back ground. He began to relax, too. Hopefully, they should be safe without a security detail. Luxury hotel with its own security; then the game with more security everywhere! Church Sunday morning, before flying back to Dallas Sunday afternoon. Not sleepy for some strange reason, he attempted to corral his thoughts away from the tragedy of the Arabian mare. 'Corral' his thoughts! What a figure of speech to pop into his consciousness now! He sighed, and pulled the tickets from his pocket. Not the best seats in the stadium! But good enough; straight out from center field. Maybe in range to catch a 'Home Run'! One of her cherished dreams! He smiled; as soon as he divulged the plan, she had started wheedling to go to a sporting goods store to look for a glove. He kissed her head.

-⧼ ⧽-

Daniel and Diana pulled into the garage of their new cabin and unloaded into the country chic space.

"Can we go ride our bikes?" the three eldest questioned eagerly in unison.

"May we go ride our bikes?" Diana corrected.

"Yeah, sure," Jeremiah teased. "You're the parents! You don't have to ask us for permission."

Daniel shook his head. "Yeah, but come back when the dinner bell rings. We can all eat in the chow hall. It doesn't look like David and Mallory are here yet. Be careful of your clothes. Don't get all dirty, in case they want to go out." He gazed at Diana. "I'll watch Zave and Nod ride their trikes, if you want to relax a little. Or you and Ry can come out with us." He took note of every nuance of her response. Sometimes, she nearly thawed out; and then other times, he found himself back to square one.

"That sounds nice. I'm going to brew a cup of coffee. You want one?"

Shade, a misting device, and a fan helped dispel heavy afternoon heat, as Diana filled him in with some of the details of the newest employees. She paused. "You haven't said much about Rhonna and how her audition went."

He rushed to grab Xavier to prevent his tumbling off the edge of the blacktop before responding. "Well, it wasn't really an audition. All my contacts are for instrumentalists, and not vocalists. Steve is always the same way; we can't really talk if we're not members of the musicians' union. The same way with Rhonda! He didn't care if she could sing a note; he wanted those dues paid in full!"

"Her name's Rhonna; she's named after her dad, Ronald Abbott. You know, maybe we should all join the union, if not being members is holding us back!" She said it fearfully, because it was something he strongly opposed. He was staunchly non-union about everything. And he had a real problem with the musicians' union in particular.

His gaze met hers. Just when their relationship seemed on the verge of 'normalizing', he didn't want to start an argument. "Okay, Rhonna. Her voice sounds pretty, but as you said yourself, she doesn't know the first thing about music. She doesn't know the basics of bass and treble clefs. But all she has to do is plunk down so much money, and she's got a card stating she's a musician?"

She nodded, a smile tugging at the corners of her mouth. Her husband tended to be a little snobbish about his ability. She could see his point about it; she had heard the same argument from him throughout their married life.

"Well, you always thought Cassandra was a gifted 'musician' because she could play the violin; but she didn't know 'music' per se, either. I mean, Rhonna's gorgeous, melodic voice can charm music lovers if she never learns theory. She's a musician; just not in your purist sense of the word."

206

He moved to slow Nadia's reckless speed before grinning sheepishly. "I guess I should enroll all of us?"

"Maybe; it doesn't cost that much; does it?"

"Well, no; it's just been the principle of the thing."

She laughed. "Yeah, I get that!"

⚔ ⚔

Deborah bubbled with enthusiasm as she tried to fill her parents in about her first week on the job in Dallas. They were having a tough time comprehending. They couldn't figure out why the company wanted Deborah to travel to Spain, much less have her mother accompany her.

She slowed down, trying to explain everything fully as she understood it. 'The Rivera family, in Spain, owned a leather company. Señor and Señora Rivera both spoke good English, but some of the relatives spoke only Spanish. Part of Deborah's job would be working with this valuable family and their fine line of products. Mallory wanted her to travel to meet the family and establish a relationship. The Rivera's were so old-school and conservative, that they would be impressed by a young American accompanied by her mother.'

Mrs. Rodriguez was dazed, trying to curb excitement about the sudden adventure opening before her. Deborah's dad didn't know. What if neither of them ever made it back? He said he would worry. True, but he seemed to feel a little left out.

"Mama, you must come to Dallas with me for Monday. They want to have dresses and things fixed up for you before the trip. Your passport is still good? I told Mallory it is. I mean, Mrs. Anderson. Look. See their designs they have fixed for me?"

"Yes, they made you get your hair cut?" Her dad expressed what he had been studying since her return.

"No! Papa! They very specifically told me it was my decision. Mrs. Anderson told me my hair is very beautiful. She said maybe they could give it a little more shape and style! See! It comes to the middle of my back, still."

⚔ ⚔

207

Mallory was all smiles as she tried on every mitt in the sporting goods store. She was pretty much settled on one she liked, except for the price tag.

"Okay, let's get that one so we don't miss the game." David's voice was teasing, but he didn't know how much time to allow for the L.A. freeway traffic. She sparkled and her enthusiasm was genuine. A middle aged guy rang up the sale. "Have fun. I hope you catch your homer."

"Me, too!" she bubbled. She held up crossed fingers, taking David back to childhood memories.

"This is so much fun!" Her eyes danced as they walked toward the stadium hand in hand. "Look, there it is," she squealed. "It looks just like it does on TV! I can't believe I'm really here. We're in time for batting practice, too. She prattled on about the starting line up and that of the Angels. "It should be a real pitchers' duel."

※ ※

Dinner in the chow hall consisted of pizza, followed by ice cream. Diana watched her kids attack it ravenously. They had all been playing hard. Surprised, she found it tasted quite good.

"Jeff's pretty sure David and Mallory aren't coming this weekend," Jeremiah offered. "He thought David had worked out some other kind of surprise to take her mind off of *Zakkar*. He doesn't know what, though. Can we still stay? It's so much fun here."

"It is fun; isn't it?" Daniel still cringed at every mention of Mallory's horse. He felt responsible for the injury resulting in euthanasia for the beautiful, expensive animal. "Yes, we'll probably stay until Sunday afternoon." He tackled a large slice of pizza, his mind moving to the mystery of where the couple might have gone. He made a call.

"Hey, Darrell; where are y'all?" He forced his tone to sound normal.

"Well, I'm in Dallas. It's my week end off, but I just heard that David and Mallory snuck off someplace, and Collins didn't accompany them either. You think they're in trouble?"

Faulkner groaned inwardly, a sense of alarm filling him. "I hope not. Did Collins have any idea-"

"No, she assumed they planned to go to Arkansas for the weekend, and maybe they did-"

"No, they aren't here. Jeff thinks David was doing some kind of surprise. Do you have any idea what it might be?"

"I don't know; maybe shopping for a new horse?"

Daniel sighed. "Yeah, maybe; I'll call Hanson, but if he hasn't heard from them, I'm going to give Erik a heads-up. This isn't your fault, Hopkins; I just feel uneasy about them."

"Well, David's a big guy, and he knows how to handle himself."

"Yeah, but I'm gonna do some detective work. Have a good weekend. I hope!"

⫞ ⫟

"Are you going to try to eat any ballpark cuisine?" David questioned good-naturedly. "Maybe we can get something later."

"I'm definitely planning on a hot dog! And a diet drink! Let's get it now, so we don't miss anything. We need to hurry up, though. Batting practice"!

Laden with hot dogs, an order of nachos, large sodas, and the new glove, they made their way to their seats. Early, few spectators had arrived.

"What a gorgeous day for a game," she bubbled. "Boston's been blistering. Which, don't misunderstand, I would love to see Grandmother and Shay. But I've been to Fenway! A huge treat! And now Anaheim Stadium! Who would have ever guessed?"

He blessed the food, and they enjoyed the breeze, the atmosphere, and one another.

⫞ ⫟

Steb Hanson encouraged his cavalry (friends and neighbors of the close-knit community) to partake of more fajitas, *refritos,* and rice. Then, after finishing off platters of *sopapillas* with honey, they adjourned to the spacious great room for the meeting. He usually began with:

> *II Kings 7:3 And there were four leprous men at the entering of the gate: and they said one to another, Why sit we here until we die?*

And the meeting on this hot Arizona Saturday was no exception. His challenge was always to get the older people who comprised his group, to leave their comfort zones and make a difference.

"Okay, we're actually accomplishing a lot, both for the Kingdom of God, and for the United States. Let's don't get all distracted and off-course because of in-fighting. Everybody's important; from those of you that answer phones an hour or so a week, to the ones protecting Jennifer at the gallery, to the ones undercover in the yachting scene. The Lord just rewards faithfulness to the responsibilities He's given us. If you feel like no one appreciates what you do; look up! We can't forget Who it is we're working for. Now, this is kind of a downer to me, personally, but it looks like Oberson has weaseled out of serving a jail sentence. At least, he's ruined politically; let's hope and pray. We're not giving up; keeping tabs on these characters." He paused to hand out photocopies. "These are the hands that Jennifer painted of the criminals. The ones in circles are the ones who have yet to be identified. We keep watching for them to pass through Bisbee in the constant stream that seem intent on harassing Jennifer. Now, we have a new Op. The U.N General assembly! The Secret Service oversees the safety of all the entourages. The dignitaries all stay at the Waldorf. We doubt any heads of state are involved, or are careless enough to leave a trail to themselves. And maybe it's no one on their staffs." He chuckled. "Who figures a bunch of old people to have an agenda, right?"

He filled in the adrenaline-pumping-details to a crowd whose eyes sparkled with mischief and delight! 'Yeah! Don't count us down and out yet!'

෴ ෴

The stadium seats began to fill up as batting practice ended and excitement mounted. "I hope they were saving their good swings for the game," Mallory commented anxiously.

She scrunched her knees in toward David to allow a group of women to squeeze past to their seats. Juggling popcorn and plastic cups of beer, they made a point of flirting with David. Mallory tried to ignore it, but they were pretty brazen. They weren't wearing much either.

෴ ෴

Erik had been alarmed at Daniel's call, too. Of course, the FBI's resources weren't at his fingertips, but he knew quite a bit about sleuthing. He called Shay, Shannon, Sanders, his pastor, everyone he thought might have a clue. Pretty much to no avail. As a last resort, he made his way to one of the greenhouses. Suzanne was busy snipping and yanking weeds.

"Do you have any idea where David and Mallory might have gone? Jeff thought David was planning a surprise to take Mallory's mind~"

Suzannes' blue eyes blazed. "I am her mother; don't forget! And I've known David longer than practically anyone."

He smiled. "Okay, Babe, point taken. I should have asked you first and not last. You're actually a great crime-solving partner. Well, this isn't a crime, I hope. But it has me mystified."

She had rocked back on her heels. "I'm sure they're fine. They're newly-weds, and I think sometimes they~"

"Yeah, yeah, but if you have any idea~"

"A Red Sox game"!

"Well, Shay said he and Delia have barely talked to her since she got married~" Erik grappled with his wife's revelation.

Suzanne returned to her knees, attacking an errant clump of grass with vigor. "Okay, then, so they're on the road. Find out where. And you've got Mallory in your sites! I've been a little amazed by her restraint. When she first came into Patrick's money, I figured she'd use it to be a Sox junkie!"

⊰ ⊱

Steb Hanson walked slowly out to one of the stables. Usually, he was swift and purposeful. He hadn't been any help to Bransom about where David and Mallory might be, but the agent's call, and mention of the couple, had shaken him. It hadn't been his intention to cheat them; he had seriously thought the 'Gray' was fully recovered! That she would have no further difficulties. Now, he was uncertain what to do. He sincerely cared about his reputation as a businessman. If he offered to share the financial loss with the kids, it might just make him look worse. And, he had already overstepped himself arguing with Mallory about pushing his Foundation on her business web sites.

"I don't know what to do, Lord. I've kind of invested heavily in the Foundation. I don't want to cast doubts on my character, but if that agent's looking into us. Maybe I should meet with them privately and just come clean~"

⇥ ⇤

Daniel and Diana's flight touched down, and he phoned Alexandra. "Is everything still going okay with the kids?"

"Yes, Sir, we're all fine. Mardy has French toast fixed for breakfast, and they're all really putting it away. I can do this. But, if it's any comfort to you, Grandma and Grandpa just got here. Grandpa's taking Jeremiah and Xavier fishing and they're all excited. Have you found Mallory yet?"

"No, we just landed. We're on the way to the game as soon as we get our rent car. Call if you need anything. Don't let yourself get sidetracked."

⇥ ⇤

Mallory watched everything avidly. "Wow, it's hard to keep up," she murmured.

"Yeah, you can actually see and follow the action better on TV. But this is fun!"

She nodded agreement as she scrunched up to let the four women out past her. They were doing quite a bit of running around and showing off. To her chagrin, the Angels scored a run in the first inning. Boston up to bat, found the lead-off batter and the lineup not meeting with her approval. "Look at him," she moaned. "His stance is all out of kilter. Why doesn't the batting coach tell him to straighten up and look alive? This is going to be a strike! Oh no! Caught him looking! Strike One!" Her call was ahead of the Ump's.

He liked baseball okay; football was his preference. The fun of this was watching her. She was lit up. She wasn't being loud per se, but definitely vocal. And, she wasn't showing off, like he thought a lot of fans tried to do. She was just passionate! She reminded him of her dad, sitting in front of their tiny TV in the little house in Murfreesboro.

He rose and moved into the aisle to allow the women to pass again. They were pretty annoying, seemingly not aware of where the field even was. The last one in slopped beer on Mallory; then apologized sweetly. "Oh! I'm sorry! I didn't even see you there!"

212

Mallory forced a smile. "Oh, that's okay. No problem." She returned her attention to the game. "Okay, he's usually pretty good." She quoted his stats. "He does better against right—handed pitchers." She groaned when he was forced to jump to avoid being hit by the pitch. But with one out, he managed to hit a single. The next batter struck out despite her tutoring from the stands.

David was growing aware of the reactions of fans surrounding them. Well, they were pretty much surrounded by Angels' fans, for one thing. Still, he didn't say anything to her. They were at a ballgame where rooting for your team was the thing to do. Although, it seemed like a circus, with few people paying much heed to the action on the field.

"Okay, two out! Come on! You can do it! Bring him home. Get ready! Here comes a fair ball!"

The bat connected, making two men on base with two outs. She groaned with disappointment when the next batter in the line-up struck out, ending the inning with two men on base.

Animated, she complained to David that some of the hitters still needed improvement with their batting stances. "I mean, I know the batting coach has lots to focus on, but why isn't he seeing that?" Her anguished voice carried.

A spectator in front of them whirled around. "I don't know! Why don't you go down and tell him? You seem to have passed 'Coaching 101'!"

Her eyes widened in surprise. She started to make a retort; then thought better of it. The girls crowded back past them. Suddenly the nausea was overwhelming her again; the hot dog trying to fight its way back up. David noted her stricken expression. He made a grab for a discarded popcorn bucket, and thrust it into her hands.

Someone notified security, and she spent the next three innings in the infirmary, trying to convince the first-aid personnel she was fine.

"Okay, let's just leave," David suggested when they released her.

"What? No! We paid good money for those tickets. I want to see the game. I'd still like to catch a homer! If someone would be so kind as to hit one! Besides, I left my new glove up there."

Reluctantly, he followed her. "Hey, I'm sorry," she apologized. "I promise to keep my mouth shut!"

"Well, you shouldn't have to. It's a game. People cheer for their teams at games! That is, if they care. It makes you wonder why people buy tickets and fight the traffic to get here. It's like they're mostly into partying and drinking. Although, why they decided you shouldn't have fun, I can' figure out. I would have said something to that guy, but I didn't want to start a fight. You might have gotten hurt. Maybe we should forget about the glove. The odds of your catching~"

Her expression set resolutely.

Once more in the stands, she looked around for the mitt. "What happened to my glove? I left it right here."

A guy across the aisle thrust it at her grudgingly.

They sank into their seats, trying to salvage the afternoon. The Angels scored another run, but Mallory bit her tongue. 'Okay, 2-zip' Still a lot of innings left.

David sat silently next to his much-subdued bride. She hadn't bounced back, either from the reprimand or from the bout of vomiting. The Red Sox managed to load the bases, and they were warming up a relief pitcher that she really liked. The batter struck out. One out! She sat dismally; then straightened suddenly. "This is it!" she whispered. She clasped her glove, watching the pitcher and batter eye one another. Right over the plate! Then, a resounding Crack!

Somehow, she was on one toe on the stadium seat, stretching~ And~she snagged the ball jubilantly, somehow maintaining, or regaining her balance. "Whoa, that stung!" She had handed her trophy to David so she could remove the mitt and rub her fingers. "Can you believe that?"

He shook his head. "Not really. I thought you were about to kill yourself, there." Then he laughed. "That was some kind of catch!"

Then some ogre was standing next to him. "That ball's mine! It was coming right straight at me!" He plucked it from a startled David's grasp.

~⚜ ⚜~

Daniel scanned faces in the crowd from the comfort of a box. Some country club crony of his dad's had access. He lowered the glasses. "Maybe they're not here."

"Well, Lisette found a copy of the itinerary. Airline, rent car, hotel reservation, game tickets. Unless they left that to throw us off," Diana responded.

Daniel jumped to his feet. "Watch out! Home run! Grand Slam! That should make her happy if she's here."

Look, look!" Diana joined the excitement, pointing to the monitor that followed the ball into the stands.

Daniel met her gaze, amazed. "It went right to her! She caught it! Well, now we know where they are."

Right to her? It was ten feet over her head! I don't know how she kept from killing herself," Diana responded dazedly.

⊰ ⊱

Mallory's jubilation died. "Let him have it," she whispered as she fought tears. The fiasco over the home run ball was compounded by the same four women crowding her again to try to get on camera. "I'm ready to go now." She escaped the crazy women and pushed past David, charging up the steps toward an exit. "Here, you can have my glove, too." She jammed it at the guy who was showing the ball off as if he had a right to it.

She dashed toward a ladies' room, but David caught her. "No, not without Collins here, to check it out first!"

She was bent over a garbage can dry-heaving when Daniel and Diana reached them.

⊰ ⊱

Rhonna scrubbed the house from stem to stern, wearing gloves to protect her beautiful fingernails. Deborah, Anna, and Heather had all gone home to Arkansas, but she wanted to settle in here. She arranged and rearranged her possessions, stopping to finger the new items lovingly. She was a little hungry, and that made her wonder if and when she would get paid, and how much. She popped her last pack of popcorn and settled down to watch some TV. She didn't usually watch baseball games, but she was suddenly aware that this was the game David and Mallory had flown out to California for. Smiling, she found her assignment sheet where she continued to write down 'Dreams'. Her first entry had come after Mallory's trick about the steak. That was her first bite of prime beef, ever, so her first item was:' To eat steak sometimes'. Her mind had continued to expand exponentially, and where she had been blank, now new ideas and dreams tripped over themselves to surface in her conscious mind. She printed neatly: 'To be able to go to the big baseball games! And to be able to fly to California'!

215

It was hot so she opened the front door, although, it was even hotter outside. She knew she could use the air conditioner, but she hated to run up the bill when she was the only one there. Her family hadn't used air conditioning much in Arkansas, but they at least had some big ole shade trees to sit out under. She couldn't find much to watch on TV so she opened the <u>See</u> <u>You</u> <u>at</u> <u>the</u> <u>Top</u> book and began to read it slowly. Someone at the front door made her jump.

"Oh Hello, Ms. Billingsley! Am I late for something? Did I forget to do something?"

Lisette gazed around the scrubbed and polished space that reeked of bleach, and made her way to the thermostat. "This is turned clear off. I thought maybe the unit was broken. How come you're sitting here roasting, and with the door standing wide open? You should leave it closed and locked, whether you're home, or not."

She smiled at the girl's stricken expression. "I know! It was a big shock to me when I moved here from the country. I was driving by just to check on everything and saw the door open. Are the others nice to you?"

"Yes'm. Nice enough. They's never been over friendly. It got me a room of my own. Debbie has her own, and Anna and Heather are sharing."

Lisette sighed. "Okay. Look, have you been eating okay?"

"Yes'm. I just finished a whole big bag of popcorn!"

"Okay, well, my husband and Cade were going to go play racquet ball and then go running. That leaves me shifting for myself, so I wondered if you'd like to join me for dinner. You should get out while the house cools back down so you don't die from the heat. Get showered and made up; I'll be back. Remember, we're supposed to expose the merchandise to people. She found a fan. "Aim this directly at you while you get ready."

⁂

Mallory wasn't sure why she felt such relief to see the Faulkners. David was always glad for Diana's expert medical opinions, but he figured Daniel was mad at his attempts to do this solo. Diana insisted on another visit to the infirmary.

The charge nurse looked up sharply. "I didn't think you were ready to leave, earlier. Now that you've caught the ball you came for, maybe you'll let us get some fluids into you?" His expression was determined.

"Yes, Sir," she acquiesced. "How did you know I caught a ball?"

He laughed. "Well, when I'm not fighting with stubborn patients, I get a chance to watch the game. That was quite a catch, young lady! You want to see it?" He was already running footage backwards. She winced as he worked at starting the line. With it started, he pressed play, and the excitement of the home run burst onto the screen. "They're still in the lead; right?" she questioned.

He sighed. "Of course, I'm an Anaheim fan, so I'm not as delighted with the outcome as you are. But the game's over, and your team won. There's always tomorrow, though, right? You all staying for the whole series?"

No, we're going to church in the morning, and then flying back to Dallas so we can be at work Monday," David answered for her.

Then, Diana felt the need to inform the other medical specialist about the baby on the way. After scooting his stethoscope around for a while, he met Diana's anxious gaze. "I'm not hearing it. I'm having her transported where the equipment for this sort of thing is better."

Mallory was grappling with that when the General Manager for the Red Sox entered the space. "Security recovered your ball, and your mitt, uh-Miss O'Shaughnessy? Home run ball's autographed, along with the game roster autographed by all of us here with the Red Sox Franchise."

Wow, thank you." She was pretty awed. "It's Mallory Anderson; my husband David," she introduced. This was her first realization that she had labeled the new glove the way she always had, out of habit: Mallory O'Shaughnessy. "I'm sorry, David," she apologized guiltily.

"That's okay. The ambulance is here. I'm riding with you." He turned to the team manager. "Thank you very much. It means a lot."

⊰ ⊱

Rhonna was nervous! She was totally unaccustomed to Dallas traffic. Also, she wasn't sure it was okay for Lisette to socialize with her. Lastly, Lisette had parked in front of a steak house that looked expensive.

"Does this look okay? Would you rather do seafood or Mexican?" Lisette seemed open and friendly. "Try not to act so scared," she laughed.

"Well, I'm not actin', Ms. Billingsley."

Lisette laughed. "No kidding. Lighten up. You know you're really worthwhile, don't you? You're worth running air conditioning for, whether anyone else is home, or not. I wish you'd call me Lisette. If there's ever

217

any reason for you to act more formally, I'll let you know. Then, it's Mrs. We only use Ms when we're uncertain of a woman's marital status. I was planning to treat you, but since we're going to talk shop, I decided to expense this one. Order whatever you like."

"Yes'm."

"Okay, stop with the yes'm. Being respectful is great, but don't overdo it. Do you know what to order? I can order for you."

Rhonna took a deep breath and looked Lisette squarely in the eye for the first time. "Sure Lisette! That would be great."

⚞ ⚟

Mallory fell apart emotionally once loaded into the emergency vehicle. David tried to cheer her up with the autographed home run ball, and her getting to meet one of her sports heroes.

"It was just disappointing to me. All my life, I wanted to go to big league games. It looked like so much fun, and I felt like I was really missing out! And I wanted to be a grown-up! But it's so disillusioning to keep finding out that nothing is what it seemed like it would be! Why was Diana whispering? What does she think's wrong, why I have to go to the hospital?"

"It's just a precaution to make sure everything's okay."

Her gaze locked with his. "It's something about the baby; isn't it? The doctor just said everything was okay a few days ago."

He nodded. "Yeah, and it probably still is."

The Faulkners met them at the ER entrance. David presented insurance information and bolted down a corridor with an arrow pointing toward the chapel. He sank onto a front pew in the small stained-glass enclosure and tried to pray. He felt so helpless and like such a failure. Despite their efforts to ignore it, a bunch of rowdy drunks had spoiled their day. His phone rang. His dad! He dreaded responding, wondering if Faulkner had already yelled about him to his dad, and now his dad would ream him out. Trying to sound chipper, he answered.

"Hello, Son, what's going on? I was watching the Sox game and saw Mallie catch a home run and a guy grab it from you. Is she okay?"

"I hope so. Between the pregnancy and the tension of the day, she's been pretty sick, and she got dehydrated again. The first aide station at the stadium sent her here in an ambulance. They weren't sure that the-baby-"

"What? She's in the hospital? Let me talk to her."

"Well, they're doing all the checking in business. I came down to the chapel-"

"Okay, David, listen to me." John Anderson's voice cut in interrupting his distracted son. "You need to go back and stay with her. Listen, I know you don't want to hear the news if it's bad. But you sure don't want her to hear-by herself!

"Well, Diana's-"

"David! She needs you. It's good the Faulkners are there, but they can't take your place. Go now! Be by her side! I don't care how tough it is on you. You can pray from anywhere! There's nothing magic about a 'chapel'."

He knew his dad was right, but it was hard to watch her when she was so sad. Especially since everything was his fault. "Okay, Lord, like she was saying; this being a grown-up gets tough."

Chapter 17: ARTISTS

Sonia Morrison gazed at a new email anxiously. This couldn't be good. She read it through again, trying to be calm. She should probably show it to Trent. Instead, she pressed the delete button. If David and Mallory were both coming, it must be to explain that she wasn't working out, and they were cutting their losses. "It's okay, Lord, right? The last I read my Bible, Your hand isn't waxed short without Diana, and David and Mallory?"

Still, it was hard for her to imagine how they could stay in this dream of a house with the beautiful products she represented for the corporation. 'She should have worked harder at it', she castigated herself. Even now, she studied her finger and toenails, her hair with the highlights needing freshening. Maybe she could at least get to the nail salon on Monday before they arrived. Then, a bright thought: the salon was open on Sunday afternoon. Trent could oversee the kids while she treated herself.

꣠ ꣰

"There you are!" Mallory's eyes still swam with tears as David entered the cubicle. "I was waiting for you before we get this moment of truth."

He took her hand. "My dad called. They're praying for us." He looked toward Daniel. "Would you pray, too?"

"Sure." His voice wouldn't come, so they basically all bowed their heads, praying silently in agreement.

"Okay, are you ready?" The nurse seemed aggravated by the delay.

Mallory's hand squeezed David's. "Yes Ma'am!"

David stifled a sob as the soft, squishy, thumping sound reached his ears, and Mallory breathed out a soft sigh of relief. "Everything's okay," she questioned?

Diana studied the small image, turning the monitor toward the young couple. "He seems quite small; I know I keep repeating myself, but he needs nutrients."

"He's a boy?" Mallory picked up on the masculine pronoun.

"It's still too early to tell that. Did you hear me?"

Mallory laughed with relief. "I did. I promise to do better. I know I keep repeating myself, too, about eating. But, this scared me."

⇥ ⇤

"I'm going to my parents' for dinner." Jeff's tone was matter of fact. "Look after things while I'm gone."

Waylon figured his panic must have shown all over his face.

"You know the drill! Announce a thirty minute warning before lights out, and then turn them out on time. This group doesn't fight too bad. But if they do, break it up. Any questions, call David!"

⇥ ⇤

Rhonna relaxed enough to enjoy the steak, trying to absorb some truths that were mind-boggling. Lisette, true to her words, was going over a lot of business stuff, until the new girl felt like her head was spinning. Finally, she lifted a manicured hand defensively. "Okay! Whoa! Whoa! You talk fast! I hope I can get smart enough to do all you're talkin' 'bout. Cause I'm likin' these fancy clothes and nice restaurants. I wanna be successful. Really, really, bad."

Lisette laughed. "Well, that's an important element! Wanting it! And being willing to work and learn to achieve it, are even more crucial. You're smart enough. You're doing great. Okay, I need to send an email. You know how to email from your smart phone, don't you?"

"No Ma-. I guess I don't."

Lisette laughed. "It's nice manners to say Ma'am and Sir. Just don't be too-I don't know how to express it exactly."

Rhonna's eyes sparkled and she laughed, actually relaxing. "Don't act like slave and master?"

Lisette nodded. "Yeah! Look, you're bright and sharp and talented. You have lots to offer. I mean, I'm going to be your direct supervisor, so I'm your boss. But I like to think we'll be working together." She glanced at a darling watch. "Okay, I'm going to have you do this email so you know how. Then, I'm taking you back to your place, and I want you to book a flight for David and Mallory to arrive in D.C early afternoon Monday."

Rhonna looked terrified. "You want me to jump over the moon, too?"

Lisette shrugged. "That's strictly up to you." She tutored the steps for the other woman to send the email to Sonia Morrison.

"Okay, Rhonna, about tomorrow. Of course, we can't make church attendance mandatory. But, we do like everyone to get out wearing the cute clothing, accessories, and jewelry, as much as possible. Will you come to church with us, if I come pick you up? Will the other girls be back tomorrow afternoon sometime?"

⌐ ⌐

"Wow, what a day," David observed as he opened the door of their mini-suite. Mallory entered and he tipped the bellman. "Thanks, we're good," he tried not to be impolite to the solicitous employee, but he could get his own ice and get them settled for the night.

With the door secured, Mallory sagged into his embrace. "It was a good day. I don't know what possessed me to boo-hoo like that. I'm sorry, David."

"Well, all the people around us~"

She rested her head against him, shushing his words. "We'll always have 'people around us' that try to ruin our joy. I'm sorry I let it happen. I mean, the Red Sox won; I caught a home run; I got everyone's autograph, and Dick Miller was actually talking to me! And, best of all, our baby's okay. And I have you! Maybe some things in life are disappointing when you smack into reality face-first." Her earnest gaze met his. "But being married isn't one of those things. Being married to you is even better than all my dreams about it."

He kissed her ardently. "I keep being afraid I'll wake up to find it's all been a dream."

She laughed. "You know, I'm actually hungry again." She pulled out the room service menu. "Ooh; French Dip Sandwich sounds great! Wanna share?"

"H-m-m-m. I want one of my own."

When the food arrived, Mallory ate half of her sandwich and a few French fries, and David finished everything else. It was past midnight as they brushed their teeth, preparing for bed.

Mallory's phone's ringing at the late hour alarmed her. Caller ID announced Waylon Mayer.

"Hello, this is Mallory." Her tone was breathless.

"Hello, Mallory. I know it's too late to be phoning people, but Jeff left me in charge. I got the lights-out thing accomplished without too much trouble; but then, a guy showed up at the gate to tell me our fences are on someone else's property. Frank Gilmore's selling some land, and he's having it surveyed. They claim our fences are encroaching on their land by about four feet. On that north boundary"!

"Okay, Waylon. You did right calling now, in spite of the hour. I'm switching this to conference so David can hear. Okay. I'm not worried about the fence line right now. He's selling? How much? Where? How's it listed and who all knows it's on the market?"

Waylon was proud of himself for the information he had acquired.

David frowned. "Where'd Jeff go?"

"Well, to your parents' for dinner. But I think Juliet Prescott was going to be there, too. He left me in charge and told me to call you if I had any questions."

David shook his head with annoyance, and Mallory smiled at him. "Okay, Waylon, thanks for the heads up. Please don't mention anything about the fences or the property's coming on the market to anyone else. I hope everything stays quiet so you can get some rest. Good night."

Her eyes danced. "That's amazing. Let's see if we can do a title search on Gilmore's spread. David, I want that piece of land, but I don't know how we can swing it."

"Why? Do you think there are Diamonds up there? I'm telling you, the fences are all on *DiaMo* property. We surveyed it before we bought from Dorman. His fences were on his property, and we put up new where the old were."

"I'm sure it was done with due diligence. If we can get those parcels, it'll all be ours, and we can leave our fences where they are. I don't know if there are Diamonds up there. I wouldn't discount the possibility. Property's just valuable. If people ever make the realization of how rich these counties are, we'll be overrun. That's why I want legal claim to what we have, and we can be in a better position to limit access."

David nodded, but his concentration was somewhere else.

"Are you upset with Jeff for taking off?"

"Well, yeah! Pretty much! I mean the Faulkner kids are all there, and Daniel and Diana are here. Waylon's new; he's barely been there a day and a half. And Jeff just took off and never checked with me."

"Well, you treat Jeff like he's your slave. I know you lean on him a lot. Sometimes I think you're harder on Jeff than your dad is on you. He really knocks himself out to please you. He's dealt with a lot recently. Like, he really loved Empress and her baby, and that guy just slit both of their throats while he watched. So, then, he shot that guy, and he's been dealing with killing him. And he feels responsibility about *Zakkar* and all that nightmare. I didn't know he liked anyone. Juliet-hm-m. Anyway, he's a really valuable asset to all you have going on. Even if he wanted to see Juliet, I don't think he would have left Waylon with it, unless he was convinced Waylon could handle it. I've been thinking Jeff needs a place of his own. I mean, quartering in the bunkhouse, never really allows him to distance himself." She noticed David's frown. "I'm not saying anything as elaborate as the Faulkners'. I've even considered-dare I say this to you?-modular! Maybe on a slab, and dressed up. In severe weather, if he's positioned near the bunkhouse, he could get to that shelter. It looks like Waylon might turn out to be a really great assistant for him."

David laughed. As an architect, he didn't hold modular housing in high regard! Had never considered it. "You know something? You're pretty smart. I have these projects, either on the drawing board, or in the back of my mind, that I think we really need-pronto! You have my solution!"

They prayed before climbing into bed. A new request: for a miracle to help them obtain the Gilmore land.

※ ※

"Hey, are you okay?" It was the second time Trent had asked her, and he was usually kind of insensitive about that kind of thing.

She forced her brightest smile! "Yeah! Fine! That's the second time you've asked." She paid the check with her *DiaMal* credit card. "Can you kind of keep the kids from killing each other if I go get my nails done?"

He frowned. "Why get them done today? It's Sunday."

"Well, yeah, I know, but they're open on Sundays, and I thought while you were going to be at the house, it would be a good chance. I'll be back in plenty of time for choir practice. I didn't get them done this past week because you don't like me to be away that long. Although the kids are all old enough–"

"He smiled, "I know. I just remember what my brother and sisters and I did when we got left at the house together. I guess if you need to– Don't use that credit card so much that–"

"Trent! Diana and Mallory sell image! Keeping myself up is one of the reasons they issued me the cards."

"Okay, well it still doesn't make a whole lot of sense to me." He addressed the kids who had gone out to watch gold fish in the fountain. "Okay, Matt, you ride with Michael. Y'all be careful. Go straight home. Maddie, you and Meg come with me. Mom's going to go get her nails done."

Megan's expression registered horror. "But, Mom, you were going to help me review all afternoon for my big Virginia State History test tomorrow! Unless you can get Mr. Haynes to postpone it"!

"No. You need to get it over with. Daddy'll have to help you."

She pulled away, leaving them all spluttering.

⊰ ⊱

"Did you get any rest?" Diana's solicitous voice as she and Daniel met the younger couple for breakfast.

"Actually, yes," Mallory answered. She and David had agreed not to discuss the Gilmore property with anyone else, except the Lord. She paused wide-eyed as a large party made up of owners and higher up staff for the Red Sox began taking seats around a large round-top. Whoa! How incredibly cool was that? She figured that was an indication that this was the team hotel.

"Did you know this was where they're staying?" she whispered to David.

He chuckled. "No clue! I guess it's something else special the Lord did for you."

Just as they were finishing, Dick Miller approached their table, the owner and his wife following him.

"You look like you're feeling better this morning," he began.

They all stood to acknowledge the introduction, shaking hands, repeating names, responding cordially.

"I feel much better," Mallory responded as the newcomers lingered. "I apologize for being in such a pity party. You were really kind to look me up and get me all the autographs, and get my ball signed."

"Well, you did catch the home run ball; fair and square. Quite a catch, by the way! Maybe I should recruit you."

Mallory laughed, but inwardly she was jubilant! Kind of another dream-come-true! "Well, where do I sign up? I'll have my own locker room, though, right?"

"Yeah, but then you might still be too much of a distraction." He noticed the affluence of the two couples. "You know, you might want to consider a box next time. And, of course, we always have a section reserved for non-drinkers."

Mallory sighed. She didn't want to seem like a grouchy complainer, finding fault with everything. "Well, of course, you're right. I could sit in a box and be isolated from the riff-raff, so to speak. But, that wouldn't really have the ballgame atmosphere. And the non-drinking section's in the bleachers, where you'd be lucky to catch a foul ball, let alone a home run." She appreciated the help and concern, but she still didn't feel like she should have to forfeit her rights as a fan and spectator, to a bunch of obnoxious people who didn't even seem to be paying attention to the game. Diana had pointed out to her, as they had rerun the footage of her catch, that the guy behind her that had decided to 'claim' her ball, had seemed so drunk-or high-or out of it, that the ball might have killed him had Mallory not snagged it.

⚞ ⚟

Bryce and Lisette picked Rhonna up bright and early, and she clambered into the back seat with Cade.

"Did you find David and Mallory a flight?" Lisette queried over her shoulder.

"Yes, Ma'-Yes, I did." Rhonna was determined to break her habit. "The house was much cooler when I got back from dinner. I booked them on a Delta flight from L.A. to Reagan, with their arrival scheduled for about one-thirty Eastern Daylight Time. On short notice, it was expensive, but I shopped the best fare. Kind of scary to me, with the flights filling up so fast! The seats are in business class, and I emailed Mallory the itinerary."

Lisette chuckled. "Good job!"

"They goin' to another ball game?" Rhonna questioned curiously.

Lisette smiled. "I never ask. I just do what she tells me. If she wants to fill me in on details, she does."

The new employee picked up on the subtle rebuke. Not her business. Still, everything was so beyond anything she had ever imagined! Fly all the way from Texas to California, and stay in a big, fancy, expensive hotel, just to attend a ball game! She day dreamed all the way to church! And through Sunday School and church! Imagine!

-3 k-

The Andersons and Faulkners showed up ten minutes before the early service, to be met by an usher, and then the associate pastor, who explained that the senior pastor was away for a few days. "The crowd's going to be down; people are getting in last little jaunts before school starts. Even the pianist is out. Would you mind playing for the congregational singing?" His remark was addressed to Mallory, and she agreed readily. "Could you sing a couple of specials, too? It's a real treat for me to meet you. Our pastor has talked about inviting your group to come share your music, but we have a modest budget and~"

"Well, if he's serious, have him call me," Daniel encouraged. "We can probably work something out. We would be delighted to help out this morning. Thank you."

Mallory scooted onto the piano bench and ran her fingers across the keys. Not the best quality instrument, but tuned. She began the prelude with *It Could Happen In a Moment*. The lively music seemed to make people stand straighter and quicken their pace. She modulated into *How Great Thou Art*, noticing people singing the lyrics softly to themselves. She loved being in church. "Lord, bless this service, and Faith, and Calvary." She smiled to herself. "Thank You for Your promise that Your Word won't return void anyplace it's being proclaimed today." Her prayer was silent as she poured her heart into the music.

※ ※

Trent tried not to be annoyed. There was a ballgame and a golf tournament he had planned to watch, interspersed with napping. Helping Meg study for a test hadn't necessarily been in his plan.

"Why did Mom have to go get her nails done right now?" he quizzed his youngest.

"The Virginia State House," she quipped. "That's the answer to the first question."

"I'll show you," he challenged. "I'm going to mix up the order."

Sure enough, she had memorized the answers in order on her study sheet. She didn't really know most of the stuff. He brewed a cup of coffee, returning to the table where she sat, annoyed. "The tests are always like the study sheets," she argued.

"Okay, well, there's more to this than passing tests and making acceptable scores. You're actually supposed to learn some stuff. Besides, Mr. Haynes is smart. He's probably setting students up this way, and then he'll change the questions around." He frowned when his phone buzzed. Email! Intended mostly for Sonia, but someone had sent it to him as well. He viewed it dismally.

"David and Mallory were coming?" He wondered what that was about. Sonia must know; the reason for her rush to do the nail salon thing.

"Okay, Megan, go actually learn this material. Mom can go over it later."

※ ※

After church, Bryce pulled in at Arby's. He didn't mind fast food anymore, especially since he wanted to catch the golf tournament.

Rhonna was amazed to be treated like part of the group. After the rebuke about questioning David and Mallory's plans, she was slightly subdued. Finally, she asked Cade if he were a *DiaMo* employee. He explained that he was still hoping to get the call from *Sanders-Chandler*.

"Well, I sure hope all your dreams come true. I can't believe you knowin' all that Chemistry and stuff, everybody isn't lining up for you."

He shrugged. "Well, one place tells me I'm way overqualified for what they're looking for. Other places want someone older and more experienced. This trusting the Lord is new to me. Now I'm starting to talk like the people I always made fun of. Do you know Roger Sanders? Maybe you can put in a good word for me with him."

"No, I just talked to him a little during those meetings. Mrs. Sanders seemed real nice."

"You guys should hear Rhonna sing," Lisette announced when they were back in the car. Do you mind singing something?"

"Yeah! Okay. I'll sing *the Prayer*, 'cause I'm hopin' Cade gets his job soon.

It was incredible!

⚔ ⚔

Trent couldn't get much out of Sonia. "Why do you think they're coming? If they're done with you, the tenants in our house still have six months on their lease. This could turn into a disaster. I'd better stay home today and start calling apartment complexes; just to be on the safe side."

Sonia was dismayed. "No, go to work, Trent. I'm sure they won't throw us out in the street. Why are you so sure they're 'Done with me'? Maybe it's about something good."

"I don't know-both of them coming-"

She received another email. "Okay, actually, they're arriving a little before two, but they're checking into the hotel. They want us to meet them at-" She named a prestigious new steak house that was the current DC buzz. "Reservations at eight; bring all the kids."

He breathed freely for the first time in twelve hours. "Okay, I'm going to work. I'll take clothes to change into for dinner. Meet y'all in the city?"

⚔ ⚔

David settled Mallory into the DC hotel, where they were met by Darrell Hopkins and Mitch Radcliff, a new guy on their personal security staff.

"Okay, here's your laptop, your phone, and the file on the Gilmore property. Maybe you can do a few chores and still keep your feet up. I'm going to go do a walk through on the house. Call if you need anything."

229

She nodded. "Great plan. I'm going to get some room service, too, even though we're having big, juicy steaks later on."

He kissed her. "That's the great plan! Stick with it. If I know you, you'll be so excited talking to the Morrisons about everything, that you won't eat more than a bite or two."

⋊ ⋉

Diana listened, amazed, to the phone video Lisette had forwarded. She was convinced that Rhonna should record immediately. *The Prayer* should probably head the line-up, but she was thinking of perennial favorites: *He*; *Unchained Melody*; *Sunrise, Sunset*; *Fascination*; *Wind beneath My Wings*.

Daniel wasn't sure what to make of the plan. "Well, I'm sure she's never heard of most of those; she may have an opinion about what she prefers to perform. Remember, she hasn't made any profession of faith, yet. I mean, not that those are sacred, but they're a few generations~"

She nodded. "Good selections that no one has released in a while. I'm going to suggest it and go over it with her. The recording studio doesn't stay booked; we might as well put it to use. I wonder if we can get orchestrated tracks of those songs, or if Mallory can play a piano accompaniment. Maybe we can all add some strings in."

He laughed at her enthusiasm.

"What?" She sounded defensive.

"It's a good idea. Remember when you mentioned to me about getting a nanny; and I didn't like the idea? Well," he held up his hand before she could answer. "I'm still against the 'Nanny' idea, but you do need an assistant. You have so much going on already, and it's a great idea. You've always been the one with the ability to find people to help you."

She nodded. "I wonder if Mallory has all those new hires plugged in."

He laughed again. "Probably so; she usually has a plan. You'd better find your own, and not try to mess with hers."

They arrived at their Tulsa estate where he greeted the kids, brought home by his parents.

"Okay, did y'all do as you were told?" He questioned. "Sorry to pick up and leave all of you like that. I'm headed down to the office for a couple of hours to start getting unburied. I'll grill up some steaks later, and we can all

230

swim. Honey, keep working on that plan! And hiring an assistant. Maybe she can make a Christmas CD, too. We can promote them together."

She stared after him, dazed, before turning to her firstborn. "Alexandra, how would you like to have a job?"

Alexandra looked suspicious. "What? Watching the kids?"

Diana laughed. "No, actually, I'm taking back that job. I need you to be my personal assistant; you know, kind of like Lisette has been for Mallory. Your dad liked the prospect of getting Rhonna to make a recording right away, but he said I don't have enough time to deal with what I have going on now; let alone adding new projects. I'm talking about a real job, Alexandra; with salary and benefits. We can work out a package tonight with Daddy." She outlined her plan for Rhonna's album. Mentally, she had included a couple more songs that would be dynamite: *Climb Every Mountain*, and *I Did It My Way*.

Wonder dawned on Alexandra's delicate features. "Okay, so I should get busy right away and see if the tracks are available and check out what will be necessary for royalty agreements?"

Diana had scooped Ryan out of his swing. "Yes. Call Rhonna first, and try to convince her to let us engineer it"!

"Yes, Ma'am"! Alexandra was eager to start. "What about the Christmas music? Maybe we can add her voice on top of our *Wise Men Still Seek Him*, and there's this cutest Christmas song I love, but I never hear it. It's a spiritual, *The Straw Carol*, and maybe, *Happy Birthday, Jesus*?

"Okay, see what you can track down, tracks or the sheet music. Here's my corporate credit card; nail down as much as you can. Here's my password."

Alexandra was blown away. In her devotion time, she had asked the Lord to do something special for her today. She sat down at her desk and punched in a number.

"Hello, Rhonna, this is Alexandra Faulkner, my mother's assistant. We listened to the video of you singing *The Prayer*, and frankly, we were both blown away. We are really eager to have you do a recording session, well, two, actually, get them completed and promoted.

"Oh, thank you, Alexandra, that's nice." Rhonna was pleased. "Don't forget, I have a job now, so I'm not sure yet when my free time is. That's the only problem."

"Okay, well, we can find that out and work around it. My mom has sort of a roundup of songs; she has me working this afternoon on finding soundtracks and music for them. For this first session, would you mind singing what she has chosen?"

"Oh, she's chosen the songs? That's a relief! I didn't have any idea what I might pick."

Alexandra couldn't believe what she was hearing. "Okay, Rhonna, that's great! As I locate stuff, I'll get it sent on to you so you can start learning the material. Here's my number. Be sure and call me if you have any questions."

⚎ ⚏

Mallory ate half of a club sandwich and drank a glass of milk as she researched the Gilmore property. She really wanted it. She was turning into quite the land-grabber with quite a number of real estate holdings. Her two recent acquisitions in Dallas provided housing for her new employees. With their not being forced to pay rent and utilities, their salaries were lower, and she was getting equity, as well as mortgage interest deducted from her taxes. The homes sat atop the Barnett Oil Shale deposit. At the moment, the Natural Gas that it was capable of producing, was selling low. However, with the volatile price of gas and petroleum products, she figured it was a matter of time, before more and more motorists and home owners turned to the natural gas alternative. At the worst, she should get equity from the homes. The D.C. properties were harder to manage right now. Hopefully, after the steak dinner, that difficulty should be resolved. Should be! "Help it to be so, Lord" she breathed softly.

Her gaze returned to the research in the folder. She was tapped out; there really didn't seem to be any way. She hummed a few measures of *God Can Make a Way*, barely aware she was doing so. Well, she had some money, but she was now coming to the realization that the Faulkners were paying for the biggest portion of her expensive wedding. She couldn't let them do that. And she needed money to continue operating. However, for some inexplicable reason, she phoned Frank Gilmore to set up an appointment to meet him at the property at three the next day. Crazy! What was her plan? Ask him to give it away?

⚎ ⚏

David walked through; for the most part, extremely pleased. He liked changes he had made to the original drawings, thinking that the space flowed better. It was quite the place! He made a couple of calls and returned to the hotel. He needed to shower and dress for dinner.

"Was everything ready?" Mallory asked.

"Actually, yes," he responded. "Wow, are you beautiful! You're nearly ready. As soon as I get cleaned up, let's go down and have a cup of coffee. Did you eat something? I'm getting ravenously hungry."

She wore a graceful black crepe dress, featuring a square neckline with ruffled capped sleeves. It stopped mid-knee, and pedicured toes peeked from black high-heeled sandals. A Diamond brooch sizzled on her bodice and chandelier earrings flashed.

Showered, freshly shaven, and dressed in dark suit and white shirt, David made Mallory's heart throb. Was he ever cute! He pulled her into the bathroom where sparkling mirrors multiplied their images.

"I hope this doesn't make you over-accessorized." He stood behind her. "I ordered these from Herb over six weeks ago because Faulkner was right." He lifted a gorgeous pearl choker from its velvet box, securing it around her creamy throat. "Perfect," he whispered.

Chapter 18: *ACQUISITION*

Waylon sat in the executive office of the Ranch complex, holding on line one. The voice of the company's number one salesman replaced that of a receptionist.

"Hello Mr. Mayer; Rick Hibbert here! Sarah was just saying you'd like to take delivery ASAP of ten double wide modulars?"

"Yes Sir, that's correct. I've looked some of your models over on the web site, and they seem to be good structures for the dollar. When I said as soon as possible, I particularly meant delivery on your in-stock item. J-300762. I believe it's top of the line, but last year's?"

"You got that right. Great deal"! He used some profanity, nothing new for Waylon, except that it was taboo for *DiaMo* employees.

"We need delivery north of Hope in Montgomery County. Then, we'll take delivery of additional units over the next eight or nine months. I'm working with a guy to give me the specs, since you custom build. We don't require all top of the line." He ironed out some of the details for immediate transport of the close-out model. He felt a sense of accomplishment. Now, it was time to tackle some of the college course-work. Well, it couldn't be all fun. After thirty minutes of concentrated effort, he made his way to the kitchen. The aroma of chow's being prepared wafted toward him: spaghetti, garlic bread, and Caesar salad. He checked the grocery delivery off quickly in his head.

"Looks like it went smoother this time, Mardy, "he spoke encouragingly, "I told you you'd get it. It smells so good it's making me hungry. You need me to taste-test anything?"

"No! You get out til the bell rings!"

Laughing, he placed a call to Jeff's phone: when there was no answer, he left a message. "Looks like you'll have a place of your own set up by Friday." He attached a couple of photos.

⚜ ⚜

Trent Morrison was a few minutes early to the Steak Restaurant. People were already waiting, and he took in some of the well-known faces of the nation's capital. He nodded toward a couple of people he knew slightly. He watched proudly as Michael drove up smoothly to the valet stand in the Yukon. The vehicle was washed and waxed to a glossy shine, and his family looked like royalty as they alit. Michael pressed money discretely to the valet, and Trent moved in to claim his clan. He clasped Sonia's hand. "You look gorgeous! The kids look so great! You are incredible!"

A limousine appeared and Lisette hopped out, helping open doors for the passengers. Expecting to see David and Mallory emerge, he was shocked to see Sonia's mom and dad. Lisette helped get his father-in-law moving forward with his walker, and then she cut a swath through the crowd to get them seated. The next limo unloaded David and Mallory, and they all made their way to a semi-private room featuring a large linen-covered table, sparkling with a dazzling array of stemware, china, and silverware. Mallory hugged everyone but Trent, and David shook hands around before speaking softly to the Captain.

No menus. Beverages appeared; somehow Mallory knew Michael liked Dr. Pepper, Meg drank root beer, Sonia and Madeleine took sweet tea. Iced water with lemons and steaming coffee arrived for him, and following suit, he thanked the server as graciously as possible. This was an amazing experience from people who knew gracious entertaining. If they were here to can Sonia, they were laying out a lot of money first. Besides, if you're firing someone, you don't bring that person's parents in on it. He relaxed. Maybe Mallory was right, and he needed to learn to worry less, and enjoy moments. Bread appeared, smelling divine, with huge squares of butter pressed with the restaurant logo. He was hungry, and his two boys always were, but they managed not to attack the basket like slobbering wolves! Sonia must have given them an extra crash course in etiquette on the drive into the city. Chilled shrimp cocktail, platters of crab cakes, seafood fondue, and calamari covered the table.

"Trent, would you bless our meal?" David invited.

With the blessing finished, the wait staff carried the various appetizers to each diner, serving them meticulously. On cue, they served a second round, but since David and Mallory refused, Trent followed their cue.

More hot fresh bread and soup arrived: lobster bisque, or golden squash. Trent couldn't resist one of each. Coffee and water seemed to be discreetly replenished after every sip.

Mallory was a charmer, bringing each kid expertly into the conversation. It was effortless because she really liked them all, and remembered their interests.

Finally, Michael couldn't resist. "I couldn't believe you really caught that home run. That was some kind of snag! Got it signed, too. I'm jealous, and I don't even like the Red Sox."

Mallory laughed. "Hey, watch it."

That intrigued his grandpa who started talking baseball with Mallory, amazed that she knew all the stats and players from way back. Still, the conversation led from one subject to the next, sometimes serious and other times frivolous and hilarious.

Salad choices materialized: Caesar, house, Mozzarella and tomato. Mallory chose the latter, eating most of it. She had managed a crab cake and a shrimp, too.

Side dishes arrived: creamed spinach, kernel corn, garlic mashed potatoes, asparagus, sautéed mushrooms. And then everyone's steak arrived, cooked to their preference. Trent gazed at his. Usually, with his rationing system, the amount of meat in front of him would feed his entire family a meal. And was it ever superb!

᛭ ᛭

Lilly felt a case of the nerves. Her timing showing up in Dallas had been providential, in one sense. The business training sessions seemed like something sadly lacking in the gobble-gobble world of big-business. Of course, Mallory's companies, the Faulkners', Roger Sanders', were small potatoes-insignificant potatoes on the world stage. And yet, they were growing and being blessed, kind of like little plants drip-irrigated in the Judean desert.

Now, she studied her glossy card, marred and bent. A schedule of appearances by Cassandra that she had labored hard to put together, that would earn the violinist a ton of money. (Lilly, as self-appointed agent, wouldn't fare too badly either.) She shrugged grimacing bitterly. Sadly, the Faulkner family didn't need any more money. Cassandra, having never felt a pinch, seemed oblivious to what it even was. When Cassandra and the Faulkner family had steered far clear of her, she had hoped Mallory would be her ally. But, Mallory had David, now. And then that entire ordeal about the horse~

Even Herb, was doing so well now, that she couldn't bully and badger her way with him. She stopped herself. Bullying and badgering had been her modus operandi for so long, that she habitually forgot it wasn't the Christian way. That if you remembered, and turned situations over to the Lord, He was always faithful to help. Without much faith, and with few other options, she asked the Lord to help. Then, with Sabbath drawing nigh, she hurried out to accomplish some errands.

Finishing quickly, she found a table in an emptying sidewalk café to relish an early dinner in the afternoon sunshine. Her phone rang; an international number she didn't have in her log.

"Hello; Lilly Cowan," Her answer was gruff, rasping with a voice abused by years of heavy smoking.

"Hello, Lilly!" It was Cassandra's upbeat voice. "Are you finding plenty to keep you busy these days? Do you ever see any of my kittens? I thought you would stay longer when you were here."

Lilly didn't know what to make of the unexpected contact. "Hello, Dear." Trying to gush cordially didn't really work for her. "It's so good to hear your voice!"

Cassandra's tone sounded dubious. "Right Lilly! Why did you come for me that day? I was an awful disappointment; wasn't I?"

"No! Not at all"!

"Come on, Lilly. Be honest! You always were. Now you got saved; don't get me wrong; I'm glad. Now, you're trying to be kind, but I need the truth. Here's why I'm calling. My mother hired my sister to be her assistant. I mean, a real job, with money and benefits. What are benefits, Lilly?"

"Uh, vacation time, sick days, retirement funds, insurance. Your sister's older~" Lilly was confused. "Why? What's your angle?"

"I want to earn my own money, too." Cassandra sounded almost annoyed; like Lilly should have understood without her having to say it.

Lilly was so blown away she was speechless.

"Lilly? Lilly! Are you listening to me? Am I hopeless? Are you tired of fooling with me? Come on, Lilly; don't give up on me before the pay off!"

A chuckle escaped. "Yeah, you were pretty much of a pain; but you got better. I haven't given up, and my plan was always the 'payoff' as you so indelicately put it. I have ten performances scheduled for you world-wide, beginning in September. I risked a lot, and thought I was going to have to cancel, which would cost me. I suppose I should be dealing with your parents since you're a minor."

"What are you talking about, Lilly? I'm not a miner; I'm a violinist-"

Diana appeared in the doorway. "Who are you talking to, Cassandra?"

The ten year old frowned. "I'm talking to Lilly. We're working out a deal. I'll tell you and dad about it later."

Diana's blue eyes widened and she smiled. "Well, we'll be eager to hear about it. Tell Lilly 'Hello' for us."

Cassandra nodded, waiting for privacy before continuing. "Okay, Lilly, can you e-mail that schedule? I'll probably need it to try to explain everything to them. So, these concerts, did any of the people talk about paying me any money?"

"Of course, Cassandra! A great deal of money! I represented myself as your agent-"

"So, what-? Does that mean you get a cut? That's fine, Lilly."

"Well, if your parents consent to this, your father might want to be your agent. That's sometimes customary."

"Okay, Lilly, I'll talk to him. Send me the email. I'll call back when I know something."

⚘ ⚘

Over dessert, David and Mallory addressed their reasons for the visit. Product orders were increasing dramatically from the D.C. area; for clothing, jewelry, and home interior products. They were recruiting additional people to represent them the way Sonia had been doing, and they were promoting Sonia to head the division.

Agape, she glanced at Trent pleadingly.

"It's a position she can do from home?" Trent felt bad for assuming his wife was doing a poor job, when she was tearing it up. He was proud of her success, but the kids–

Mallory's gaze penetrated his. "Yes, for the most part. We are actually here to move y'all again, too. The house is bigger, and she'll have an office complex; state of the art. She will have some traveling occasionally, mostly to Dallas. Until now, the housing, maintenance, outfits, jewelry to use, have been the salary package. Now, she'll also have a monetary salary. Not a huge salary, but enough to cover the extra tax-bite, and a little over. Now, Trent, I know this makes you nervous! But we want her to get out a lot! We like for her to spend money on her expense account, because when she does; we make money! You want her to stay home and cook budget meals, but we want you all to be where you're in contact with the public. That doesn't mean eat every meal at a steakhouse like this; however, it's a clientele like this, that we want to make contact with. Since we offer products across a price spectrum, McDonald's, Denny's, Starbucks, the malls, anyplace is good. People aren't going to beat your door down to see our stuff."

David took over skillfully. "Now, when we relocate you to the larger house, it features a caretaker apartment. You'll still have the maid and landscapers on a regular basis. Since you won't have live-in help, we've fixed the caretaker space for your parents. We know their needs have increased, and that it's gotten harder to look in on them. When we move them and your family, we'll have those two properties empty, and we've acquired a couple of others in this area. We were wondering, if you, Michael, would be interested in managing our properties here. You can still finish your degree, and also help with the care of your grandparents. It will familiarize you with real estate and the building industry; knowledge that will always come in handy. You'll either love it or hate it, but that helps you with your life's choices."

"Well, I'm not sure I'll know where to start–"

"I'll get you started," David's words were relaxed and confident. "And I'm pretty sure you'll be a quick study."

⊰ ⊱

Cassandra sat nervously at the kitchen counter. She needed to have a word with her dad as soon as he stepped in the door, before her mom and everyone else surrounded him. She studied the email from Lilly. At first, she had figured her daddy would be a push-over for her and Lilly's plan; now as she viewed the musical selections dismally, doubts began to hover. A couple of the pieces were incredibly complex, and three were by new composers; she had never heard of them, or heard their works that she would have to learn. She fought tears. Maybe she should fall back on a lemon aide stand like other nine year olds.

She glanced up as the latch clicked.

"Hey, Cass, what's up? Something on your mind?" Daniel took in his daughter's dejected bearing "Your mother told me you were on the phone with Lilly. What's this?" He tugged on the corner of the print-out.

"It's a concert schedule Lilly came up with." She released it for his review.

Usually one to carry his jacket and brief case to his office, he set them on the kitchen counter instead, and sank onto a stool next to her. "Wow! They're spread out all over the world. You'll need to wax your surfboard."

She giggled, knowing he referenced Nick and his stories.

"You'll need some shark-repellent, too."

She sighed. He sobered up, too. She was like him. A little levity went a long way. And then it was time to be serious. He was confused.

"So, does Lilly know any of these people? Has she tried to contact them?"

Cassandra's serious eyes bored into him. "Of course! It's actually all arranged, and if I don't go, she'll have to pay fees to cancel me out."

Daniel's brain was trying to absorb it. Pretty nervy! On Lilly's part, to assume! But then, that was how she had been from the beginning! Nervy and assuming!

"Well, I think I need to call her and talk to her for myself. What time is it in Israel?" He glanced at his watch.

"Are you going to tell her I can't?"

"You want to try it; don't you?" As a father, he desperately wanted to protect her. It was easy for him to see her frailties; he knew her limitations as a violinist. And he longed more than anything to keep her here; keep her little, keep her sheltered.

Her features were a study in anguish. "Yes very much! No, not at all! I don't know! Am I ready?"

"No. You are not. Can you get ready? That's up to you. We haven't pushed you~"

"And, I haven't pushed myself. I~I~can't do it; can I?"

He shook his head negatively. "You can't do it if the symphony directors are locked into these pieces. If they're looking for a nine-year old prodigy that can perform these difficult, difficult selections flawlessly enough for world-wide critics~you're not there. Your hands are little; you're little~" His voice broke. "That's why I need to talk to Lilly. She has no clue what she's asking you to do. If I can select the music, and the various venues agree to my choices~"

"Does that make you my agent then?" Her tone was worried.

"No! It makes me your father! Why? Does Lilly think she's your agent?" He stared at the schedule the woman had pulled together. If she could arrange his changes, she would probably deserve the position, and the money. "I'll call her and see what we can arrange. Don't worry. I'll be nice. Your mother thought Lilly was upsetting you, demanding your return to Israel."

He gathered his jacket and possessions as Diana entered the kitchen.

"Hey, I didn't hear you come in." She offered a welcoming kiss. "Is everything okay? Are you still going to grill steaks?"

He kissed her. "No, I'm going to be on the phone; I may be awhile. Why don't you order pizza? Be sure to give them directions."

"Well, I know how to grill~"

He paused. "I know you do. The steaks will save. Just make it easy on yourself. Okay?"

⊰ ⊱

Trent and Sonia kept exchanging glances and squeezing hands as the tour of the 'new' house progressed. It was palatial, top of the line, finishing touches and trim beyond imagining. It perched deeply within its own acreage, something extremely rare this near the city. The apartment for Sonia's parents exceeded the square footage of the current town home where they resided. Trent was nearly speechless. 'Why would they do this?' He focused back on Lisette, who was conducting her upbeat tour. Like this place needed its own cheerleader to sell itself. Another dazed smile met Sonia's.

"I can't wait to call Teri," she chirped.

He shook his head, and she picked up on his subtle disapproval of her plan.

"I guess I should hold off on that. You're right! Are you worried about what the new job will entail for me?"

He laughed. "No. Evidently I've been underrating your ability. I've kept thinking the carriage was going to turn back into a pumpkin. Instead, it's been traded up. I don't know how I can, but I keep forgetting how good God is, and how He always blesses obedience. Not just ours, but our kids'. Sonia, you've done a wonderful job instilling our values into them. I guess that's been one of my concerns about your having any other job."

"Well, Mallory and the Faulkners stepped into our lives when we were in crisis~"

"Well, we were in crisis because of Lilly and her ~"

"That certainly exacerbated it, but~"

"Yeah, we were in financial trouble. This is an expensive area to live in, and government salaries don't crash through any ceilings. Then, with Meg's asthma and your parents' getting bad in California, I was frustrated and trying to blame you. The Lord intervened for us, and He used the Faulkners and Mallory as His instruments. We need to be careful not to lose sight of Who's behind all this."

⚓ ⚓

Delia set her empty tea cup in its delicate saucer as she closed her Bible. "Lord, I keep trying to turn this over to You, but I can't stand seeing Shay hurt day after day. I want to call Roger Sanders and tell him off. Shay isn't like his father was, if that's Mr. Sander's problem. And he isn't like Connie's husband. Lord, bless Brent and Connie. Lord, if Emma isn't the right one for Shay, show him another girl. I must admit, I'm confused. I'll put it in Your hands for another day, and leave the sorting out to You."

⚓ ⚓

Mallory paced nervously. David sat in the cab of the truck, reluctant to exchange the air conditioning for the scorching heat. Mallory looked cute. Having fallen in love with the batik print Diana had incorporated into Rhonna's wardrobe, she had requested a dress utilizing the print. With exquisite results, or course! Softly grayed blue-green flattered her eye color;

the linen print falling to dropped waist and box pleated skirt. Tan stacked wedges matched the beige in the print. She glanced at her phone.

"What are we doing here?" she fretted nervously.

He chuckled. "I'm trying to stay cool, and you're trying to bring on a case of heat stroke. And, also, we're waiting for Mr. Gilmore and his real estate agent. We're early. Would you relax?"

"I can't! What are we going to say to him, David?"

He laughed. "I'm sure you'll think of something; you usually do."

"Like what? We asked him to come meet us out here because we want all this acreage-but we don't have any money?"

He shrugged. "It might at least be good for a laugh. Maybe we're here so you can see this place is a dump, and realize you don't want it."

She tried to scowl, but he was so cute. He knew the ramshackle buildings weren't what interested her.

They watched as an older model Suburban shot rocks and dust before pulling in front of their vehicle and stopping by the back porch. One of the men emerged from the vehicle, nicely dressed in slacks and dress shirt with rolled up sleeves. "Electricity's off to the house, so would you like to join us in the larger vehicle?"

David briefly considered the safety angle. His pistol was holstered beside his seat. Hopefully, Mallory's was in her handbag. He nodded. "Sounds like a good plan."

The young couple shook hands with the men as they introduced themselves. "So, you're Patrick's girl," Gilmore observed. "I'm sorry for your loss. It was my loss, too. I really liked the man. I guess he left you pretty well fixed up. I used to see him around at auctions, so I wasn't as surprised as most people around here, to learn he had been accumulating a fortune."

Mallory nodded, still praying for wisdom-or for a sudden windfall. "Yes, Sir, all the stuff that looked like worthless junk, was really worthwhile junk." She laughed. "And, he was always tinkering and inventing stuff."

He nodded. "And a Red Sox fan. That was the man's main fault."

Mallory tried to look severe, but the twinkle in the guy's eye made it hard. "That's something I inherited, too."

"Well, you sure get around. Saturday, you were in California; yesterday in DC, and today back in rural Arkansas. You're quite the ball player. Well, enough of that. I take it you're here about some of the parcels of property. Well, I was kinda trying to keep it under wraps about my selling out, until

I worked out in my mind, the best way to parcel up the lots. You're looking for what? More room to spread out for your Alpaca? You want the acreage adjacent to you? Some of the land gets pretty inhospitable and hard to get to. Nothing for farming or livestock. I'm not sure how I'll unload it. It's quite rugged even for hunters."

David spoke up. "Actually, she wants all of it."

Gilmore eyed them steadily, trying to keep his 'poker face' in place. "All of it," he finally echoed. "Have you even seen it?"

Mallory plunged in, "No Sir, not most of it. I've looked it over on all the maps I could get my hands on."

He squinted shrewdly. "You're a Geologist; right? You're talking about buying, mineral rights, and all? What do you think is here? You study Geological maps? What about all the environmental concerns about mining? Are there really Diamonds to speak of in Pike County?"

She plunged in. "I have this verse:

Ecclesiastes 11:6 In the morning sow thy seed, and in the evening withhold not thine hand: for thou knowest not whether shall prosper, either this or that, or whether they both shall be alike good.

Yes, there are gem-quality Diamonds in Pike County, as well as many other varieties of gem stones. This entire area is fascinating from a Geological standpoint. And of course, we are always open to expanding the Alpaca ranch. We would enjoy taking a tour of the property, but, um~" she hesitated. "We don't have much cash on hand right now. I'm really afraid we've wasted the time you've given us." She felt totally foolish.

The realtor wasn't one to let a prospect escape. "Well, we can do the credit check; maybe you can walk away today with one of the prime parcels!"

Gilmore glared at the loquacious salesman. "Tell, you what, Paul, we'll drop you off at your office; Abe, I'll take you back to your room." His flint-hard gaze met David's. "You two want to follow me? I'll go on to the lodge at Daisy. You can at least buy my dinner in exchange for my time!"

David shrugged. "Yes, Sir, we'd be happy to do that."

Lilly was nervous when she found she was dealing with Daniel rather than Cassandra. Surprisingly, he conversed normally, expressing his concerns, but not opposing the schedule. Well, definitely, he needed details. His major concern was about whether Lilly was trying to coax his daughter back to Israel to live. The next issue was the travel details: safety and lodging. Lilly was still working on the logistics, but for the most part she planned to fly El Al. He discussed the orchestral numbers, suggesting other pieces Cassandra could master by the performance dates. Lilly had no desire for her protégé to suffer any humiliation.

⚞ ⚟

Lisette held a short closed-door meeting with Sonia in the spacious new office suite. "You'll need a part-time assistant. We don't really have time to vet applicants, so you can find someone you'll enjoy working with. By the way, Diana just hired Alexandra as her assistant. It's working out great, so far. Well, I'd better run! Plane to catch! I'll be in touch. This division's a new thing, so we can feel our way through it together." She was gone, leaving Sonia with her heart skipping for joy! 'Maddy had been a little jealous of Michael getting a job handed to him. Hey, if Diana Faulkner was hiring her daughter~' She ran in search of Madeleine.

⚞ ⚟

"Well, he was pretty nice about stuff; don't you think so?" Mallory questioned as they approached the lodge at Daisy. "We'll treat him to the best steak in western Arkansas, and hopefully, we'll have a new connection. Maybe we can offer to help show the property, or something."

"You know, I've been thinking about something," David changed the subject. "I have a corporation, too, and it's never occurred to me to add you in. The buildings at the Ranch are free and clear; maybe we can borrow against that, for a down payment."

Mallory's countenance brightened more. "H-m-m, I never thought about that. Maybe we can buy part of the property. I just can't decide which part I'd be most interested in. I mean, the adjacent land to ours, makes sense~"

"Yeah, and I think that's the part Gilmore considers prime; he'll be pricing it high, to compensate for the rough undeveloped portions."

Mallory nodded agreement. "I kind of tipped my hand when I mentioned maps. I mean, I'm not sure what minerals there are-but it seemed to pique his interest. He'll probably decide not to sell at all now."

With their steaks ordered, David asked Gilmore if he minded that they bless the food.

The guy consented somewhat awkwardly. Then, buttering a roll, he posed his question.

"Okay, let me get this straight. You want to buy all four hundred of my acres, but you don't have any money?"

Mallory sighed. "Well, we have money, but it's all kind of ear-marked. We have quite a few operations going, and we need to keep operating capital on hand. I can't think of any way to obtain your land without jeopardizing what we have going on; and consequently the people who work for us!"

Gilmore nodded, liking what he heard. "Okay, well, I don't want to bog you down with details, but my wife Linda and I aren't getting any younger. We moved to Little Rock about four years ago, and my man Abe, has been running things. Well, he's been with me for twenty-five years, but he's getting really crippled up with Arthritis. Linda and I, neither one want to move back to the country. Now, we have plenty of money, so if you two kids are really serious about this, I can carry the financing, for say, up to five years-"

Tears sprang to Mallory's eyes, and he held up his hand, laughing before continuing. "Well, I guess I've come to consider the place an albatross, just seeing the problems. But, you're a Geologist, and for some reason, you're interested in it. Really interested! Here's what I'm thinking and if you like it, our attorneys can get it all refined on paper."

He straightened, allowing the server to present his salad.

"Okay, you have tight security around your place, right? Cameras, and everything?"

David nodded. "The best we can make it-"

"Yeah, Abe and I had some expert come out and start talkin' about cameras, and this and that, until we were just confused. Here's what I'm thinkin'. I'll carry the financing, in return for you keeping up my cattle operation, and keeping security about some valuable stuff I need to keep storing. You can buy the mineral rights, too, in exchange for twenty percent of any profit you realize from mining or drilling operations, for as long as my wife or I survive."

"How soon can we close?" The question burst from Mallory's lips.

David laughed. "Okay, whoa, hold it. I don't know the first thing about running a cattle operation. I mean, the Alpaca are one thing; they practically raise themselves, but—"

Frank Gilmore shrugged. "How much do you have to know?"

David's gaze traveled from a crestfallen Mallory to the sly rancher. "Duh! I don't have to know much, except to find someone who does know! Your guy, Abe, can he get around on an ATV or golf cart? Can he keep running things if I find some young guys to follow his orders?"

Chapter 19: ANTICIPATION

Proverbs 28:20 A faithful man shall abound with blessings: but he that maketh haste to be rich shall not be innocent.

Another visit to the doctor showed the baby developing normally. It seemed that the nausea was more sporadic, and for the most part, Mallory was getting her appetite back. "We need to fix up a nursery," she mentioned as she and David headed back to the office together.

He nodded agreement, saying he had been thinking about some options. He hadn't charged ahead with the project, because the first trimester was the time when most miscarriages occurred. And, he thought they should wait until they knew the baby's gender and decorate the space accordingly.

They descended to the café, and Mallory frowned, noticing Rhonna seated by herself. "Okay, let's join her and see what's going on." Without waiting for a reply, Mallory made her way to the table where the girl ate alone.

"Hey, Abbott, 'tsup?" David questioned. "I want to give you a head's up that I'm going to be invading your room with a crew of guys for the next couple of days. Mallory wants the interiors of the houses updated. So stash away anything that's not for our eyes."

Rhonna's eyes widened. "Thanks for the warning. How are you going to fix it?"

He bit a sandwich, chewed, and swallowed. "Well, I really won't know much until I get a good look at it. Do you have any preferences?"

"Black"!

He laughed. "Okay; in a word! As I remember, the bedrooms are quite small. Black will really close it in. You thinking. maybe black on the narrower wall, or maybe a wallpaper with some black in it?"

She frowned thoughtfully. "No, I'm thinkin' everything should be painted black!"

"Okay, then, black it is!" Mallory's decisive mode! "Now that that's settled, I need to go over some things with you. We want all the new women to come to the Ranch this weekend. We're going to test your driving proficiency. If you're good in the country, then, we'll try I-30, and finally Dallas. Everyone needs to be able to get around. And, since most everyone has a license, they'll still need to get a Texas one now that y'all live here."

Rhonna tried to mask her anxiety. Her family had one derelict car, she hadn't driven yet; insurance was prohibitive, for one thing.

"You'll do fine," Mallory reassured. "I'm taking the lessons, too. I learned how before I moved here, and had a tiny bit of experience. Dallas was pretty terrifying to me. Then, Mr. Faulkner decided that for security's sake, my team should drive me. David thinks I should be able to drive, though, in case of emergencies. Okay, and also, I have CD sets of common grammatical mistakes in spoken English. I issue a set to every new employee and expect them to master it. I don't want to hear about any of my employees telling a contact 'that they seen something,' or making any other egregious grammatical blunders. Also, Diana's coming next week to go over some of the clothing details. You'll need to be familiar with all the textile terminology by then. Also, the Faulkners and David are hoping you can get started this weekend on a CD to release as soon as possible. I guess Lisette has informed you of some of the projects she wants you to do?"

Rhonna smiled mildly. "Some phone calls and letters. Ma'am, I'm still worried about when my job's gonna start, and what I'll be doing."

Mallory was taken aback, and David tried not to snicker. "Well, you've been doing your job for nearly a month: attending meetings, making calls, reserving flights, taking care of correspondence, reading the books, wearing the fashions, learning the various aspects of the business. Mostly, you're Lisette's assistant, to do what she needs done."

Rhonna shook her head wonderingly. "We-ll okay but if you need me to mop or vacuum be sure and say so."

"Well, that's a great attitude. Sometimes David and I vacuum and clean stuff up. Mostly, for cleaning, if you keep the house neat and tidy between the maid's visits, that'll be a help."

⊣ ⊢

David phoned his attorney in Little Rock, regarding adding Mallory to his corporate hierarchy. Often feeling that he had little to bring to the table, he was annoyed with himself for not having thought of sharing what he did have! With that accomplished, he made a couple of calls to begin the remodel of Rhonna's space. An idea was coming together in his mind, and he doodled some sketches. Nothing definite until they could actually get there in the morning, and measure! Still, he went on-line to shop for a small garden tub and separate corner shower stall, noting down the measurements they were available in.

When Mallory buzzed him, he was amazed that it was nearly three o'clock "Hey, the afternoon's going by fast–I mean, quickly. What's up?"

"Well, you were right about where we have Heather assigned."

He laughed. "Could you please try not to sound so surprised?"

She laughed, too. "Well, I'm sorry I was skeptical. I didn't think I'd find enough of these fraudulent charges to merit another employee on the payroll. But–uh–she's going to pay for herself. You're right, just little questionable charges and fees here and there–you don't have time to analyze all of it! Well, it adds up to lots of money! And Heather's a perfect fit! Just a meticulous plodder! Well, I have plenty to finish; are we still leaving at four?"

"Yeah, I'm finishing up some stuff, too. Four still sounds good to me. Have you been gathering up the financial documents for Mr. Gilmore? I'll dig out my stuff this week end at the Ranch."

Seized with inspiration, David suddenly remembered a bed he had seen in a catalog. Rhonna's bedroom was tiny; maybe this was the solution. He redid his drawing with the 'loft' bed on its high stilts. Below it, he tucked a computer desk and chair and a love seat with coffee table. Kind of like a double-decker bedroom. He buzzed Todd, giving him instructions about which bed to purchase, and where. "Have it at the girls' house in the morning," he instructed. He was humming to himself as he joined Mallory at the elevator. He kind of felt like Rhonna felt. If this was his job, when was the tedium going to start?"

250

Erik Bransom kept at it on his own time. Somewhere, Darius Warrington must have his own yacht. A 'sailing yacht' according to what Cy had boasted to Mallory. The FBI agent figured when he located the vessel, it would yield evidence. Not a matter of 'If', but 'When'. Dawson, his superior, had told him to forget about it. Hence, his spending his time on the search. Erik had carefully searched U.S. marinas and coastlines and those of her territories~no small task. Not physically, but cyber-searches, turning up nothing registered in the name of either man. Now, he scanned satellite images of some big oceans. He brewed more coffee; then returned with a full mug. 'Okay, Darius lived in Laguna.' He sipped the hot beverage, returning his cursor to the L.A. area. 'Okay, past American waters into international; Dawson's reason for not keeping at it. He smiled at the flotilla of the Seventh Fleet, out from San Diego.' His images were undated so he couldn't know in real time where all the American fleets were located. 'A little ridiculous, since, doubtless, the Russians and Chinese had the data in real time, if they wanted to use it.' He shrugged. 'Maybe the precautions kept a few lone nuts from targeting the American ships.' Back to the task at hand! 'Warrington's boat wouldn't be anchored along shipping lines, but surely it wouldn't be too far out into the vastness; would it' He tried to recall Mallory's exact words. 'Cy had tried to persuade her to go sailing on the weekend. The Gulf of Mexico was more convenient for sailing from Dallas; but Cy was newly moved to the Dallas area, and the Uncle, owner of the sailboat, lived in California. Cy must have planned to fly with Mallory to the west coast for the week-end excursion.' He scanned the Pacific Ocean. 'Catalina Island and The Channel Islands National Park! Warrington wouldn't leave the vessel where people were.' He zoomed in, enlarging the expanses, studying every possible anomaly. He raised his mug, still moving the cursor; then plonked it down suddenly without sipping! 'Could this really be it?' Even zoomed in completely, he wasn't sure. 'Where were the images where you could read the logos on golf balls?'

Lilly was elated! With the exception of one orchestra, the scheduling staffs had agreed to her changes. So, the tour was on; with the blessings of the Faulkners, who would be present in Toronto for the first of the nine performances. From then on, Cassandra would travel with one person from her family's security for each performance, accompanied also by Lilly and her small entourage. Faulkner had agreed to appointing Lilly as his daughter's 'agent' for this concert series.

⚜ ⚜

Madeleine screeched with delight! "You're serious, Mom? They said you can hire anyone you want, and you're giving me a chance?"

"I can't think of anyone I'd rather work with. The thing is, though, it's a real job. That means that parts of it, you'll like more than others. If I need you to help me with something you don't enjoy, I don't want to hear, 'Oh, I forgot'."

"I won't do that, Mom, I promise! Do I get clothes and jewelry?"

"Okay, I don't have all the details. Lisette told me we'll be forging new trails. I'm not sure if they're paying you directly, how much, or how it works. I'm pretty sure they'll do you right, and then some; or they'll do very well by me, so I can reward your diligence."

"Mom, this is extra-exciting, because I prayed about it. You know, you and Dad have been teaching us in James chapter four about not being jealous of each other, and fighting, and carrying on? That we have not, because we ask not? Well, I was so jealous of Michael when they just handed him that dream job! But I told him he's a great guy, and he had earned their trust-well, that was hard to do. Then, I thought about praying, but they were already all gone back. I didn't have any faith at all, and I know how Daddy's been about me working."

"Well, he isn't against your working, Maddy. He's against having you in the work force with all kinds of bad influences."

Madeleine sighed. "Well, yeah, but, sooner or later, you have to face it and take a stand-"

Sonia's eyes danced. "Well, maybe not!"

⚜ ⚜

Erik tried to convince himself that the dot was the object of his search. The way these maps were, he couldn't determine the exact coordinates. 'Let's see, fly past the Channel Islands, Zig left and up a bit-' He fought feeling defeated by the odds. Dawson would never go for this. Lots of reasons, probably masking the real ones! Even as he stared at the dot in the immensity, certainty infused him. He had to know! He had to find out!

⊰ ⊱

David grinned as he stepped into the 'Cave'. "Okay, let's not do any more until we're sure this is really what she wants. I have the measurements, and I'm ordering the bathroom fixtures. That sliding glass door's atrocious; wish we could remodel and put in French doors. At least it lets light into the gloom. Why would anyone want such a small room all black?"

Damon took in the tiny patch of neglected yard through the expanse of glass. "That outdoor space could be pretty neat. Maybe some vertical blinds in something natural looking, and repairing the screen will help."

David nodded. Not bad suggestions from a new guy.

⊰ ⊱

Rhonna's eyes sparkled. "Yeah, that's great! It's comin' along. Y'all forgot something, though." The young woman hated being a pain, but David kept asking her.

"Okay, what?"

She rolled luminous, large eyes, upwards.

"You want the ceiling black, too? I should have guessed. Well, I don't like those outdated, textured circles. Okay, black it'll be." He showed her the broad, black, plank sample that would be the floor, She nodded approval, and he showed her his drawing.

"We have this loft bed; it's queen sized, has this railing all the way around so no one tumbles; there's even a gate here at the top of the ladder that allows for access, and then fastens securely. The problem is, that the mattress is thinner than standard. It may feel a little hard; of course, you can't sit up in bed." He showed her his alternative ideas.

Tears sparkled. "That there's a bed? David, I ain't never seen nothin' like that for cute! This here material, in the drawin', on the bed and little couch; is it kinda like the clothes Ms. Faulkner fixed up for me?"

He surveyed his drawing. "Well, maybe a little bit, in my artist's rendering. We can find upholstery swatches for whatever you want. Solid, striped; zebra might be nice. Are you listening to that grammar course Mallory bought for everyone?"

She folded her arms. "A little bit. David, that isn't me."

He folded his in response, leveling his gaze on her. "No, but it's going to be; right?"

"Let me look at those pictures again." An attempt to change the subject back!

"Look, Rhonna, we like who you are." David changed imperceptibly from pal to boss. "We have great respect for you as a person. But, don't you want to be as sharp as you can be? We're trying to bring out the best in everyone; not just for our sakes, but for theirs as well. You can't make us look good without looking good, yourself. And it isn't that hard. Just listen to it over and over again, until the right usage comes more naturally than what you've always said. We know you know what's right. Because you got good grades in English"!

"Yeah, I could figure it out, the rules and stuff, and fill the blanks in with the right choices, but then when I'm talkin'-"

"It'll come together if you work at it a little."

He smiled when Diana appeared in the doorway. "What do you think? She already said she wants the ceiling black."

Diana tipped her head thoughtfully before reaching for the sketches. "Oh! Cute idea! About the loft! Great use of the small space! I agree about the ceiling. It's too atrocious for words, anyway. Rhonna, do you know what crown molding is? How about the comforter and love seat upholstery in a large leaf print, similar to the batik designs in your clothing? In black and beige, and put in crown molding in beige enamel for a little contrast with the black?" Her hands moved over the sketch book, using the oil pastels.

"I'd like to get rid of the sliding door in favor of French doors," David commented. "But that's messing with the entire wall, then."

"Yeah, that's pretty major. You sketched a vertical blind? That's a good idea. Just do it in textured, black linen. It might fade quickly, but it'll blend with the wall and be less of a jarring note." She stepped into the bathroom viewing stained fixtures and cheap linoleum tile that rolled up at the edges. She shuddered. "Lisette has chosen better real estate. And this is the new plan?" Her laughter revealed her delight. "Ooh, this is fun!"

Rhonna stood, gazing from one to the other. "You know what? When they said this would be my bedroom, I was so happy. It's nicer than any room I ever had, and I wasn't sharin' with no-anybody! And havin' a bathroom of my own-" She fought tears. "And I thought it would look nicer painted with black, but-this-. See, that's the thing. I'm supposed to be dreamin', and I don't know how!" She tapped the picture. "That's dreamin'! Livin' like you're in a magazine! I have three brand new pairs of shoes. I never dreamed of having one pair as nice as those. Eatin' steaks and havin' credit cards? Maybe I'll leave the dreamin' to y'all!"

Diana's eyes were filled with tears in response to the emotion. "You know what? It's just the Lord. He does exceeding abundantly above all we can ask or think. I never had anything this nice growing up. You know David and Mallory didn't. That's how God is! He gives! He gave His only begotten Son to die on the cross for our sins. And the Bible tells us that if God would give that, why would He deny us other things that cost Him less? He's on our side, and He blesses us as long as we obey and honor Him. Cute, cute room!" She stepped to take in the view beyond the glass. "You're going to dress this up as part of her space, too? David, you're amazing!"

⚜ ⚜

"Jed, listen to me, please," Erik pled with his immediate supervisor. "Who are you afraid is going to get snared in this? More Washingtonians?"

"Calm down, Erik." Dawson used a few expletives. He usually tried not to swear around Bransom, so Bransom wouldn't think he needed the 'getting saved thing' so bad, but Bransom was the one who usually made him want to cuss the most. "Hey, if people who live in D.C. are committing crimes, I'm for apprehending them. If there's really a boat full of evidence someplace, I'd be in favor of finding it! What I'm afraid of, is wasting a ton of money to come up with nothing! You said yourself, that you can't be a hundred per cent sure that you've really spotted a boat, and that you can't get the coordinates! What do you want me to do?"

"Get me a better satellite map and then authorize a task force to get out there and find out what's there."

"That's what I was afraid of."

⚜ ⚜

Let's all go have lunch at the café in Mallory's building," Merc Carlton suggested to his dad. "It'll give us a change of scenery, and the food's pretty good."

"Yeah, and you're hoping to run into David and Mallory?" Linda, his father's wife, and Mallory's aunt, registered her suspicion. "Why should we have to chase them down? I thought David was serious about learning jewelry."

Merc sighed. "I'm pretty sure he was serious. They both stay busy. I'm not 'chasing them down' by going over to a public spot for lunch. Would you two relax? They like us; they like being with us. But, they only have so much time, and lots to do. You two get so~"

"Paranoid?" Herb supplied the word. "If you say so"! He winked at his wife. "Let's do it, just to prove that we aren't."

"Well, they serve a good Reuben."

⊰ ⊱

Erik Bransom had felt better. He was quite sure his superior had ordered him to forget Warrington, the possibility of his having a yacht, and the entire scenario. Now, Dawson himself, Erik, and special agent Caroline Hillman were aboard a USCG Cutter headed to a speck beyond the California coastline, into international waters. The Coast Guard crew felt the sailing was routine and smooth, but it was choppy enough to make Erik question his own sanity in insisting on coming out here. He sensed that Hillman was more miserable than he was, except for her need always to come across as a female tough enough to make it in the Bureau.

"Coming alongside," Dawson announced. "That's a disaster looking-relic if I ever saw one. If the Warrington's were luring women onto something like that-uh-wouldn't have worked."

Bransom sighed. Dawson was right. Unless the women were drugged or dead long before they reached this remote anchorage. He had a moment of lapsed reality; suddenly anxious. Which would be better? For the vessel to simply be a benign piece of wreckage? That he could live down the razzing about? Or for him to be correct, finding disturbing evidence?

A Coast Guard officer conversed with Dawson. The large, vintage, wooden craft rolled seriously to port.

"She looks ready to sink beneath the waves forever, taking whatever secrets she holds with her to the bottom." Dawson relayed the report.

256

"They're taking a chopper up for more of a birds-eye view of her, but she's too unstable to try to board."

Erik fixed his view on his search target. Surely, they weren't arriving a scant few hours too late. "Can they start pumping her out, and get her under tow?" He knew it was a lost cause, and his request a desperate last straw.

His superior, either didn't hear him, or pretended not to.

He watched as the chopper ascended above the Cutter deck, then hovered over the deck of the other ship. A crew member descended on a cable, specialized camera in hand. Bransom's stomach didn't feel any better as he watched the cable spin and swing in the wind. He was surprised to see the winch drop lower, the crewman, barely skimming above the rising starboard deck. Erik moved closer to the window for a better look, his queasiness forgotten. There must be something, for the guy to drop down lower for a closer look.

The Captain received comm from the pilot, who repeated the words of the photographer.

"Okay, can you start pumping her out, and get her under tow?" Dawson's terse words!

Dawson turned to face Bransom and Hillman. "I guess it's awful!"

⊣ ⊢

Mallory stopped by to glimpse the remodeling for her newest staff. "Wow! What a difference," she gasped. It was amazing. The aged, stained bathtub/shower with sliding doors rather than shower curtain had been removed. The mildewed wall behind it had been ripped out, and new sheet rock would go into place once the plumber and electrician made changes. The old sink in its wooden, Formica counter was in the yard, that wall already sanded and retextured.

Diana was there, excitedly into the new decor.

"I'm surprised you're in Dallas!" Mallory gave her a hug as she spoke.

Diana laughed. "Well, I'm excited about the trip to Spain, and I don't want to miss out on anything. Deborah and her mom are meeting me here in a few minutes. She said something about 'having a confession to make'. They were nervous. Now I'm nervous, too. Maybe they can't go on the trip."

Mallory smiled. "Well, all the new kids are pretty nervous. Which, I'm never sure if that's good or bad. Here they come now." Her tone turned alarmed. "It looks like they're both crying." She made her way to the kitchen as they both entered. "Deborah, what's wrong? Hello, Mrs. Rodriguez. Is everything all right?"

Deborah proffered her cute new jacket wordlessly.

Mallory took it, confused. "What? It all came apart?" She turned toward Diana. "Have we had this happen before? Okay, well, y'all don't cry. I'm sure we can get it fixed. Right, Diana?"

Diana fingered the damage unbelievingly. "What happened? It looks like someone took it apart on purpose."

The two cried harder; finally, Deborah gasped out. "You can fire me because it's ruined. It was a very nice outfit." She dabbed at tears with her fingertips. "Or I can repay from my checks."

"Okay, please stop crying. It's nothing to get fired over, or to deduct from your check. It's okay. We can fix you up with another one that hopefully, won't fall apart."

"Well, it didn't just simply fall apart," Diana argued. "Everything we produce is the highest quality!"

Mallory responded, "Yeah, I know, but you're not helping me here, because I'm trying to get them to stop crying. We can replace the jacket. I'll replace the jacket."

"Okay! I can tell what happened." Deborah's voice broken by sobs. "I showed Mama my new clothes. Mama sews, and she likes the pocket! She say, 'Let me take apart. I can learn how. I can put back! No one ever know!' My mama is a good seamstress. Always she takes things apart to fix them, and no one can tell it's fixed, but~"

Diana's expression brightened. "Okay! That makes more sense. So, Mrs. Rodriguez, you're a seamstress? And you were trying to figure out how to make a Besom Pocket? I can get you the step-by-step instructions if you like."

Deborah's mom reached for the garment. "Always, I can~"

Diana nodded. "You can always get garments put back together. That's amazing. But you couldn't with this, because the seam allowances are trimmed completely out. That makes it lie nice and flat, without any bulk and bumps. But it didn't leave anything to work with for sewing it back. We understand. I think it's amazing you wanted to learn the procedure." With the misunderstanding cleared up, Diana brought up the trip. "Deborah can come, can't she? And you're accompanying us, too?"

Mallory could see the joy returning as Deborah and her mom realized they hadn't scuttled their opportunity. They all began chattering around the kitchen table. Mrs. Rodriguez' first name was Juanita, but everyone called her Nita, and although Deborah had to interpret a lot, Diana and Mallory both liked her. A lot!

⊰ ⊱

The old boat was a conundrum. An old wooden superstructure belied the new state-of-the-art mast and rigging. Powerful new motor and generator had ceased to function for lack of fuel. There was plenty of surplus fuel, but no one had been on board in months, to keep her up and running.

As information arrived, Bransom shared his thoughts. 'All the surplus fuel aboard was reminiscent of the shrimper in the Gulf of Mexico. Use something so abandoned-looking that no one would pay any attention~?'

The Coast Guard Commander explained that the aged wood allowed some leakage, but that she did okay as long as the bilge pumps functioned. She had taken on quite a bit of water since fuel to the generator had run out, making the pump stop.

"She's on the edge, Special Agent Dawson. It's risky to try to send someone down there to put fuel to the generator so we can pump out the water. We can't tow her if she's filled up with water. What the ensign saw was gruesome. Someone will have to board her and go down into the hold. They'll try not to damage any evidence~"

"I'm not sure anyone should go aboard," Erik cautioned. "If I'm right in my suspicions, that doctor played with some pretty powerful toxic substances.

⊰ ⊱

Jennifer tensed, eyes dilating with fear. She pressed a button and ran from the gallery through the back exit. Down the street and into a cute bistro, she slid into a booth and called Nick.

"Whoa, whoa, slow down. You alerted Steb and you're in a safe place?" Nick's voice always had a calming effect.

"I'm in a busy, public place! I'm still not certain it's safe! Nick, this was one of the really bad ones. Maybe you should let the police know, so they can back up Steb's people. Nick! I don't want anyone hurt because of me! Is this never going to end?"

"Okay, okay. Maybe not until we end it. I'm almost downtown. You got your gun, right? Don't be afraid to use it on him!"

Steb and his people didn't need any back up. They had the perpetrator cuffed and riding out of town in the back of Hanson's pickup before Jennifer's call to her husband ended.

⚖

David and Mallory met Frank Gilmore at a title company in Hot Springs! And the out-of-reach tract of land was theirs! "That was just the Lord! That was just the Lord! That was just the Lord!"

Mallory had made the same statement so many times leading up to, and since the completion of the closing, that David had finally teased her with one of her old expressions, "You're starting to sound like your needle's stuck in a groove."

Her eyes danced with excitement! "Yeah, but whoever heard of a seller carrying the financing for five years? He didn't even want the earnest money, so we can use that immediately to begin some improvements to the place! You're right. We need to level the old house, get a modular on site for Abe, and get him an ATV to use. Jeff really wants to keep Waylon for his assistant. What do you think about placing Luke here to help Abe?"

"M-m-m, I don't know. You have a spot for Luke, and I'm not sure he'd be a fit here. Let me give it some thought!" He kissed her lingeringly. "It's nice of you to offer, though."

Chapter 20: ADORATION

David ran interference to get Mallory up to their master suite past everyone who clamored for her attention. She was captivating! People were drawn to her. He was acutely aware that there hadn't been enough time to heal her heart about *Zakkar*. Perhaps they should have stayed in Dallas for the weekend, which he thought was incredibly boring. And there was much to do here. Still, he didn't want to be selfish and unheeding of her feelings. He brewed a cup of coffee, whitening and sweetening it the way she liked it.

"You mind if I make a few calls? I need to make sure Brad's got everything for the crews to get a lot done on those two houses while all the kids are home this weekend. Then, Damon told me Jason Johnson asked if we need to hire anyone else. Jason might be interested in the job with Abe; he doesn't like the retailing he's been doing. Maybe he'll like building fences and tending to cattle." He ripped open a package of cookies, biting one, and offering them to her. "Then, Sanders left me a message; I guess he has a couple of questions about his facility in Houston. He still really wants your gymnasium, you know?"

Her countenance hardened stubbornly. "I know. If it were for sale, it'd be listed. I bought it because I like it."

He laughed. "Yeah, but why do you like it so much? If you want a gymnasium, we could sell that one to Sanders and build one in Dallas. Or here! We don't have anyone in Houston to manage our property. And if you want to shoot hoops, how often will we be down there?"

Cool green eyes met his.

⊰ ⊱

Jurisdiction of the crime scene on the boat was up in the air. Dawson acquiesced to the Coast Guard, as they disengaged the Cutter, and a tug boat pulled her into dock at the base. Heeding Bransom's warnings, investigators in full protective gear began photographing and documenting everything. Seasoned coroners seemed dazed by the scope of the crimes.

"What did they need with old people?" one of them addressed Hillman.

She shook her head, battling her own emotions. "The alleged felon is a cosmetic surgeon. I think he was doing research with some of the poison substances, like making his own version of something like Botox. He commented to me something about fixing my labial folds for me. Maybe he used older people for guinea pigs to test his substances on. I'm only guessing.

"There was a refrigeration unit filled with units of blood. When power failed, it really spoiled. Why did he have units of blood?"

Erik joined them, exhausted. "Insurance in case the surgeries he performed went south, I'm guessing. Universal donors, type O. My guess is that he targeted his prey by blood type. The organs are more likely to match, and having the blood would be advantageous. I'm not sure there's been any 'research' such as this since Joseph Mengele. As a physician, he could access information like blood types. None of this gives us Probable Cause to get a search warrant for his house, because we haven't been able to get a definite link between him and the boat. He has to have a launch or tender to get back and forth, but we haven't been able to locate anything like that."

⚔ ⚔

Daniel felt like his week had been extremely productive! Convincing his dad to read the <u>One Minute Millionaire</u> had fired him up, too. *GeoHy* was strong and productive for a small corporation, but Daniel had been feeling like it was stuck, mired in three generations of tradition and satisfaction. 'Satisfaction' was good; 'contentment' sanctioned in the Bible-unless it amounted to doing less than your best. Then, it bordered on slothfulness.

Romans 12:11 Not slothful in business; fervent in spirit, serving the Lord;

So, he and his father had been busy; re-interviewing employees, reassigning, cleaning house and releasing 'dead wood'. A senior Geologist who was a great employee, had been promoted and was beginning a recruitment campaign at some local colleges and universities. *GeoHy* had been growing, but Daniel was certain it would have grown more with some carefully planned measures. Of course, he had excused himself since taking over guardianship of Mallory and being involved with her company. But that was the thing; he should have hired a comptroller, rather than trying to do it all himself. The money coming in from *DiaMo* and *DiaMal*, along with compensation from serving on various boards, had made him willing to coast with the family business. The same with his dad, who had their home paid for and a generous retirement coming in.

Arriving at the cabin late Friday afternoon, he felt like he had really earned the rural retreat.

"Okay, Honey, you just feed the baby. We'll unload stuff," he directed. Actually, with their cabin so complete and stocked, they needed to bring very little but themselves. Still, the vehicles always seemed to collect stuff and trash.

"What do you think about sandwiches and chips? We're a little late for 'chow' and Mardy's probably getting ready to clean up. Besides, it's fun to be with our family."

"Yeah, let's make sandwiches and do a picnic in the woods," Jeremiah suggested. "There's a stream that might be fun to fish. David keeps rods and reels ready over in the mud room of the bunkhouse."

All doused with insect repellent, they ate sandwiches and chips as purple filtered into the sky, the pines deepened, and night sounds rose.

"I didn't catch anything, "Jeremiah lamented. "I lost a couple of good lures. I don't even know what kind of fish there are, or what they bite on."

Daniel shrugged. "Don't look at me. I have no idea. It was still a good idea; a lot of fun!"

⚐ ⚑

Steb made sure his prisoner was secure within the town jail. "Looks like you've messed yourself up pretty good," he observed. "Nothing that scary has even happened to you-yet. I guess you're only brave bullying women and children. You aren't a match for men."

"I was outnumbered and overpowered, taken off-guard. You, old man, are going to regret having ever seen me!"

"Outnumbered and over-powered? Eh? Guess you don't like having the tables turned. You enjoy being on the bullying end? Why are you in Arizona? Kind of off the beaten track for you! You're usually New York City to Connecticut and back."

"I demand to be released. You should at least be decent enough to let me clean up."

"You made a big mistake, my friend, when you came here to hassle Jennifer! We plan to give you a taste of your own medicine."

"Jennifer? Who's Jennifer? Oh, do you mean Veevee? Why would I come harass her? What difference does it make? I know about you and your crazy web site! You're deluded if you think you can change things!"

Steb settled back in his chair, arms folded, eyes mere slits. "Not very clever are you? So, you do know Jennifer and that she lives near here and works at the gallery is Bisbee? And, you know I'm out to get criminals like you! And, here you are! Maybe I can't make a huge difference world-wide, but I can rearrange you!"

"Ansel, come here and help me, will ya?" he summoned one of his deputies. "Let's get our guest here over to the garage and hose him down!"

⇥ ⇤

Nick attempted to console a distraught Jennifer. "Okay, you're safe; you're safe," he soothed. "If it helps you feel better we can go to Tucson and check into a hotel until we find out what happens with this guy."

"Nick, I'm not safe! Your life is in danger, too. I shouldn't have married you! They're going to win!"

"No, they are not! Come on. Let's pray. Greater is He that is in you, than he that is in the world. Come on, say it with me! Let's sing it!" She was crying too hard to join in.

⇥ ⇤

Mallory sent a text to Diana. "Hey, I know it's getting late, but do y'all want to come over for dessert?"

264

Diana phoned her back immediately. "Yes, we'd love to. We love it that y'all fixed us up as neighbors out here. We don't want to be in your faces all the time."

"Yeah, we don't want to wear thin with you guys either. But the other night, we ate at Daisy Lodge, and they had this blackberry cobbler. It tasted so good that I ordered another one. Well, they were closing for the night and had just thrown out the rest! Since I was disappointed, David ordered this huge frozen one and baked it. It's enough for an army~"

"Enough said. We're at your door."

"What did you think about the drawings I did for your home expansion? Are you still thinking about moving instead?" David had wondered about it for weeks, and finally broached the subject over cobbler and coffee.

"No, we're refinancing, and it's a pain. I think they have everything they need and we're ready to close, and then, we have to hunt up something else. I think I'm pretty organized, and then~" He gestured despairingly, and they all laughed.

"The refinancing and adding on are good, though. We'll have more space, lower our interest rate, and even reduce our payment," Diana chimed in."

"We did have a question, though." Daniel hesitated. "The plans are amazing, but we wondered why you moved my office and Diana's design studio to the third story. It seems like it makes more sense to leave them where they are and add bedroom suites to the new floor."

"Well, yes, Sir." David gazed from Daniel to Diana and back. "And I can draw it that way. I was thinking in terms of emergency evacuation~"

Diana looked startled. The young architect seemed to have considered things they hadn't. A fire, and the kids up another flight of stairs? "And that's the reason you've used some of the square footage for another stairwell. You know, in all of our years living in our home, we've never talked about fire drills and getting out." Diana's tone revealed that she was shocked with herself at the safety oversight.

"Yes, and besides, you both need more space for the studio and offices," David agreed. "Also, we redid our sports room and took out that practically brand new black leather furniture. In your remodel, can you use it? Or, do you want it in your house here? I picked things out in a hurry. I can use the leather in the third cabin that's nearly finished. We can move things around."

Daniel laughed. "Hey, if it's up for dibs, I want it in my newly expanded office."

⚜ ⚜

"Nick, we can't go to Tucson! I have to paint! Let's go home!"

He put the truck in gear. "No, we can't. I'll get you some supplies. Come on; it isn't like you to give up."

⚜ ⚜

Erik spoke briefly with Suzanne. "I guess I'll be in the L.A. area a few days more. I sure miss you. Everything okay there?"

"Yes, fine. Is this any closer to wrapping up? It seems like it just gets deeper and more hopeless."

"Seems that way from my angle too! But the Lord promises to be on the side of the righteous. Make sure everyone keeps praying about it. Mention it Sunday in prayer request time. Okay, Dan Wells from the Phoenix office is on the horn. Love ya. Call if you need anything."

"Hey, Wells, what's goin' on in your corner of the world?"

Bransom banged his chair down onto all four legs, letting out a moan that made everyone in the office look up. "What? You're kidding! Okay, I'm on my way there!"

"Book me a flight to Phoenix as soon as I can fight my way through traffic to the airport!" He roared the order as he bolted for the door.

Fighting the freeways towards LAX, he placed a call. "Hanson, do you know anything about a Robert Saxon from New York City? His wife has reported him 'missing'. I guess he went to Risa Perkins' art gallery to shop for some of her work, and never came back."

"Well now, I've heard of Risa Perkins. What was that other name? I don't recall if I've ever heard it, or not."

"Okay, listen, Steb, so far you've been helpful. Don't cross over a line here, where I can't help you get back! Missy and Christine need you. So does your foundation! You'll have a hard time running it from jail. I'm on my way to Phoenix to spearhead the search for this guy"

"Yes, Sir, thank you, Agent. Who did you say went missing? Robert?"

"Saxon! He's a big East Coast money management guy."

266

"Well, I'll keep my eyes open. Why don't you join us for dinner when you get to the area?"

⊰ ⊱

Rhonna appeared at the ministry headquarters at ten fifty-five, relaxed and calm. David took charge of the gathering crowd. "Okay, let's just kind of jam a little to get warmed up. Rhonna, you brought the tracks back with you, didn't you?"

"What? Was I supposed–" She laughed. "Yeah! Here they are! Gotcha"!

"Funny!" He snatched the proffered stack, trying to act annoyed. "Okay, spectators, other side of the glass. Everyone auditioning to perform with this fine vocalist–"

The crowd divided up accordingly.

"Okay, Phil; am I ever glad you made it!" David was relieved beyond words to see Phil Perkins. "Okay, you're the engineer. Let's hit it!"

Phil started the background for *The Prayer*, astounded at the girl's voice, even in just the first few measures. He stopped things. "Okay, Daniel, why don't we add your violin in here live, you can ad lib it and make it sound even sweeter; right?"

The session went smoothly, for the most part with no stops or redos. Phil talked everyone through each piece prior to the actual recording. Alexandra, Mallory, and Diana formed a lady's trio to do some 'Oooh's and Aaah's for backup in *He*.

"That song's real pretty," Rhonna commented. "I never heard it before, but my mom said she used to hear it some and liked it."

The vocalists of the group filled in live with the chorus and orchestra backgrounds of *Climb Every Mountain* and *My Way*, and Cassandra accompanied *Wind Beneath My Wings* on her violin. For an assortment of amateurs, they produced an amazing product.

Diana snapped a picture of the girl's radiantly smiling face for the cover design.

"Should we get a group picture to put on the back?" Daniel's question.

No one answered him, and the only credits on the cover were the usual ones. This was about Rhonna Abbot.

267

꘎ ꘎

It took over an hour to reach the airport, but Bransom used the time as fruitfully as possible. At his instructions, agents in New York City and Greenwich, Connecticut seized all the electronic devices relating to John Saxon. Well, the Feds would need to know if the guy had received any threatening emails, or if some clues to his disappearance might appear in his data. Erik grinned. If his hopes panned out, they should get plenty of incriminating material.

In his moments before the plane's departure, he checked in with Wells. "I'm on my way. What have you turned up?"

"A scared girl and her husband! We have them in a safe house again, and she's frantic about painting some more. She's turned really fatalistic about this, and she wants to incriminate as many of the guilty as possible, before 'they get her'."

Dread clutched at Bransom. "Well, no one knows what these people are capable of more than she does. Double up their protection and let her paint!"

꘎ ꘎

Meanwhile, back at the Ranch, David went to work, insisting Mallory nap. She was keyed up about Rhonna's recording, her mind popping with ideas to promote and get it 'out there'. But exhaustion soon chased away excitement, and she dozed. Within forty-five minutes, she was awake and refreshed. She nibbled cookies with milk before going out to see what was happening.

Waylon sat in the deserted chow hall with a text book before him when she entered.

"Hi, Waylon, studying, I see," she greeted.

"He nodded, "Yeah trying. There's so much reading~"

She laughed easily. "Tell me about it!" When there was no laughing response, she sat down across from him. Of the new hires, he had been the poorest student. Maybe he wasn't ready to handle a full freshman class schedule.

"Why is reading a problem? Are you a slow reader? Or you have a hard time comprehending? Maybe there's a course of some kind."

"Look, Mallory, I really need a job. This job! really, a job that doesn't require me to do college work. I'm not smart enough-"

"Well, are you dyslexic? I mean you got through thirteen years of school. You must be fairly smart if you could fake past being a poor reader. You know what you might try? An iPad, that you can load your books onto and play audibly!"

He stared back at her in amazement. "Really"? He felt pretty overcome. When he had felt hopelessly stupid, and that there was no solution- "Yeah, it isn't that I don't want a college degree"-Vistas expanded before him.

"Do you know where David went?" She tried to sound more mildly curious than like a domineering wife.

"Yeah, he and Jeff rode up to the Gilmore place to look things over again."

She exited, fighting a wave of tears. This was the first time David had ridden *Cap'n* since *Zakkar* had been put down.

❧ ☙

Jennifer worked with pen and ink, not her usual medium; creating a *cartoon* genre, not her normal style. Finishing, she stood back. "Okay, can you email a picture of this to Agent Bransom?" she questioned.

Hands shaking, Nick captured it on his phone. It was gruesome and violent! Cruel! With the image on its way, she collapsed against him, sobbing.

He was able to give little comfort before she tore herself from his arms. "No! I must keep working! I must!" Still, further attempts served only to frustrate her.

❧ ☙

Mallory fought emotions as she made her way back toward the house. 'It was okay for David to ride; his going to the new property probably meant he was working. He was a hard and good worker. Without him, she would never have dreamed of taking on more ranch land.' She cut around the house to take advantage of more shade and stopped short with a cry!

'It couldn't be! Could it?' She tried to remember. Making her way onto the porch, she approached the illusion, afraid it might vanish. 'It was! It really was! Her old porch swing for as far back as she could remember!'

More tears! But they were of wonder and joy. 'How could David be so nice to her? So thoughtful'? She gave the swing a gentle shove, and it moved noiselessly on new chain. Her gaze traveled upward. It was bolted securely to the porch ceiling. She curled up on it, pushing it with one toe as her habit had been.

David hurried. He hadn't planned to be this long. He didn't want Mallory to worry about him, and he hated being apart from her. He ground gears and winced. Not much practice with standard transmissions. "I can do it, Abe," he grinned.

"I'm sure you'll do better wrangling her than I will this horse. I haven't ridden in a while."

David headed the dilapidated truck onto a county road while Jeff and Abe rode the horses back along the trail.

Mallory watched curiously as a beater of a truck made it through the gate and came toward her. It was David! "Afraid to come riding up on *Cap'n*?" she challenged.

He laughed. "Not too much! Did you get a nap?"

She nodded. "I did, for nearly an hour. Then, I went hunting you. Did you know Waylon can't read?"

He started to pull her close, then, remembered he was sweaty. "Well, I can't say I'm surprised. He's turning into a good worker, though. I see you found your swing."

"Yes! I love it. I'm surprised there was that much left of it, to refurbish."

"Well, you're right. There wasn't. The original hardware was all rusted. It's basically a copy. It's a little different; I couldn't find the exact hardware."

The bell rang, summoning campers for supper. "I'm starved," David announced. "Nita came to help Mardy with authentic Tex-Mex; homemade tortillas and everything I'm sorry I got so dirty; I just planned to look things over. I'm afraid there won't be any food left if I shower first."

Mallory laughed. "Well, let's go then. I'm starved, too!"

Rhonna's voice filled the chow hall as they dug into plates full of excellent and attractive fare. "That didn't take you long," Mallory commented on the musical background.

"Yeah, well people need to be aware," he answered. "It's on the answering machine here, and is background music while people hold. On Monday, I'll fix *DiaMo* the same way."

She laughed. "Knock yourself out, but at *DiaMo* we don't put people on 'hold'. Now, you can add it to the CD changer of background music in the two suites."

⊰ ⊱

Erik studied the image emailed from Nick. Although the image was small, he got the story. He phoned Hanson. "Okay, I'm here to join the search for this missing guy."

Steb's laugh was dry and mirthless. "Well, wonder of wonders! He showed up out here! They're not offering a reward for him, are they? Why don't you bring a friend or two out here for dinner, and you can take this sorry-well-you can take him off our hands?"

"Okay, Wells and another guy are meeting me at the airport. Take good care of him. You think he has a strong connection to our cases?"

"I'm pretty sure he's a ring leader. A real coward, though!"

"Okay, well, we're coming. Don't do anything-" Even as Erik finished the warning, he was aware of information coming in from the New York office. Some of John Saxon's files, barely encoded, were incriminating in the extreme. The money trail! And quite an extensive client list!

"Bingo! Now, those are some leads to follow up on!"

⊰ ⊱

David pulled a folding chair into his workshop for Mallory. "Okay, not the most comfortable," he fussed.

"I'm fine. Go ahead and start on your project you said you're excited about!"

He nodded. "Can I get you anything? Did your dinner settle okay?"

She laughed. "Yeah, great! I would have eaten another plate full, but it was gone. But, I'm not hungry, really!"

He lifted an old, worn out saddle onto his workbench and began saddle-soaping it. Grime came off, revealing lustrous leather grain. Still, Mallory was perplexed. The saddle was done for, with stuffings sticking out, and everything. Still, he worked meticulously, conditioning the aged skin; then polishing it to a shine. He shoved the stuffing material in and stapled the edges. Then, making a paper pattern of the circumference, he cut pieces from hand-tooled black leather to trim it. He cemented the trim

271

in place, doing the same with the leather coming loose from the horn. It looked cute, but Mallory questioned if it could handle any further wear and tear. He finished by cleaning and polishing the metal fittings and stirrups. He held it up, surveying it proudly. "Gilmore's place has junk everywhere. Some of it, he wants to keep warehousing; you know, with us keeping an eye on it. Other things, he just wanted hauled off; stuff that accumulated in the bed of that truck. But some of it is awesome!" He held the saddle against the logs above his workbench. "Whadaya think?"

She caught on, and her eyes danced. "No! Put it on the front of the house next to the front door! The porch will protect it from the weather! David! That's beautiful!"

⚜ ⚜

Erik checked his emails, startled by the small image from Nick's phone. "Can you transfer this to your laptop so we can see it better?" His question was to Dan Wells, who always had tech stuff with him. Wells whistled in amazement as the larger image produced greater detail. "Wow! That captures some drama! Looks like one of the leading roles is played by our man, John Saxon! He spooked Jennifer far more than any of the others have!"

Erik was driving, but he diverted his attention to the screen. "H-m-m, yes, and it looks like the man with his back turned, is our good doctor. Looks like his build and hair; ah and there's one of his hands with his big gold and diamond ring. How do you interpret the story?"

Wells was silent for several moments as he studied the cartoon. "Well, I wouldn't swear to it, but it looks like they have a girl who'd be real cute without her thick glasses. Saxon stomps the glasses. Uh, our plastic surgeon tries his luck as an eye surgeon, the girl loses her sight completely, and they kill her?"

Erik returned his attention to the highway. "Forward that to Hillman. See if she can find a record of that girl's disappearance. And her medical history with her vision! Also, have her start looking into lists of people who were awaiting organs, who withdrew their names before they found matches. I'm thinking that if they couldn't use this girl, after they blinded her, and they killed her—"

"That they would have harvested her organs"? The third agent sounded shocked.

272

"Anything that converts to money"! Bransom's tone was bitter. "Anything"!

⚔ ⚔

Mallory watched as David mounted his latest handiwork. He stood back, surveying it. "What do you think? Does it look like someone just stuck an old saddle on the front of their house?"

"No! I think it looks amazing! Like everyone would want one if they saw it! David, I'm serious, things like that and your horseshoe furniture and sculptures! Well, and the really cute sports memorabilia, too! As more campers stay on as employees, you should produce more and circulate a catalog."

"Come here, and let me show you some of this stuff before it gets completely dark."

She watched as he excitedly displayed pieces of junk to her: an old fishing creel that he planned to clean up and varnish, along with an aged fly rod, to adorn the cabin just being completed. Then, there was another saddle in bad shape. "Look, it was for a miniature pony. Isn't it cute? Only really small toddlers can ride them. Anyway, I thought it would be cute to incorporate into a rocking horse. Girls like rocking horses, too. At least, my sisters did. What do you think?"

She laughed. "I think you're brilliant! You are, however, reminding me a little of my dad!"

He laughed, too. "Oh, yeah, the inveterate junk collector. Speaking of, some of the stuff Gilmore has warehoused looks like some of the stuff your dad had around."

Mallory shrugged. "I guess it was all kind of up for grabs after I moved to Dallas. At least you discovered all the Diamonds. If he ended up with some of my dad's stuff, at least he has kind of the same appreciation. And he is financing the land. Jeff's home looks pretty good; don't you think?"

"Absolutely! You had a great idea about that. Let's go in so I can get a shower."

"Yeah, and find something to eat! I'm starved!"

Chapter 21: ACCELERATION

It was ten-thirty Saturday night when Daniel's phone vibrated, showing a number he wasn't familiar with. He answered as civilly as possible, although the late call was impolite. "Daniel Faulkner."

"Hello, Mr. Faulkner, let me start by apologizing for the late hour. This is William Pennington with Melton-Vanderhoff, Corporation. I hope this call finds you all well. Do you have a few moments?"

Daniel settled onto the sofa in the great room. "Yes, Sir, how can I help you?"

"Well, Herb Carlton brought your wife to our attention when he was crafting the jeweled bottle for her. And you're familiar with the campaign we're launching for the fragrance and refillable atomizers?"

"Right! Launching before the Holidays in ten different cities around the world! I remember." He was trying to be patient, not sure how this pertained to him.

Pennington continued. "I'm coming to my point, and I'm not really sure why we contacted you rather than your wife. We were doing more brain-storming today and refining of the launch and all the preliminary marketing. And we all agreed, we could use a spokesperson for the fragrance."

"And you thought Diana might be interested. Is it okay if we talk about it? She'll be in touch as quickly as possible, whatever we decide. We know you have a deadline. Thanks for your call."

Daniel sat quietly, gazing admiringly around him at the richness of the logs with stars sparkling beyond. That was scary. 'Diana with a modeling job? Oh, no: spokesperson job!' His temptation was not to tell her about the opportunity. Just call Pennington back with a 'we're not interested'.

"Lord," he whispered. "My wife is beautiful. Thank you for her, and thank You that you gave her such perfect physical attributes. You know, she has always tried to use her gifts and talents for You. Is this a door opened by You? That we should walk through? Have You given her favor with these corporate people, or is it some evil snare of the devil to derail her and hurt our family?"

She appeared at the railing of the loft opposite him. "Hey, I thought you were right behind me. Are you coming to bed?"

He laughed. "Yep; got a phone call"! He made his way up the stairs. "Let's go out and star-gaze; want to?"

"I guess, if you do. Who called so late? Is everything okay?" She followed as he pulled the telescope onto the balcony.

"It was William Pennington; remember him? They were working on the marketing and launch of the fragrance and bottles, and they started talking about the possibility of your being their spokesperson."

"H-m-m, I wonder if they asked Mallory and she turned them down."

"Honey, why would you wonder that? Do you not know how beautiful you are? You are a lovely, lovely woman who wears their fragrance. Your beauty and honesty together, well-I guess they can tell you'll make sales."

"Well, what do you think?"

"Well, I don't know. I mean, I don't want you to do it. But I know that's just selfish of me. I don't want anything to upset the status quo. I love us, and I'm scared of any change that could skew us. But, it could be something beautiful. I don't want my petty and groundless fears to hold you back from being all you can be. Does that make sense?"

"But you don't really want me to pursue it?" Her countenance was aglow at the invitation.

He took her hand, bowing his head. "Lord, we know this hasn't taken You by surprise. We don't want to jeopardize our family or our testimony for You. But, if this is something we can use to glorify you-We're confused."

He raised his eyes to meet hers. "I know. Let's do it this way. Call him back. If he answers, we'll take that as a sign to move forward with this. If he's turned his phone off, or he's on another call, if he doesn't answer, we'll forget about it."

She nodded agreement, pressing the redial key on his phone.

Pennington connected on the first ring. "Hello, Mr. Faulkner. Thank you for calling back! I hope you're going to accept."

"Hello, Mr. Pennington. Diana Faulkner. We admit that we're intrigued. Can you add any details? We're leaving for Spain next week, and we'll be gone for twelve days-"

"Oh-oh! When do you depart next week?"

"Thursday"!

"Okay, although it's late, I can shoot you a preliminary contract. If you like it, we can send our corporate jet for you tomorrow. We can shoot quite a bit of footage before you leave. I'm sorry our deadline's tight and this is sudden."

"We can't come tomorrow. We have church commitments." Diana's voice was firm. If this prospect wasn't the Lord's will, this should be the acid test."

"Okay, then, early Monday? We'll make arrangements at the Waldorf. I know it makes it tight for departure for your previously planned trip. It's just, our clock's ticking toward this deadline. How many will be in your party?"

"Ten." Diana's voice was sweet. "There are eight family members, and we'll have two people from our own security. We actually depart for Madrid from JFK, so it won't be necessary for you to arrange our return to Tulsa. Will that be acceptable with you? We'll plan that way, pending the terms of the contract."

⇥ ⇤

Erik and other agents took Saxon into custody without staying for dinner with the Hansons.

Their prisoner was livid, making threats against Steb and his personal, vigilante police force.

"Actually, they're a real police department of an incorporated town. Hanson said you were properly Mirandized." Bransom was hoping the sketchy arrest wouldn't get his case thrown out.

"They threw me in the back of a personal vehicle, a pickup truck, and slung me around for a wild and terrifying ride. I'm bruised everywhere."

"Yeah? Well, they don't have money yet for a fleet of official cars. I'm sure you've been inconsiderate of a few prisoners, yourself." He produced Jennifer's cartoon. "Why'd you stomp on this poor little gal's glasses?"

"Where are my attorneys?"

Bransom leered. "Oh, I'm sure they'll be here eventually. Do your attorneys represent your son? Or does he retain his own counsel?"

Saxon seemed to blanch. "My son? Are you trying to pin something on him, too?"

"Pffft, No! I guess maybe you involved him! I don't 'pin' stuff on people. You or Dietrich, or someone had him watching Jennifer and Mallory out on the desert one day. He left his trash out there. A plastic water bottle yielded his DNA. If we can't link him to attempted murder, maybe we can slap a bunch of fines on him for littering. You know, Al Capone never got convicted of racketeering but only income tax evasion." He smirked. "You and your son filing your taxes correctly? Speaking of~"

⇥ ⇤

Daniel whistled in amazement. The remuneration article of the contract sounded good! Very good! Diana was concerned about some of the hazy details. The Corporation reserved the right to choose what she would wear in the photo shoots.

"If I can't wear my own designs and our jewelry, I'm going to back out," she fretted.

Daniel laughed. "Well, if they're smart, they'll allow you to wear your designs, because you'll give the campaign a classy look that way. But let's not be extreme. As long as they want you to wear~you know~something decent, that again, presents a good testimony~"

She nodded at his wise voice of reason. Still, she hoped she could wear her own and Herb's products.

⇥ ⇤

Tammi Anderson became Mrs. Kerry Larson in a ceremony that was sweet and moving. Taking place at Calvary, officiated by Pastor Ellis and John Anderson, Mallory and David both performed their parts, with no acrimony toward the couple who had refused to attend their nuptials. At the end of September David turned twenty-two, and he and Mallory celebrated quietly together.

⇥ ⇤

"I can't believe how the summer flew by." Mallory snuggled in front of the fireplace in the master suite at the Ranch. "We've been married four months already. I'm excited about our trip! I know I'll miss Daniel and Diana, but I'm glad Nick and Jennifer are coming. Diana said the crews are making fast progress on their addition."

David nodded. "Yeah, I'm sure they're in a mess. Adding on overhead is different from having it all going on at one end. They're basically living crowded together on the first floor." He laughed. "'Crowded together', being a a relative term."

⚔ ⚔

Lilly beamed. Concert one on her agenda was a success! She returned home to Israel with satisfaction and extra cash. In three weeks, they would travel to Tokyo, where the audience would be tougher. She sighed. It was lonely, being with Cassandra and her family, and then leaving them behind, again. Well, at least now, she could look to her Messiah for solace.

⚔ ⚔

Erik and Dawson ate breakfast at a downtown hotel in D.C. "Well, we have a ton of evidence, and more and more people are being implicated. At least people finally wised up about going down to hassle Jennifer. We haven't had any complaints since Saxon was arrested."

Erik perched his knife on the edge of the plate. "Okay, but tell Wells not to get complacent. I'm like you; I couldn't believe the different guys were careless enough to keep showing up. But just because Nick and Jennifer aren't aware of being watched-"

"What? You think they're still on the radar?"

Bransom's features were a study in anguish. "I'm positive! These masterminds had no idea Jennifer was so smart and that she was gathering so much information! I know the DA says he's positive that Jennifer won't be forced to take the witness stand! I'm not that convinced. Defense attorneys can cast doubt on the paintings; even stating we had them done, after the fact, after these people were arrested. Of course, they'll do every mean trick there is to discredit her as a witness. That is-if she agrees to testify and lives to try it!"

※ ※

Mallory skyped with Callie, "I can't believe how fast she's growing," Mallory commented about Victoria, who was all dimples and smiles. "I wish you could come home and show her off in person. When does it look like you can get away?"

Callie listed off a long agenda of projects and events that were coming together. "You just can't imagine how happy and fulfilled I am! My life was so pointless! I thought there was absolutely no rationale for my existence! I do wish we could get together, but I wouldn't trade what I have for anything! I hear you and David are quite a team, and you're tearing it up!"

Mallory laughed. "Well, I don't know about that, but we keep busy. We're actually getting away for ten days. David's taking me to Yosemite. He knows I've always wanted to go there. Seeing Half Dome and El Capitan intrigued me before I even decided to become a Geologist. The only people going with us are Nick and Jennifer. Which, my relationship with Jennifer was strange~even before the weirdness with Cy. Nick's fun"!

Callie shook her head, mystified. "So, why don't you and David go; just the two of you"?

"See, I shouldn't have said anything. Anyway, David and I will have lots of private time together. We're staying at the historic lodge in the Park. Ah-wan-hee! I'll let you go, but promise you'll stay safe."

Callie laughed. "Well, we always try to be careful, but truthfully, the US seems more dangerous than here."

"Yeah, how weird is that? Give Snookums a sugar from Aunt Mallory and tell Parker to contact his big sister. Later!"

※ ※

David and Mallory loved the vacation. Lisette was so capable that they were able to enjoy being away. The new employees were hitting stride, Rhonna's recording was selling, and things were over-all going in positive directions.

"Let's go see the giant redwoods while we're this close," David suggested as they ate breakfast. "You know, the forty-niners didn't mine all the gold."

His mischievous comment was toward Mallory, who basically missed his point.

"Well, maybe not, but they get paid plenty! All the professional guys do!"

David laughed. "Uh, I wasn't referring to the football team."

She frowned. "Well there isn't a baseball team named that; or hockey?"

"Right, I was teasing my fortune-hunting bride that there's real gold left by the miners, who were called 'forty-niners', because the gold rush here in California took place in 1849."

Nick laughed. "See, Anderson, when you have to explain your jokes, they weren't that good in the first place."

"Well, he's right; it would be fun to go try panning." Mallory's eyes shone. "Of course, when there's gold in the streams, it's eroded out of a vein higher up. I love the verses:

Psalm 121:1&2 I will lift up mine eyes unto the hills, from whence cometh my help.

My help cometh from the Lord, which made heaven and earth.

I know the primary meaning is to look up, beyond the hills to God, for His help. And I know the high elevations were strategic military advantages. But, I don't think it does the passage a disservice to suggest it means for natural resources. God made heaven and earth, and he chocked them full of valuable mineral deposits. As rocks erode, the valuable substances get carried down by streams, giving us alluvial deposits."

They laughed at her earnestness, but she continued, warming to her subject. And look at:

Genesis 49:25&26 Even by the God of thy father, who shall help thee; and by the Almighty, who shall bless thee with the blessings of heaven above, blessings of the deep that lieth under, blessings of the breast, and of the womb:

The blessings of thy father have prevailed above the blessings of my progenitors unto the utmost bound of the everlasting hills: they shall

*be on the head of Joseph, and on the crown of the head of him who
was separate from his brethren.*

The utmost bounds of the everlasting hills produced Gold for Joseph's
crown, and gemstones to adorn it. *Blessings of the deep that lie under* refer to
wealth hidden deep within the earth's crust and on the sea floor."

"If you wondered why she chose Geology-" David swept dramatically
with one hand. "Of course, she cares about the wealth, but more than that,
it's the excitement of discovery. That's cool how you made the connection
of those two passages about the hills."

Mallory smiled at Nick and Jennifer. "Gold is every place in Arizona,
too. If I lived there, I'd be out every day with a metal detector."

Nick shrugged. "Yeah, I saw the program about that. Of course, that
guy could do that because he had a camera crew and a bunch of people he
was teaching and stuff. But people are always out to get Jennifer anyway.
I'd be worried out prospecting by myself, that someone would kill me for
my metal detector, whether I'd found gold or not."

She shrugged. "I'd tote my gun."

They all gave her strange looks. "Yeah, I know. It isn't that simple."

⚐ ⚑

David placed the finishing touches on a project. He thought it looked
kinda cool. With the remodel finished for the girls and the one for the
guys nearly completed, he was solving a final issue. The house had been
divided up kind of strangely, so they had removed several walls to open up
the space and allow light in. It was drastically better, but then he decided
a screen would make a nice divider between spaces, providing privacy and
a design feature.

He surveyed his handiwork. Screen print on burlap of a photo he had
shot down the center of the stable. Hazy stalls on either side muted grays
and browns; a guy thing! He cemented leather trim around the edges
and left a pair of reins hanging down on one edge. Rustic, western! Why
not?

"You made that?"

The suddenness of the voice, when he thought he was alone, made
him jump.

"Dad! What are you doing here? Oh, Yeah; I was just finishing up and admiring my handiwork." His gaze traveled to the entry of the shop. "Hi Mom! I was just getting ready to go inside. My project's done, and it's gotten really cold." He led his parents to the golf cart. "Y'all follow me." He jogged briskly toward the house.

"Y'all have a seat. I'll find Mallory." He didn't have to find her; she appeared, amazed by the arrival of guests.

"Would you all care for coffee? This is a treat!" She pushed a button to brew a cup. She loved her pastor and wife, but it was pretty different calling them mom and dad.

"I'll have coffee, if it isn't too much trouble." John Anderson was amazed at the warmth and atmosphere of the beautiful space. "If not for Jeff, we wouldn't have a clue what happens up here."

"Well, then; good for Jeff." David tried not to be annoyed by everything his dad said, but he had begged his dad for five years, to come up and check on the progress going on here~to be answered by excuse after excuse. Maybe he had stopped inviting them; why did they need an invitation, anyway?

"Well, we're glad you're here." Mallory laughed. "We're glad we're here. We've been so busy that we haven't had a chance to get here, ourselves. I'm sure you know we've been between Houston, Tulsa, and Dallas, overseeing David's different construction/remodeling jobs. And we went to California for a few days of vacation. You guys need to see Yosemite. We took a ton of pictures, but El Capitan on a four by six picture isn't the same. And the General Sherman tree, you can't even get in a picture; it's so tall. Then we went to Toronto for Cassandra's first concert on her tour, and we've performed a couple of weekends at new churches."

David watched as Mallory visited sweetly. After five months of marriage, he loved her more hopelessly than ever. "'Tis true we've been busier than a one-armed paper hanger, but we've gotten things in place so we can get here easier every week-end, or at least nearly that often. I'm glad you came up; what do you think of everything?" As soon as he asked, he was sorry. His dad couldn't just compliment him, and say, 'Amazing job! We're proud of you!' It had to be, "Couldn't you have tried harder to make the camp happen?" And, "Pastor Wilcox and other area preachers still don't understand why you didn't build a Bible Camp like Patrick stipulated."

"Let's go to the chow hall for lunch," Mallory intervened smoothly. "Nebraska's playing in just a bit." She knew her Pastor's passion for college football, and Nebraska was his alma mater.

"Well, if we're not imposing—"

"Mom, you're not. I've begged y'all to come up here. We usually eat over there unless we go out."

Tuna sandwiches and chips were the fare, followed by small containers of pudding. They all ate hungrily as the conversation grew less strained.

"Well, look who wandered in." Jeff's response to his parents' visit matched that of his older brother. "Have y'all toured the whole place? Give me a chance to eat, and I'll drive you around."

Waylon joined them. "Hello, Pastor and Mrs. Anderson; it's nice to see you."

"Good to see you, too, Waylon." The Andersons had worked hard in their small community. The cyber-ministry continued to grow, but local people were hard to reach, so they were extremely proud of this convert. "You seem to be a quick learner, really growing in grace."

Mayer chuckled. "I can't say I've heard that very often. Ask Mr. Haynes. I was pretty much the class dunce. Well, I guess not really, but we all thought I was. I had a hard time reading. I just got more and more behind; which, I guess, being so discouraged about academics made me act up, get in more trouble, and do worse. I was really shocked when David and Mallory hired me, and more surprised when they kept me on. Well, they expected me to do college courses when I barely made it through high school. Well, when Mallory realized I can't read, instead of making fun of me, or telling me to 'hit the road', she just told me to start using an iPad playing audibly." His voice filled with emotion. "Now, I listen to it constantly, trying to catch up! I have the Bible and several commentaries loaded, as well as my college texts and reading for enjoyment."

The pastor laughed. "No kidding! You know, I make all kinds of excuses for not reading and studying more than I do. It's amazing to think how much I can still learn, if I'll be that smart about wanting to and making it happen. The Proverbs speak, through all thirty-one chapters, about gaining more and more wisdom and knowledge."

Following the lunch, Jeff took his parents on the tour. David went to work on the nursery talking shape next to the master suite, and Mallory spent a couple of hours talking to Diana's dad about the logistics of the Patrick O'Shaughnessy Foundation starting up operations in yet another third-world country. Permits and visas were coming together, but Mr. Prescott worried about the staff's being spread too thin. "We need more laborers in the harvest," he commented.

"Yes, Sir, we do. But if the Lord's opened this door so miraculously, He can staff it, too. We just need to ask Him to do it." She breathed a quick prayer.

She was aware of Pastor's being back because she could hear him and David cheering raucously as Nebraska dominated. She loved sports, but she decided to phone Diana rather than joining them. "Hi, I'm disappointed you aren't coming this week end," she opened.

"Well, no more than I am," Diana's rueful laugh. "I'm nursing a houseful of sickies. I don't want you to get this nasty cold. It's bad enough when you can take all the OTC meds, but when you're pregnant, and can't take much~. And Cassandra hasn't gotten it yet. Now I'm worried she'll get it just in time for the concert in Prague."

"Oooh, there's a prayer request! 'Lord, please don't let Cassandra get sick, especially during the concert weeks'. Have you gotten any updates on how our silk print is progressing?"

"It's stunning! I'm not sure why they sent it here. Do you want me to ship it on to you there? Hopefully we can make it there next weekend."

Mallory was disappointed. "Next weekend's fine. It does look good, though?"

"Yeah, you're a genius! This baby's gonna have the cutest room in history!"

Mallory was silent.

"Are you okay?" Diana queried.

Mallory laughed. "I am! I want her to have the cutest room in history! But, I don't want to spoil her! You know, I actually believed that because my dad never gave me much materially, that I wasn't spoiled."

"M-m-m, stick with that thought! He really invested himself into you, but you had him wrapped around your little finger."

"Yeah, I did."

Just as she disconnected, her phone rang again. "Caramel! Hey, what's up with you? I've tried to catch you a few times~"

"I know, and I'm sorry Mallory! I think I'll get a chance to at least return your calls, but my life as an intern is frenetic. I'm callin' you about this guy~

"Ooooh"! Mallory giggled excitedly. "And does this 'guy' have a name? Is he cute? Not that looks are everything, but they don't hurt, either!"

"Calm down! Calm~this isn't a romantic thing! Just friends"!

"Right"! Mallory sounded unconvinced. "Okay, so why are you calling me about him?"

"Well, this is probably way out of line~tell me if I am. But, Amon Williamson's his name; he just finished his residency. He has these debts~and with all this Federal insurance mess~he can't decide what to do."

Mallory was processing. Caramel wasn't asking her for money, because she had plenty.

"Well, what? Are you wanting me to hire a doctor? It just so happens that we're expanding into another African nation, but~"

"Would you consider him?" Caramel's words were eager.

Mallory laughed. "Okay, hold on. We were just praying for laborers into the harvest. But would this guy, Amon, you said? be interested in this rough form of practicing medicine?"

"Yeah, he's a major Christian! He's all familiar with the Foundation~Well, I follow everything, and I've bragged on it a lot."

"Wow! That was the sound of my jaw dropping! I don't know why I still get so amazed when God answers my prayers, but~have him send me his information. Love you; it's great to hear your voice. Hey, Erik told me that college rep's out of jail already. At least he's a registered offender now."

"Hopefully that'll make a difference. I'm glad now, the Lord worked things out for me differently. Thanks, Mallory."

"Yeah, thank you. Take care."

⚔ ⚔

David sat on the porch in a weak circle of sunlight. The wind was calm and a fire in the Chiminea lent warmth. He sipped coffee as he idly checked his phone for messages and emails. Scary; his dad and mom were already nervous about Tammi and Kerry's relationship. He sighed. Why would his dad think he could help? Why should it be his job? He was relieved when Mallory joined him. He stood, smiling. "Ready? You look gorgeous!"

"Thank you. Diana's steady supply of cute outfits helps immeasurably. I'm hungry. Since the weather warmed up some, I hope I don't cook in this."

He took her elbow to guide her down the steps. "Yeah, that place can be like a sauna. My dad runs the heat up to blistering when the weather's cold. And then, when we exert ourselves with the action songs for the kids-"

Mallory laughed. "My dad used to say he turned the heat extra-hot every time he preached about 'Hell'."

David's laugh, "Yeah, and since he always preaches on that, it's always way too hot in there. He always got mad at me for not wanting to wear a suit and tie-Oh well. We're supposed to start being better friends to Kerry and Tammi."

Her serious gaze met his. "Okay, well, let's invite them here next weekend."

He shook his head wonderingly. She was such a trooper. If his dad thought she should climb Everest, she'd have it done within the week.

A quick buzz up the blacktop brought them to the chow hall. Breakfast would be juice, cereal, and toast, so the kitchen crew could get ready for church, too.

Chapter 22: ABDUCTION

Special Agent Caroline Hillman didn't like what she was hearing! A wealthy Dallas socialite whose child had been snatched! Local police had contacted the FBI, and the Feds were in initial stages of the search and investigation. The beautiful Cynthia Diane Hicks-Livingston, overwrought, was in a tirade about her ex-husband. From a large family and with scores of loyal employees across the US, he could easily be behind the kidnapping. Hillman didn't think so, but the woman's statements would force them to investigate every angle of her allegations.

"Okay, please, Ms. Livingston~"

"I go by Hicks!" With plenty of abusive language about her ex, Delane Lee Livingston, "He swore he'd get even with me!"

As assertive as Agent Hillman tried to be, she couldn't take charge as readily as she would have liked. "Okay, Ms. Hicks, we understand your concern~"

"You do? Do you have children, agent? And an ex-husband with means and motive to make your life a living~"

Hillman didn't answer the question. She didn't need an argument. "Okay, may I call you, Cynthia? The agents will take your statement about all the people you think might possibly be involved. My concern is, that, if your husband isn't behind the disappearance~"

"My EX-husband! What are you? Deaf? My ex-husband has my daughter, and you think I don't know what I'm talking about!" More abusive language!

"Okay, but what about your son? Delane is his father, too; right?"

"What? You think I sleep around? Yeah! He's Devon's father, too! What's your point?"

"Okay, Cynthia, my point is, that if their father was behind this, and he's as capable of an abduction as you think him~"

"I KNOW him to be capable of this!"

"Yes, Ma'am; so then why would he not grab both of his children?"

Tear-reddened eyes shot sparks! "I don't know! When you catch him, maybe you can ask him!"

⇥ ⇤

Erik worked the altar at Faith as three men from the camp expressed their need of the Savior. It still amazed him, with his background in law enforcement, that some of these guys were actually kicking free, overcoming odds and obstacles, to become hard workers and functioning members of society. Not reformed by any program of man; but transformed by the regenerating power of Jesus! It was surprising to him that so many local people still lamented the Bible Camp for kids. Obviously, God had overridden Patrick's plan, to institute a better plan of His own!

"Do you kids have time for lunch?" He caught David and Mallory as they exited the church, figuring they would be in their usual rush to get to Dallas in time for the evening service at Calvary. To his amazement, they accepted! Just as his phone rang, summoning him to the abduction case.

He laughed bitterly. "Just when you two are free, duty calls me. I better get on the road. It'll take me four hours to get on scene."

"No, eat at Hal's with us," Mallory insisted, "and join us for the chopper ride to Dallas. You can eat, and still get there sooner. Whatever we do, let's hurry. My cereal wore off more than an hour ago."

⇥ ⇤

Nick watched as Jennifer glued herself to the TV screen, taking in every detail of the new 'Amber Alert'. Her features were a study in anguish. Danay Hicks-Livingston, aged six, missing; probably in a custody dispute!

"Call Agent Hillman, and tell her the father isn't responsible! They're wasting time! She's probably already in Canada!"

"Canada? Dallas is closer to the Mexican border." Nick was amazed that there might be a different angle. Shaken, he phoned Bransom. Jennifer was usually aloof and far removed from this type of drama. He couldn't guess why this so resonated with her. Usually her nerve endings seemed numb. Could it be that life was returning? And with it, maybe too much pathos?

Bransom answered immediately. "Yeah, Nick, what's up? You guys okay?"

"Yeah, we're fine. But, this kidnapping in the Dallas area-it has Jennifer shaken up! She thinks you guys are wasting time considering the custody thing and a parental kidnapping. She mentioned that whoever snatched the little girl might already have gotten her to Canada."

"Canada?" Bransom's reaction mirrored Nick's. "Will she talk to me?"

"No, she doesn't want to." Nick was perplexed as his wife backed fearfully away at the suggestion she talk to Bransom directly.

"Okay, well, maybe you should encourage her to paint something. Call me immediately if she says anything else." He disconnected and made a call, placing agents on alert to check all flights, commercial or private, destined for anywhere near either US Border. With the heat turned up at the Mexican border, the northern boundary was more porous! Of course!

Mallory phoned Steb Hanson. "Hey, I'm sure you're aware of this new 'Amber Alert'. Jennifer's really shaken by it; has Missy seen it? I'm sure you already have, but if not, can you put it on the *SOC* web site for people to pray for her safe return? Jennifer thinks the kidnappers might take her to Canada."

"M-m-m, yeah, initially maybe, and then to Europe? Maybe on a Canadian passport? They may try to pass her off as a boy, since everyone's on the look-out for a little girl. I'll get on it, and on the prayer request part, too."

Bransom sighed. Maybe there needed to be more vigilante-types beating the bushes for the missing child! He wasn't sure! He issued orders to re-interview all of their suspects who had been arrested in connection with the human trafficking. There was quite a list.

⊰ ⊱

David and Mallory smiled greetings to several of their employees as they slid into a pew a few minutes before the service. Bryce was there; which was a good thing. If he was growing in grace, it was a jerky ride, and 'for better or for worse', Lisette was in the journey with him.

"You look so cute," Lisette whispered. "You give the maternity-look a lot of class."

"Thanks. Well, having six kids, Diana has experience in this department. She always looked amazing! I think I'm gonna be bigger than a house! And now, I'm starving all the time!"

Lisette tried not to be envious of her friend and employer. She assumed she herself, would never be able to have children; what kind of dad would Bryce make, anyway? She joined the congregational singing, trying to redirect her thoughts.

᳇ ᳅

Erik continued working the Danay Marie Hicks-Livingston case, handling the media and overseeing the agents who were interviewing possible witnesses and working the 'crime scene'. Not much to it, which was another reason to assume the abduction was smooth and professional. Delane Livingston seemed as overwrought as his ex-wife, accusing her of negligence. Their hatred of one another seemed genuine. It was hard to believe the couple could have at one time been in love. The phone lines rang with tips from well-meaning people to pranksters. When an unknown number called his cell, he answered. To his amazement, it was a research department at a well-known university making a bizarre request. Bransom didn't have time to deal with it at the moment, but it was so strange he wasn't sure he understood.

"I'm pretty sure Treasury won't be auctioning that off any time soon. For one thing, it's evidence against the doctor, to help convict him of criminal mal-practice, murder, and whatever else. I'm not sure it should ever be available to the public. I'm very busy right now~"

"But his findings are so valuable. For all that research and learning to be wasted, would be even more criminal~"

"You know, it would be hard to find anything 'more criminal' than his crazy, deluded experiments! He'll never publish either, because laws have been passed to prevent crazy inmates from making money on their activities!" He hung up as the professor argued in favor of 'gleaning valuable information'.

᳇ ᳅

An army of senior citizens manned their battle stations. Maybe they weren't the best eyes and ears~with bifocals and a few hearing aids~but they were mighty in numbers and determination. They turned out to work surveillance in communities across the nation. Gas stations, airports, bus and train terminals! They were armed with pictures of Danay and reproductions of Jennifer's paintings, which were incriminating many members of the kidnapping ring. They just might help rescue a little girl, and what else did they have going on? Steb had suggested that people on the coasts keep an eye on tenders making runs to yachts anchored off-shore. As an afterthought, he contacted a company manufacturing submarines for private use, posing as an interested buyer. And while his contacts spread out to keep watch, many of them prayed.

⚔ ⚔

Sonia Morrison listened to updates as she returned home following the evening service. She was curious about whether it was a custody dispute, or something more sinister; not that children didn't stand to be harmed, either way. The little girl was beautiful. She returned her attention to matters at hand. Several people were coming over; most of the preparation had been completed earlier. Michael and Megan helped her with a few last minute things as the caterer arrived. Food was spread attractively by the time the guests trooped in. With the larger home, there was really space for entertaining. Trent was more relaxed about everything, too. It was just fun; they were making new friends, and hopefully selling Mallory's products. Even more important, and something they were totally unaware of, they were extending their influence; a sweet grass-roots-values-influence that the DC area needed desperately!

⚔ ⚔

"What's that? Arizona plates? The kidnapping took place in Texas! Estelle Norman lowered high-powered binoculars to address her husband, Jack."

He nodded acknowledgement and eased his Jetta into traffic a car or two back. "That may be a rental car. Think about it. Rent it; return it; they clean it up real good. There are records of who rented and when, but fake documents~. I'm calling Hansen. You call 911."

Jack was still talking to Hansen, who was interested in his information, when Stell disconnected from the dispatcher. "He patched me through, to the sheriff, who was very condescending. He claimed for a fact, that the dad's family is behind it. How can he know that for sure? From clear up here"?

"Listen, my wife just spoke with our local sheriff. You think there's a chance he could be in on it? I haven't ever liked him much."

Steb was alarmed. "Well, that's a scary thought. Listen, you guys watch yourselves. If you question his integrity, don't be in contact with him or his department again. I'll alert the Feds."

⊰ ⊱

"Are you okay?" David was watching the Sports on the big screen in the master suite. Usually, Mallory was more into all the scores and rankings than he was.

"I'm fine! I just get a little nervous about stuff." Usually chipper and upbeat, this was an unusual admission for her."

He beckoned her down beside him. "Oh yeah? What kind of stuff?"

She sighed. "I'm sure it's silly. It's all still a ways off, anyway."

He wasn't sure whether to press her, so he didn't. Wrong decision! She burst into tears!

She was worried about the baby, and about labor and delivery, and whether they could be good parents and not raise heathens! Not sure of what else to do, he held her. At last, he turned her toward him and met her gaze. "Me thinks thou art trying to swallow the steak whole! Remember thine own illustrious illustration?"

She giggled through tears. "I know, but it does all weigh on me."

He nodded. "Yeah, believe me, I understand! We have plenty of responsibility, and we ain't seen nothin' yet! But we can do it; we have all the guidelines in the Bible that the majority of the world doesn't have a clue about. We'll do okay. We'll work at it together, and pray about everything. Come on; you're tired." He knew it was still hard on her about *Zakkar*, although she seldom mentioned it.

⊰ ⊱

Each suspect the FBI interviewed passed the initial test! All of the relatives and employees loved lively little Danay, and they all asserted the same thing. Delane was as happy as he could be under the circumstances, with the custody and visitation arranged by the court. He wasn't one to break laws and risk losing everything he had! They all insisted that the authorities should get busy and find the real culprits before it was too late.

⊰ ⊱

Erik was awake early, his head throbbing. He felt like he hadn't slept, yet he had managed to miss an email from Nick. He opened it, and to his surprise, the style of Jennifer's artwork was different again. He stared at it blankly. It was a pretty enough scene. Rocks, mountains, forests, and a lake; with a somewhat ramshackle, half-timbered lodge or resort! It kind of looked like any 'starving artists' landscape'. If it had significance, it was lost on him! He poured a cup of coffee. Did the serenity mean he should chill? Not with a little girl missing! He couldn't! And Jennifer wouldn't want him to! He forwarded it to Hillman, and then to Steb. 'I wish Jennifer would just talk,' he mumbled to himself as he finished dressing and made his way from the hotel room. He stopped himself. She was! This was her way of communicating! Actually, quite effective! She had helped him put figurative nooses around quite a few necks.

⊰ ⊱

Steb opened the image from Bransom, who was evidently awake. He called the agent as he sent Jennifer's picture to his computer and enlarged it on his monitor.

"This is Bransom! Did the picture mean anything to you?"

"Nah, is it supposed to? Listen, I got a call from a couple in Vermont late last night. They thought they were watching something suspicious with the Danay Livingston case. When they contacted their local sheriff, he kind of made fun of them, insisting they should go home and forget about it. And claiming decisively that it was a family feud! Why wouldn't he at least look into their allegations? There's a reward up."

Bransom idly wondered the same thing. Except he knew by experience that there wasn't anyone alive any more stubborn than a lawman with his mind made up! He made note of the county and the names of the couple.

293

But it was strange; when he tried to phone them to get more details, neither cell phone was turned on!

⧉ ⧉

Steb and Christine moved about, doing their normal Monday morning routine. Steb met with his ranch foreman, outlining weekly priorities while Christine gave orders for some closet and storage chores and met with the staff that would be in charge of the *SOC Foundation* for the remainder of the week.

Coming inside for his mid-morning cup of coffee, Steb was met with a series of piercing screams from the direction of his office! He thought it was Missy, and he felt like he was plowing through wet cement trying to get to her.

Likewise, Christine, digging out an upstairs storage area, couldn't imagine what was going on.

Steb reached his overwrought daughter a few steps ahead of his wife. "Missy! Missy, Honey, what is it?"

"No! NO!" Her voice was a nerve-jangling screech. "No! You can't make me! You-can't! No! No! Nooooo! Oh, oh, please, no! I'll do anything-"

Cornered behind Steb's massive desk, her frantic gaze sought an escape. Her screams changed to whimpers. "No, please don't make me go back! Please! Please?"

Steb stared helplessly at his only child, tears streaming down his own face. "You don't have to go. It's okay, Darlin' It's okay. Daddy's here. I'll take care of you. Look, here's Mom, too."

Christine did a little better, coaxing her back to her own suite of rooms, trying to reassure her.

Drained, Steb sank heavily into his leather chair. He couldn't figure what had set Missy off so. True, she hadn't emerged from her dazed torpor; but they hadn't witnessed anything like the scene which had just transpired. His screen saver showed the seventeenth hole at Pebble Beach. A beautiful spot like that shouldn't have rattled her. He touched a key, making the beautiful course go away, and revealing the scene Bransom had sent him. He regarded it steadily. It didn't look that threatening. He phoned Bransom.

"Hey, is this painting of any place in particular?"

294

"Beats me! Jennifer told Nick that the kidnappers would probably take their victim to Canada. Which, we've always concentrated on the border with Mexico. But, she freaked out about talking to me. I don't know if they threatened her not to talk-so she's painting pictures instead. Anyway, when she wouldn't say anything more about the Canada-border thing, I kind of kiddingly told Nick to have her paint a picture. He emailed it to me in the night, but it's meaningless to me. And, I've spent hours trying to contact that elderly couple; I can't raise them. Have your heard anything more?"

Steb's heart sank. "No, not another word! I sure hope they're okay. I called about this picture because I think it might be what just put Missy into the most awful emotional fit!"

⊰ ⊱

David and Mallory arrived at the office late-morning, following a routine visit to the doctor. The two suites hummed with activity. Two gifts had arrived; Mallory's twenty-second birthday and she emitted screeches of delight! "Look at that," she gasped to David.

He nodded. It was awesome. After Jennifer's strange reaction to painting a formal portrait of the two of them, she had created a beautiful oil. She definitely possessed talent, with infusions of her own inimitable spirit! "That is so perfect!"

The piece was indeed gorgeous, capturing Yosemite, with El Capitan bathed in glowing light, autumn foliage, and David and Mallory sitting at a picnic table in the foreground. With a capricious breeze ruffling her hair, and enchanting light haloing her, David thought Mallory rather eclipsed him. Nothing new there! The portrait captured her mid-sentence; glossy lips parted ever so slightly.

"Well, she was right, about painting what she wants, when she wants to, the way she wants," Mallory acknowledged. "I liked the picture Diana took of us, that we wanted Jennifer to copy; but this is far better! I need to call her."

"Okay; come call her from my office." David's eyes danced.

"Oh, I'm finally allowed into your sanctum?" David Anderson had been up to something for months; something so top secret she had been barred from the mystery project. "Okay! I'm dying of curiosity!"

She halted in wonder, clasping both hands to her heart. "Oh! Oh, Wow! Oh, that's for me? That's the most beautiful-"

David laughed. "Well, maybe you should try it out!"

She patted at tears springing up, before flinging herself into his arms and pressing her lips on his. "Oh, thank you! I love it! I just absolutely~ Oh! David! I love you!"

He laughed again. "Come on; sit down and see if it sounds good."

He watched; she seemed stuck in slow motion, but finally she sank onto the bench and caressed the glowing wood of the cabinetry. In a daze, she reached for the card perched on the music rack. It was a beautiful card with a hand-written message and a gift certificate for a year of lessons from a prestigious professor. So perfect! Who had she cried to when she couldn't take any more lessons? But her best friend, David! A fleeting moment of panic hit her: how could she add lessons and practicing to her hectic mix, with the entrance of a new baby? She'd have to get more organized, for sure!

She smiled a bewitching, breathless smile. "What should I play? I'm kind of a blank!"

Before David could make a suggestion, fifty or sixty people erupted from nowhere! Hats, noisemakers, and balloons! "Happy Birthday"!

David lowered the top of the baby grand, leaning toward her. "Play *Happy Birthday!*" So she did, as friends and family squeezed around singing.

"What a surprise," she laughed. "Uh, ya got me again!"

☙ ❧

Jack squeezed Estelle close to him, trying to warm her up and control his own shivering. He fought panic and accompanying nausea. He wasn't sure how long they had been without any food or water. With Stell's diabetes, he was doubly concerned. "Okay, Lord, please help us," he whispered. "And the little girl, too! Give us wisdom. We're ready to die, as far as bein' saved; but we aren't eager to."

"Sh-h," Stella cautioned. "I hear 'em." They embraced one another, terrified, as someone shook hard on the padlocked door of their prison. Evidently making sure the couple couldn't escape. At last, Stella thought she heard car doors and an engine start. Then silence!

"I think they've gone." Jack's hearing was poor, and their captors had laughingly thrown his expensive hearing aids away before stomping on both of their pairs of glasses.

After an interval of what they thought was silence, Jack pushed himself to his feet. The cold was numbing, and he could hear the wind picking up. That's right, the forecast had predicted this. The space was unbelievably dark as he eased around the circumference of their prison. If he could find a blanket, tarp, rags, anything to insulate against the cold.

"Be careful, Jack."

He grinned in the darkness, despite the gravity of their situation. For over fifty years, this woman had been cautioning him the same way.

"Bein' careful, Stell," he responded good-naturedly. Just as he spoke, he stubbed his toe painfully on an unexpected obstacle.

"Ungh, uh," he moaned. Still, he felt a sense of jubilation. Some kind of home-made wooden tool carrier; his hands searched eagerly. Screwdriver, hammer, flashlight! Didn't work, of course! The stuff was pretty rusty; evidently left here and forgotten long ago. He continued, feeling his way along. Cinder block, best he could make out. Then, he came to a spot where something seemed to be bolted to the blocks, plywood, or something. He pulled firmly at one edge with the claws of the hammer. "Let me know if you hear 'em comin'." He applied more pressure. They had to get warm and get food! And get word to the FBI about Danay!

-≒ ≓-

Mallory took in another surprise! A portion of the extra office suite was beautifully turned into a nursery/daycare! Amazing! "So, this is what you've been up to! I love it! So we can bring the baby to work with us. No wonder you didn't say much when I was trying to get you to worry with me. You already had it figured out."

"With that, everyone trooped out, reconvening at a party room in a popular steak restaurant."

Erik gave Suzanne a kiss on the cheek as he sat down next to her. "I'm glad you came to Dallas. Otherwise, I'm not sure when I'll see you again. I may be here awhile."

"Well, then, I'm glad, too. It's hard for me to believe Mallie's twenty-two. Sometimes it seems like she should still be just a little girl. I'm glad they're so happy. Too bad you missed the stuff at the office. Jennifer painted an incredible picture of David and Mallie at Yosemite-"

"Hey, speaking of Jennifer and painting-" Erik didn't mean to interrupt and change the subject. He brought up the email Nick had sent him. "She painted this. Steb and I can't exactly recall this place. But I guess Missy got really emotionally upset, and Steb thinks seeing this might have been what set her off."

Suzanne glanced at it, and handed it back. "Looks like it could be practically any~" She paused, mid-sentence to take it and gaze at it again."

"I have seen this, on your laptop~ This is like, uh, the stationery letterhead; remember, when you were checking out about Otto Malovich, and his eyes?"

Erik squinted at her, and then at the image. "Hunh? That place was where? Albania? Romania? Why would Jennifer be aware of an orphanage there, going way back? Why would she paint it now? When we're looking for Danay?"

Suzanne smiled, blue eyes alight. "Guess you just answered your own questions."

⚏ ⚎

Jack applied more leverage, not sure whether to tackle the bolts, or the plywood. He whacked the board, and it seemed like the racket reverberated forever. His hammer swung through, though, and he felt a surge of triumph! Brittle in the cold and rotting from damp and weather, it was pretty weakened. He ripped and clawed away at it, pausing so Stell could listen for anyone approaching. Even all of the exertion wasn't warming him up much. He needed to hurry, not sure his efforts would get them any closer to freedom.

"Stell, it looks like someone tried to board up and cover a door. Maybe we can get out."

She mumbled an indistinguishable acknowledgement, and he went to work with fresh vigor. The door was an old metal affair, secured in a metal frame. It seemed defeatingly solid, but the metal building attaching to the frame seemed rusty and fatigued. He pressed against it, and it seemed like it would give way easily. He wanted out, but he didn't want to pull the whole place down around them.

"Stell, we may be able to get out," his whisper carried in the country silence. "Come over here; we'll get you our first."

"Like this?" She was horrified; the criminals had forced them to remove their shoes and most of their clothing.

"Yeah, if any of them are still here, it's not gonna matter. Hurry"!

She complied and he peeled a corner of metal upward with the hammer claws, cutting himself in the process. If he survived this, a tetanus shot would be in order. Drifted snow covered the opening, and he wrenched the protesting metal up higher. They clambered through the opening together into the freezing snow.

"Maybe we should have stayed put. It was at least sheltered in there, and dry."

"If it's our best option, we can come back. Let's at least look around and see what's here and try to figure out where we are. You need food and your Insulin, not to mention warming up. He pulled the tool chest out and dropped the items back into it. He swung it ahead of them to cut a path through the deepening snow. At the corner of the building, they paused.

"Okay, snow was deeper there where the north wind made it drift against the building," Jack observed. On the west side, nothing was visible but a large field with a line of trees on the far side.

"Come on, Hon," he encouraged. The metal building was long. "This used to be an airport back in the day," he noted as he got his bearings. "I guess they didn't really bring us far; maybe seventy, seventy-five miles." He grasped her hand, pulling her along, as he continued carrying the tool caddy.

"You're bleeding!" Her voice sounded alarmed.

"Yeah, we're both a sight to behold, I'm sure." He was winded by the time they reached the end of the building. "Look, there's another building. Where they spent the rest of the night; I'm positive. It's bound to be warmer and more comfortable than where they dumped us. Come on; you can make it!"

Her doubtful gaze met his. Without her glasses, she couldn't' see another building, or anything else but driving snow. Still, she stayed with him as they plunged through more deep drifts, finally gaining the porch of another decaying building. It didn't look like any improvement, but they entered anyway.

Flipping light switches didn't bring any illumination, and ashes in a Franklin stove were cold. A broken window on the front of the building allowed the wind to howl in.

"Maybe they'll come back for us." Her voice sounded old and defeated.

"They won't." His voice was calmly assured on that score. "And if they did, it wouldn't be good. Listen, we aren't giving up. We threw them a curve that cost them time, and now this storm front's gotten here. I think they planned for someone to fly in here, grab her, and fly across the border; but with no way to de-ice-well, it'd about be suicidal, anyway. They're stuck somewhere, and nothing's flying today or tonight, even out of the big airports. We have to notify the Feds. It's up to us! That little girl's whole life-Lord, ya gotta help us! Please help Danay!"

⚜ ⚜

Erik sorted through old emails, finally giving up with a defeated sigh. Evidently, he had deleted the missive that Suzanne claimed used the same scene as Jennifer's picture. Maybe Col. Ahmir, in Turkey, could find it, and confirm it. Sadly, it was the middle of the night in central Turkey. Erik closed his eyes. 'An orphanage?' Suzanne had originally commented that the picture looked forlorn. No people, children, graced the space. There was no evidence of toys or playground, like you might hope to see where children lived together, hoping to be taken in by kind families. He shivered involuntarily. Okay! Definitely not a happy place! A hard existence that had turned Oscar and Otto Malovich into hardened criminals a generation previously, and which caused Missy Hansen to scream in terror at the sight! He tried to remember the name of the place. Some kind of Nursing Home sounding name: *Pleasant Hills*, or some such. "Help me, Lord," he whispered.

⚜ ⚜

Cold rain pelted Trent's windshield as he headed home from downtown DC. He was hoping there wouldn't be freezing precip so early in the season, so he tuned the radio to find a forecast. An update Amber Alert update surprised him. He figured Bransom was too involved to chat and satisfy his curiosity. He placed a call to the *SOC Foundation*, and a chatty volunteer filled him in; probably with information that they shouldn't have divulged. Vermont? And an older couple seemed to have disappeared after reporting suspicions to the local sheriff's office? He was the director of the US Forestry Service Law Enforcement and Investigations. He placed a call to Ed Murdoch, who was over the US Forest Service LEI, Northeastern Division.

"Thought I might be hearing from you before this," Ed responded, laughing. "How far am I supposed to stick my neck out?"

Trent didn't laugh. "You have daughters; don't you? How far would you want people to stick their necks out for them?"

"You have to put it that way. The problem is, my kids like to eat and keep living in a safe warm house."

"I hear ya. But you can give your guys in the White Mountains a heads up. They need to watch out for the sheriff of Essex County, and help find out everything they can about this couple, Jack and Estelle Norman. A couple of civilians who involved themselves, and they may have found themselves in trouble. Just act like you're on your way skiing, stop in Island Pond and do a little snooping. Think these racketeers and the little victim are in your neighborhood, trying to sneak into Canada and fly to Europe from there with her. We'll never get her~"

"Yeah, I hear ya. We'll get on the stick. Weather's wicked up here, though."

"Yeah, hoping and praying that slows their plan. Later!"

⊰ ⊱

The other building was slightly better. Through the front windows, Jack could make out tire tracks, quickly blurring beneath the snow. "They're in our car," he observed calmly. "They'll have returned the rental; our car isn't reported stolen. So, unless they get stopped and a cop asks why the car and insurance aren't in their name~" He tried to cover his hopeless sensation. "Okay, you stay wrapped in this old mattress as much as you can." He gave Stell a stern look when she tried to protest the filthy item. "Better than freezin'! Come on; help me out." He jerked down an equally filthy vinyl shower curtain. "I'm goin' out to look around at what's here. I'll stay where you can see me. He tore the shower curtain apart, securing pieces around his bare feet the best he could, and wrapping the remaining piece over his head.

"Don't know what you think you'll find."

"Don't know either," he flung over his shoulder as he grasped the tool kit and made his way across the rickety porch. Everything was slick and he moved gingerly. His getting injured would really reduce their chances of making it. But without some miracle, they couldn't survive a night in either one of the buildings. It was just too cold! In spite of his caution, he went down and floundered in the drifts, trying to get back on his feet. That was when he noticed! About thirty feet ahead of him, down a pretty steep incline, was a rough patch! A patch that looked like the earth had been freshly turned just as the snow started falling. His heart lurched, and he clasped at his chest. Surely they wouldn't have killed her! Well, she hadn't been going along with her captors calmly; what had made him and Stell notice the scenario. But out here, with him and his wife locked away where they'd never be found, and no one within miles, the girl could carry on, resist, scream, whatever! It wouldn't make any difference. He gazed at the spot, suddenly heedless of the cold, feeling sick dread. He turned and waved at Estelle. This would take him from her sight line. He hoped she'd understand he was fine, and not come traipsing after him. He stumbled in his awkwardly devised slippers. Reaching the spot, he attacked savagely with hammer in one hand, and screw driver in the other. The frozen earth seemed reluctant to yield up its secret, but the ground was warmer as he dug, and mud began to give place. At last, he viewed a big black trash bag, bound securely at the top with its neat plastic fastener. After a struggle, he managed to pull it free. With no blood in evidence, he had already decided this wasn't a shallow grave; there was no little body. He un-notched the fastener, and there on top lay his boots and socks. Quickly, he removed the tattered pieces of vinyl and pulled the boots on! Followed by his thick jacket!

"Hallelujah, Lord, maybe we can make it!" He turned and charged up the hill with renewed purpose!

Chapter 23: ANTAGONISTS

*Proverbs 29:1 He, that being often reproved hardeneth his neck,
shall suddenly be destroyed, and that without remedy.*

"Why are you calling me?" Mel Oberson's voice dripped
with angst and disdain.

"Well, this bratty kid's been nothin' but trouble. She got those nosy old
people involved, and we had to take care of them. Then the snow started
so we had to delay the pickup. Maybe the Canadian border in wintertime
was a bad idea~"

"I'll take care of your loose ends. Don't ever phone me directly
again!"

꒳ ꒷

Erik was jubilant when the call was picked up! Oberson, free on bond
awaiting trial, evidently believed the slick lies his defense team was feeding
him, about the charges not sticking, and how he would emerge a free man.
Still, arrogant, to barely pause in his criminal activity! If he considered
himself another Teflon™ type guy, he was wrong! His bail was about to
be revoked, and he was going to Federal lockup! Bransom passed on his
information and issued new orders!

꒳ ꒷

Back in the scant shelter of the smaller building, Jack and Estelle emptied
the trash bag. Most of their possessions, taken by their captors, were

accounted for. Except for his wallet and Stell's purse! They located both cell phones in their coat pockets, but the batteries were drained.

"Maybe the purse and wallet are buried out there someplace." He doubted it, but he was considering another expedition. His wife's handbag would have a Snicker's Bar™ and her medication.

"No, they would have taken our ID's and credit cards."

Jack nailed the old mattress across the broken window, and insisted his wife wrap up in his coat, too. When he was dressed, he pulled the garbage bag around him. He tried to settle against her; he was tuckered from all his efforts.

"We haven't checked what's in the attic." Her tone sounded inspired and hopeful.

He sighed. "Yeah, you're right. Maybe there are a couple of steak dinners up there waitin' for us." Still, he couldn't ignore a possibility, however slight.

⊰ ⊱

Jarod Murdoch and a couple of other Forestry Law Enforcement guys paused, panting with exertion. They all enjoyed cross country skiing; they just didn't do it often enough

"Let's keep moving," Murdoch urged. "It's cold when we stop, and every second lost–"

They kept going, pressed on by urgency!

⊰ ⊱

Erik Bransom emitted another yelp of delight! "Thanks, Lord," he breathed silently. First, there was the call placed to Oberson, traced to a caller in Vermont! And now! Signals from the Normans' cell phones, showing the location of the phones, hopefully where the elderly couple was! Agents were on their way to the indicated coordinates; but travel was snarled up, due to the weather. He hesitated briefly before calling to confide in Hanson.

"Did you find her?" It was Christine's eager voice, answering Steb's phone.

"No, Ma'am, I'm sorry. Is Steb available to talk to me?"

"Afternoon, Agent; are there any developments you can fill me in on?" Steb's voice took a few minutes coming on the line.

"Maybe a couple," Erik answered softly, not wanting his conversation overheard. The FBI was supposed to stop vigilante groups; not seek their help. "We got a call intercept from the people behind the abduction; Vermont! And we have locater signals from the Normans' phones; not that far from the first location. We're trying to get our guys in, but it's nearly blizzard conditions up there. I don't want anyone else to end up in trouble~" His voice trailed off. Who was he to ask another old couple to put themselves in peril, seeking the Normans?

"I see," Steb responded. "Well we had that Forestry department big-wig call here, askin' questions~"

"Thanks, Steb! You're a genius!"

⚔ ⚔

Steb placed a call and got immediate responses. He sent everything across the *SOC* web site, and thousands of people prayed over the update. Two hundred sprang into action, looking for the 2007 blue Volkswagen Jetta, Vermont plates Echo-Charlie-nine-one-zero Alpha with a Purple Heart decoration!

⚔ ⚔

Trent Morrison sent the information from both Erik and Steb via sat phone to Murdoch and his guys.

"You have got to be kiddin' me," Murdoch responded. "We're practically on top of where they're holding the little girl!"

"Okay, great!" Morrison hated to douse their enthusiasm. "When you locate, pull back and watch! Don't! I repeat, do not go in with just the three of you!"

"Well, we'll have the element of surprise~"

"We don't know that for sure. Follow my orders! Remember your kids like to eat! Scope the place out, look for this vehicle! And wait until you get a 'Go-ahead'!"

⚔ ⚔

"Good birthday?" David finished studying some reports and headed for the master suite.

305

Mallory moved into his arms, laughing. "Yes! Fabulous beyond words! I love having the beautiful piano at the office, and I'm really excited about lessons with a Classical pianist! Everybody else was so kind, too! I'm overwhelmed. I already started a few thank you notes, but they seem kind of flat and inadequate!"

He gave her a gentle squeeze. "Well, it's because you're always so thoughtful and giving. You deserve everything you got, and more besides. You're such a great pianist; I hope you don't feel insulted about my hiring you a teacher."

She fought happy tears. "Believe me; I don't think I'm that good! It's perfect! You remembered how disappointed I was when I had to stop taking lessons."

He tilted her chin up and gazed deeply into her eyes for long moments. "Well, I know you were feeling overwhelmed by our work load, in two locations, and everything else we do, in addition to the baby's coming. If you want to wait to start the lessons, I get it."

"No, I'm ready to start! Like you said, I made a big mountain of everything in my mind. I guess, one of the things I've wrestled with the most, is about how I can be a good mother and still work. I'm not sure why; you take so much off of me! And, now that beautiful nursery right at the office! You think of everything!"

Ready for bed, they knelt together and David prayed. "Lord, we sure love You. We're grateful for all You've given us. Thank You for Mallory and her birthday, and bless all our friends for their kindness. Protect us, and give us a good night's sleep; may Your angels encamp round about us. Please protect little Danay, and bless our country. In Jesus' Name, amen"!

⧉ ⧈

Bransom was in close contact with agents in the Northeast, moving into positions slowly, delayed by the storm. With Hillman running the local operation from Ms. Hicks-Livingston's lavish North Dallas home, he slipped away for lunch with Herb and Linda Carlton. His food had barely arrived when Hillman called him.

"What?" His voice registered his surprise at her update. "That doesn't make any sense!"

"Tell me about it," the other agent agreed. "Danay disappeared four days ago, and a ransom call comes now? I tried to tell Ms. Livingston this is someone else trying to cash in! But she's determined to do everything this caller said. A million dollars in non-sequential twenties"!

"Well, you're in charge there. Maybe getting money together will occupy her. I think we're within a few hours of retrieving the child. The ransom call may be a ploy of Oberson's to deflect suspicion from himself. He's been behind who-knows-how-many kidnappings? But he's never made ransom demands."

"No," Hillman agreed. "Because it's always the children he actually wants, and not cash. You're probably right. Maybe he's trying to make this look like a different MO, and if he gets the ransom money, it's all the better for him! So I should just let her and the ex, work on getting the money together?"

"Yeah! Should take them some time! Step in, though, before they actually attempt to make the drop. Keep me in the loop."

"I'm sorry," he apologized to Herb and Linda. "I mostly wanted to touch base with you, and invite you to come see us in Arkansas one of these weekends. I don't enjoy hunting particularly; I get shot at enough on my job-" He laughed at his own Agency joke. "But Herb, I know you and Merc enjoy it. I'm pretty sure you could use one of the cabins up at the ranch, but you're welcome to stay with Suzanne and me. You could be at a blind within an hour from our place. Linda, you could go antiquing while they freeze."

"Thank you, Erik." Herb responded. "Merc mentioned that to me months ago. Now the season will be past, and I didn't make the arrangements. I have been, in my spare time, working on project for Mallory's birthday. Now-maybe Christmas"!

"It's beautiful," Linda remarked. "Herb is such a perfectionist; he's finished it and redone it three or four times."

"Well, this will surprise both of you, and also Merc, but we will come this week end. Thank you for the invitation and the reminder," came Herb's gentle voice. "A break from this is what I need."

Suddenly, David joined them. "Hey, look who's here! Y'all should have called us. Well, maybe you didn't want to eat with us. I came down to get our order, but then I saw y'all and called Mallory, she said she'd be right down." He nodded at the café manager, who brought his order over.

"Hey Erik, Aunt Linda, Uncle Herb"! Mallory greeted warmly. "I couldn't believe it when David called and told me you were down here. Uncle Herb, we were wondering the other night, if you and Merc were going to get enough of a break to come up during deer season. The welcome mat's always out for all of you; you know that, right? I know the jewelry orders are always back-logged! I guess if there's a down side to your talent and popularity, it would be the problem of keeping up with so many orders! At some point, maybe you should walk away for a few days."

The lunch was fun, but Bransom got tough when David tried to pay. "Let me; just this once. I invited Herb and Linda, and I'm glad you and Mallory joined us. You guys always pay. I'm gettin' this."

He made it out to the parking lot as his phone rang again. "Yeah, what's up now?" He listened, interested, to another tip on the hot line! This time from an airport control tower! The controller had picked up a comm. between a private jet pilot and a radio operator on one of the frequencies.

"The guys on the ground were real nervous, trying to get this pilot to make a 'merchandise' pick up. The pilot's response was that he didn't dare risk any damage to the aircraft, stating that none of them, or the merchandise, was as important to Mr. O as the multi-million dollar jet."

Bransom called Dawson. "Mr. O, hunh? And his sweet bird? I want that craft seized! You know, according to his reported income, there's no way he could own a fast, long-range jet like that! Call our friends at Treasury again."

⚔ ⚔

"Let's head home and beat the traffic."

Mallory glanced up at David, her face a study of earnestness.

"Gather it up; we'll work on more at home. There's no sense getting stuck in bottlenecks because we stay here."

"Well, everyone else has to stay-"

David laughed. "Yeah, They do. They work for us, and that's the way it is. We don't have to stay! We're the bosses! We take care of business, and we were here earlier this morning than any of them were. Which, is beside the point! You worry too much if everyone likes you and if they know you work harder than any of them. That's something Faulkner always yelled at me about. Evidently, he's afraid to holler at you. He was right, though. Sometimes leadership's lonely. At least now, we have each other!"

⚔ ⚔

Commercial flights finally made it into Montpelier, where Forestry Service guys awaited the Federal Agents with four wheel drive vehicles and heavy clothing. "Suit, top coat, and loafers won't get it today. We're driving as far as the roads are cleared. Then snowmobiling, cross country skiing, or snow shoes, are the options. These guys trying to get off the beaten path have mostly shone a spotlight on themselves. People in these tiny, isolated communities know one another, and strangers sets off alarm bells with them. We have guys in position who are keeping us in the loop with sit reps. Eyes are on both the elderly couple and the perpetrators with the victim."

⚔ ⚔

Daniel settled into the family room, where Jeremiah was engrossed with a heavy volume in front of a cheerful fire. "Game of Chess?" he challenged.

"Yeah, sure," Jeremiah's agreement lacked enthusiasm.

"You go first," Daniel encouraged his son, who shoved a pawn forward.

"Sure about that?" Faulkner's eyes sparkled. As with golf, he played a psych game, as well as every other skill he could muster. He was competitive.

Jeremiah calmly refused to take the bait. "Yeah, I'm sure. I mean, 'Yes, Sir'. Dad, can we talk? You know? Without you getting mad?"

"Do we usually get mad? As long as your attitude stays respectful?"

Jeremiah shrugged. "Yeah, sometimes"!

Daniel moved a pawn. "Okay, I'm summoning all my calm and rationale. Put it on me. What are you wanting? An apartment and a car"?

Jeremiah's turn to sparkle mischievously! "Is that on the table?"

"NO! Do you want to play Chess; or don't you?"

"Can we talk; or not?"

"Yeah, I said, 'Put it on me'."

Jeremiah sighed. "Okay, usually before kids want an apartment and car, what do they want?"

"Mmmm, a new bicycle?"

Jeremiah summoned his patience, ignoring the jibe at his youth and immaturity. "No, Dad. Usually they need a job before they can get an apartment and a car."

Daniel grinned. "Ah, well, if you're interested in working for what you want, that's a good sign."

"Yes, Sir, I hoped you'd be impressed with that." The fifteen year old was trying to be serious-with some degree of levity. Against his will, he suddenly fought tears. "I don't know how to tell you, but I don't really want to be a Geologist, at all! I'm sure you're really dis-" He couldn't go on.

"Whoa-ho, Son! Evidently you've got me pegged wrong. I won't be disappointed if you decide not to be a Geologist. I'll be disappointed if you decide not to become a good Christian man. If you've decided not to pursue Earth Science, is it because your interests lie elsewhere? Are you serious about getting a job? Now? Why? You're barely fourteen."

"Well, Alexandra has the job, being Mom's assistant."

Daniel realized the need to proceed cautiously. "Well, she's nearly three years older than you are. But you're big enough and mature enough to begin taking more responsibility. Do you have something in mind?"

"Kind of; like every day, when you go to work, you don't do mostly Geology stuff; do you?"

"Well, Jer, it's a Geological company. I'd be lost if I weren't a Geologist. I mean I do all the administrative things, too."

"Yeah, Dad, the administrative stuff. Do you ever need any help with any of that? Payroll and bill-paying and stuff like that?"

"Accounting? You think you'd be interested in that? Okay let me think. Your computer skills are better than mine, probably. Maybe I could start you out with some data entry. It's possible that Mr. Haynes can get a business math course into your curriculum. Added on top of what you're already doing."

Jeremiah flinched. His school load was already rigorous. "Well, could I go to work with you every day, and have a cubicle and do my school from there, and do some jobs for you, too?"

Daniel regarded the earnest face, gazing eagerly across the Chess board. He nodded, barely perceptibly. "Yeah, Jeremiah, I'd like that."

♘ ♞

The combined agencies in Vermont accomplished the rescues and arrests with little additional drama. The Canadian authorities grounded the private jet, ready to turn it over to their American counterparts.

Jack and Estelle Norman were rushed to a nearby clinic for treatment and further assessment. Danay Livingston-Hicks, exhausted, traumatized, but basically unhurt, was being questioned gently by agents as they headed home with her.

Agent Caroline Hillman was ecstatic about such a positive outcome. Bransom was in a good mood about it, too. She decided to bring up an issue she had been wrestling with.

"Could I ask you something?" She approached him as her team dismantled their post in Livingston's dining room.

"About that 'organ recipient list' assignment I gave you?"

"Yes Sir, as a matter of fact! How did you know?"

Erik was tired, but this fired him up. "I could tell it didn't set real well with you when I told you to get started. Then, you haven't gotten started. Glad you brought it up, because now I don't have to. When I tell you to do something, I expect results."

"Well, it's just that there are some happy stories. People, kids, whoever, get a shot at life!"

"At the expense of someone else? You're talking about these rich people that go around the rules! Yeah! They get to keep their kids, or whatever, while other parents with as much love and longing, and whatever-have-you, lose theirs! I'm not trying to put an end to 'happy stories', here, Hillman! I like happy stories as well as the next person. But I'm saying, 'the ends don't justify the means'! And any racket that puts money into the pockets of thugs who traffic in people, and parts thereof, stinks! And I'm asking, make that, telling you, as a federal agent, to investigate criminal activity! Look at it this way, too. The people going off-shore for organs and surgeries are victims, too. Say, they pay, half a million for a kidney and the entire procedure; how do they even know what they're gonna get? Who oversees this black market industry; for professionals, the facilities, even the condition of the organs? Pretty sure organs were harvested from Warrington's elderly 'guinea pigs'. If these illegal entities put a ninety year old heart into a patient, how does he know? As long as it keeps ticking a little while longer? Who does he sue if he ends up worse off? Do the job. It isn't yours to decide what to look into, and what not to."

⊰ ⊱

David and Mallory headed toward the Ranch following the board meeting at *Sanders, Corporation.* They planned to spend as much time in their country retreat as possible, through the Holidays and the first of the year. Then the second week of February, they planned to stick close to Dallas, the doctor, and the hospital while they awaited the arrival of the baby.

"Wow, my mom told me Cat's been doing an awesome job at the *Chandler Plant,*" Mallory commented. "She revealed some good numbers, and she's been a genius, helping all of the *Sandler* people make the adjustment."

David nodded agreement. "Yes, you're right. She has the economy working in her favor too, though. The employees don't feel optimistic about finding comparable jobs if they walk away. I mean, even Holman! With his credentials, he would have been snapped up immediately by some company. But the way things are, Cat and Roger had plenty of time to mess around before they made him an offer. It's helping us, too. To hire easily and keep people on."

Mallory smiled. "Well, yes, but our people are loyal to us, too."

David grinned at her. "Treasure that thought."

"Okay, I will," she responded defensively. "You need to give people more the benefit of the doubt."

"Your dad didn't. He didn't trust anybody! Not banks, not the sheriff's department. He knew that when the chips are down, people seek their own best interests. I mean, everyone betrayed Jesus! The people He healed and helped; even all of His disciples! I wasn't trying to start an argument. I was basically pointing out that, even though the slow economy hurts our sales and revenue, it helps us with our personnel. I'm just noticing that in every area of life where there are positives, there are negatives, too; and vice versa."

⊰ ⊱

"I'm done, Mom," Alexandra announced. "I've missed Jeremiah since he started going with Daddy every day. And now that Cassie's left for another concert, it's really lonely."

Diana grinned. "Yeah, and there's nothing to divert Frances' attention from you so you can goof around."

Alexandra blushed. "Well, I really do miss them, too."

"M-mm, no one to fight with! I have a stack of faxes for you to send, and I need you to pack up some fabric samples to return. That should keep you busy until the guys get home."

Alexandra's cool gray eyes met her mother's. Most of her jobs as assistant were boring and routine. She knew better than to complain. And she liked receiving pay checks. "Okay, well if I'm finished before that, I know where to find you for more assignments. Also, I've thought that things are a little messy and disorganized~"

"Yes, you're right about that! Business has picked up for the Holidays, and I've let things get jumbled. If you can bring order from the chaos, that'd be a relief. Oh, and by the way, when Dad and Jeremiah get here, we're packing up and heading~"

Excited yips burst forth from the teenager, and Diana didn't get a chance to finish her sentence.

-≒ ╞-

Erik mulled over hand written notes he had jotted down in the course of his on-going investigation. O'Shaughnessy, Oberson, Otto Malovich, Oscar Malovich! Which one was the mysterious Mr. O? He sighed. He had assumed it to be Mel Oberson; he still leaned that way in his thinking. Evidently Missy's terrified response to Jennifer's most recent picture, had mentioned 'Mr. O'. "It was always bad, but then, whenever Mr. O showed up~"

Well, evidently the guy ran a 'tight ship', dealing harshly with whatever infractions might have taken place. Erik scoured up and down his face with both hands. Wilhelm Dietrich? A big gun? But not a top echelon person? Erik penciled a rough management diagram, indicating what he now thought the peck order to be. He twiddled the pencil. "Okay, Ryland O'Shaughnessy died in custody. Apparent suicide? Yeah, right! Almost simultaneously with Oscar Maloviches' meeting his demise in a similar fashion! Okay! No coincidence then! The guys in charge, the ones who gave the orders, didn't order their own executions, obviously. He crossed through O'Shaughnessy. One eliminated of the four. He phoned Nick.

"Aloha, Agent," Nick's voice was always chipper. "Not bad news, I hope. Any new developments?"

"No, seems like I'm spinning in the same circles. Jennifer hasn't made any comments on her latest painting, has she?"

"I guess the paintings are her comments. She never talks about stuff. She tells me I'm better off not knowin'."

"So, she's never mentioned anything about a Mr. O? When Missy Hansen saw Jennifer's picture of that orphanage, she went berserk; mentioned Mr. O a couple of times. Jen had claimed she was never aware of Missy, yet, when she sent those coordinates that were encrypted in those numbers, Missy showed up. Anyway, I have Oberson and Oscar and Otto, who could feasibly be called, 'Mr. O'. "Okay, it probably isn't Oscar either. He's been in prison under close scrutiny for nearly four years. He was kind of the wimpy follower of the two twins. And Otto! Not sure where he can be hiding!" He paused, remembering a tale related to him by a Boston homeless man. "Thanks Nick."

With the call ended, he circled Oberson's name in heavy black!

Chapter 24: ACTUALITY

Nita Rodriguez completed some finish work with fine, hand-sewn stitches. She stacked bodice-front pieces she had been working on; an array of colors, styles, and sizes. She patted the pile affectionately. What she and Deborah had felt was disastrous, was turning out to be amazing! A good seamstress who enjoyed (make that, loved) sewing; she had taken one of her daughter's new jackets apart to learn how to make the awesome Besom pockets. She was so skilled that it usually worked. When she and her daughter had confessed to Diana, that the garment was ruined, instead of getting mad, Diana had seen past the debacle to a talented woman. Now Nita stayed busily and gainfully employed finishing piecework. And, as if that weren't totally too much, *DiaMal, Corporation* supplied a state-of-the-art sewing machine! An eye exam with new glasses made the work even more enjoyable, and David was remodeling a house just outside of Murfreesboro, that would provide the seamstress and her family with bright, efficient space! She and Manny had always been renters. Now the agreement on the bigger house was that they would pay the same rent to David and Mallory that they had paid to their former landlord. A great arrangement for everyone involved, giving the Andersons more Arkansas property without raising too many red flags.

In Israel, Lilly took note of the developments with satisfaction. 'Yes, the Lord worked miracles on behalf of Mallory, yet Mallory continued to see new possibilities and move forward in faith.' Lilly realized she had kept her defenses up against the Lord and His obvious planning, for far too long.

She smirked at her own foolishness; her attempts to avoid admitting the obvious. No one could have that much luck, or coincidence.

༈ ༈

David paused to study the drawings. "Okay, who framed this in this way?" His question directed itself toward Waylon. "There are supposed to be a couple of big bay doors here."

Waylon pointed towards the far end of the cattle barn that was going up on the Gilmore property.

David tried to do a slow count, remembering the young employee was a really hard worker, if somewhat spatially challenged. The entire framing of the structure was going up, basically in reverse of the plans. "Okay, Waylon: North, South, East West! The doors are on the wrong end of the building. Knock some of this out, and leave the bays; close in the other end except for a single door."

"Well, does it really matter?"

"Yeah, it really does. This end is nearest the road, and trucks can get in to load and unload. The other end faces the pasture, and there isn't room to make truck access around there. That would be costly and unnecessary anyway. It's just a few hours and board-feet wasted; it could be worse. I'm going home to check on Mallie. Jeff's on his way."

In his truck, he pushed up the heater. He was frozen. He'd be home before the truck warmed up much. He tried to get his anger under control. If Jeff had been on-site, the bays would be in the right spots. He checked himself. Not Jeff's fault. "It's me, Lord," he whispered. "I need to be on-site more. Thank You for the good workers. Thank You that You're always patient and kind to me when I blunder."

༈ ༈

Delia glanced up as Shay passed her office door. "Good morning, Shay. You've missed a couple of calls." She filled him in with details about the woolen mill contact.

"Thank you, Grandmother. It sounds like you handled it better than I would have. I hate it that you've been fielding my phone calls. What was the other?"

"Roger Sanders. He wouldn't give any inclination of what he wanted. For you to call him when you get in"!

Shay blanched visibly, hazel eyes widening. "Well, what did he sound like?"

Delia couldn't help being tickled. "Oh, like a roaring monster! He sounded like he usually sounds, Shay. Call him and find out what he wants. Remember to be extra-courteous."

Shay nodded. Sometimes his frustration with Roger's stance regarding Emma rankled. "Was he at the office this morning?"

"He didn't say. He called from his cell. Call him back on it."

⊰ ⊱

David's phone rang just as he made it in the back door of the Ranch house. "Hey, Shay, what's going on in Boston?"

"I just got off the phone with Roger Sanders. He said nothing about Emma, but he was nice to me as could be. His company's been working on fabric dyes, particularly for animal fibers. Making him real interested in my wool and our alpaca! He's flying me to Arkansas to meet with him and Cat and Holman about the project. You aren't surprised." Shay liked to be the first to know and share information, and he seemed slightly deflated.

"I'm not surprised, because we discussed the entire thing in length at the last *Sanders* board meeting. Just because he's interested in partnering with us, doesn't mean he's changed his mind about Emma. My dad actually called Roger's pastor. Maybe they all need counseling. But especially Brent and Connie! Okay, don't mention that to anyone else."

"My lips are sealed." Shay laughed. "And you accuse me of being a gossip."

⊰ ⊱

"Hi, I thought I heard you." Mallory moved forward to give David a hug, and he embraced her.

"M-m-m. Did you get any more sleep?" She was beautiful and he hated releasing her.

"I did a little bit. Then I woke up and enjoyed leisurely devotions. The morning's been relaxing, even if I didn't sleep late. How's the barn progressing?"

317

"One step forward and three back. Some days are like that. I walked away to keep from losing my cool. Waylon was building the thing backwards, and I have no idea where Jeff's been. It's freezing cold out there, anyway."

"Yeah? I have a fire going. Do you have time for coffee and cobbler?"

He shrugged. "Yeah, I should take a breather. I thought something smelled good. Have you eaten anything yet?"

"Just half the cobbler! It's probably best you came in when you did, or I might have finished it off. I started a puzzle. Listen, it's starting to rain. I love the sound of rain."

An hour and a half later, he saw the truck of workers return to the bunk house.

"Is it too rainy for them to work?" Mallory's trying to understand the building industry.

David sighed, watching from a wide window as the workers unloaded. "No. It's cold and miserable, but they could have stayed at it. It's like if I'm not on the job every minute~"

"Yes, you're the best worker, and you know what needs to be done. You're a natural leader, but still fun. People want to be where you are. But take a break. The weather's supposed to be better Monday, and they can hit it hard then."

He smiled. "I guess I needed to hear that. Maybe I will put it up in neutral and help you with your puzzle. I hope Jeff's okay. Maybe he just saw the socked in weather and went back to sleep. He really never gets too much time to himself. I'm glad you thought of a way to get him a place of his own."

Mid-afternoon, security called David, informing him of unexpected visitors claiming to be inspectors. He pulled his boots on and zipped out in the golf cart to meet the officials. To his amazement, it was a surprise visit from OSHA. David was a stickler for job safety, and he complied with OSHA guidelines. Still, he felt a sense of awe as he escorted them to the work-site. No slave-labor going on here! No labor of any type. He explained to them that he and Mallory were both sticklers for doing things correctly and insisted they go to the store for a complimentary coffee.

Conferring among themselves, they decided that might constitute bribery. David shrugged. "Well, it isn't like you found us in violation of anything and you're fining us. If that were the case, we wouldn't offer a bribe. I assume bribery usually means something more than a few coffee beverages, though.

Still, the store glowed appealingly through the chilling afternoon murk. Mallory appeared, exuding her usual warmth and charm; and they all went away with significant purchases.

⊰ ⊱

Erik was aware of the fact that the Hicks-Livingstons were preparing a civil suit against Oberson. Of course, he hoped the criminal charges would stick and the guy would go away for the rest of his days. He was certain that the benign-seeming politician had orchestrated numberless murders, but had probably kept his hands clean of the actual dirty work. Getting the death penalty for him probably wouldn't happen. He knew Treasury was hard at work, sorting out the financials and tax issues. All of the investigations and cases should bring a lot of pressure to bear. Saxon, and his son, too, were finding themselves implicated and in deep trouble. Right now, one of the agent's biggest prayer requests was that the Federal judge would allow Jennifer's paintings as evidence. That would be incredible. But even if it were disallowed, the artwork continued to implicate more and more felons. Evidence continued to surface. As each domino fell, it hit another, creating a chain reaction of events. Warrington's boat implicated people, whose electronics led to others. Nooses were tightening; nooses of their own making.

⊰ ⊱

Marion Weatherby stood to his feet, offering his hand across the broad expanse of his desk to the new clients, David and Mallory Anderson. "What can I offer you? Coffee? Water? Sodas?"

Mallory asked for water, impressed when the chilled plastic bottle was presented with a crystal goblet of ice. Elegant touch! Weatherby brewed himself a single cup of coffee, equally impressed with the young couple.

He conversed pleasantly, remarking on the relentless drizzle, a few comments on the economy, before falling back on the age-old topic of sports. To his surprise, Mallory became more animated than her husband. She was definitely a knock-out. He changed the subject to Mallory's obvious

319

condition. "When's your baby due? Have you learned the baby's gender, or are you going to be surprised?"

Mallory liked his laid-back style, but she was glad when David spoke up, steering the conversation to their reason for being there.

"Well, Sir, we have an accounting firm that handles all of our corporate finances. We like them very much, and trust them. Still, we thought we might prefer some separation for our personal business. We know our present CPA keeps confidences, but~"

"I understand." Weatherby leaned back, relaxed, steepling his fingers beneath his chin thoughtfully.

David continued. "I have a corporation and I haven't really gotten Mallory on it yet. Which we have an appointment with our attorney about the legal part of that. Maybe we have the cart before the horse, visiting you first."

The CPA leaned forward, motioning for the stacks of documents as he slid on reading glasses. He sipped at his coffee as he shuffled through the pages, then, glanced up sharply.

"Wow! You two kids seem to be doing okay! Wow!"

Mallory frowned slightly. Their personal money was actually a narrow slice of the pie.

He studied the paperwork more closely in silence for several minutes. "Well, there's a lot here to digest, but on the surface I'd say your charitable giving is way out of line, even as high as your income is. You can't claim nearly this much~"

"Yes, Sir"! David's response was quick. "Of course, we want to get all the exemptions we can. We don't want to evade paying taxes, but we don't want to overpay, either. Our charitable giving isn't motivated solely on tax breaks. We believe in the causes we support, especially the furtherance of the Gospel. We find that when we try to be generous, just for generosity's sake, that the Lord heaps more back to us."

The money man tried not to show as much skepticism as he felt. "Can you actually quantify that?"

David laughed easily. "It's a lesson I've learned from watching Mallory. It's added up in my mind. I can't begin to list all the examples, but here's a big one. Okay, see this stream of income from Melton-Vanderhoff?"

"Uh-yeah; impressive!"!

David leaned forward, excited and earnest. "Well, that's coming in because Mallory decided to give a generous gift to her best friend. She commissioned a perfume bottle; Diana collects fragrance decanters. Well, Mallory has a Diamond company, *DiaMo*; and her uncle is a world-renowned jewelry designer. So, she had him make this rock crystal decanter, all encrusted with gold and gemstones. Well, she wanted Diana's favorite perfume to come in refills that fit into it. So, when Herb contacted the perfume-maker, a subsidiary of *Melton*, they were all blown away by the entire concept. They contracted with Diana to model for the fragrance, which got her more money coming in; like they're not already super-rich! But here's the really amazing thing! Our attorney called us, and said *Melton* wanted to pay Mallory, too, for the initial idea! Which none of it was that innovative! Kerry Larson, our attorney said it's pretty unheard of for a corporation like that, just to purchase a concept, without being sued for it. Which, we would never have considered suing for something as obvious as that was. Mallory didn't order a gift for her friend, knowing all of that was going to work out that way. She's just loving and generous, and God blesses that."

⊣ ⊢

Shay was nervous. His brother, Shannon, laughed at his fretting. "Look, you know your stuff. You'll do fine. Try to put Emma out of your mind and concentrate on how important the deal is."

"Easy for you to say! Do you even like anyone?" Shay's anguished response.

Shannon shrugged. "Let's just say I've been more goal-oriented lately. Dad challenged me to get rich being a teacher, remember?"

Shay dropped his head into his hands. "Not my favorite subject there, Bro. But, yeah, I remember. He's a fine one to mock education, seeing he got iced sitting in prison."

Shannon shrugged. "The classic definition of 'irony'"!

"Spoken like a true literature teacher. Do you mind sparing me? So, were you starting to say you've figured out a way to get rich teaching school? Please tell me your scheme's legal. Grandmother's finally proud of both of us."

"Well, little brother, you should be relieved to know it isn't a 'scheme'; it's a plan. There's a difference. I'm glad Grandmother's proud of me; and I want to be a credit to Mom's memory. My plan isn't dishonest or novel. It's hard work! I teach in the high school every day, and the junior college two nights a week. I bought a house, which I'm fixing up a couple of other nights a week and Saturdays. I'll move into it, so I can stop throwing rent money away every month. I plan to slowly accumulate rent houses, or flip them for profit, whichever works. In this economy, it's a good plan. There are several foreclosures coming to auction; are you interested?"

Shay started to laugh it off, then met his brother's serious gaze and paused. "Re-cal-cu-lating," he laughed at himself for being short-sighted. "Okay, ya hooked me. What are the properties and when's the sale?"

Shannon chortled gleefully. "Sorry. Time for your meeting! You better scoot along. Sanders won't be impressed by an unexcused tardy. Meet me at McKenna's when you're done. You can buy me a steak, and I'll fill you in."

"Deal"! Shannon slapped his brother on the back, making his way to his rent car. His mind spun from the possibilities! 'Yeah, he loved his grandmother, and Boston, and her mansion, and the work they did together. But, maybe that was Beth and Roger's big concern. That if he married Emma, he'd take her all the way to Boston to live with him and his grandmother in some dank mausoleum! What if he owned two homes? Operated between Boston and western Arkansas? Emma could commute back and forth with him, and the Sanders could make sure he was treating her great! David and Mallory owned two homes; so did the Faulkners. He hadn't intended to get in any kind of a race with them! But Shannon made sense.' He was bright, optimistic, and exuberant as he entered the meeting with Holman, Cat, Beth, and Roger Sanders-and Emma!

⚐ ⚑

"Are you hungry?" Mallory questioned as they pulled away from their appointment with the CPA. Barbecue sounds really good."

"I'm always hungry; great plan. Oops, phone's ringing." He looked at the number. "Yeah Waylon; what's up"?

"Well, all the new trespassing signs came, and we're posting them around as each section of the new fence gets completed. But, I had an idea."

"Well, we're always interested in new ideas," he responded. Secretly he wished, Mayer would talk to him when he was at work. He often felt like the other guy got bored, trumping up reasons to call and chat. David didn't particularly care to buddy up with the employees, especially now when he could be with his wife. Still, he perked up visibly as the other guy continued.

"Okay, slow down."

"Well, the way I see it," Waylon tried to speak more clearly. "You Christians get all exercised about not being able to put the Ten Commandments up in the different public venues: town squares, court houses, the schools. But y'all aren't putting them where you can. I was thinking, 'yeah, put up the **No Trespassing** signs, but post the Ten Commandments, too. Or that verse about *As for me and my house, we will serve the LORD.* I've actually cut out a big board, and thought I'd start wood burning the first one as a prototype to see what you think."

David laughed. "Yeah, it's a good idea, but don't you wood-burn anything. Remember you're dyslexic and can't spell. Okay; the idea's better than good! And you're right! Start cutting out more! If Steb and my dad get on this, we should have orders from all over the country. And you're right; we get so stuck on what we can't do! That we fail to do what we can!"

David disconnected, turning his attention to Mallory. "Go get a table. I'll go through the line; you want ribs?"

She nodded. "Yeah! Get double meat. We can eat it all between the two of us."

He joined her quickly and they prayed before attacking the stack of ribs. "So was Waylon's idea really good, or were you being nice?"

He buttered an ear of corn and a roll. "It was really good! I mean; a brilliant no-brainer. Is that an oxymoron? He hasn't even gotten saved yet, and he's providing wisdom for something the Christian world has missed. What was Jesus' parable about the steward that lost his stewardship, and that the unsaved often use better sense than the 'children of light'?"

Mallory dabbed her chin and fingers. "These are messy. So, what was his illumination?"

"They are. I better eat them all. Corn's messy! It's all messy." He pulled the food toward him and she slapped at him playfully.

"Okay, he's posting the **No Trespassing** signs on the Gilmore land, and he's thinking about maybe posting the Ten Commandments, too. And about how Christians all get in an uproar about our eroding rights to freely express our religion; when the Commandments and Manger Scenes and such are banned in public spaces. Which, I think we should speak out on that. But here's the absurdity he pointed out. We do absolutely nothing to promote righteousness and the Gospel in the ways we can! He suggested that Christians should mark their homes with:

Joshua 24:15 b . . . but as for me and my house, we will serve the LORD.

Wide, expressive eyes met his! "Yeah; is he ever right! Look how many properties we own, that the Lord has given us, and we haven't even~" She giggled delightedly at the opportunities that presented themselves. "Take that, in conjunction with what the CPA just told us!" Her voice was charged.

"What are you talking about? That we produce different signs with Scriptures, for home exteriors? There's a surplus in Christian book and gift store for ones to put on interior walls~"

"Yeah, and they're good. Except usually the people living in the houses are familiar with the truths, whereas, people jogging or driving down the streets, wouldn't be. Waylon's right! We're missing a huge opportunity, not just to share with others, but for giving the Lord the glory for what we have!"

"But you lost me." He dabbed at sticky fingers and the napkin stuck, making a bigger mess. "What does that have to do with what the accountant just told us? We manufacture the plaques, push them on the web sites, and make a fortune on them?"

"M-m-hm-m," she answered brightly, her eyes shining with mischief. "No! We just make a small amount of profit on each one! What kind of money-hungry person do you take me for? Okay, the CPA cautioned about money in off-shore accounts, but he didn't say we shouldn't earn money on foreign investments."

He frowned. I can't even follow the AMEX and NASDAQ, let alone the foreign markets. Besides, which, I thought they were all in a lot of trouble."

She laughed. "See, you follow it better than you thought. Okay, he said we should accrue more expenses, business-related expenses."

"Okay, we'll take more vitamins and health-supplements." His dark eyes danced.

"No, we travel more."

"Sounds fun; how will it count as business-related?"

"Well, we go someplace we want to see anyway, and we buy property there."

"Overseeing property isn't that simple," he cautioned. "Especially across distances"!

She nodded easily. "Probably, but it isn't impossible. Look, the European property market's depressed now, too, so it's an opportune time to buy. We purchase properties, and we can display some sort of Gospel witness in the exterior decor. We rent or lease the properties; even if we lose money, it'll help us. It will give us an excuse to send our staff overseas; they get the benefit of seeing places. I don't know; what do you think?" She trailed off, almost sheepishly.

"Well, now that you explain it to me step by step, I think it's sheer brilliance. I didn't glean that much from listening to that guy. But you're absolutely right. We have money sitting in accounts, doing absolutely nothing! Our own personal money, and not the assets of our corporations. How can you think of such fun ways to make money?"

She shrugged, bathing in the heaven of his praise. "It's just the Lord. If we purchase run-down properties, we'll have to buy materials and use local labor, which should help a few people with jobs. We need to be careful, though, because some of the Europeans countries are on the verge of destabilizing."

"Yeah, maybe we should forget about villas on the Greek Isles."

Mallory dug out her phone. "I need to call Risa. I love the idea of wooden signs with wood burning, for our rural properties. But maybe Risa could do like Calligraphy on tiles and all kinds of artistic slants. You know, some people put out those brightly colored banners; what are they? Nylon? You can get them at the craft stores that say things like 'Spring's Here'!"

"Yes, and while we're on that subject, we should get flag poles and American flags for both of our houses."

"Yeah, what's wrong with us? Also, I need to call Enstrom's and order gifts for Mr. Weatherby and his office staff."

"Have Lisette get it done."

She smiled. "Well, I'd agree with you, but we don't necessarily want everyone to know we've hired another accounting firm."

"You want this last rib?" He thought he should offer. To his chagrin, she did.

Her eyes shone. "Go get another order."

Chapter 25: *ASSIMILATION*

Thanksgiving was lavish at the Ranch. David and Mallory gathered a crowd of family, friends, and co-workers, and the chow hall was warm and festive with a special atmosphere for the campers.

Erik expressed his concern about the campers and the threat they might present to Mallory's safety.

"Erik, we've talked about it; especially about Mardy. And we know you're right. Most of the guys have some type of criminal background. We try to be careful, and I know we can't foresee things. But, we've prayed about it, and it's as close to what my dad bought this property for, as we can come. After a few days here, most of them seem more loyal to us, than our regular employees." She smiled. "I know; we don't want to get confident in that."

She piled whipped cream on top of pumpkin pie and joined her cousins who were engrossed in the Cowboys game. "How's your real estate investing working out?"

Shannon answered eagerly. "Mine's great! I'm nearly ready to move into a home of my own. My brother's a little too snobbish for the venture."

Mallory nodded. "Yes, I imagine. Not many homes like Grandmother's, in Hope. Especially in foreclosure! I thought I checked out a pretty decent-looking frame, four-bedroom with brick exterior."

"I showed him that one! He wouldn't bite!" Shannon's response!

"I'll go in on it with you if you need a silent investor." She tried not to sound too eager.

Shay's temper kicked in. "Okay, you don't have to undercut everyone on everything!"

Mallory's Irish ire fired up in response. "Hello, Shay O'Shaughnessy! What have I ever undercut you on? Or anyone else, for that matter? I try to seize on opportunities. Shannon just said that the house in question isn't good enough for you!"

"I'm still considering it–"

She blew a disgusted sigh. "Well, be sure and take your time. It isn't like it's going to wait for you. Make an offer. If the seller declines, then assume that's the Lord telling you, 'No'. One of David's crews can turn it into a dream, and one with plenty of room for you and Emma getting started. Not that, she's that close to becoming yours. You super-analyze everything too much before you act. Like, you're trying to see how the climate is with Roger and Beth, infusing layers and layers of meaning into every word they say, instead of taking charge and telling them you plan to marry her."

Shay folded his arms belligerently.

"She's right, Dude. We probably lost the chance for getting that house."

Shay strode out, his interest in the football game forgotten.

⚔ ⚔

Xavier was David's buddy, following him around with his own hard hat and little set of tools buckled around him. Mallory watched them with amusement, Zave's little legs pumping as hard as they could, trying to keep up. It was what he needed, though; a place where he could bang and hammer and run off boyish energy. Nadia pushed a doll in a stroller up and back along the asphalt.

Diana joined Mallory, pulling a throw around her, and drawing a chair nearer the Chiminea. "I ate entirely too much."

"So did I," Mallory admitted. "Everything was delish! I love Thanksgiving."

"We do too." Diana's fervent tone! "And who would have ever guessed, but we adore coming to the country. I'm grateful for the upgrading at our house, but it's extra nice to be able to get away and come here. What project is David working on now? I told him he doesn't have to keep an eye on Xavier. John and Daniel and the bigger kids went to practice at the archery range."

Mallory sighed proudly. "I'm not sure. I can't keep up with all his projects. But one of the newest ones, thought of by Waylon, is different signs and ways of stating faith on the exteriors of property. To begin with, they're erecting flag poles: we need to fly the American flag, Arkansas', and the Christian one. Risa's coming up with some ideas of tiles and wrought iron, and other various artistic media. They're working on an elaborate Nativity Scene, too."

"Waylon thought of that? Did he receive the Lord?"

"No. Sometimes we think he's close, but then other times~ David said it reminds him of *Luke 16:8* where Jesus said the children of the world are sometimes wiser than the children of light. I guess Waylon, and a crew, were posting **No Trespassing** signs, and Waylon thought the Ten Commandments would be an appropriate addition. So, then he started thinking that Christians get in a turmoil about our rights of expression of our faith; but we don't express it very well in ways that are not Constitutional and Supreme Court issues. I mean, I think the Framers of the Constitution were very much Biblicists, but we do get stymied by what we can't do, so we don't do what we can. I've been thinking about banners, too. Do you know what I mean?"

Diana nodded noncommittally Mallory laughed. "Relax! You know it's a good idea! You're worried I'm thinking of pirating our seamstresses and tailors from our clothing production. I hardly think I'd do that. We barely keep up with our orders. I'm working in my mind on a proposal for Steb Hanson. Surely some of his retired Christian followers could start producing cute and bright banners as a cottage industry. I'm not talking about the Commandments necessarily, but 'Praise the Lord', 'God is Good', 'I am the Door', 'Trust Jesus'. Erik said that Jack and Estelle Norman who helped rescue Danay Livingston, are retired and barely make ends meet. He's a decorated war hero, too. I tried to convince them to come here; I really want to meet them. But they seemed a little apprehensive. I'd go there and talk to them, but I'm not supposed to travel that far until after the baby's born."

"But you want to assimilate them, too? You're remarkable, Mallory."

"Do you mean that in a good way?"

"Of course! What else would I mean?" Diana was perplexed.

"I don't know. Shay just said something a little while ago that kind of hurt my feelings. I wondered if other people feel the way he does. I mean, I know I get excited, and making plans, and I get carried away~ I see opportunities that seem like they're from the Lord; I don't try to undercut anyone."

"What exactly did he say?"

"I don't know, but it made me mad and then I responded in kind and smarted off to him about Emma and her parents. Now I really feel ashamed of myself."

❈ ❈

Bryce placed a stack of shirts in the suitcase. "I'm excited. This should be fun."

Lisette nodded agreement. "I'm pretty sure Mallory planned for us to have fun, but her major thrust is for us to find some decent properties." She fanned through a stack of computer print-outs. "This is kind of complicated to the ninth power. Not just seeing if the houses look okay, but figuring out the foreign currency and the intricacies of legal differences in purchasing real estate. Mr. Prescott can assist us some."

"I'm eager to see my twinky and Samuel. Don't tell her, but I've really missed her."

"Your secret's safe with me, although she'd probably like to know that. What's with you for always trying to act unfeeling? Why do you always play the tough guy?"

Bryce looked wounded. "Sorry. I didn't realize I do that. I don't know if it's the way I lost my parents, and trying to cope with that. It'd be hard to get mushy with Blythe, and she'd make fun of me."

Lisette shook her head in wonder. "Well, you're probably right. She wouldn't know how to behave if you ever acted human. Once she regained consciousness and adjusted, she'd probably like you better."

❈ ❈

David found Mallory to show her the wooden sign with the lettering stenciled in. "Here's the rough draft. Daniel told me Shay took a jab at you. What was that about?"

"Wow! That looks awesome, already! Then the burned out letters will be darker? Then what? Stain and coat it with something to protect the wood and make it shiny? Maybe I should take a picture and send it to

Steb." She gave him a condensed version of her plan to involve Hansen and his retired *SOC Foundation* followers.

"You know, Christmas is on top of us, and there's no time to waste. I mean, I know a lot of times a formally written out business plan is necessary. But if you give Steb your sketchy idea, he'll have people all over it this weekend. People with cramped budgets can earn some extra for Christmas, and other people, who can't find a Nativity Scene anywhere for any price, will find that they've become available all across the country. Synergy! But we can't sit on it. I'll go email him right now. I'll deal with Shay later, since you obviously don't plan to tell me what he said."

⚜

"Weather's changing our itinerary," Bryce announced to Blythe. "Our layover in New York is going to be shortened. Our getting into Manhattan is impossible now. We really were looking forward to getting together."

Blythe was taken aback by Bryce's obvious disappointment. "Well, we only came North to get together with the two of you. We'll check out here, and be at the airport by the time you land. We'll eat and talk at the airport, and when y'all leave for London, we'll check on getting an earlier flight home. Herb and Linda and Merc and Nell all want us to come to Dallas for Christmas; so maybe we can spend more time together then."

"That would be awesome. I know Lisette would love that. Okay, see ya at the airport."

⚜

Shay refused the baked goodies left over from the Sander family's Thanksgiving meal. "I shouldn't have charged down here this way, with this being a holiday, but Mallory accused me of stalling; I thought I'd been looking for the time to be right."

Roger Sanders laughed. "A delicate thing! Sometimes we do wait for a perfect moment; usually it never comes. Still, you hate to charge in without considering timing at all. What's on your mind?"

"Emma!" Shay blurted out the answer without laying any groundwork. "She's always what's on my mind! I really love her, Sir, and Ma'am. I'm not sure what your difficulties are with that. Is it the fact that I plan to keep looking after my grandmother and living so far away? I thought my brother had come up with a plausible solution, but now I don't think so."

Beth smiled. "Well, first of all, about caring for your grandmother; we're very impressed by the deferential way you treat her. She's a great lady. What did Shannon say?"

Shay motioned defeatedly with his hands. "Well, he's gotten interested in Real Estate here in the Hope area, foreclosures and getting houses at auction. I thought maybe I could have a home here and Grandmother's in Boston."

"Why is that not a good idea?" Roger's expression was impassive.

"Okay, it is a good idea. For some people! Many do very well at it, I guess. I'm too busy with what I have going on, and I committed about the deal with *Sanders* and the new dye-stuffs and that project. Managing real estate is so 'out there'!"

"It doesn't really dovetail with your business model. I agree. And Shannon's first remodel doesn't look the best-"

"It looks awful, but he's so proud of himself-" Shay sighed. "I hated to say anything to him, but he doesn't have a clue. And I sure don't. So, I backed away from the entire concept. I had thought that you might not be against Emma marrying me, if we owned a home here. But my grandmother's home is huge, and she feels like there's plenty of room for Emma and me to live our lives, pretty much in privacy."

"Well, we've been against her marrying anyone. She isn't even twenty. I guess I have let Connie and Brent's situation color my reaction to any suitors for my other two girls. And, I'm sorry to say, but I let the facts affect me about your being a 'novice' Christian, and your father."

Shay spread his hands on the edge of the kitchen counter. "I'm pretty sure my dad was behind my mom's death! Believe me, I had a problem with him, too! But it's what is, and I can't change it. I really respect you both, and I'll abide by what you say; or try to- I can't even imagine trying to love anyone else, though."

⚜

Rhonna sorted through emails; nothing of importance to address. She poured a cup of coffee, while going over some priorities mentally. With David and Mallory and Lisette all out of the office, she was overseeing things. She called a meeting. "Okay, just touching base with everyone.

The TV news crew is going to be at *Gemhouse* tomorrow for the Christmas Gems Extravaganza. Of course, Davis is on top of the details, but I'd like it if you, Anna, and Luke, would be there also to make sure David and Mallory are nicely represented. Davis sometimes likes to give the impression that he's still totally in charge. It begins at one-thirty, but be there an hour early to make sure everything's first-rate. Of course, look your best, and make sure you review the Christmas line so you can address questions. Deborah, I need you to book a flight to Vermont. The Normans are interested in making signs and banners. You need to meet with them, and get them whatever they need to get started. They'll get a credit card so they can handle their expenses. Then, Mrs. Faulkner and Alexandra were both already busy ordering fabric in all different colors for the banners and having some of it shipped up there. You'll see to obtaining a sewing machine, and Mr. Norman needs art supplies and wood and stuff to paint his signs. They have a friend who works in glass to make door insets and sun-catchers. Kind of make sure they can all make it happen. David wants to help them out, but he wants decent-looking stuff in return. Do you think your dad can go with you? Is he a good driver on snow? He'll get paid for his time and all of his expenses traveling with you. Heather, keep doing what it is that you do. Looking for fraudulent charges and scoping out opportunities. Damon, you and Todd plan to work in Arkansas the rest of the week. Security's going in on the Gilmore place, and David wants you all to be versed in everything. Any questions, call me. Bryce and Lisette are hitting a few bumps in the London real estate arena, so she's a little frustrated."

"What are you going to be doing?" Damon's question seemed to reflect genuine interest.

"Don't worry 'bout the mule goin' blind; just load the wagon." Rhonna rose and moved past them.

"Hunh? What was that supposed to mean? What wagon are we supposed to load?" Damon's question was directed toward everyone in general.

"I think she was telling you in so many words, to mind your own business," was Luke's response. "She answers to Lisette; not to us. When Lisette's gone, she's in charge. Let's go down and eat in the cafe, then we can go change before we head to the Ranch."

"Actually, you should stay decent-looking to travel, and change to work clothes when you get there." Heather suggested. "It's what we're about; remember?"

Damon started to protest, but Luke agreed. "Good point. Do you have time to join us for lunch?"

Heather accepted readily, while Deborah, surfing air fares, shook her head negatively.

"I'll bring something back for you," Heather offered. "Chef Salad?"

⊰ ⊱

Bryce and Lisette finished dinner at a restaurant in Victoria Station. "Well, I'm feeling beat, and we don't have a whole lot to show for it. I usually feel peppier than this."

"Well, factor in jet lag and the weather," Bryce suggested. "We should still take the Tube to Knightsbridge and shop at Harrods before we go back to the hotel. We can take a cab back from there; what do you say?"

Lisette summoned a bright smile. "Sounds like fun!" And it really did. Sometimes he could be fun and take interest in things.

⊰ ⊱

Rhonna checked her makeup before entering the salon. "I think I need the works," she confessed. "I get so busy I don't take time for myself." She chose a polish color and slid her feet into the swirling water.

"How's your CD selling?" The shop owner remained suspicious about the girl's employment.

"You know, better than I thought it would. Did I ever give you one? If you want to make a little extra, I could fix you up to help move them on commission."

"Cash money?"

"M-m-m, I don't know about that. I have this Uncle, Uncle Sam? You ever heard of my uncle? He always likes to make sure he gets his slice of the pie. I can handle the paperwork, though, so you just receive a form reflecting your earnings from me, for when you file your taxes. Think about it. You have contacts I'll never meet; it could be beneficial to both of us."

"How's that lady that came in with you the first time?"

Rhonna smiled. "Diana Faulkner. Yeah; she's nice! She's doin' fine. I wish you could meet David and Mallory Anderson, too. Hey, are you interested in getting jewelry for anyone on your Christmas list? I have complimentary passes to a Christmas Gemstone Extravaganza at *Gemhouse, Inc.* It's a nice shindig with great food. The jewelry's exceptionally nice; from classical to whimsical, and across a price spectrum."

"Sounds intriguing, but I hate to show up places I haven't been before, solo. And with the Holidays and parties coming up, I can't really let anyone off to go with me."

Rhonna flipped magazine pages, not wanting to be pushy and override the other woman's every objection. An hour later, getting her hair redone, she tried to re-approach the subject casually. "It's a come-and-go affair. If you like, I could meet you about two-fifteen, and we could attend together."

⊰ ⊱

David frowned in concentration. Usually tuning his violin didn't make him nervous; but around Daniel Faulkner~ He winked at Mallory who was seated on the front pew with her mouth ajar. She was still as awestruck by the Faulkners as she had always been. Well, they were very impressive.

"Are you two planning to sing, *It's a Miracle?* It's a real winner with people."

David studied Daniel's expression; deadpan. "Well if you want us to, and there's time." Faulkner was a nice guy and an awesome Christian, but he could get possessive at times, of the repertoire.

Faulkner was impressed. David Anderson was developing a great sense of when to back off and, conversely, when to take charge. "Okay, plan on it, second number. It's a great addition; it conveys a great message light-heartedly."

David nodded. "Yes, I agree. It would be even better with your kids singing it with us."

Of course, Daniel agreed with that, but he held some reservations "I'm not sure any of them even know it."

"Xavier does. He sings along with me when we're working."

Daniel bounded away to confer with the sound man. Xavier on the platform was a scary thought.

⊰ ⊱

Deborah was enjoying time alone with her dad. He didn't necessarily have experience driving in snow, but he had more of a feel for driving, in general. They were both awed by the Vermont wonderland. The Normans and their friend Greta Jorgenson were waiting for them, and forming a bond was easy. The visit required several days of hustling, but Deborah and Manny felt a sense of jubilant accomplishment as they boarded their flight back to Dallas. Estelle had completed three brightly colored banners, had learned to photograph them on her cell phone, and email the pictures to the *SOC Foundation* web site. Greta, doing the same with glass suncatchers, learned the same process for sharing her gift with a market eager for it. Jack patiently cut out each piece of a manger scene with a jigsaw. His projects required more time, but he was excited about the prospects presenting themselves.

⊰ ⊱

Xavier was adorable singing with his older siblings and David and Mallory. On the final stanza, he held the mic determinedly in chubby little hands.

"But God knows my name,
And He cares about me!"

⊰ ⊱

Bryce and Lisette returned home with one property in London, and one in Paris and a handful of contacts. "I just never felt like I could really get with it," Lisette apologized to Mallory by phone. "At least Rhonna did a bang-up job here. Maybe you should have sent her. Bryce was kind of thumbs-down to everything we looked at."

"Listen, you did fine. You're right; Rhonna is turning out to be even more amazing that I thought. And, you've done a great job training her. If you can turn people under you into amazing leaders, they won't take your place! I plan to send her someplace, in the very near future, to represent us. That's a credit to you, and not a threat. Do you think you need to see a doctor?"

"Well, I don't think so; I'm not really sick. Sort of zapped; kinda hard to explain"!

"Oh yes, believe me; I know the feeling very well~" Mallory's voice was loaded with meaning.

"Okay, well, yeah! You're~" Lisette paused. "I'm not! I'm sure that isn't my problem. I'll fill you in more later; okay? About the properties, and the contractors we met with." She escaped the call and sank weakly onto her sofa.

"Are you okay?" Bryce was watching her from the dining room. "Was the boss not happy with our results?

"Yeah, I think she is; we didn't really go into detail." Her eyes met his as tears escaped down her cheeks.

⚜

Harold Foster, President of Tulsa University, escorted his visitor to the outer offices, returning to his desk with some items to clear up. He summoned the dean of the Earth Sciences Department, who appeared as quickly as possible.

"What's going on?" Concern was etched in his features.

"I just had a visit with an esteemed alumnus, Daniel Jeremiah Faulkner."

"Okay, is that good? Are they going to endow the University? I guess they really have the money. You're talking about the senior guy, right?"

"Have a seat." Foster sat grim-faced while the professor complied, before continuing, "Their money is frankly, none of our concern. Our faculty and staff are. Faulkner came to register a complaint against David Higgins and his conduct. Off-the-record, between the two of us, as old friends"! He steepled his fingers and regarded them critically, clearing his throat several times. "I'm trying to word this carefully. The Faulkner family, as you know, all had a-a-a religious experience."

"Oh, yes, Sir. We all know about that! Gone to seed on all that Creationism-garbage~"

President Foster straightened commandingly. "If you'll allow me~ I'll let you know when I'm ready for you to speak. Okay, coming straight to my point, David Higgins has turned into a loose cannon. Because he was buddies with the younger Faulkner in their college years, he seems to think they're still friends and peers. Because of that, he has begun taking liberties, trying to revive and cash in on an old friendship which no longer exists. His antics, in spite of the class and grace of the Faulkner family, have become impossible for us to overlook. He's tried to coerce Faulkner into sending his son here, and he's suggested heavily that Daniel give us funds. The University handles that; hopefully, with more taste and class than Higgins has exerted. He's practically become a thug."

"Pffftt!" The derisive expression delivered scornfully.

"Unless you would like to turn your resignation in with that of Professor Higgins, I suggest you remain respectful. Higgins, for some reason that defies my logic, has stirred up a woman from the past to make trouble for the family. Something akin to blackmail and extortion! Higgins misrepresented to both Faulkner and the woman. Now, she won't leave Daniel alone; he's changed all of his contact information to be rid of her harassing emails, phone calls, and other attempts at contact. Of course, that caused all of their correspondence with their customer base to be disrupted, and she can probably get the new information. In the meantime, *GeoHy* has been dealing with all the nuisance Higgins set in motion: new stationery, business cards, and so forth. Now, the woman is trying to make contact through his involvement with Mallory O'Shaughnessy's company. I'm at a loss as to how to make it stop, but I'm outraged at the person who started it! Such unprofessional and unbecoming behavior will not be tolerated by the University! I'm sure Higgins will fight his termination, but a review is under way. He'll lose. Put out feelers to find a replacement for his position. That's all."

⊣ ⊢

Steb and Christine laughed at a few crank emails sent to the *Foundation*, criticizing the Hansons for becoming commercialized and using the non-profit status fraudulently.

"We aren't making a cent on this, neither is the *Foundation*, although, if it were, it wouldn't be fraud as long as the funds went to our mission statement. Part of our mission is to wake Christians up to the plight of this nation. People of faith, proclaiming it on their doorsteps; what could be more inspired? It's amazing, really. Christian people all around the country are going to work with hobbies or cottage industries, to supply this demand we're creating. Using our *Foundation* as a clearing house, a way for the buyers to be in contact with the sellers, is helping thousands of people, and getting more attention to what we're doing. *Romans 8:28* at work once again"!

⊰ ⊱

David and Mallory met Frank and Linda Gilmore for dinner at a prestigious old hotel in downtown Little Rock.

"This is a treat for me," Linda beamed as they were all seated.

The captain moved forward, unfolding the ladies' napkins and placing them across their laps.

"It is for us, too." Mallory was genuine. "Nothing from the bar"! Her words to the captain were delivered firmly, but with a smile. She wasn't sure about the Gilmore's stance on alcohol, but she and David were buying the meal.

With their order turned in, David began. "We actually have an installment for you." He drew a check from his jacket pocket. "Things are actually going smoothly up there. No more cattle rustling within the past two months. I know Abe keeps you in the loop. He's a good man.; devoted to both of you."

"Well, we haven't been worried about this." Frank's eyes glinted good-humoredly as he tucked the proffered check into a compartment of his wife's handbag. "We're so glad you've recognized Abe's value and kept him on. Sometimes, when folks get old and kinda crippled up~" His voice broke.

"He's a treasure to us," Mallory spoke hastily. "He knows cattle; we sure don't. He knows all the vets and everyone at the feed stores, practically everyone in five counties. All the other guys that work with him like him, too, as well as respecting him"!

"Well, I'm glad things are settling down. All this cattle rustling! Well, it's always good for cattlemen when the price of beef is good. It's just sad; it seems like there are more and more people that have no qualms about taking what isn't theirs. You've made the place state-of-the-art to discourage that kind of thing. I guess I just felt too old and gutted to tackle it. When Abe's arthritis kept getting worse, we weren't getting any younger, the house was about to fall through, I just decided to get out! But, even getting out seemed daunting! All those fast-talking realtors saying do this, do that! Fix this; parcel it up."

Over dessert, Gilmore leaned forward. "With the completion of that big barn, David has informed me I can bring some of my stuff back out there to store. Some of it's kinda valuable, and now that someone's watching the place twenty-four/seven~"

Mallory felt a moment of panic. Taking responsibility for other people's valuables concerned her.

Gilmore laughed. "Okay, relax, girlie, and give your husband some credit. I have my stuff insured to the hilt, and he has everything spelled out in detail about liability. Not that any of it matters much. Linda and I don't have any heirs; we planned to leave Abe taken care of, but we didn't really want to leave everything we have to him. Of course, we're both in fairly good health, and we want to enjoy what we have together. When we both pass on, we want you two to inherit our estate."

Mallory gasped in amazement, speechless.

"You know, we credit your daddy for what we now enjoy. I was basically a hard-scrabble farmer, and I was about to lose my tractor. Linda and I went to an auction to clear out some junk that had been on our place for longer than we had owned it. Well, your daddy, he was real intrigued by some of it. He told us not to unload it, but that he'd come to our place. We would gladly have sold him every scrap for a hundred dollars and felt lucky at that. But, your dad, he was the most honest man I ever met."

Mallory nodded through tears. "And some of the (junk) was valuable antiques, and he knew the value to the penny, and where to find buyers who would offer top dollar. My mom and everybody thought he was kind of crazy; I guess I did, too. But, we really loved each other. I still miss him so much. I'm excited about our baby, but every day it makes me sad that my dad's gone. He would have been even a more amazing grandpa than he was a dad."

"Yeah, and he loved baseball and the Red Sox. He talked almost as much about them as he did about you. You know, when that fancy Faulkner family hauled you off to Dallas, did you ever wonder what became of the stuff lying around your house and shed?"

Mallory's eyes widened as she dabbed at tears. "As a matter of fact; not really! A hauler came, trying to get my old tractor, but the wasps stung him and ran him off. Then it sold for a lot of money. The shed~the people from the Treasury Department~there was still stuff strewn everywhere a couple of days before the will~"

He chortled. "I cleared it away and warehoused it. I figured if someone wanted it, they could speak up." He paused, his eyes glinting. "Diamonds were falling out of every cranny of that house, so David moved it up to the camp property and dismantled it. I know you keep the Diamond production low-key~" He shrugged.

"Is any of the stuff valuable; do you know? I think it should belong to you now. Even though I found out a few pieces of it were worth a lot, I still thought most of it was part of the subterfuge. I've never given it another thought. Well, I say I haven't. My dad left files and files of paperwork; some of which related to purchases and sales of his 'stuff'. I spent quite a bit of time going through it; I'm not sure why. But then, it all got stolen from rental storage in Dallas."

"You might mention it to Lilly Cowan." Linda's suggestion made nonchalantly, like she hadn't delivered a bomb-shell!

Chapter 26: *ARREST*

Bryce and Lisette sat facing one another in wonder. "Wow! I don't know what to say. Wow!" Bryce looked and sounded dazed. "You've kept saying you were sure you could never have children, and frankly, I didn't care. Well, I thought I didn't. Did a doctor tell you you never could?"

Lisette shrugged. "I've tried to block most of it out. I'm not sure. I mean; I wasn't a Christian. I believed in God, though, and I was so sure He would punish me. I guess I figured it would serve me right, to be unable to bear children. Even when Mallory suggested I might be expecting, I was sure she was wrong, or that it would be something strange. I can't believe the report that everything seems fine, and my scarring, in view of what all went on, is minimal. It's amazing when you figure God will punish you forever, and He reminds you you're forgiven. I'm emotional."

⊰ ⊱

Steb and Christine were bursting with excitement. There was no end of the creativity and whimsy Christian people were bringing to light. Churches were getting on board, too. And not just Baptist churches, but all types of denominations were working harder to proclaim the Savior's birth. Living Manger Scenes, elaborate drive-through and walk-through musical dramas, extra groups of carolers. "Let's work on changing what needs to be changed, but let's do all we can, in the meanwhile," seemed to be the battle cry. Not, 'We can't', but rather, 'We can'! Especially through Christ"!

It's so exciting." Christine's beautiful features were alight. "But remind everyone to keep praying for our country, too. It's so easy to only pray, or only work. We need to remember both."

Steb rose with his perennial coffee mug. "Yes Dear, you're right. You always are." He laughed. "I'll go post it right now, and then we'll head to Tucson to get the Normans. I'm sure glad they're coming. It's thanks to them that Danay gets to enjoy Christmas at home. They really suffered for trying to help, but they created just enough delay to Oberson's team, that the storm got bad." He broke off, realizing Missy was listening.

Christine turned. "Hello, Honey; do you need something?"

Missy's face was chalky. "Oberson? Is he coming?"

Christine rose. "No, he won't be spending Christmas at home, not this year; and hopefully never again. He's in jail. Jack and Estelle Norman are coming here. They are the couple who helped rescue Danay Livingston. They're good people; not bad ones."

"Is Sheriff Roberson coming, then? Who's supposed to come for me?"

"Roberson's in jail, too." Hanson's voice was a fierce growl. "No one's coming for you, Missy. You're home. You're here to stay."

"Sheriff Roberson is the sheriff. He isn't in jail. He has the key. He puts people in jail."

"He isn't sheriff anymore." Steb labored for a patient tone. "They took his badge, and his gun, and his key, away! He can't hurt you." He was amazed by his daughter's words. He and the FBI were convinced that the former sheriff had been instrumental in Missy's disappearance, but her words now were the first she had spoken to confirm it.

"Would you like to join us, Dear, going to Tucson to meet the Normans?" Christine's voice sounded hopeful, but Steb's heart plummeted. Changing anything about their daughter's routine could be terribly upsetting for all of them.

"Is there enough room? Will they have suitcases?"

"Of course there's room for you, Missy. The trunk of the car's real big for their luggage. Once we pick up our guests, you can ride in front by Daddy. I'll sit in back with Jack and Estelle. Then we want to have dinner at a nice restaurant and ride around and look at Christmas lights and Manger Scenes."

Caroline Hillman and another agent tailed a suspect: one who was shopping fiendishly for expensive stuff. Since they weren't actually working under cover, they weren't set up to fit in with the other up-scale women around them, who were grabbing things to try on.

"Keep an eye; I'm going to report to Bransom." Hillman moved from the busy department.

"Learn anything?" Bransom's tone was tense.

The other agent laughed. "Oh yeah. I found out people can spend fifteen hundred dollars on a cotton blouse without blinking. Oh, you mean about our person of interest? She's trying on twenty armloads of things; she gets attention; she is gorgeous. She's a jerk, though, to the salespeople. Okay, the rejects, I think she just left in the dressing room. I think that's what all these gals do; not accustomed to picking up after themselves. Okay, she has a big pile she's purchasing. She already bought out the lingerie department. She wrote a check there, now she's presenting plastic. You want us to move in?"

Erik hesitated. "Not yet. This is enough to nab her for fraud, but if we let her keep on, we'll have more. Just don't lose her."

⊸目 圼⊱

"I love Christmas." Mallory's eyes glowed as they exited their gates, passing their elaborate Christmas displays. "But now, when these decorations comes down, we can put up some other type of witness. It's fun to scan through all the options. Sam fixed up a web site for the artists and buyers to get together, and Missy's learning the system to oversee it. Christine told me that it finally got through to her, that she was home and safe. I guess, whoever took her, just drummed and drummed on her, that her mom and dad didn't want her, didn't care what happened to her. All those years, while their hearts were breaking, she thought that." She stopped herself. "I'm sorry. I was talking about loving Christmas and went all morose on you. I'm excited about the things I've gotten you. I wish you could open some of them now."

David laughed. "Right! You're just trying to find out if I've gotten you anything yet, and what it is."

"I mean it, David, please don't get me another horse."

He kissed her fingers. "Don't worry. As good of an idea as that was, I have some others. I don't want us to get in a rut when we've only been married six months. The Anatole just texted me a picture of the banquet set-up!" He displayed the image. "Sadly, it looks like all the doors are on the hinges."

She laughed. "I was so upset with that Turkish manager; it was like, he understood English, but he didn't understand why we would want our meeting to be private. That was literally an 'open door' of opportunity. Then, you were a genius to announce to people about Faith's web-site."

"Well, thanks. I guess it was the Holy Spirit. I seldom visit the site now, since we're so busy and we're usually there each Sunday morning, but there are a lot of Turkish followers, and quite a few Iranians."

"That's amazing, David. The internet causes lots of problems, and it's easy to forget what a valuable tool it is, for both business and ministry."

He nodded. "Yeah, hey, you know what? Let's ask the Lord to do something incredible like that through this banquet tonight." They bowed their heads and joined hands as David worded the short prayer.

※ ※

Professor David Higgins left from the meeting; a lynch mob! Tension and fury emanated from every pore. He wasn't guilty of any of the stuff they said. If he had ever had a plot, it had certainly backfired. He tried now, to remember what exactly had transpired with his last meeting with Faulkner. Short! The guy had ticked him off bragging about having a country home! He got his parking validated~ How was it his fault if Nan Burnside had turned stalker? Who wouldn't want to be stalked by a gal like that? He couldn't help it if the woman still carried a torch. He pulled in at a liquor store near his home. He'd sue the University, sue Foster, sue the Faulkners!

※ ※

Bransom, resplendent in his tuxedo, gave last-minute instructions to his task force. "This suspect has crossed over a line. She's guilty of fraud. Arrest her and read her her rights, like you would any other lowlife who isn't gorgeous and dressed to the nines. If I had more female agents, there wouldn't be a guy in this group."

"I've collared good-looking women before, Bransom. You treat us like we're kindergarteners. We promise not to succumb to her charms.

344

Not nervous because it's personal, are you? I mean, if this woman's really stalking Faulkner, they should file a restraining order and let their LEO's deal with her."

"Yeah; they've been prayin' about it; hopin' she'd give up and go away. Which, if she were a person with good sense~well, a person with good sense would have given up when it ended years ago!" He laughed at himself. "Stalkers are not people with good sense! But, she's made herself a nuisance across state lines, causing snafus for both *GeoHy* and now making problems for *DiaMo*. I mean in this economy, how long can a person just keep on making trouble for people just trying to conduct their own business? And, this isn't her first time writing insufficient funds checks, and getting credit cards fraudulently. She's begged her way out before; never even been put on probation."

"What will keep her from throwing herself on the mercy of the court this time?"

"I'm not sure. Sometimes, charges do stick, and people are dealt with for their misdeeds. I just keep at doing my job. David and Mallory and DiaMo are bringing a civil suit. There's always that when the criminal system fails."

"That sounds like a three-ring circus. If the Andersons win a judgment, how will Burnside pay up? With a bad check?"

"I hope so; then we could arrest her again. She hasn't gotten off this time, yet, though. Don't forget. Alright Hillman's in charge. I'm meeting Suzanne for our big shindig."

"Look, there are the Faulkners!" Mallory's voice was charged with awe. That always amazed David, in a way. Of course they were here! They were part of the same corporate enterprises. But Mallory was right! They were A-ma-zing!

"Yeah, see the bellman is unloading. They're checking into their suite first; which is what we're doing, too." Hopkins pulled the vehicle in behind the Faulkners, waiting for a bellman to unload David and Mallory's things. David hopped out, offering a hand to Mallory. "You look sensational."

She grinned at him as she stepped down. "Thank you. I feel like a beached whale."

"Well, you look better than the ones I've seen. How do you know how beached whales feel?" He knew he could make her laugh, and his original assessment about her being a sensation was on target. She wore a taffeta skirt of ivory and cinnamon plaid, flared, with large ruffle, swishing softly with her every movement. A cute cinnamon-colored sweater flared over her tummy, finished with taffeta cuffs and collar. Glossy heels and evening bag complemented, and a white mink cape warded off a definite chill.

Mallory paused, watching Daniel and Diana unload their family; Daniel, in his tux, and Diana in the Sable coat; her hair down, but clipped back, spotlighting Diamond chandelier earrings. Daniel carried Ryan, and Al and Cass had Zave and Nadia clasped firmly by the hand.

David hung back. "You're right. They're incredible."

Daniel indicated a comfortable-looking conversation area in the spacious lobby, and Diana and the kids turned aside; he could complete their expedited check-in.

David nudged her gently toward Faulkner's family, moving toward the check-in counter himself. Diana was intrigued with her children, but Mallory frowned as some woman swooped dramatically to the exclusive check-in and grabbed Daniel's arm. Before he could register any response, FBI agents moved forward and grasped her.

"FBI! You're under arrest!"

Chapter 27: AWARDS

In their suite, Mallory trembled in David's arms. "Wow, that was a show I hope I never see a rerun of. Maybe I shouldn't have mentioned her to Erik."

"Why not? I mean, the FBI didn't arrest her for being a nuisance. When you brought her to his attention, and he checked her out-well, she's had a few brushes with the law. I guess she thinks she's too gorgeous, or smart, or something, to work a job like everyone else has to do. Faulkner isn't the first guy whose assets she's targeted. She's kind of a Jekyll and Hyde; a real mean streak one minute when she's crossed, but then a sweet, tragic victim when she faces a judge or jury. You okay? We have a busy night bearing down on us in less than thirty minutes."

She patted tears. "I'm fine; I'm happy for Lisette, but that means I'm taking some of her responsibility back." She forced a brave smile. "Okay, tonight's awesome. Lord, don't let weird stuff ruin it."

Rhonna rushed to meet them as they appeared for the banquet, her iPad in the crook of her arm, marking off a 'to do' list. "I think we have everything ready. I tried to visit with the Blairs. Does he have a problem with black people?"

"Not necessarily. He doesn't like anyone much," David responded quickly."

"Rhonna, you look really cute!" Mallory took note of the deep, luxurious, black velvet. The only adornment was a black velvet rose with a trio of pearls in the center, clasping one corner of the square neckline. Pearl posts accented with small diamonds glowed on her earlobes. "You have incredible taste."

The Faulkners, getting out their instruments, tuning up, being so totally normal, helped restore Mallory's nerves. She wondered if they felt more turmoil than they showed outwardly.

After the strangeness of the opening act, the evening was awesome! David was incredible as MC, maintaining the balance between humor and emotion. The year had been astounding, and the Andersons shared generously with those who worked to make it happen. The businesses were family-oriented, the new hires being joined by parents and siblings. Deborah and her mother, Nita, earned a trip for their entire family to visit relatives in Costa Rica; Waylon's family received a ski trip to Steamboat Springs; Rhonna and her family were Hawaii-bound, where they would take a cruise to four of the Islands. The other employees were rewarded with similar destinations of their dreams.

The food was marvelous; attractive salads, large portions of Virginia ham, scalloped potatoes, Brussels sprouts in a cheddar sauce, and candied yams.

During break, David and Mallory visited animatedly with various friends.

Following the break, John Anderson presented a devotion; the familiar theme of, 'Don't get so frenetic with Christmas activities, that you crowd Christ out'. Mallory crossed her eyes impishly at David. Church activities were the main things filling up the December calendar. It was a good reminder, though. With his message finished, and more carols and Christmas songs sung, he made more presentations. Eight different pastors and their families had been invited as special guests: The Ellises, the Blairs, and the leaders of six other churches, started or being helped by John Anderson Ministries. None had ever made the trip, and it was a dream most had dared not dream of.

Psalm 35:27 Let them shout for joy, and be glad, that favor my righteous cause: yea, let them say continually, Let the LORD be magnified, which hath pleasure in the prosperity of his servant.

Mallory introduced Lilly, who loved the attention, and who was acting as liaison with the Israeli tourism industry. An added bonus was the choice of two *DiaMal* ensembles for the ladies to enjoy on the trip. Also included in the guest list were Nick and Jennifer.

During the final break, desserts and more beverages appeared in abundance. David got Mallory a piece of pumpkin pie loaded with whipped cream and fixed a big sampler plate for himself. The Faulkners provided musical background as people spent the remainder of the evening socializing.

Shay approached his cousin bashfully, offering a gift. "I'm sorry for what I said Thanksgiving. I really didn't mean what it sounded like. It's just, Shan got me all hyped, about real estate and investing, and maybe an angle with Roger Sanders. And then! I saw his remodeling handiwork! I didn't know what to say to keep you from investing with him!"

Mallory shook her head, perplexed. "Yeah, well, biting on the property was the main thing. Opportunities don't just sit and wait while you decide. I wouldn't have to move very fast to 'undercut' you."

"Well, maybe I am cautious. I can't afford to lose money on snap decisions."

Mallory laughed. "Whatever, Shay! We don't make 'snap' decisions, but we do make decisions. We made a joint offer with Shannon, we bid low and sold the property two days later, making over five thousand, without applying an ounce of paint. I know it doesn't always turn out that way." She peeked into the gift bag, then, ripped the tissue out of the way. "Isn't that adorable? This is our first baby outfit! Oh! That's so cute!"

Shay looked dumbfounded. "It's the first? I figured she already had a nursery full of clothes!"

"No! A nursery full of toys! Well! Three nurseries full of toys!" She smiled happily at David. "We never had many toys. This is so adorable, Shay, and soft. Alpaca! I love it."

"Yeah, I wasn't sure Dallas would still be cold enough for her to wear it by her arrival in March. If it isn't, you'll have to come see Grandmother and me in Boston! It stays cold there year round." He blushed at her praise.

"Mallory, do you and David feel like having more coffee?" Daniel's voice at her elbow.

"Oh, I think we're always game for that." Her eyes met David's for assurance, and he agreed readily.

A small group assembled in one corner of the lobby, and Daniel and David secured a pot of coffee from the bar tender. "It's amazing that a huge, convention hotel isn't set up for guests to be able to have coffee beverages," Daniel observed.

"Well, they have a coffee bar, and probably it's busy in the mornings. They have the coffee shop closed up and the bars open at night, in response to what the majority of the clientele wants. They're interested in their bottom line, like we are. The bars make money in the evenings, and the coffee shops don't. It's another indictment of our society in general." Roger's assessment. "Where did your cousin go?" he questioned Mallory. "Emma's coming back down in a minute."

Mallory seemed to be listening to the lively conversation and banter, but her thoughts churned. Erik had tried to ignore his phone throughout the evening, but then had finally left. She wondered idly if Daniel's idea of coffee and extending the party was that he didn't really want to face Diana with the weirdness of what had happened.

"What do you think, Mallory?" Shay's question brought her back to the moment.

She flushed, flustered. "Uh? About what?"

"When did you stop listening? Do I need to go back over the whole thing?"

"Yeah, I guess."

"Okay," Shay laughed. "Look me in the eyes. I brought you a baby gift, an Alpaca set, and you said it's so soft, and non-allergenic, and you haven't bought baby clothes because you've gone crazy on toys-"

"Well, I didn't say 'Gone crazy'," she protested.

"Well, no, but you did say three nurseries full-"

"Yeah, so"?

He laughed. "Oooh, aren't we defensive? But you made me think of a great idea! It's so great I don't even have to mull it over for weeks. Everybody else agreed with me the first time, but you were in Lala Land! I have this concept of making toys from Alpaca. I'm thinking of an adorable little Alpaca animal to begin with. Or how about a little baby doll dressed in an Alpaca sweater set, with the felt shoes and beret? I see I have your attention now!"

She laughed. "Yes, Shay, you do, and a variation on a theme. We should get into doll clothes. There's a really popular doll line, right now, and that company is so enterprising. I admire their business model." Her gaze directed to Diana, whose approval she usually sought. "Why don't we produce a cute doll, too? And we can offer doll dresses to match our little girl dresses."

Diana sighed slowly. "I don't know. It's kind of copy-cat."

"But not piracy! And not many people seem to be copying, for as great of an idea as they have. And we have really gorgeous designs. The dolls can sell us, and we can sell them. Kids always want more toys! They get them, too."

Diana laughed. "Well, evidently yours will! But you're right. We've had cute designs, too. As the one who conceived many of them, it's sad for me to see them fade away."

"Yes, and I loved that Linen Damask dress I had; the one in pale yellow. Just such cute things! And we have contacts in China~"

-⚏ ⚏-

Dawson was more furious with Bransom than he had been in a long time. "What's that about, Erik? Is this some personal witch hunt of yours to help your friends? Mallory complains to you, and you fix it for her?"

Erik tried to remember the verse about a soft answer turning away wrath. "If that's what it looks like, I'm sorry. Mallory made me aware of some of the things the suspect was up to: I had her investigated because she's a law-breaker. Isn't that what we're about?"

"Well, there are a lot of worse people out there, who demand our resources."

In spite of good intentions, Erik lost his cool. "Okay~ So~what? Just expend our energies on the ten most wanted, and forget everyone else? Make sure we only nab the very worst, even if others are really, really bad, and a menace to society? Nan Burnside is a white-collar (if you will) criminal. She writes hot checks and gets credit cards and runs them up, not intending to pay them back. She's taken bankruptcy before, but usually she finds some poor chump to charm into helping her out of scrapes. She doesn't care if she leaves broken families in her wake! She's crazy! Doesn't take 'no' for an answer, and she's gotten more desperate! David and Mallory's company shouldn't have to keep making expensive changes in their security and firewall because this woman is so desperate to get at Faulkner. I mean, how many members of society does she have to victimize, before someone decides 'it's enough'? I mean, it isn't just the Faulkners and Andersons she's hurting! Who pays for all of her defaults? Thefts, if you will? I do! You do! Every rich person in America; and every poor person, gets hit in the pocketbook because of irresponsible credit. Every time Nan Burnside gets something she doesn't plan to work at paying for, just because she's pretty, and spoiled, and wants it; I help bail her out! You define for me, who's a public menace, if not this thief? Yeah, there are people who have written larger hot checks. But explain to me why a woman has to have six thousand dollars-worth of expensive underwear, when she's flat broke and in a deep hole! I mean, if she was a single mom, using fraudulent methods to feed her kids, it still wouldn't be right."

"Come on, Erik. If that check's good by the time the bank opens Monday morning, then it's not hot. A lot of people 'kite' checks. It isn't the best practice, but if they make it to the bank, or their money does, they're home safe. And you had her nabbed when you did, because it's hard to make deposits from jail."

"She has no money! Nothing coming in before her bank opens. She was gambling! Gambling on getting to Faulkner, to get something out of him"!

"My point, Bransom! You can't be selective in your law enforcement to protect your friends!"

Bransom's entire body language reflected his frustration. "Look, I didn't know her plan was to show up at the Anatole and waylay Daniel when he checked in. Although, the way she's stalked him, she would have known where and when to be in his face. He was with his family; his friends were all gathering there, he was holding his baby. He's a man trying to keep his defenses up!"

"Yeah, I know. There are millions of people out there that don't care about the sacredness of marriage vows. If you try to arrest all of them, the jails and prisons will be overcrowded! Your judgment got blurred. Don't let it happen again." Dawson walked away.

Bransom found a quiet corner. "People should care about marriage vows, Lord. I know our country's in trouble. And when folk in law enforcement think fraud and theft aren't so bad because other people are doing worse~ I'm glad You're for righteous judgment."

He raised his head, grinning. Although Dawson had told him off in no uncertain terms, he hadn't told him he had to cut Burnside loose. He sighed. He felt like the other culpable entity was the credit card companies. They were so eager to get people trapped in their high-interest business, that they were basically unscrupulous. Proving Burnside defrauded them would suggest they cared. As long as they could show accounts receivable, even on bad debts, it helped satisfy their shareholders.

-H |-

"Dad, did you know that woman?" Jeremiah's question freed itself the moment the door to the suite closed. "What did she do? Why did the FBI arrest her?"

"Yeah, I knew her a long time ago, Jeremiah."

"Is she the same one from last summer?"

"Get ready for bed, kids." Diana's clipped voice sounded tired.

"They will, Honey; we're all tired and it's late. But I need to answer him. He deserves that. Everybody sit down."

Her cheeks damp with tears, she complied.

"Her name's Nan; she is the woman who contacted me last summer. I've tried to ignore her, but she won't let go. Grandpa went and complained about Professor Higgins' role, stirring the pot, to the President of the university, Harold Foster. We have a lot of people rooting for our family, and that's good. But, I want you to know, that no matter how much they care, I care more! Your mother is a treasure to me; she's the one who gave me the Gospel and I got saved. I care about my testimony for the Lord, and I don't want to hurt you guys more than you've been hurt, by the things I did a long time ago. Things, I'm so ashamed of. Because, even when people are unsaved, they still really know when their behavior is wrong! I knew it, but I didn't care. I mean, maybe it bothered me some of the time; I guess I always tried to justify my actions to myself."

"So, do you think she still loves you, even though you're married to mom?" Alexandra mopped at her own tears.

"That I don't know about, Al. I think she's more interested in money and position; things she wouldn't have, if she managed to lure me away. If I did y'all wrong like that, my prestige would evaporate faster than a dew drop in the desert. She wouldn't step into being the 'lady of the house' in a home like ours. Your mom would boot me out; I'd be in an apartment paying rent and expenses on an additional household, and trying to hold everything together for y'all to keep living where we do. Nothing would be like she supposes it would be. You guys all know the verse:

I Samuel 15:22 And Samuel said, Hath the LORD as great delight
in burnt offerings and sacrifices, as in obeying the voice of the

LORD? Behold, to obey is better than sacrifice, and to hearken than the fat of rams.

The Bible is clear that it's better to obey the Lord because when we disobey, we immediately sacrifice more than we ever can imagine. God has blessed your mother and me as we've worked together, so we have a lot! This woman wouldn't really want me at all, if she knew how little I have to offer without God's blessings on my life. I don't know why she got arrested. That was a scene, but I think she planned to make a worse one. The Lord helped me. Like I said, Grandpa has been trying to help, and evidently, Mallory and Agent Bransom, too. We have a lot of great friends that care. I don't want to let them down, either. Any more questions?"

⊰ ⊱

Rhonna sat alone in her suite. Her family had been invited to the banquet celebrating a successful year; then she had told them good-bye as they headed back to Murfreesboro. She would see them all in a couple of weeks for Christmas. Then, mid-January they all planned to travel to Hawaii. She swiped at happy tears as she pulled tattered pages from a folder in her notebook. Her 'Dream' pages. Staying in her own suite in a large and luxurious hotel! Fabulous things kept happening to her that were beyond her ability to conceive of! She had never dreamed of going to Hawaii, let alone taking her parents and siblings; staying in world-class hotels; with money hardly an object!

She laughed through tears as she gazed heavenward. "All right, God, You win! I'm in college and doin' okay; my room at the house is cuter than I ever dreamed of havin'; I have beautiful clothes and jewelry to wear! A year ago, I was afraid of graduatin', afraid I couldn't make it. My best idea and dream was for gettin' on at the Sonic, part-time. But it's true, that verse David and Mallory and Ms. Diana are always sayin':

Isaiah 55:9 For as the heavens are higher than the earth, so are my ways higher than your ways, and my thoughts than your thoughts.

Like we learned in science classes, the heavens are light years and light years away! Millions and millions of miles! That's what You offer me! A life far transcending my best plans. I've been real silly not to accept You before this. I want You in my heart and to be Lord over my life. Thank You for dying for my sins, and what You've done for me to get my attention. I guess I've been hard-headed. Um, Amen"!

⚔ ⚔

"Hey, Dad," Jeremiah studying credit card statements, had come across a puzzling transaction. "We just now got billed for all that stuff you charged at Wal-Mart a long time ago. There's a little explanation with it. It got kicked back automatically for verification of the card holder, and then, for some reason they aren't sure of, the transaction never got processed. They're not sure what happened, but they say we still owe the money."

Daniel reached for the statement frowning. In this electronic age, snafus like this were practically unheard of. He remembered the Sunday afternoon well, being called back to answer a security question. One which the stress of the moment– He gazed at the amount. Not something he had budgeted for, and inopportune now, at Christmas.

"Do we still have to pay it? They're the ones who lost track of it." Jeremiah's logic!

"Yes, Son, we do. We bought the merchandise, signed on the line, guaranteeing payment."

The statement reflected the lump sum, not itemized, but he pretty well remembered each purchase, as panicked, he had torn through the store, trying to prepare–

"'Roll Back the Pages of Memory Now and Then'! Wow, this was from before Xavier was born; Cass was gone; we thought we were going to lose you and Al, too." He choked up. "We didn't know what Mallory would do while we hid out; we worried about that!" He tried to remind himself that worrying had been needless then, and it still was. Just, this was a lot! They were adding on to their home, trying to pay their part of Mallory's wedding they had agreed with Erik on, providing Christmas for treasured people on their list.

"You finding anything else, Jer? Any big credits someone owes us?"

Jeremiah laughed. "Well, quite a few things corporately; questionable charges like Heather looks for, at *DiaMo*! Sorry, nothing in our personal stuff."

⚑ ⚐

David stared at Daniel like he was off his rocker. "Hey, I wish I could suggest something. I'm never sure what to get her and good ways to surprise her. She's still disillusioned with professional sports and after the college scandal about abusing kids; well, so much for those ideas. I mean, MLB was what she was about. Jewelry; well, we're better off with the corporation's owning it, rather than her personally. Cars just need to be big and safe! And again in *DiaMo's* name."

"Yeah, kind of the same conclusions we came to," Daniel agreed ruefully. "Does she want another pet?"

"M-m-m, she made me promise not to get her another horse! I'm pretty sure she meant it. I mean, Tammi tells Larson stuff all the time, when she means the opposite. He kind of stays in trouble, just because he can't figure it out- But Mallie has four macaws and Dinky. I know that when the baby comes, she's eager to travel someplace. But she wants to do it for a corporate meeting and claim the expenses."

⚑ ⚐

"Mallory does such nice things for her employees," Beth commented to Roger as they returned to Arkansas. "I wish we could afford to do something like than."

Roger glanced at her sharply. "You know, we should. I mean, not anything that elaborate and upscale, but something to show our gratitude for them. What?"

Her expression belied her words that had begun the entire conversation. "Well, it's just that it's Christmas-"

"Right! I think that's what gives Mallory the spirit of giving and sharing. Come on, Beth, you were right. Don't backtrack now. We have more already that most of the world will ever have! We've had our best year, earnings high; not one set-back, to speak of, with the *Chandler* acquisition."

"Well, yeah, but you've tithed on all of it, haven't you?"

He sighed. Sometimes he felt like she resented that. "I have; that's doing what it's our duty to do. Our tithes help spread the Gospel and keep our church and staff functioning. It doesn't give back to our workers for what they contribute."

"Well, they have generous salaries and benefits."

"Beth, I can't believe you! Our income outstrips the highest of theirs by thousands annually. And if you're looking forward to having extra to spend on Christmas, they would be thrilled with extra, too. I'm going to get with Wes and work out a scale for cash bonuses, order a box of that Enstrom's Almond Toffee for each family, and have an awards dinner. I'm going to call Mallory and ask her if we can pay the way for our pastor and his family to go to Israel when the others go."

Her jaw dropped. "Israel? For the whole family? How much will that cost? We always give them a hundred dollars for Christmas, and I think that's more than they get from most people."

He nodded. "We'll tell them we can't send them on a trip every year. But this year, we can, and we should. He's always wanted to go. I'm calling Suzanne right now. With its being such a short time until Christmas, I don't know what kind of facility she can reserve."

⚅ ⚅

Suzanne called back within the hour. "Okay, I'm getting things nailed down! Two venues, actually! With the short time-frame, I decided to do Houston and the *Chandler* people this coming Friday night. Mallory agreed to let us use her gymnasium. That's a good start. In Hope, on Saturday night, I connived my way into using the high school lunch room. Both places will look good with Christmas decorations, table linens, and fresh flowers. Hal agreed to cater for our event in Hope, and Cat is working on finding a caterer in Houston."

⚅ ⚅

Mallory sat lazily in front of a cheery fire. She was supposed to be relaxing, but with everyone around her scurrying, she felt like she should help. David winked at her. "Don't even think about it. Can I bring you something? How about some eggnog"? He returned quickly with a tall glassful. She watched amazed, as he added more festive decorations and began carrying in poinsettia plants. She knew Diana was in control in the kitchen, directing the putting away of groceries; she and Daniel were cooking Christmas dinner. Most of it to be supplemented by favorites from David's mom and dad, and other menu items from Erik and Suzanne! Everything smelled divine, and stacks of gifts tumbled from beneath two Christmas trees.

"That looks beautiful, Grandmother," she observed as Delia deftly folded linen napkins to sit jauntily atop each place setting. She held each piece of glassware up to the light, watchful for any smudge or speck. If she were at home, she wouldn't be lifting a finger, every smudge and speck banished by a well-trained household staff.

"It does! This is such a beautiful place." She smiled at David. "Since you have so many poinsettia plants, why don't you take some down and dress up the chow hall for the men? I can't help thinking they must be homesick for something, for someone. If any of them would like to call someone to wish Merry Christmas to, they can use my phone."

"Those are both stellar ideas! Alexandra and Jeremiah baked them all special Christmas cookies yesterday. You know, I used to feel so sorry for myself, thinking how poor we were; that we didn't have anything! Meaning, I couldn't get the latest, most expensive, athletic shoes or sunglasses. I had so much then, but I just never took stock of it, to be grateful." He stopped and kissed Mallory. "Now I have so much more; it's incredible. But these campers; most of them come from unimaginable poverty. I'll be right back; taking flowers down there and checking on Mardy and her Christmas cooking."

⊰ ⊱

"You make Merc nervous every time you open that box," Linda warned Herb. "It should be traveling in an armored car, but hopefully no one would imagine we have anything of such immense value with us. I should have Christmas wrapped it."

"It looks okay, though?"

"Yeah, it's gorgeous, sublime~ What are you worried about? Davis Hall's assessment of your work? He doesn't hold a candle~"

"No! No, I do not care about that man!"

Linda was unconvinced, thinking his staunch denial belied his words. "Who then? Lilly? Why does she have such a hold over you?"

"No, not Lilly; I hope Mallory will like it. Well, and professionally, I would like my work regarded well by both Mrs. Cowan and Mr. Hall."

He broke a chunk of toffee from a larger slab. "This is very good candy. I can hardly quit nibbling."

Linda's piece broke off, larger. "Yeah, you should leave the lid on the candy box, too. I can't resist gobbling. We're going to be eating a huge Christmas dinner in a couple of hours. I don't need extra calories from candy. It is the confectioner's art, though!"

⫸ ⫷

Lilly frowned at snowflakes beginning to fall. "Are we getting close? We have been riding endlessly! You better not be thinking of kidnapping me!"

The driver of the hired limousine regarded the woman steadily in his rear-view mirror. He didn't have a clue who she was! She was annoying. He drove people around the Dallas area all the time, who were richer, more famous, and certainly better-looking. If he planned to kidnap anyone, she wouldn't be his choice."

"Yes, Ma'am!" Trained courtesy! "About five miles now. You're in plenty of time for you dinner! This is way out in the sticks!"

They paused before electronic gates, and Lilly regarded a beautifully calligraphied tile secured on a stone gate-post:

Deuteronomy 30:17b . . . if . . .

Lilly regarded it with wonder. She was familiar with the verse and the context of the small, but highly significant conjunction. That God's blessings are conditional, and it lies within the power of each person, to open the floodgates or cut them off.

The gates swung open, and she was at her destination without mishap.

⫸ ⫷

"Great ham, Erik! Wow, everything tastes so good. I love the Waldorf salad. Mom, it wouldn't be Christmas without your jell-o stuff."

"Yeah," David agreed with Mallory. "And, Mom, your mashed potatoes are the greatest on Planet Earth! Look! It's starting to snow!"

"Mallory, your table looks beautiful," Linda observed.

"Thank you, Aunt Linda. Grandmother fixed the table, and mom provided the fresh flowers and candles. Rhonna always talks about her 'Dream Sheet', and how hard it is to dream, with her narrow frame of reference, but I never imagined surroundings this elegant! Let alone living in them!"

Everyone nodded agreement and the conversation hummed pleasantly.

"How did Roger's staff get-togethers go?" Daniel questioned Suzanne.

Suzanne laughed. "Great! I even got a nice bonus!"

"You did?" Mallory's eyes danced. "You should treat yourself to something special, Mom. Why don't you and Erik take a cruise together?"

"Well~"

"Because Erik is always working! The bad guys never back off! You never slow down, either, Mom. It's still a good idea."

"Speaking of bad guys, are there any new developments in any of your cases?"

"As a matter of fact, Missy Hanson suddenly started improving emotionally, and she's provided some astonishing information. She's actually working some to help with the home decor items and people wanting to purchase them. Colonel Ahmir is working on getting information about that orphanage, or whatever it is. Missy saw Oberson's mug shot and said, 'Oh, he's grown old!' Meaning, that he has been deeply involved in this enterprise for a very long time! Since the time of Missy's abduction, at least"!

"And he's been serving in public office for most of that time?" Diana looked like she might be sick.

"Ya know? A cruise might be good at that," Erik returned to the original subject. "You know? Around the Caribbean"?

Suzanne laughed. "What? So you can check for black market organs and see the yachting set more up close and personal?"

Erik laughed. "I'm hurt! I was just thinking of the time alone with you."

"You know, we got a bill on an account the other day, from several years ago." Daniel's voice filled with incredulity as he changed the subject. "It kicked out for security purposes. I went back and came up with Diana's mom's maiden name; I'm not sure how. Well, then after that, for some reason it never got run through. Until now"!

"Wow, God helped you all there." Erik was amazed. "I'm pretty sure the ABI and the Feds were looking into your doing anything suspicious. They came up empty. If they had been able to track that sale, they would have known you were camping somewhere nearby. They wouldn't have given the search up as easily as they did."

⚔ ⚔

With the meal finished, they gathered in the great room and Mallory seated herself at the piano. David passed out sheets with lyrics. "I still mix up all the verses of Frosty," he admitted. They sang songs and Christmas Carols until they exhausted suggestions and requests. Then Pastor Anderson read the Christmas story from *Luke 2*. Faulkner prayed, thanking the Lord for the free gift of Eternal Life heralded by the angels over Bethlehem, and they began distributing gifts.

The gift giving was fun, as wrapping paper and bows flew, amidst oohs, and ah's, and thank-you's!

"Mom, let's just throw the trash away. You can quit saving wrapping paper and bows now," David reminded.

Daniel opened a small box from David and Mallory and gazed at both of them, amazed. "Are you sure?"

"We are," David assured "You're the only one gifted enough to merit such an instrument. We've wanted you to own it, all along. Now the insurance will be on you," he finished with a laugh.

As the large stack of gifts dwindled into smaller, individual piles, Mallory regretted not having purchased gifts for Herb and Linda. They could be so different. Sometimes, they were barely civil, and now, earlier in the week, they had called and kind of invited themselves to the Ranch for Christmas dinner. She loved and admired them both, but they could be thorny. She was kind of mystified as to their reason for coming. She hoped they hadn't fallen out with Merc and Nell and the boys.

It was fun watching the three youngest Faulkner kids open their gifts, and cry when there weren't more. Mallory loved them; they were an honest study of human nature.

"Wow, thank you, everyone! I think it's dessert time!" David's eyes sparkled as he prepared to lead the attack.

361

"One moment, please!" Herb stood and produced a flat velvet box from Linda's handbag. "I have been preparing for Mallory, a gift~" His tone filled with drama. "I regret not to have completed it by your birthday! The scope kept~" His voice trailed off as he handed her the box.

Even before she opened the lid, Mallory was gasping for air. "Uh, thanks, Uncle Herb, Aunt Linda." She raised the lid, and gasped, her eyes widening, with dismay! This wasn't good!"

"You don't like it?" Herb had watched her expression carefully, hoping it would infuse with extra wonder. Now he felt profound disappointment. Even embarrassment.

She held it wordlessly toward David, and his heart plummeted. It eclipsed all his gifts to her by galaxies!

Daniel let out an involuntary whistle as his gaze met Bransom's.

Wordlessly, she passed it to Lilly.

"It's beautiful! What's wrong with you people?" Linda's indignation erupted, breaking the stunned hush.

"Beautiful hardly describes it! Words fail!" Mallory fought tears. "I can't accept this, Uncle Herb! I mean, I love it, that you crafted something so exquisite, just for me! I can't afford to insure it, and I don't think I could hire enough security to safe guard it!" She stared at the glorious creation glowing from its velvety nest. "It belongs to a bigger arena, Uncle Herb! It's world-class!"

"But, you are world-class~"

"Well, thank you, but I'm not~ Lilly?"

Lilly was in too much of a trance to respond.

"Hello, Earth to Lilly! Earth to Lilly!" David's voice was teasing with staticky noises, and the humor brought a few chuckles to break the electric moment.

Mallory's thoughts chased each other frenetically through her mind. 'She couldn't hurt Herb's feelings again; it was yearend and the IRS would appraise the gift in the millions; she hadn't gotten gifts for them, at all; people killed for less than this; how could Herb have afforded to make it?' She retrieved it from Lilly's hands and sank down next to David, surveying the gift with wonder. At last, she passed it to her mom, Diana, Delia, Pastor and Lana.

Back to her, she touched the piece gently. "I'm speechless, Herb!" She knew she needed to tread carefully: *Artistic temperament ahead!* "I know the Lord inspired you to create this! It's absolutely exquisite. I remember how disappointed you were, when you made a piece to enter into a contest, and it was disqualified, because it so totally eclipsed all of the other more-amateur pieces. Well, they were only amateur compared to your work. The judges felt like you were in a class by yourself then, and you still are! I couldn't afford to accept that as a gift, and I can't afford this, either. I wish I could, but like I said, this should be for the world, and not for me! I think we should let Lilly auction it! That will bring more notoriety to you among the world's rich and famous. Most of them will never see our catalogs, until your name becomes even better known. This is your opportunity for that. Helping your business will help ours, too! And I love seeing another piece in your *Orchid* theme. Maybe you can make them your hallmark design, like Lalique did with dragonflies and frogs. Personally, I much prefer orchids. But that's just a suggestion. I don't in anyway want to try to curb your creativity."

Even as she spoke, she realized that Herb and Jennifer were much alike in their insistence on freedom of expression in their artwork. Herb was behind on the perfume decanters, and backorders were piling up for his other designs. And he was expending his energy and precious materials on this gift to her! She figured she needed to contact Davis to fill in some of the gaps Herb was leaving, and then he would act threatened by her doing that. And speaking of using gems and metals~ He didn't have them! Hurt feelings or not, the jewelry suite had to go!

Chapter 28: *AUCTION*

On the return to Dallas, Linda was relieved that Herb could see Mallory's point, and he wasn't injured and licking his wounds.

"Well, I did want to give for Mallory, something nice. She could see, though, that I allowed the scope of my gift to take me into very deep water. I have depleted much stock, with no real way to replenish it. I know Merc was nervous! He was nervous it would be stolen; Mallory would have nothing, and *Carlton, Inc.* would go under!"

Linda nodded. A concern she had shared. "Yes, Mallory's pretty savvy for someone so young. She continues to amaze me. Her actions on the other piece of donating it to the museum in Israel, has made your name famous. We all got tax credits for the gift, rather than owing taxes. But now, selling this piece at auction is even more brilliant. We'll get cash infused back into the company, and Lilly will make a nice commission. Mallory doesn't even want part of the sale price. She wants our bottom line healthy, and for us to continue making many of their jewelry designs. And also, not to squawk any more about *Gemhouse!*"

Herb grinned at her slyly. "Yes, I got that!"

〜

Lilly spirited the valuable jewelry set away, much to Erik and the security personnel's relief! Darrel was busily interviewing applicants to add to David and Mallory's details, someone whose primary responsibility would be safeguarding the baby. Such high-profile and valuable jewelry would make the Andersons' homes very enticing targets, indeed.

Within a week of the set's appearance on the market, exclusive clientele were submitting sealed bids. Top bidder was the Israeli museum, with an offer of a million and a half. The amount was staggering to Mallory. Herb's touch on the pieces was magical. She continued to be amazed that he had been contented, spending most of his life in the pawn business. He still seemed barely able to grasp the talent he had been endowed with.

"Well, Lilly, now that you're moneyed up, where are you headed next?" She couldn't resist teasing. "We're headed back to Dallas in the morning. You're welcome to come stay with us longer."

"Nick and Jennifer have invited me~"

Mallory laughed. "Yes, I know they have, and they meant it, too. Their accommodations for you won't be the best, but Arizona's beautiful. You'll see them when they come to visit Israel in a few weeks."

"Arizona is a desert; Israel is a desert: if you've seen one desert, you've seen them all!"

Mallory didn't agree, but arguing with Lilly was a losing battle. Her real reason for not going was the reminder that there would be no luxury. "Come to Dallas," she repeated.

"Yes, I should impose upon you and David until you reveal to me, the whereabouts of the 'pink'. I keep thinking I shall see it reappear at some point in time."

Mallory's wide eyes met the other woman's, startled. "The 'Pink'! Uh, yeah; I forgot about it. I hope it didn't accidentally get thrown out."

"Thrown out! How could it possibly be thrown out?" Lilly's first thought was that she was being played, but Mallory seemed pretty serious.

"Calm down, Lilly. It might not have been. I just haven't even thought about it in so long. When we get home, I'll check. Are you coming with us?"

David didn't mind the fact that Lilly was accompanying them back to Dallas. She couldn't stay too long! Cassandra was performing in Sydney Friday night; a long flight, and she would need to get her feet under her and rehearse before the concert. Besides that, Lilly could be a hoot!

⚔ ⚔

"Going someplace?" Several agents circled around Robert Saxon and his immediate family as they prepared to board a private jet bound for Rio de Janeiro. Erik had been against releasing the father and son on bail, stating they were a flight risk. They were proving him right, and now they were headed back to jail. With their passports confiscated by the courts, they were attempting to travel on carefully forged documents. Another figurative nail in their coffins! He felt quite a bit of satisfaction, although it amazed him how cleverly counterfeiters managed to make acceptable forgeries, despite government attempts to thwart the practice.

⚔ ⚔

Bryce and Lisette met Blythe and Samuel in Atlanta. "This is a nice surprise," Blythe bubbled. "What's up that you didn't want to talk about on the phone?"

"Well, I've been thinking a lot about Dad and Mom and the businesses. I haven't talked to Agent Bransom about the advisability of doing this, but I think we should step into being more active in running things, hands on!" Bryce spoke softly, still concerned about being overheard.

Blythe stared at him, unsure what to say. It was a transition for her twin, wanting to rocket from wannabe playboy bum, to corporate executive.

"Well, that's interesting. Do you have a plan?"

Bryce laughed suddenly, a spontaneous sound she hadn't heard since they hit adolescence and he got too cool to laugh. "Well, I feel like the Lord has a plan." His gaze turned toward Lisette. "He gave me this incredible partner before I even had a grasp of getting anything beyond just real cute! She's real cute and real smart, too!"

"That's the plan?" Blythe was unconvinced. "So what? We send her in, and if she doesn't get her head blown off, we advance to phase two?"

Bryce laughed again. "Yeah! Whadaya think? No, seriously, I'm enrolling in business courses. I thought maybe we could ask Mr. Sanders and Mr. Faulkner to mentor us in the best approaches for getting an audit and start assessing where things are."

Her gaze met his. "You're serious."

⚔ ⚔

Mallory showed Lilly to her suite. "You have time to rest or take care of business, or whatever you want. We're going out for dinner. You can join us, or have dinner here. Your choice"!

Lilly took in the lovely space, very inviting. "I'll decide. What about the Diamond? Is it thrown out? How can you be such a stupid girl-"

"Yeah, Lilly; let me know what you decide!" She escaped. It annoyed her for Lilly to call her stupid. She made her way to the master bedroom, hoping she hadn't lost track of the valuable gem.

"Okay, Lord, please let it still be here," she breathed. It should be; except that Diana had such a penchant for keeping everything uncluttered. That basically meant that everything Mallory had worn once or twice disappeared, to make room for new things. She ran her gaze across rows of shoe boxes. "Yes, clear at the left, on the bottom!" She pulled the box out, remembering the shoes, a pair she had purchased at Galleria shortly after her move to Dallas. They were cute, high-heeled pumps in a soft turquoise she no longer had anything to match. Evidently, Diana had let them stay because they were barely worn and still pretty much in vogue.

Pulling out the paper stuffed in the toes, she unrolled it to expose the lovely uncut stone. "Thank You, Lord," she breathed. She replaced the valued item carefully and snapped a picture of the shoes with her cell phone, then sent Diana a text.

Hello, Diana,

Remember these cute shoes? I really liked the color. Any chance of my getting an outfit to go with them? Preferably springy, for after the baby comes.

Love, Mallory

Hopefully the shoes (with the hidden diamond) would be safe for a while, if they went with something else. The hiding place seemed as good as any. But it fired her desire to really hunt for more.

David came in search of her. "Hey, Larson called me. He and Tammi want to join us for dinner. Is Lilly coming too?"

"I don't know. I was giving her a choice about it, and she started calling me 'stupid' again, so I just got out. I hope she does. The more the merrier."

David laughed. "Yeah, you mean, what's one more, weird person? Lilly kind of goes together with Kerry and Tammi." He pulled her near. "Tomorrow night, we're going out for a nice dinner together, just the two of us. Why on earth was Lilly calling you stupid?"

She melted against him, meeting his kiss. "I don't know. I guess it doesn't matter."

Chapter 29: ANALYSIS

Mallory finished her devotions and scooted her Bible and notebook to the upper right-hand corner of her desk. "Okay, Lisette, what's on the docket?" Her manicured nail held down the intercom button.

"Are you sure you want to know? Rhonna's wanting to talk to you; like asking me every other minute. I think she has some kind of problem. Then, the usual paperwork for you to sign! Herb and Linda are coming to lunch down in the café, and they would like for you and David to join them. Then, you have an appointment about the health insurance quotes and updating our package, and someone from Governor Bateman's office wants you to call."

"Okay, thanks, Lisette. Go ahead and send Rhonna in. Bring coffee and some Danishes, will you please?"

She stood to greet her employee and help situate the refreshments. "Thanks, Lisette."

When the door closed she sank down in the conversation area with a cup of coffee, and pastry. "Help yourself, Rhonna. Have a seat."

"You not goin' on the other side of the desk?" Rhonna's voice was tinged with humor as she fought for composure."

Mallory laughed easily. "An obvious power play! I guess not. I thought you wanted to talk. This seems more conducive to conversation. What's on your mind? Please, don't cry, or I will, too." She reached for a tissue box.

"Well, I owe you so much~ My mama's real mad at me right now~"

Mallory nodded comprehension. "You're wanting to leave. It's okay, Rhonna, and you don't owe me anything. Of course, we don't want you to leave! You're a great member of the team. I'm concerned, though. Is this about that Jim Whitley that pays so much attention to you down in the café? He wears a wedding band; is his interest in you professional?"

"Yes Ma'am! He wants to hire me; I don't know why I want to make a change. I figured if I'm going to, though, that it would only be right, before we all take that fancy trip to Hawaii."

Mallory nodded thoughtfully. "Okay, Rhonna, you earned that trip for your efforts last year. No wonder your mom's mad at you. David's been checking out *Whitley Enterprises, Inc.* Jim has things rolling and going; we're impressed. If you've prayed about it, Rhonna, and you feel like it's right for you, we have no hold on you. I hope it works out for a stellar career for you. If it doesn't we'll welcome you back. We'll give you great recommendations for your performance."

"You and Ms. Diana have done so much for me."

Mallory shrugged. "We really haven't, Rhonna. You're kind of like Caramel Du Boise. Roger Sander was looking for someone to really help. But all Carm needed was the barest nudge."

"Am I wrong? Wantin' to work for a company that's comprised mostly of black people?"

"I don't think so. You're a good worker, and they need great help. I've wanted you to feel comfortable here, but I can't force something, if the time isn't ready. It's an adjustment from the dynamics of Murfreesboro and the schools there, to the real world. And the 'real world' stays in a state of flux. I haven't been able to tell if you were shutting the other girls out, or if it was them, making you feel like you don't fit. If you have to spend hours a week at a job, it should probably be one where you feel comfortable."

"You won't be mad at me, then? And you'll refer me? And we all still get to take the trip? Will Ms. Diana be upset?"

"Well, upset at losing you as an employee. Hopefully, we can keep you on as a friend. We'll keep pushing your recordings, and hopefully, so will friends and associates at your new company. We'll continue to discount our merchandise to you, if you're interested, and maybe you can develop customers for us from the new contacts you're going to meet."

Rhonna smiled broadly. "Now, that's real smart of you! If it was me, I would have gone and gotten mad-"

Mallory smiled. "We've sort of seen this coming, so my response is planned. I've been known to lose my temper; it takes a long time to undo damage. Herb and Linda Carlton are coming to lunch later; I'd like for you and Mr. Whitley, and some of his key people to join us, if it isn't too short notice. I'd like to familiarize them with who we are and what we're about, and get acquainted with them. My treat on the lunch"!

⚜ ⚜

David clicked from link to link, doing some research that could be highly profitable for their companies. He tried not to be annoyed as his phone interrupted his search.

'Ah, Jeff, he needed to hear from him.' "Hey, how are the world travelers? Are you and mom having fun?"

Jeff laughed. "Is it okay to admit it; since we're here for business?"

David laughed in response. "Yeah, Mom probably isn't racking up the dollars too much with her wild partying."

"Yeah, she always worries about the extravagance of getting Starbucks. With the exchange rate here, she really feels like it's wasteful and sinful. Hey, the properties look good. Sorry I didn't have much confidence in Billingsley's choices. We met with one of our missionaries; he knows a contractor to fix the blemishes. Then, he said he can oversee getting it leased. Our sign that quotes:

> *John 11:26 And whosoever liveth and believeth in me shall never die.*

*h*as sparked a lot of interest in the neighborhood. In the morning, we take the Chunnel to Paris, and we'll see what we have there. Tell Waylon this is brilliant, sharing the Gospel in ways we can, while we change other things that need changing."

⚜ ⚜

Jed Dawson was concerned. Senator Oberson wasn't going down without a fight, and he didn't care what he said, or who he hurt. He had claimed all along that Bransom's pursuit of him was politically motivated: the attack of conservative Christianity on his liberal agenda. When he caught wind of Nan Burnside's arrest, it fueled his rhetoric that Bransom picked and chose his cases to benefit his friends and his crusades. Dawson, who knew Erik, knew it wasn't true, but it could be spun that way. It seemed doubtful if the senator's criminal activities would even unseat him from his office, let alone get him put in prison.

Reluctantly, he picked up the receiver to call the agent. Bransom interrupted him triumphantly before he could say much.

"Well, we'll see! Saxon and Son broke and confessed; it implicates everyone more deeply, that we've been investigating. Backs up Missy's words and Jennifer's paintings"!

Dawson was stunned. That was almost enough to make him believe in miracles!

⚔ ⚒

"Okay, Mom, I finished everything on my list. It's still fifteen minutes before Daddy and Jeremiah get here. What should I do next?"

Diana looked up from her sketch pad, impressed. "What did Davis Hall have to say?"

"He sounded really excited and told me he'd look into it and send us an email by first thing in the morning." She tiptoed forward. "Wow, Mom, that's gorgeous. Is that kind of based on the silks we saw in Lyon? That visit was an eye-opener. I mean Americans make fun of the designers and haute-couture; which they do make some of their designs 'out there', past the 'cutting edge'. But some of the designs and fabrics are amazing! No wonder you say you get tired of denim, denim, denim. There really is so much more."

Diana laughed. "Delia was amazed, when she first got saved and started reading the Bible, that it referred so often to linen and fine linen. That got her attention each time, since she had dealt in linen all of her life. There is more, and God gave us the ability to utilize stuff and design and create; one of the ways we're made in His image. I like to have fun with it."

⚔ ⚒

Valentine's Day found the Faulkners in Rome, with Diana promoting her fragrance and refillable, jeweled bottles. From there, they joined Lilly in Prague for some sightseeing and Cassandra's sixth performance of her ten concert tour. When the Faulkners returned home, Lilly and Cassandra

371

continued on to London for the next performance. Cass was lighting it up, making friends, overall, and receiving good reviews.

Following the London performance, she returned with Lilly for a few days in Israel. They joined Isaac and Rebekah for dinner on Ben Yehuda Street, and then Cassandra and Rachel moved to their own table for filter coffee and dessert. They used more milk than coffee and laughed and shared secrets as long as they could.

"You're so lucky to get to travel and see the world," Rachel observed wistfully as they were about to part."

"It isn't luck, Rachel; I prayed. My mom hired Alexandra to help work for her, for money. I asked the Lord to help me get a job and get paid, and Lilly called me about this tour."

"Well, I don't think praying made it happen. You have a lot of talent."

"Well, I know it's prayer. Trust me; there are a lot of violinists who have more talent, and have worked harder and longer than I have. I remember my first time praying. There was something inside of me that made me want to be part of a symphony. I didn't even know how to phrase what I wanted. Well, I had kind of my own made up language, and my parents really didn't understand me. The way I described it, was that I wanted to go with the *violin people*. My daddy told me I should pray for Jesus to come into my heart, and I asked him if that would make the *violin people* come for me. Anyway, I got saved that morning, and then I asked Jesus to let me go with the *violin people*. Well, then, Lilly showed up at our house, and I went with her and came here, to Israel. She wouldn't even give me my violin, and I thought she was so mean! Well, she was. Anyway, then one morning, when I was wandering around on my way to school, I heard a violin and it led me to your house and your daddy's helping me. I kept trying to remember all the things I had ever heard about Jesus; I thought my dad and mom probably would never want me back. Jesus always helps me; sometimes He just does it ways that seem weird, like Lilly. Do you think you could come see me in Tulsa sometime? I'm going to pray that you can."

⚜

Shay proposed to Emma on Valentine's Day and they began making plans for a June wedding. Where the event should take place was the first order of business. Beth and Roger had friends from all over the country, between other college alumni, their yachting friends, and colleagues in the chemicals industries. Hope was a small town, and their church plant was modest in size. Lodging for out-of-town guests was problematic. Still, Roger pointed out, that all their church friends were closest and most likely to attend.

"Remember how you and Merc fixed up tents for some of the Faulkner's concerts? Maybe we can have it at the church, but outdoors, to make room for more people." Emma's solution!

"That's a great idea! We can get something really nice, a large white pavilion. We can put down astro-turf or outdoor carpet on the parking lot. Suzanne offered to provide flowers. Maybe we can hire the Faulkners to perform string music. Maybe David can help us come up with a way to fight the heat. We don't want to use fans that are so loud no one can hear your vows. Maybe a misting device if it won't make y'all's hair frizz"!

Emma's eyes sparkled with anticipation, and to Roger and Beth's relief, Brent and Connie were getting along again.

-≒ ≒-

"So, do you think it will work okay for Shay and Emma to live with Delia?" Lisette tried to phrase her question casually, but Mallory glanced up at her sharply. They were in the middle of a ton of work, for one thing, so they hadn't been indulging in idle gossip.

She straightened up and the baby started doing summersaults, or something. "Where did that come from? They have all decided to make it work: commitment, that's the first step for making anything work. Sorry, I guess that sounded lecture-y. Grandmother's home should accommodate everyone with as much privacy and as much togetherness as they want. Are you trying to figure out if you and Bryce can move in with Blythe and Samuel? That place could quarter an army."

Lisette's cute features flushed slightly. "We're uh, we're just thinking."

Mallory nodded knowingly. "That, I understand. While you're making up your minds, I wish you'd focus."

"Well, if I leave, do you think Heather-"

"No. Heather's good at what she does. You aren't gone yet anyway. What else do I need to look over tonight?"

"Rhonna should have stayed."

Mallory laughed. "Why do you think so? People come and go. You've been amazing to work with; but it's crazy, with Bryce attacking the corporate world on such a grand scale, for you to keep your loyalties here. He needs you and your talents, and you are his wife. So, if Rhonna were still here, what? You'd feel less guilty about what you need to do?"

Lisette grinned sheepishly. "Yeah, I guess. I mean, the way I acted before~"

Mallory's laugh rippled. "Yeah, Girlfriend! The way you acted before brought David charging into my life to help me. I'd say that's a *Romans 8:28* event! Even more amazing is what's going on with you and Bryce."

"You are going to make me cry; aren't you? God made things work together for my good, even when I didn't deserve it."

Mallory laughed again. "None of us ever deserve it, Lisette!"

"Oh yes! I keep forgetting that!"

⚓ ⚓

Mallory's eyes took in the people lunching at the in-house restaurant. She and David were meeting with Gabe Pritchard, but David wasn't there yet. She hesitated. Gabe was better than the guy he had replaced, but he still made Mallory uncomfortable. He tried to come across as a gallant ladies' man, but instead, he came across as a fop. Not sure where that term had come from, or exactly what it meant, she came up with an acrostic for it, *fool on parade.* Not very nice, but~

He caught sight of her and she advanced toward his table, hoping David wouldn't be long.

⚓ ⚓

Kenneth Wilson realized he should look sharper to conduct such an important interview. He needed a haircut, but had kept putting it off. Then the morning had started out with a lot of drama and escalated from there. Some days were that way! He splashed water on his unshaven face and poured another mug of coffee.

Talingua announced the applicant without benefit of an intercom. Grinning, Wilson hollered back. "Send him in!"

⊣ ⊨

David arrived in time to squint quizzically at Pritchard. Conversing with the guy was just weird. He talked in circles and metaphors. David questioned whether he had ever come up with a thought of his own. So, Mallory said something that made a lot of sense, and Gabe came back with, "Which came first? The chicken or the egg?"

Mallory's cool green eyes met his momentarily before she answered, "The chicken, but what does that have to do with anything, Gabe?"

Pritchard acted condescendingly smug. "That was a rhetorical question, with no certain answer. People can argue it back and forth without forming a consensus."

Mallory sighed. "So, in your round-about way, you're saying you don't know when you can have equipment on site? So the chicken and egg thing is a dodge. Look, who can we find out from? Because we need to know without playing word games"!

"Ooooh, hormones making us a little testy, are they? See, that's why women should leave business to men."

"Well, Pritchard, my hormones are in balance, and I want to know, too" David managed to keep his tone controlled. We have a contract, and we lose money every day we can't drill. Pretty sure that was Mallory's concern, too. And the chicken came first! No debate! Read it in *Genesis 1:20*. God created mature fowl, and told them to bring forth after their kind. An egg could never hatch and nurture itself. The earth was filled with mature plants to drop seeds to bring forth after their kind. Adam and Eve were man and woman; not babies. Now that I've satisfied your curiosity about that, could you satisfy ours as to when your company plans to perform according to contract?"

The guy was left stammering. "You see everything so cut and dried."

Mallory nibbled on a chip. "What exactly does that mean? 'Cut and dried'?"

⊣ ⊨

"Mallory, what are you doing?" Lilly's aggravated question was as direct as usual. At least she avoided calling her stupid.

"We're drilling a core sample, Lilly. When Mr. Gilmore agreed to carry the financing for us to buy his land, we agreed to check out the minerals and cut him in twenty per cent. Hence, the drill"!

"Mmm-m," was Lilly's response. Mallory could envision Lilly's pinched lips.

"We aren't looking for Diamonds, per se, Lilly. Although, should we find some, I'm pretty sure you'd find it interesting. I know you are totally Diamond focused, and whereas, I like them a lot, as a Geologist, I just find it fascinating to explore anything hidden beneath the earth's surface. I'm excited about it, and we're keeping our word to Mr. Gilmore."

Failing to convince the other woman, she disconnected, then called her back, on a hunch.

"Yes, Mallory? Did you decide to call back and tell me the truth?"

"Lilly, I did tell you the truth. Now, I want you to tell me the truth. Do you know who took all of my dad's records and paperwork from a storage locker?"

Lilly's turn to stammer! "Why would I have anything to do with the disappearance of piles of trash?"

"Uh-huh! So! You do know!"

"I said no such-"

"Right Lilly! I want every scrap back!"

⚔ ⚔

Wilson studied the man seated before him with the accompanying paper work. "I'm sorry. I can't figure out why you're here. With your credentials, you can make it anyplace."

A broad flash of white teeth lit the other man's countenance. "Any place I want, including here? If my credentials will get me in anyplace I want, and this is where I want; then does that mean I get the position?"

Wilson leaned back tiredly with his hands behind his head, showing wide sweat rings on his scrubs. "Du Bois told you about our work here? You two romantically involved? If it's none of my business, I understand. Yeah, you have the position. I'm sure you won't stay long, but I can use the help. You didn't ask about the pay scale."

"Caramel said Mrs. Anderson treats people fairly. I'm not expecting to get rich. What keeps you here?"

"The Gorilla."! That was the easy answer, and they did still fascinate the doctor. He wasn't one to share emotions, especially with a new acquaintance. "A lot of other medical reasons! It's always a challenge; never boring. Some days, it's pretty heartbreaking. I stay because most people are hoping to get rich; consequently, they give places like this a wide berth."

"You haven't changed to the new church Parker and Callie are trying to start?"

Wilson surveyed the earnest kid. "No. They need people who can work in the church and really help them build it. My ministry, if you will, is this clinic. I stop long enough to run into church in time for the services, and run right back out. I tithe and give, but that's the extent of my involvement."

"But this *Foundation*, it's a Christian organization; right?"

"Yeah, funded by Mallory and a few other contributors; Independent Baptists. We can witness, but others have strong holds over the minds of the people. Tribal leaders, Pentecostal ministries, cults! They'll work to keep people from seeking the medical help they need, if we seem only interested in proselytizing. As most things in life, it's a tight rope."

"Mallory knows it's like that, though; right?"

"I'm not sure exactly what she knows. She isn't here. I try to run things the best way I can, as someone with boots on the ground here. I don't mind if you get involved with Parker and Callie's new church. As a matter of fact, Pastor John Anderson is coming to preach an evangelistic meeting there in a couple of weeks. They're excited about him coming. You know, he decked me once!"

⊰ ⊱

"That's what all the stories say. They're basically in agreement." David tried to curb the enthusiasm in his voice." They started out with poor equipment, regrouped with updated stuff, were on track for a really lucrative year, and then switched to mining Vanadium because its price shot way up."

"That doesn't even make sense." Mallory returned her attention to a picture of a sumptuous cut Diamond. "They left a Diamond-rich deposit in order to prospect? That's why people 'prospect', looking for rich deposits. Once they find one, the search is usually over. It's like looking for a misplaced earring. Once you find it and put it on, you don't keep moving furniture and looking under stuff. The site was rich, they had mining

377

concessions, rosy forecast, and now it's abandoned and totally reclaimed by nature? We should research Vanadium and its price history and production in Colorado."

He nodded. "Sure, maybe we can get in on that, too."

She laughed. "I'm not sure that's what I was thinking. Look, I'm really eager to fly up there and look everything over once the baby comes. It sounds exciting, but I'm thinking Lilly probably knows more what the real story is. Don't forget my and my dad's ambitious longing to search the Little Missouri, to the Atchafalaya, to the Mississippi, to the gulf of Mexico."

"You won't even look in the little streams on the Ranch."

She sighed. "Because of Lilly and her spies! They want American Diamonds hushed up. Americans are the major consumers of the world, and we're supposed to keep thinking they're rare, exotic, and from far-away locales. That's in our best interests, too."

"Yeah, but she'll barely let any of ours into the market."

"True, but she could block us out completely. She ended up liking us, against her will. Go ahead and schedule the trip. Where should we fly in? Laramie? or Fort Collins?"

"I'm saying Denver. We'll have more driving, but I don't want us flying in small regional jets over the mountains in early spring. Too many storms and stuff can pop up."

Chapter 30: ARRIVAL

"Okay, that does it! I'm going home. Thanks for everything, Diana!" Diana's blue eyes blazed into David's as she flounced from the suite.

He looked around helplessly. "Yeah, thanks for everything, Diana"! Under his breath. She was gone anyway. He ran his hand through unruly hair and gazed out the window. "I'm pretty sure she isn't going home to Tulsa tonight. The rain turned to ice a couple of hours ago. So, you doing better now?"

Mallory sniffled and dabbed her nose with a tissue. "Yeah, I'm fine. I wasn't trying to be difficult." Tears flowed freely again. "If that was textbook labor and delivery, I wonder what it's like to have a hard time."

He neared the bed. "Yeah, textbook-routine for them! They do this time after time, day after day. They could have a little empathy for young couples that are scared and don't know the drill. I guess we should have found time to take the classes. It's my fault. Can I get you something?"

"No! Just don't leave! I don't know why my mom didn't come! She~she's just never~" A fresh deluge came.

He gazed at the little bundle starting to move and stretch. "You ready to hold her yet? She's waking up. That'll help you feel better."

"No it won't. I want my mom!" Her voice rose in a wail.

He was at a loss, envying Diana for making her escape.

⛬ ⛬

John Anderson had felt that he was prepared for Abuja, Nigeria with total and instant immersion in the culture of the third world country. Even after dinner with Parker and Callie and Wilson and Wilson's new protégé, Amon Williamson, in one of the nicer restaurants, he was homesick. He was eager to preach and excited about another church being started, but he was missing the entrance of his first grandchild. He should have timed this better. The city, in some ways modern, was still raw and unsettling. He had always respected missionaries and their willingness to serve the Lord, far from home and family, but this gave him a bigger-than-life taste. A bitter taste! He was amazed at Callie's ability to handle it.

⚏ ⚎

David pulled out his phone; his battery was low. Caller ID told him Suzanne was calling. "Here, it's your mom. Stop crying."

She grabbed the phone, crying harder. "Mom, where are you? Why weren't you here for me? I wanted you–"

David heard Suzanne's voice, but couldn't understand what she was saying.

Mallory's woebegone voice broke in. "Why are you in New Orleans?" She listened, sniffling. "Oh, because of the weather? You were trying to come, and got routed all over because it got bad everywhere? Yeah, I'm okay. I made Diana mad at me. I was scared; I wanted you here. I wanted Daddy. Then, after she was born, I nearly shook to pieces. What am I gonna do, Mom? Are you still coming?"

She listened, mopping tears. "The baby? Yeah, I think she's okay. She looks real teeny; she didn't feel teeny though. Okay, I'm glad you're safe. Did David send you pictures? I don't know why I can't stop crying."

⚏ ⚎

A timid tap on the door preceded Lana with all David's siblings. David moved toward them to greet his mom with a kiss on the cheek. "Are the roads real bad? Did Jeff drive you? Suzanne tried to fly in and got rerouted all across the south."

Lana patted David's cheek. "You look tired, Honey. I hope you aren't coming down with anything." She moved past him for a closer look at the baby. "Oh, hi, Mallory Can I hold her?"

"I guess. She's fussing a little bit."

"Well, that's because you have her all unwrapped."

380

"That's because they had the blanket so tight she couldn't move," David's defense.

Lana was wrapping the receiving blanket tightly again. "Well, that's for a reason. It's reassuring to the baby to be swaddled. They're used to being confined in the womb."

"Okay, that's enough, Mom."

"Did she have a cap? Babies can lose body heat~"

"Yeah Mom! We were looking her over to see what we've got. Mallory wanted to make sure she doesn't have red hair, and I was kind of hoping she would."

"Well, she is adorable. Such sweet, tiny little hands! Long fingers, maybe she'll be a pianist like her mommy. Did you settle on her name?"

"Well, we're definitely settled on Amelia; I like Erin for her middle name."

"Yeah, that's pretty! Amelia Erin Anderson!"

David felt a stirring pride for his little cub, and he trusted his mom with her. He wasn't so sure of his sisters passing her around. He wished Mallory would come to herself and rescue their child.

The crowd grew exponentially when Diana came back with Daniel and their children. At least Diana had sense enough to stop passing the baby around like a football.

"I need to get a lot of pictures to text to John. He's so disappointed to miss all this," Lana' voice carried above the confusion. "He figured you'd go past your due date, and he'd be back."

Mallory's response was a shuddering sigh. 'That's right. Her pastor was in Africa. She wanted to talk to him, in private.' More tears came.

"Mallory, have you tried to nurse her yet?" Diana smiled as she watched the baby gnawing hungrily on tiny fists. "Have they brought you two, anything to eat? You should give it a shot before she gets really hungry and they just start her on a bottle."

Mallory shrugged. "Maybe they should do that, while I decide~"

"Oh no," Lana chirped. "If she gets used to a bottle, she might not~"

"Okay, well we haven't really had a chance~" David's objection was drowned out.

"Well, if she starts on formula, she's likely to get all kinds of allergies and asthma, and she won't have the immunity to disease that breast milk gives her."

"Yes, that's true, Mallory." Diana's agreement made Mallory feel really ganged up on. "Why don't y'all go down and find David something to eat, and I'll help her get going?" Diana was already shooing everyone out.

David hesitated.

"You too! Shut the door behind you."

⚎ ⚌

Caroline Hillman made her way carefully into a boggy area, fighting a cold, whipping wind, where a body had been discovered. Badly decomposed, but the ME on site informed the investigators that it seemed to be a young female, early twenties.

"Remnants of the clothes would seem to indicate it's the missing nanny," a young agent informed her. "She died trying to protect her little charge?" he assumed innocently.

"Maybe! It's hard to say. Why don't you go try to talk further to Danay? Nanny might have taken a payoff to look the other way while Danay was kidnapped. Then they might have double-crossed her so she wouldn't talk, and grabbed their money back. Don't tell Ms. Livingston yet, that she's dead. Just ask Danay again where she was when the abduction took place. The little girl was extremely vague before. We weren't sure if she didn't notice the nanny in the confusion or if she felt some loyalty and was trying to protect her.

With a pair of agents on their way to the Livingstons and others skillfully working the crime scene, she made her way back to her vehicle to report to Bransom.

"Mallory had her baby!" she exclaimed gleefully when Bransom connected. "Congratulations in order for you?"

"Yeah, thanks, Hillman; is that the reason for your call?"

Rebuked, she blushed. No one there to notice! "No, Sir. The body south of Dallas appears to be that of the Livingston's missing nanny. Looked like blunt-force trauma to the back of the victim's head. I have one team re-interviewing Danay, and the others are finishing up with the crime scene. Oberson may be facing a murder rap now."

"Yeah, and he planned for Jack and Estelle Norman to die, too. He isn't a man to let anyone get in his way. Be careful, Hillman. Get me the report of the new Danay Hicks interview as quick as you can."

The conversation completed, he gazed moodily out his office window. Seventies the previous day; ice storm today! He had been out of contact with his own three girls when they married and gave birth to their children. He thanked the Lord for reestablishing the broken family ties. At least, he had been blissfully ignorant of their birth pangs. Tracking with David on Mallory's progress had nearly overwhelmed him. Now, Suzanne was stuck in New Orleans with Mallory in Dallas crying for her. He buried his head in his hands. He wished he could fix all the hurts of those around him. As an FBI Agent, he tried hard. Usually tough, he suddenly wished his pastor hadn't left the country.

⚜ ⚜

"Okay, Mallory, that's enough. There's no one here to be impressed by your theatrics. You have the beautiful gift of a healthy baby girl; labor's over; so are the shakes. Now turn on your side and tuck this pillow~"

Tears continued to slide down Mallory's face, unabated. 'She wasn't trying to, *Impress anyone with her theatrics.* She didn't know why she still felt so overwhelmed and unable to stop crying. She suddenly needed to confide in her pastor, to get some feedback from him. Could he just walk into her room when she needed him, with the rest of his family? No! He had to be in Africa. And Lana and all the rest had to stomp in, telling David he looked tired!

Diana was offensively hands-on with the process.

"Do you mind?"

"Come on now, Mallory. I'm a nurse and a mother. Get over yourself." Diana was acutely aware of post-partum depression, but she had studied enough psychology to take a tough approach, rather than a sympathetic one.

"Why did you run David out, too?"

"Because when you nurse, especially getting the hang of it, you need to relax as much as possible. Besides, you've used him as your whipping boy all day. He needs some dinner and a little break."

The attempt at feeding didn't go well.

"A little pinch!" Mallory's surprised screech and her jerking responsively caused Amelia's little face to pucker. Then the baby began screaming in earnest.

"Mallory"! Diana's tone was a rebuke, and for the second time in one day, she walked out, leaving Mallory staring stupidly at the howling, squirming infant beside her.

The din brought an aide in to ask Mallory if she needed anything.

"Um, do they take her to a nursery where people feed her and look after her?"

"Well, usually when people have a suite like this, they keep their newborns with them. That's the point of it. And your husband's real jumpy about someone taking your baby or switching her. Your friend said you were going to try feeding~"

"Yes, Ma'am, but she left, and I want my baby to drink formula out of bottles."

She was met with a hard stare.

"Please," she added. Maybe she was being a pain!

"Okay, here's a fresh diaper and some wipes. You change her while the charge nurse finds out what formula your pediatrician wants to try her out on. He was under the impression~"

"He was under the wrong impression, then, okay? And can you change her? I don't want to do it. I'm not ready."

⚔ ⚔

"How'd everything go? Where's Diana?"

David's return brought more tears. "She got mad at me~and stomped out~again." She could barely talk. "Why were you gone so long? You didn't have to leave. She's not our boss~"

She broke off as David's family traipsed back in followed by Daniel and his kids. The suite seemed like a three-ring circus when Pastor and Mrs. Ellis arrived. They had a planter for her, but they eased back out, relieved that they had done their duty and there was good reason for their not staying.

The baby was really unhappy by the time the charge nurse contacted the doctor's service and got a call-back about the formula. Lana was more than happy to grab her new granddaughter and feed her her first bottle. "John will be so jealous," she crowed happily.

Daniel wasn't sure where Diana was, but in her absence, he decided to take over as patient's advocate. "Okay, David and Mallory are pretty exhausted. We should all go, so they can have some family bonding time, just the three of them." He rose, pointing his kids toward the door. "Where are you and the kids staying, Lana? Maybe we can help y'all get settled since John's not here."

Cassandra turned at the door way. "She's a really nice baby, Mallory. I hope you feel better soon. Come on Janni and Melody. You guys will get some turns later."

Daniel paused at the foot of the bed. "Good night, Mallory. You'll feel a lot better tomorrow. You guys call if you need anything. Anything I can do?"

"Tell Diana I'm sorry. I didn't mean to make her mad-"

"It's okay. She'll be fine tomorrow, too. But, I'll tell her. Anything else"?

"No, I guess not, unless you can blink Pastor Anderson here."

"Would if I could! He's missing getting to meet his first grandkid."

Tears flowed freely. "It isn't about that. I'm in a spiritual crisis. I don't know what to do."

"Well, here's your Bible. Reading it always helps you. But so will a good night's sleep! Did you ever get a dinner tray?"

"I wasn't hungry. I sent it back. Thank you. I think we're good."

-ᚻ ᚼ-

"Mallory asked me to apologize to you. I wish you wouldn't just take off. Even our security people weren't sure where you went. Are you over being mad at her yet?" Daniel felt weary, worried about David and Mallory, and needing Diana to be her usual perky self.

"Well, she should be ashamed of herself."

"Okay, Honey. She apologized. Everything was stressful for them. Remember how young they are. Because they're both so successful, and so together, and such hard workers, we forget how green they really are about many things. You and Lana shouldn't have pushed her so hard about nursing. Evidently, she and David have never discussed the issue. You had it planned out years in advance, because it's what your mother did, and as a nurse, you were technically aware of the benefits. Mallory isn't you. It's okay if she isn't you. And don't let your feelings be hurt because she still wanted Suzanne."

"That had nothing to do with it."

He pulled her close and searched her expression. "M-m-m, are you sure?

She laughed suddenly, the tight strain easing on her features. "I guess you're right. She got so wound up that she pulled me in emotionally. It's been a tough day. Are you ready to go to bed?"

"Not yet. You try to get some sleep. I'm going to try to set things up for Mallory to have a Skype conference with John. She said she's in a 'spiritual crisis' and that concerned me. Maybe it isn't just the typical post-partum depression. When I asked her if I could get her something her response was, 'not unless I could blink her pastor here'."

Diana laughed again, sounding even more like herself. "Skype is nearly that magical. We should have thought of it earlier so John could feel more involved with what's happening here. It can feel very isolating, being in a different culture far from home."

⊰ ⊱

David listened, chagrined. He was trying to settle Mallory and his new daughter down; he felt drained, and everyone was saying Mallory would bounce back after some rest. Now Faulkner had called to talk to her.

She disconnected and handed the phone to him. "Get out your laptop; your dad's gonna talk to me on Skype in fifteen minutes."

"No, come on, Mallory. Let's just get some sleep, please. Everyone said that's what you need, and you'll be fine~"

"Yeah, that's what they think; what they hope. I won't be fine, David. Please! What's another half hour?"

"I don't know. Look, I'm your husband; I try to be the priest of our home. I don't know why we can't just talk about whatever is on your mind."

"I can't, David. I'm sorry. You mostly want to go to sleep anyway. Just get the laptop up here and go to sleep. Except that I want to talk to Pastor privately."

His eyes met hers, dark, inscrutable, like she had wounded him. He placed the device on her tray. "You think the battery will last long enough? Or do I need to connect the cord?"

"Well, the battery should work, unless it's already nearly run down." She turned the computer on, and looked at him pointedly.

386

"We'll be back later," he mumbled as he scooped Amelia up and made his way into the corridor.

⊰ ⊱

John Anderson felt a deep sense of dread as he logged on for the conference with his daughter-in-law. Of course his concern was for the stability of his son's marriage. He silently pled for wisdom.

"Greetings from Nigeria, Mallory," he opened as her picture appeared. "Congratulations on being a mommy. Is David there?"

"Hi, Pastor," she struggled for enough composure to speak. "He's-um-here, but I sent him out with the-um-the baby."

He laughed. "Okay, Calm down, Mallory. Did y'all officially decide to name her Amelia? That's pretty."

"Yes Sir! Maybe-um." She sniffled. "Maybe this was a bad idea. I don't know what my problem is. Everyone thinks I'll bounce back to the top by morning."

He waited. "And you may. I'm praying that way. But what's on your mind? Are you enjoying your baby?"

She broke down even more, shaking her head negatively. "And don't tell me what a gift she is! That she was born with all her parts in the right places and she's normal and healthy."

He laughed, "I won't. That sounds like Diana Faulkner's sermon, and she might sue me for using her material."

"Well, I know all that, and I didn't forget and need the reminder. She is very beautiful and perfect, but-"

"But what, Mallory"? Even as Anderson probed, he felt like the Holy Spirit gave him some desperately needed insight. "What? She's beautiful and perfect, like your horse was? Like *Zakkar*?"

She sat sobbing and shaking.

"That's why you sent David out so you could talk? So he won't feel worse about that?"

"I-um-guess so. So he won't be mad at Jeff. It wasn't Jeff's fault; it wasn't David's or Diana's. It just happened! It-it's my fault."

"Well, sure it is. You're too mature of a Christian to blame God, right?"

"Well, isn't that how I'm supposed to be? I-I don't want to sound like a smart aleck to you. But, um-aren't we supposed to trust God that it's according to some plan-even when-we don't-"

387

"Understand? Yes, but in trying not to blame God, it isn't very fair to Mallory to blame her for everything. Mallory, do you still think it's your fault about your dad?"

She nodded heart-brokenly. "I know it is! That's why I'm so scared."

Her eyes mirrored the fear she confessed.

"Okay, Mallory, let's pray. I should have started with prayer."

She bowed and he voiced a prayer for wisdom and for the Holy Spirit to fill her heart with His peace.

"Okay, Mallory, the coroner's reports indicated your father was gone before his body hit the floor. If you had found him immediately, it's uncertain anything would have done any good."

"Yeah, I know. I'm wasting your time. This is dumb. I'll be okay with some rest."

"Okay, be patient with me. I'm trying to understand what you're saying. Okay, you know what the coroner said, so why do you still feel so strongly that you're responsible for his death?"

"Well, it should be obvious."

"To you it is, Mallory, because you've wrestled with it for so long. Please explain what you mean. I'm sorry to be dense."

"Well, it's my fault, because I adored him! I loved him so much. He was just-! God gets jealous when we love anyone or anything more than we do Him, and- my dad was an idol in my life, and so was *Zakkar*! I never meant that to happen. I want to love Him supremely-that's why I'm afraid I'm going to lose David. I'm afraid I'm either going to run him off, or the Lord will take him-"

"And the baby? You're afraid to let your heart fall in love with her?"

"Yes, I'm bad luck for her-"

"Okay, listen to me, Mallory. All your dad's years of believing in 'luck' are still carrying over in your beliefs, in spite of your knowing the truth. You aren't 'bad luck' for her. She needs you to adore her and bond with her. Mallory, you do love the Lord supremely, and although He's jealous over us, He never becomes vindictive. You do put Him first in every decision you make. You are exhausted and hungry, and your hormones are all over the map. But in trying not to assign blame for what happens, to God or other people, you can't heap it all upon yourself. Does that make sense? Mallory, you don't have to be a 'nursing' mother, to be a good mother. You don't have to be like either Lana or Diana-or like your mother. Just be yourself. You and David together are competent to decide for yourselves.

Don't box her out, Mallory. It's okay to give her your heart. I'm sorry you've been hurt and known such loss. I guess I wasn't aware you were still hurting so much. I'm sorry."

She wiped her face again and summoned a smile for the first time. "I know. I thought I was doing a pretty good job dealing with it."

"You were. You're a strong, vibrant Christian. It's good to deal with issues, just with the Lord and your Bible. As you know, I often have the same people in my study for counseling, week after week. They don't do anything I recommend, and they don't search out answers for themselves as they should."

"Again, it's about balance," she acknowledged. "I shouldn't be overly dependent or your wisdom and counsel, but I shouldn't try to be so independent of it, either." She heard Amelia's little squawks as David paced past her doorway. "Hey, you can come in now. Your dad wants to see her better."

Chapter 31: ASSURANCE

"Hey, Erik, what's going on?" John Anderson's response to an IM from Bransom! "I just finished a Skype session with Mallory. Have you seen the baby?"

"One picture! I'm conflicted about doting on Mallory's newborn when I didn't even know my daughters were married and having kids. I heard she had a hard time, and that tore at me. She doing better? Since your talk? She and David are doing okay, aren't they? Whenever I'm around them, they seem to complement one another like cookies and milk."

"M-mm-m! Don't say 'cookies and milk' to me. I've been starving since the second I left home. Why did you message me? You know I'm not at liberty to divulge confidences."

"Yeah, that's not what I'm after. This is probably stupid. You got time for this?"

"I do, but turn on your camera and save ourselves the keyboarding. What's on your mind that's really very valid? And not stupid at all?"

Erik's face popped onto the screen as he laughed. "I get so annoyed with people. I have my devotions in the morning, and I feel so good, like I love everybody~. But then, everybody's doin' stuff wrong; not according to procedure; about to get themselves, or somebody else killed. I've never doubted my salvation since that afternoon in your office, but this passage keeps going through my head, 'that they'll know we're Christians by our love'! I feel like I'm at odds with practically the whole human race. Would I feel like that if I were a true Christian?"

"People have an odd propensity toward being annoying, Erik. You're life's marked by love, even from before your conversion."

"Okay, now I know a line of garbage when I hear one-" Erik's expression registered frustration.

"Okay, you wanted my input, so please do not interrupt me. When I said your life was hallmarked by love, I wasn't saying you're a mushy, emotional ball of snot-slinging, huggy junk. I don't know why people think that's what *Love* is. Too many goofy movies and storybooks! Woo-oooo-ooo-ooo. And although people annoy you and try your patience, it doesn't mean you don't love them. Like Tammi. I don't know how many times she has backed into the same tree leaving the church! It costs me, and it drives me crazy; it doesn't mean I don't love her. Why did you decide to risk your life every day, being in law enforcement? But to protect America and her citizens? What would motivate a choice like that, but love? The other agents' being careless is hard for you to deal with, because you care what happens to them, when they seem so impervious. Loving people isn't grabbing everyone you know with a hug and a kiss. That can be very phony; like Judas Iscariot, greeting Jesus with a kiss. Look, I love my whole body of believers. I try to help them and protect them, fight the devil himself for them. That doesn't mean I want to hang out with all of them and be best buds. Remember the Bible definition of *Love* is far different than the World's"!

"Okay, you're right; that clears up a lot, but I try to keep from just being a grouchy old guy."

"Don't worry about it, Erik. Your personality is businesslike, maybe serious and slightly gruff. It's what makes you ideal for the FBI. I reprimanded David more than once for making fun of Faulkner for ordinarily being the serious type. As Christians, we do have a deep abiding joy, but the Lord doesn't want us all to be a bunch of grinning, gushing idiots. When I watch some of the so-called preachers on TV, they annoy me. I think, 'No wonder the world doesn't want anything to do with Christians!' I don't know those peoples' hearts, but they seem plastic and fake. So much for my judging evil judgment"!

Bransom laughed. "Okay, you cleared that up for me bright as day. I guess I should have figured it out for myself, but since I didn't, thank you for your time. We all miss you."

"Believe me, not as much as I miss being there. I'm not sure what possessed me to come here."

Bransom laughed. "*Love*! The real kind"!

⊰ ⊱

Ivan Summers sighed wearily. Haslett was a problem. After single-handedly taking out a violent criminal, he seemed out-of-control. Summers hadn't ever cared for him too much, but he had tried to help the rookie Arkansas agent get the feel of things. He talked too much, for one thing, bragging about his escapade, glad that he had shot the kid dead, saying he would be quick to do it again in a similar scenario. It sounded nuts to the public (probably because it was), and the press continued to egg him on so they could make total anarchy seem like a preferable choice to law enforcement personnel who planned to shoot first and investigate afterwards. It scared Summers for the kid's sake, too, because gang members could easily decide to avenge their leader's shooting. If Haslett didn't care about himself, he should care that his bravado placed his wife and kid in the cross hairs. He phoned Trent Morrison, not certain why.

"Hey, Summers, you've been on my mind." Morrison's upbeat tone lifted Summers' spirits.

"Oh, yeah, why's that?"

"Just wondering if our house is staying clean after our housecleaning last year! You see anything suspicious, like they're regrouping? I mean, we did some serious damage, what with the missiles firing. I can barely believe that happened. Still, the bad guys don't just give up. The American market for their products is too lucrative. It's hard for me to believe that so many Americans choose to be strung out on drugs. Defying laws, risking serious consequences"!

"Yeah, Morrison, you're such a good guy that you can't grasp the psyches of the bad guys. Every user isn't the same and their motives for using run the gamut. Still, it makes criminal activity within our borders pay off big time. Money to the criminal element is like blood to sharks."

"Yeah, that's true. Listen, stay in touch. If you notice any signs of regrouping, let me know."

"Sure Morrison. You're like Bransom. You federal guys seem to think all the state agencies work for you. If we find crime problems in our state, we take care of it."

Morrison laughed. "Yeah, no doubt! Hey, why'd ya call?"

"I'm not really sure, but the reminder came at a good time. Guess I'll scout around and visit with the locals, see if anyone's aware of anything cropping up. With spring coming, more people will be hitting our Natural State. Hopefully, not to try to grow their cash crops."

⊣⊣ ⊢⊢

"Okay, Hillman, I thought you were going to interview little Danay again and send me the report. What's the holdup?"

"Well, Cynthia Livingston was uncooperative. She said they have Danay in counseling, and we'll upset her by dredging the whole thing up over and over again."

"We'll upset her. We'll upset her? Criminals grabbed a six year old child as she was leaving a ballet lesson, killed her Nanny, drug her across the country! And we're the villains? Go back tomorrow and tell that crazy, hysterical woman, that we have an investigation ongoing. And if we have to, we can arrest her for obstruction!" He paused. "Maybe I'm crazy, but has it occurred to you that the mother might have played a part in it?" He could hear the other agent sigh as she considered her answer.

"I suppose crazier things have happened. How do you want me to proceed with that?"

"Cautiously! Get more research into her background. Check her financials, get her phone records, tap her phone, and put her under surveillance. If someone kidnapped one of my kids, I'd want to get to the bottom of the investigation as fast as possible, see some heads roll. I'd cooperate and blame the bad guys for causing mental stress. Get copies of the divorce settlement, custody agreements, child-support. I've thought it strange all along, that Danay was grabbed alone, and her brother wasn't touched. Could be coincidental! Ms. Livingston should be aware that Danay isn't home free. If she was handpicked like most of Oberson's victims, chances are, he still wants her."

"Yeah, you're right. You know what that means; don't you?"

Bransom's chest squeezed. "That he hasn't changed his mind about getting Jennifer back, or snatching Mallory. I wonder if he knows Missy has started talking. I'll contact Nick and David and Steb and arrange extra protection details. Hillman, you be careful, too."

"Yes Sir; and Theresa Reynosa?"

"Yeah, what have you heard on Roberson?"

"Not much. I'll have the DA contacted on it tomorrow. His house, phones, computers were loaded with evidence against him; I hope nothing's stalled out." /

⊣⊨ ⊨⊢

Mallory hugged her sleeping infant anxiously. "It scares me when I can't wake her up. How do I know she's okay?"

"Because Diana told us she's fine. Tiny babies sleep a lot and they sleep really soundly. When they're asleep, you can hardly make them wake up; and when they're awake you can hardly make them go to sleep. Usually their days and nights are mixed up. Let me put her down and turn on the monitor. There should be plenty on ESPN about opening day for baseball. It feels good to be home."

"Well, in a way, it does. I just felt more secure with all the nursing staff making sure she was okay."

David laughed. "She's okay. She's eating fairly well, and keeping down a good portion, I think. In a couple of days, we take her to the pediatrician, and they'll make sure she's gaining weight."

Mallory relinquished her tiny parcel, and David kissed the little face tenderly before settling her gently into a handmade wooden cradle.

"Where did that come from? You made that? How did you keep it hidden from me?"

He smiled at her delight. "I did make it, and hiding it from Miss Nosey wasn't easy."

She ran her hand lightly across the polished wood. "It doesn't have any lead in it?"

"Not that she'll be gnawing on it anytime soon, but no. Lead-free! I used a pattern that doesn't have any design defects, as far as her getting caught, or anything. Mallory, we've done all we can to keep her safe."

Anxious eyes sought his. "What? Am I obsessing?"

He pulled her close. "No, you're perfect. It scared me when you were acting like you didn't care about her."

He was starting to relax when the call came from Bransom.

⊣⊨ ⊨⊢

Daniel listened tensely to Erik Bransom's words. "What more can we do, Erik? Hiring extra people costs a lot of money, and it's still hard to know if you can trust them when it comes to such high-value targets. I wonder if it would be possible to hire a private investigator to check into the security people we have. See who contacts them, if they're suddenly getting large sums of money. It scared me when you told me that the nanny might have been paid to facilitate Danay Hicks' abduction. I don't want to offend our long-time security by checking them out again."

"Why should they mind, if they have nothing to hide? Look, none of our privacy as Americans is like it once was. You can certainly use the proliferation of information to your advantage. Everybody else does, in far worse ways than that. And Faulkner, don't get so concerned with Mallory's safety that you leave your wife and kids exposed. You have a very beautiful family."

"Yeah, you're right, Erik, I do. Thanks." Daniel disconnected but he couldn't dispel the phantoms that seemed to have flown into the suite on Bransom's chilling warning. Suddenly, he was overwhelmed with the weight of responsibility. He had become casual about the risk to his own family. Sure, he took precautions. Their family was well-known in the Tulsa area and probably esteemed to be richer than they actually were. So he was prepared against being an easy target of opportunity. But for someone as ruthless and totally without scruples as Oberson's people, for someone determined to get his beautiful children and use them for unspeakable wickedness! He trembled. Not a fight against flesh and blood, but against spiritual wickedness in high places. His wife and kids on the line, and he was worried about offending his employees by double-checking their activities? Tears of shame burned down his cheeks. "Lord, help me be a man! Evil is overtaking us, and I'm not even caring for my own family as I should. Help me to make more of a difference!" He took the notepad and pen furnished in the room and moved to the sitting area of their room. He was disgusted with himself, remembering Chapter One of the *One Minute Millionaire* about small adjustments made at center, that carry on out to be huge.

1. *GeoHy* fleet (Not the ones that transported the family) but the other trucks should have Scripture added to the *GeoHy* logos on the doors.
2. *GeoHy* office suite: Place appropriate and attractive Scripture verse on the glass by the logo.
3. Add plan of salvation to stationery and business cards. Do a good enough job, that people will contract with us anyway.

4. Try to expand our musical outreach and be aware of pastors and churches to help and encourage.
5. Be more involved in Honey Grove. I've been a cry baby that they don't roll out a red carpet for us.
6. Put our Gospel music on our phone system for people 'holding'; but out of courtesy, try to eliminate people being put on 'hold'.
7. Post a nice plaque on our wall next to the gates. Lighted.
8. Erect a flag pole and fly the American flag.
9. Send out a memo in our building to see if any of the other tenants would be interested in a weekly men's Bible study.
10. Place an attractive plaque next to the front door of our cabin.
11. Take Diana and go out visiting and soul-winning every week. At Honey Grove, or wherever we are.
12. Check and double-check the activities of everyone who comes into contact with my family!

He rose from the desk and moved softly around the darkened suite. "Lord," he prayed, 'help me to reconcile trying to be a 'Super-nice-guy-Christian with Mean-ready-to-fight-and-kill-if-necessary Christian. I need to move past shooting the guy hassling Morrison that night. I did what I had to. Help me do it again, if necessary. I want to have a good testimony for you before men, but I don't want to be crippled by seeking their favor."

❧ ☙

Mallory checked items off her list as she assembled them in their master suite. "Am I forgetting anything?" Her anxious gaze met David's.

He laughed in response. "No I think that's pretty much everything she owns. She has more luggage than the two of us put together. Once we get to Denver and get the rental car, we can stop along the way and buy more diapers and wipes and formula."

She nodded, relieved. "Yeah, that's true. I guess we're ready then?"

❧ ☙

"Race you back to the cabin," Daniel challenged Jeremiah.

"Hey, no fair! You gave yourself a head-start." Jeremiah was on his heels.

They were neck and neck as they burst in the back door. "I won!" Daniel's voice was filled with laughing jubilation.

"Yeah, whatever, Cheater"!

Diana glanced up mildly. "Who won the game?"

Jeremiah thrust a tumbler under the spigot on the refrigerator door and gulped thirstily. "We lost by one bucket! One lousy bucket! But we showed them that white guys can be in the game."

Diana laughed. "I'm sure you did."

"I'm hitting the shower so I'm ready when the chow bell rings." Jeremiah refilled his water and headed for the bathroom.

"Don't use all the hot water!" Daniel filled a mug with coffee and sank down at the counter. "How's my beautiful girlfriend? Did you miss me?"

"Of course. Did you really beat Jeremiah in a race?"

He laughed. "Absolutely! Why would you doubt? Of course, I gave myself one small advantage. You know, to offset my disadvantage of being twenty-five years older than he is."

She nodded, amused. "I see. So, you didn't really cheat; you just evened up the playing field?"

"Yeah, hey, Jeff was in the gym and he was kind of griping. David told him to go to Kirby to the lumber yard, and see if he could assemble another crew. I guess they plan to build on the Dorman piece of land. He said David and Mallory were on their way to Denver. You know anything about that?"

Her eyebrows raised slightly. "Didn't have a clue, but I'm glad if they're having a chance to get away. They really didn't go anywhere for a honeymoon. Maybe they're going skiing."

Daniel looked at her morosely.

"What? They don't have to take us with them everywhere they go. If you want to ski, let's go. We're big kids; we can make our own plans. But this is pretty fun, just being able to come here."

"Well, who will they have watching Amelia while they ski? I don't expect to be invited everywhere they go, just because most of the time, we have been. There are these fresh concerns with security~"

Alexandra and Cassandra appeared, snapping helmets on. "Mom, you need us to do anything? Or can we go ride our bicycles?"

"You know the rules. Stay on this property. Be back in an hour," Daniel's response. "Where are the little kids?"

"Ryan's down for his nap and Nadia and Xavier are watching a movie. You want us to bring them?"

"No, go on. I may take them out and let them swing. We're gonna eat lunch in the chow hall; maybe we'll drive over to Daisy for dinner this evening."

"Are David and Mallory coming?" Cassandra's face lit at the prospect. "Isn't Amelia sweet? I could eat her up."

"No they aren't coming. I guess they went to Denver. You better go ride before your time's up."

"Oh, to check about the Diamonds," Cassandra nodded sagely as she followed her older sister into the garage.

⊰ ⊱

Lilly reread a confidential directive from her director, her expression grim. It was a scarcely veiled threat to her for not having prevented David and Mallory's trip. She paced, aggravated, trying to marshal her thoughts so she could frame a measured response. Evidently, the Powers above her were giving her little credit for having the situations under control. They inferred that they were aware of her conversion, and felt it not beneficial to the Diamond Industry, nor to Israel. She was as much in the loop now, as she ever had been! It was her job, and she had always done it extremely well! Extremely Well! Since her accepting Jesus as Messiah, she felt that she was doing a better job. From the platform of genuine enlightenment! Being able to see beyond her nose! She sighed! She had David and Mallory very well in hand. Considering what they could try to do, they played along extremely cooperatively.

She sat down to word a reply:

To the Director, Shalom,

As you know, Mallory O'Shaughnessy has played our game very willingly. With no disrespect, Sir, you seem to think that you are alone in your grasp of the situation.

For decades, our combined efforts have marketed both Diamonds and the Jewelry Industry to the American Public,

398

creating an aura of mystery and allure. An image that we have maintained most carefully, even since 1906 when D were first discovered in West. Ark. We were able also to squelch the revelation of the find in No. Co.

With DiaMo also aware of the need to maintain prices for their stones, they have no desire to destabilize prices and our industry. The last thing they would want to do is cause damage to Israel. When firing on the range, it is wise to discern friendlies from enemies.

Your loyal friend and servant,

Lilly Cowan

⊰ ⊱

"Dawson, what kind of strings do we have to pull with Treasury to get Oberson and some of these other guys' assets going to the victims as restitution? I hear about its happening occasionally."

"Yeah, I don't know, Erik. Treasury prefers to keep the proceeds of the auctions for the government. It helps pay our salaries."

"Oh yeah? I thought they ran the printing presses for that. Listen, I know I've heard on the news of crime victims starting to get more than having their perpetrators put behind bars. I know an attorney I can call about it."

"Yeah, Erik, but if the government goes broke, we won't even have resources for putting perpetrators behind bars."

Erik sighed. Oberson's financial scores were in the millions of dollars. Millions he owed back taxes on and that Treasury could seize due to the illegality of the enterprises. But it wasn't a drop in the bucket to begin making up for the national debt. He dropped the issue with Dawson, making a mental note to check it out with Kerry Larson.

⊰ ⊱

Snowfall in Northeastern Colorado covered the ground-and Mallory's plan-with a wet blanket.

She gazed out the window forlornly, "Remind me, that when the Lord skews my plans, it's because He has something far better. It's one of those days, when I just want what I want. Well," she laughed. "I guess they all are. This is one of the times when my response is either: *Know God,* or *No, God.* Let's finish getting ready and go down and read our Bibles while we eat breakfast."

David nodded agreeably. She had a good balance, knowing that *Matthew 6:6* instructed about having devotions in a secret place so that God, Who sees in secret, rewards you openly. Jesus gave the example of the Pharisee who made a big to-do of his public prayer to be seen of men. But Mallory liked to stay where she wasn't ashamed of her Bible, either, and she was willing to let her light shine that way.

David was always happy to show off Mallory, and now, Amelia, too. And, breakfast enticed!

❈ ❈

"Ivan Summers, here. What can I do for you, Jeff?"

"Yeah, Mr. Summers. David told me to go back to the lumber yard up at Kirby and see if anyone was hanging around that needed work. That really scary gang guy that you and David thought you killed? He's alive! And! He's back working there! I shifted into reverse and got out, but he saw me! He was calling someone the last I saw!"

"No way he could be alive, Jeff! Just with the tats and stuff, they can all look the same. You didn't even stop for a really good look, did you? I mean, it definitely bears checking out. Morrison called me a few days ago, asking if the problem was cropping up again. We'll make sure it doesn't. For you to be on the safe side, forget David's assignment and stick to the Ranch until we make sure. The Faulkners are there right now, too, aren't they?"

❈ ❈

David was satisfied with the amount of attention Mallory and his infant daughter garnered. Mallory wore a deep grayed, blue green suit knit of Alpaca and Mohair. The jacket, short and molded, buttoned to a Nehru collar; and the skirt flared into a mid-calf sweep, meeting shining brown boots. Amelia matched mommy from boots to beret; and from the diaper bag, peeked a baby doll, dressed identically. Quite a number of restaurant patrons stopped to ask whether the famous doll company now also created clothing for real mommies. To which Mallory responded with her brilliant smile, handing over a business card, "No, my cousin thought of this."

Other people noticed the opened Bibles. One man pastored a local church. "Hello, you don't know me; but I'm familiar with you. I've often wondered what it would take to get you and the Faulkner family to come perform your music at our church. We're kind of small, though, so we just figured~"

"Well, we try to go where the Lord wants us to," David responded. "The sizes of the churches aren't our determining factor. My dad pastors a little church."

"Uh, yeah! Little, and world-wide! That I could be like your dad"! The man's tone was wistful.

"Here's my card. Call me if you're serious, and I'll work out a date between you and Daniel, when we could come." David was the contact person for bookings since Faulkner's information had been switched to avoid stalking. "Where is your church? If we're still in the area, we'll probably visit Wednesday night."

Pastor Don Brookings, of Northshore Heights Baptist returned to his table, happy for the new contact.

"Are you ready to go back up? We aren't getting much reading done," David noted.

"One more cup of coffee?" She was irresistible.

His phone bonged an email. "It's from Frank. He just auctioned off something that used to belong to your dad. He's keeping ten per cent for his trouble of rescuing the junk, warehousing it, and making the sale. Your part's only nine thousand dollars! And, he hasn't cashed the check we gave him that night because he wants to carry the financing on the entire amount for the whole five years. He trusts us."

Mallory's eyes widened as she grasped the whole thing. "Okay, not my part, but <u>our</u> part, is nine grand. That's why the Lord held us up this morning. He wanted us to meet Pastor Brookings and He wanted us to know about this extra money in place, in case we need to make any offers."

David grinned. "And, a restaurant full of patrons knows about our products. You do look sensational, by the way."

⊰ ⊱

Dan Wells checked in with Bransom. "We've done everything reasonable to find Zeb Matthews' remains. If Epson shot him that night, like Jennifer thought, he didn't bury the body in proximity to the trailer. She said what? That he called in a posse of his friends? Maybe Epson wounded his son, but then they got him across the border and harvested his organs?"

"Yikes! That's macabre! I mean, it would be one thing, to shoot a son in the heat of an argument. But-"

"Well, yeah, but Matthews worked with tough characters, and he needed them for his miserable existence. He wouldn't have been in a position to dictate any terms. Maybe they buried the remains in Mexico, or just left them to the coyotes. Or maybe Zeb's still alive and well somewhere, and Jennifer just assumed he died."

Erik was able to fall asleep after the conversation, but he dreamed he was receiving a heart transplant in the middle of a sandstorm on the northern Mexican desert.

⊰ ⊱

"Hey, Jeff; what is it?" Back in their suite, Mallory was dozing, and David's phone volume was all the way up.

He moved to the living room, trying to un-jumble Jeff's narrative and talk without disturbing her. Jeff's second try wasn't much straighter.

"Well, maybe Summers is right. With the tattoos and overall scariness-"

"I'm not crazy!" Jeff interrupted angrily. "And I'm not just some punk kid that doesn't know what he's talking about!"

"Hey, Man, I'm sorry. I sure didn't mean to come across that way! Well, Summers was right about you watching yourself. Keep the guns more handy. Look, Jeff, all I know is that those two guys were dead and they were calling out for body bags." Something occurred to him suddenly. "Maybe I figured out the mystery. What if it's another case of identical twins? Like Oscar and Otto. Why can't heroes ever come in pairs?"

"Good question. That makes sense, and at least I know I saw flesh and blood and not some apparition."

"Maybe flesh and blood, but if he's like the other one, he's still spookier than all get out. Call Summers back and tell him what we think. Maybe you should call Morrison, too. And see who's nearby of the Forestry Service law enforcement"!

"Could you do it?"

"No! If you want to be treated like a man, you have to be one!"

Bob Porter answered Morrison's cell. "Hey, Jeff. Thank you for giving Summers the heads-up. Trent's still finishing up some paperwork. We just finished taking nine really hard core guys into federal custody. We're thinking the leader of the pack was an i~"

"dentical twin," Jeff finished.

"Yeah, and blaming Ivan Summers for his twin's demise. Totally loco! We've ramped up enforcement in the major national forests, but keep both eyes open."

"I will! Even to sleep"!

Morrison shoved his phone back into his pocket. Things shouldn't be like that, here, in America.

Chapter 32: APLOMB

"Hey, snow's all gone. Do you still want to try to see stuff today?"

Mallory nodded eagerly. "Yeah, let's check out and go view the site; then we can stay in Ft. Collins tonight. Maybe go back again tomorrow, if necessary. Then get back to Denver in time to go to Northshore Heights."

They hustled to load the vehicle and check out by the noon deadline.

♯ ♮

Risa created a gorgeous piece to grace the wall of *GeoHy's* office suite. A bas-relief sculpture of a mine pit, with a Geologist wearing a hard hat, and citing three verses Daniel liked from the book of Psalms:

> *Psalm 95:4-6 In his hands are the deep places of the earth: the strength of the hills is his also.*

> *The sea is his, and he made it: and his hands formed the dry land.*

> *O come, let us worship and bow down: let us kneel before the LORD our maker.*

♯ ♮

Accompanied by Jason, Katy Graves appeared at the Federal Courthouse in Omaha and gave a deposition regarding illegal activities she had been involved in at the convenience store in Kirby. With her statement, all charges against her were dropped. Miraculously, that included the charges of child endangerment. With a clear record, she agreed to marry Jason.

"Thank you for your patience with me," she whispered, as he slid a ring onto her finger.

"You were well worth waiting for. You were something to keep me reaching forward as Tim slipped away." He laughed suddenly, smile crinkles by his eyes chasing away the haunted look. "Well, you're far more to me than that."

She nodded seriously. "I understand that, Jason. Now let's pray about Chad. I know what you promised Tim, and I agree. It's just that fighting his mom in court can be so ugly-for him to go through. And I feel a little sorry for her. She is his mother; she made mistakes. I made mistakes I can't believe, as I look back."

He nodded. Neither of them had money for a custody battle. And they probably couldn't win, anyway. Maybe Tim's ex had made a mistake, and now she could be a great mom! Still, her behaving the way she had when Tim had come home so busted up~ Tears filled Jason's eyes. He just had a problem with that!

⊰ ⊱

"Mr. Billingsley?" Bryce glanced up at the hesitant receptionist. Being called 'Mr. Billingsley' still made him glance around, expecting his father to appear. "Yes, Sandra, what is it? Did you get that report I asked you for."

"Yes, Sir, it took a while for them to get it into the binder. I thought you might also like similar information on *Wharton*." She placed the neatly bound report before him.

"Yes, I guess so. I'm not familiar with *Wharton*. So, whatever it takes to bring us up to speed on them would be greatly appreciated. You set up an interview for me with Archie Ward?"

"Yes Sir! In the morning at nine! He's out on the links right now."

Bryce frowned. Your boss wanting to meet with you should surely take precedence over a golf game. But this was probably best. More staff would be around in the morning, in case the meeting grew testy. Employees were already filing out for the day. "Set it up with Marie to re-interview in the morning with Blythe. That's all. Oh, and Sandra, send out a memo that

405

unless there are urgent matters, everyone should plan to be in from eight 'til four."

At precisely four, he loaded his brief case with work and headed down the elevator.

◄ ►

In Ft. Collins, David and Mallory checked into a hotel suite, changed Amelia and fed her, and headed out again. "We need to get burgers and eat on the way," David observed. "Take advantage of daylight."

Mallory nodded agreement and with food purchased, they chatted happily as they headed onto US 287 N.

"Who called you when we first got back after breakfast?"

"Jeff! You're not gonna believe! He thought that guy I killed was back from the dead. So scared he couldn't talk straight. He had already contacted Summers. Anyway, guys from the various federal agencies took nine guys into custody; one of them an evil twin~"

"You're kidding~" Her eyes sought his, concerned. "They just keep coming."

He nodded. "Yeah, sadly! They never give up, is the reason why we can't either. What are you thinking you're going to see when we get here?"

"Probably not much! I just want to look at things as a Geologist in the field. One of the few weaknesses of studying on-line is the absence of enough field experience. It's a pretty place."

He nodded. "But are we looking to buy more property?"

Her eyes glowed. "Well, not really, until we got that word from Frank Gilmore."

He nodded. "Yeah, that was good news, but the five years will go by fast, and we'll owe him the money. We could put this payment into an escrow or savings account, or something."

She nodded. "Is that what you think we should do? Keep the money safe?"

"Well, there's something to be said for that. What are your thoughts?"

"Well, when I woke up this morning, my only plan was to come up here, and look, and leave. And I was disappointed that the snow changed my plans. But the delay was just enough to get Frank's email, and for me

406

to read farther in my Bible than I usually would for one day. I read about the three stewards' being left with the money to invest."

He cut his eyes at her quizzically "And the guy who just kept the principal safe was an unprofitable servant. The ones who were commended were the investors. The risk-takers"!

She shrugged.

"Okay, so we <u>are</u> looking to buy."

And they did! The cutest place imaginable! David was amazed! With the price of properties in the Mile High State, it was unbelievable that the sellers of this one had dropped their price twice. They hadn't had one inquiry in nearly a year, and were desperate to unload it.

After signing the contract, they ate dinner at a cute western-themed restaurant and drove back to Ft. Collins.

"I'm amazed!" Mallory's countenance sparkled more brightly than ever. "It's another instance of *I Corinthians 2:9:*

> *But as it is written, Eye hath not seen, nor ear heard, neither have entered into the heart of man, the things which God hath prepared for them that love him."*

⊰ ⊱

Daniel noticed regretfully how much attention his son garnered from different women in the Sullivan Building where *GeoHy's* offices were located. Jeremiah's voice had deepened as he had shot up in stature. Always dressed nicely, thanks to his mother's efforts, he was cute. With a serious, but pleasant demeanor, it seemed like the world lay open before him! ~If they could keep him from snares and pitfalls.

"Good morning, Becky," Jeremiah greeted a girl in the elevator as he and Daniel descended together for lunch in the Bistro.

She blushed and answered shyly.

With their food before them, Daniel took the conversational plunge. "Son, I can't help noticing you're starting to get quite a bit of attention from the opposite sex."

Jeremiah shrugged. "Yes Sir. I think they all think I'm rich. Which, I guess I kinda am. But I don't want to get involved with some social-climber."

"Well, is there anybody you like? I want you to feel like you can talk to us."

Jeremiah smiled. "You mean am I getting over Mallory? I guess I don't really 'like' anyone. I think Megan Morrison's real cute, but she's young."

Daniel nodded, trying to keep a straight face. 'Like Jer wasn't young himself'. "Yeah, she's pretty cute, and she's a nice Christian girl, too. I mean, I don't want to push you; it's a long ways off."

"Yes, Sir, and the thing that scares me about Megan is her asthma. I wouldn't want anyone who's about to die on me."

Daniel chewed a bite of salad slowly before responding. "Well, I guess we try to insulate ourselves from heartache. The truth of the matter is, life is risky; with no guarantees. Megan might live to be eighty, in spite of her asthma, and someone else who seems the picture of health and vitality can suddenly be gone!"

Jeremiah nodded and retreated into silence. At last, he started to say something, but then sighed instead.

"What's on your mind, Jer?"

"Well, how do I know for sure if I'm being called to preach? I mean, how do I know the will of God for my life?" The questions erupted from the depths of his soul. "I mean, do you and grandpa and mom want me to be a Geologist? I know I'm supposed to honor you all."

Daniel leaned back while the server refilled his coffee. "I'm sorry, Jeremiah, if I've acted like I expect you to take over *GeoHy*. Of course, I love it! But not nearly as much as I love you! What I want for you is to do the Lord's will. If He's calling you to preach, that would make us ecstatic! You've seemed interested in the numbers and accounting aspect of the business."

"Well, yes, Sir, because if I become pastor of a church someday, I'll need to know how to handle the finances. I know I'm barely in high school courses, but I want to study Theology and accounting, together. I want to keep working with you every day. I love *GeoHy* too." Tears freed themselves against his will. "I can't explain it!"

Daniel's eyes filled with tears in response. "It's okay, Son. You don't have to."

Lilly listened to the most recent report, amazed. Even with her conversion, she continued to be astounded by Mallory and the mystifying manner in which things opened themselves up to her. Another piece of property, located right at the edge of the Diamond-bearing land of northeastern Colorado. Not more expensive, as the treasure buried not so deeply beneath the surface would suggest; but price-reduced for quick sale. The trendy cabin, nestled on seven acres at the edge of the Roosevelt National Forest and the Front Range, was in itself, a jewel. Yes, Mallory's sharp eyes were quick to see Diamonds amongst the gravel, but she also had a sense of value of everything else surrounding her. She was like her father, who knew the value of junk to be obtained for a few dollars, held and sold as great treasure to the right buyer. Then, she was able to see potential in people. David and Mallory's Colorado purchase was for the value of the property, in and of itself, if they never pulled out one Diamond. But if, eventually, American Diamonds should be acknowledged and mined, she had a foot in the door at two very promising locations. Smart girl! Smart couple!

And all the people, surrounding Lilly, who could get so nervous, were calming down, too.

That was a relief, because she had three more concerts on the schedule with Cassandra.

⊰ ⊱

"Well our day went well; how about yours?" Diana greeted as Daniel and Jeremiah entered from the garage.

Daniel grabbed her, kissing her hard. "Our day was good; better now that we're home with you! Smells good in here; thanks for starting the soup."

"Yes, I started it, even though I received a call that Jim's in the hospital with pneumonia. I thought we should go visit him and take him some. He's grown frailer than ever. I wish he'd let his defenses crumble and let us witness to him."

"Well, we should pray about it," Jeremiah was the one who tried to make a habit of praying about everything.

"Well, it kind of was a prayer, what your mom just said."

Jeremiah frowned. "Well, Mom was talking to you, and I know God hears everything we say. But it isn't the same as talking to Him. We let

God know what we want Him to do; but He's more motivated when we ask Him."

"He's right," Diana acknowledged. "Jeremiah, why don't you pray?"

And he tried to, but his heart was so broken that words wouldn't come.

⚏ ⚎

Back in the hotel, Mallory spent a long time on the phone with Jack and Estelle. "It may be too much of a change from what you're used to. If you can give six months, then if you want we'll help you move back."

Estelle fought tears. With the unbelievable compensation Mallory was talking about, she felt like she could accustom herself to the jungles of Panama.

"Also, I'm concerned about the altitude. My friend Diana is a nurse and she said if you don't have any serious respiratory problems, you can probably acclimate fairly quickly. It's a dream location, for beauty and things to do. It's even better than Arkansas."

⚏ ⚎

Erik awakened again with the pain in his chest; only this time he wasn't dreaming he was having heart surgery. He tried to stay calm; the pain was definitely there, although it didn't seem to be intensifying. He sat up slowly, massaging the area gingerly.

"Are you okay?"

Before he could answer, Suzanne dialed 911.

⚏ ⚎

David stayed up late, making plans with Jeff and arranging for utilities in their name to be turned on at the new cabin. It was in unbelievably good shape, less than ten years old and well maintained. David had good ideas to add signature élan, but that would be later, if ever. He combed through the newspaper for modular housing, and looked up directions to the dealers that seemed promising. He hoped he could accomplish a lot in the week so he and Mallory could get back home. Although they were having a ton of

410

fun! He moved softly to the mini-fridge to grab a Dr. Pepper, and Mallory emerged with Amelia.

"I thought I heard her stirring around. Did I wake her up?"

Mallory laughed. "No. It's the middle of the night. Her time to howl! Are you getting things nailed down? Why don't you order something from room service?"

"Are you hungry?" his voice sounded hopeful.

"I could eat a little something. You know, I used to daydream about things like this. Like staying in a really cheap motel would have been an outing for me. But I'd see on TV, really nice hotels and room service~ Let's do it." She finished changing a diaper, shaking a bottle to mix water with formula. "We're going to be up for a while."

While they played with Amelia and ate and talked, they both received text messages. One was about *the Maestro's* being hospitalized with Pneumonia, but that he had received the Lord. The other was that Erik was in the ER with more chest pain.

-⊰ ⊱-

David chose an attractive double-wide with nice amenities, signed the paper work, and arranged for rapid delivery. Jeff and a crew were arriving as quickly as possible to create a spot on the new acreage for the pre-built home. They could get it set up and skirted, ready for Jack and Estelle's arrival. He checked messages. All of the final touches were in place at the *Chandler* facility in Houston. Roger was inviting him and Mallory to a banquet celebrating the acquisition and its face lift.

Almost immediately, Suzanne phone Mallory, giving her an update on Erik's condition, and asking if Sanders could use her gymnasium to house the banquet. It still bothered her that Roger wanted the gym so badly, but she consented and was glad for further news about Erik. He was still in the Hope hospital ICU on nitro drips and heart monitoring equipment, waiting to be transported to Baylor Dallas for a heart cath. It made Mallory nervous.

"Mom, please don't be so involved with this banquet that you don't take care of him."

Suzanne responded sympathetically, that he was in good hands, the transportation was set up, and if he required another stent, it would be in by Friday; he could be home Saturday, and the banquet wasn't scheduled until Tuesday evening. And Cat Sanders and her personnel were doing most of the work. Then, she actually thought to ask about Amelia.

Even though, the question seemed like an afterthought, Mallory bubbled enthusiastically. "Oh, she is so adorable, and so much fun. I'll send you some more pictures. She seems to change minute by minute. She's still mostly a night owl. She has her daddy wrapped around her little finger already. Love you mom. We're praying for you and Erik."

"I'm curious about something," David's eyes were alight and mischievous. "Why won't you sell that gym to Roger? It's a natural fit for him and the *Chandler* branch. With the money, we could build a similar gym at the Ranch. Well, maybe more on the Gilmore property so people in the community could rent it and we wouldn't actually have a bunch of extra people being a security concern at the Ranch itself."

Her troubled gaze met his. "I don't know, David. I guess since I own it and can't really use it much, and Roger wants it so bad- I guess I feel like I should just give it to him. But, we can't really afford that. Do you think we can?"

"That's been your hold up? Roger has money like you wouldn't believe. Mallory, he doesn't expect you to donate it to him. If you did, he'd be in a tax turmoil like we have been since Herb's gift to you. Let's just sell it to him; we don't have to make money from the deal."

She nodded, convinced. "Okay, you want to call and tell him?"

⚔ ⚔

Daniel gazed into Diana's laughing eyes. Their anniversary presented a chance for an elegant dinner, just the two of them.

"Really? He said that? He thinks Megan's cute, but her asthma's that much of a concern to him? I'm glad you opened the door on the conversation. Let's not push him about the call to preach. I'm thrilled, but I want him to be sure it's the Lord."

Daniel nodded. "What about Al? Does she ever say anything about Tommy Haynes? Or anybody? She does a good job helping you out; doesn't she?"

"Yes, we have a lot of fun working together, and she's getting good phone and people skills. She frees me up more to look after the little ones and play with them."

His hand covered hers on the table. "Yeah, they're all so cute and so much fun. Being married to you is an incredible adventure. You're so special and you've brought dimension into my life like I could never have imagined."

"Well, thank you, but it's the Lord! I mean, wow, I loved our home before, but the new third story is incredible. And David thought about the safety and evacuation plans and drills. I hope we never have an emergency, but as a nurse, I should have thought about our advance planning."

"As a dad, I should have. I've even been careless about keeping the batteries checked in the smoke alarms. David has so much talent; I always underrated him, I guess. He and Mallory seem happy, don't you think? All except for the day Amelia was born."

"Yeah, I didn't handle her too well. I'm still not sure what had her so out of character. What her spiritual crisis could have been. I mean it could have all been the hormones. They go all over the charts."

"Well, she seems topside now. I think it hurt David's feelings that she didn't just tell him whatever it was instead of his dad. They bought a place in Colorado, and they're moving that couple from Vermont to oversee it. They think they can pretty much keep it occupied by vacation renters year-round. It should more than pay for itself, and it's right on top of more Diamonds. They've named it the 'Sparrows' Nest'. Look at a picture of the sign they're putting on the gate." He opened the photo on his iPad.

"Oh! That is adorable! That day seems like it was yesterday and yet eons ago. So much has happened."

He regarded her seriously. "Such an inspired picture: we've done a sermon, jewelry, clothing, all of Caramel's projects, and now this. I mean, I love all the different aspects that various Christians bring to these signs. Love the Ten Commandments! But they seem austere. This just shows the Lord's tenderness."

The sign, painted brightly, featured birdhouses on either side. Between them sat the same little row of sparrows from Diana's photograph, taken five years previously on the Saturday before they relocated Mallory to Dallas. It bore the lettering: *YE ARE OF MORE VALUE THAN MANY SPARROWS.*

"And, if you pay close enough attention; the one in the middle has the cutest little face!" Daniel's comment, as he repeated her lilting observation from the past.

⚏ ⚎

Mallory opened her eyes, squinting in the gloom. She couldn't remember where she was, or what she should be doing. She finally focused on a bedside clock. Seven-thirty. She stretched. Oh yeah, she was married to David and they were in a hotel in Colorado. It looked like he was up already so she slid on her robe, noticing Amelia wasn't asleep in her pack and play. She halted in amazement at the sight that greeted her in the living room. David was feeding the baby and reading his Bible aloud to her. He looked up. "Good morning, Gorgeous!" He patted the sofa next to him. "Care to join us? Coffee's made."

She poured herself a cup and curled into the indicated spot. "M-m-m. Keep reading. I love the sound of your voice."

"M-m-m. Okay. I was reading her the part about the sparrows."

"Yeah, I like that part too."

He pulled the bottle free, watching the little countenance pucker in protest.

Mallory reached for her. "I'll get her to burp while you read. Did you change her diaper already?"

"I did. Do I get some sort of badge for that?"

"Well, I think you should."

He read a couple of chapters and they prayed together.

⚏ ⚎

David and Mallory tried as delicately as possible to get Rhonna out of the house. Mallory wanted the girl's transition away from *DiaMo* to be as smooth and painless as possible. Rhonna still used the phone and laptop all the time, too. The laptop thing seemed particularly thorny, since company and personal information were mixed together on it. With Lisette and Rhonna both gone, she was scrambling to find a personal assistant who could handle things. David was busier than she was, leaning on Jeff as his PA, and then Waylon, Luke, Damon. Entering the mezzanine café, and spotting Rhonna seated alone, she decided to make her move.

"Hey, Rhonna, do you mind if I join you?"

"Well, some other people from our company are comin'." The response seemed defensive.

Mallory summoned a smile. "Okay, I understand. I need a chance to talk to you, though, about your plans for getting an apartment or something on your own. We provide housing for *DiaMo* employees, and since we're looking for replacements for you and Lisette, we'll need the room. We've given you a couple of months; are you finding a place?"

Jim and his wife and several top-echelon employees materialized. "Okay, Mrs. Anderson, watch yourself and don't be recruiting my employees." Jim's attempt at sounding jovial and teasing fell kind of flat, in view of what had actually transpired.

Mallory didn't bother with the pretense of a smile. "Well, it's not my business particularly, but Rhonna was under the impression that you were matching her pay."

Jim smiled broadly, stating the amount of cash salary he was matching.

Mallory sighed. "Okay, well, that's what she thought she was making. Jim, that's the amount of her net pay from us. What her checks were for each payday. We were also providing housing, use of a car, health and dental insurance, retirement, utilities, cell phone, and a laptop with wireless, college tuition with fifteen hours/week built into the work schedule for academic pursuits. We're still paying her cell phone bill and she has our files on her laptop. She can't afford to live in Dallas on that tiny amount of money. She was worth everything we were providing her with, and more."

The other executive grew testy. "Are you sure she's that sharp? Sounds like she doesn't know the difference between gross and net pay! And what a benefit package is."

"Oh, yes, Sir. She's that sharp! I don't equate mental acuity with naïveté. She's only eighteen and she grew up in a small rural town. It's unconscionable for you to take advantage of that!"

He smiled genuinely, losing the brassy bravado. "You're really stirred up; aren't you? Hey, look, believe it or not, I'm not trying to cheat her out of anything. I thought you were the one taking advantage of her ability and innocence, by paying so little."

"Oh!" Mallory was taken aback. "Well, I guess she needs to find an apartment, but I didn't want the girls in apartments because there's more danger."

Jim's facade came back up. "Okay. Well, I'm looking to hire good help, not adopt projects. I'm not paying tuition and paying her a salary for her study time. I don't know how you keep from going broke."

Mallory fought tears. "Yeah, really! Except, when you care about people and treat them the way you would want to be treated, the Lord seems to bless what you're doing."

⚜ ⚜

Mallory looked around in amazement. "Wow! This hardly looks like the same place!" Remodeling and exterior facelifts, with attention to grounds and landscaping, had brought the *Chandler* facility from urban blight to an oasis of meticulous attention to detail. New sidewalks and curbs with painted crosswalks controlled by *Chandler* signals created easy access to the office complex on the other side of the street.

Cat greeted them cordially. "Our controlling the traffic caused many of the motorists to reroute. So, there are fewer cars by here, and they have to stop. The city of Houston has, surprisingly, been on our side. They knew the traffic was out of control, but their budgetary constraints have hamstrung their ability to add signals. Of course, the better areas, with their councilmen, get the improvements, more than the industrialized places. Can I hold her when she wakes up?" she finished.

⚜ ⚜

Erik loped up. "After I get a long turn," he teased.

Mallory grabbed him in a hug and kissed his cheek. "Mom told me it went like they thought it would. We're so relieved. We were praying for you. Why didn't you say anything the first night when it hurt?"

"I thought it was that weird dream, and then it quit hurting. Doesn't this place look amazing? You need to check out the interiors. I can keep an eye on Amelia while you look around."

"Okay, not with the carrier, too. That's too heavy." Mallory worked to release the straps holding the baby securely, and pulled her free.

Erik nestled her gently in the crook of his arm, heading for a picnic area where bright umbrellas fluttered. "Look, she didn't even wake up. Y'all go on and take a good look around."

The banquet was lavish. Fresh flowers appeared everywhere, linens and fine china with candle light. Cade waved to them, but he was engaged in conversation with a group of people Mallory didn't remember. "Has Roger done a lot of new hiring?"

416

"If so, they dress sharper than your ordinary absent-minded chemistry professor. Quite a few dignitaries are here: the mayor, a couple of city council members, a city planner, and a State Senator."

"Wow, I'm impressed. I hope they aren't all speaking."

David shrugged, grinning widely. "They're all politicians; what do you think?"

"I think Amelia won't have that type of endurance. And I don't want her separated from us!" Her eyes flashed, but he was in agreement.

"Seriously. We have places reserved next to the head table, but I'll ask your mom if we can sit toward the back, instead. If the baby fusses, one of us can slip out with her; when she wears us both out, we can leave."

It seemed like a great plan, but Suzanne took the issue up with Roger. He appeared immediately. "Hey, thanks for coming! I know y'all are always both really busy! I'm thrilled you decided to let me buy this gym. You were brilliant to notice it and act so fast!"

David laughed. "Don't look at me. I just wanted to go eat! She's the one who wanted me to turn around and let her take a closer look! Since she agreed to sell, I've done a few drawings of features to tie the properties together. It might have to involve purchasing a couple of the derelict properties in between; I can show you which ones. You got a minute?"

"Only a couple? There's kind of an entire block, with run down houses on both sides-"

"Come on; only take a minute!"

⊣ ⊢

The food was fantastic. Salads, breads, then David devoured his steak and loaded baked potato and gazed hungrily at the remains of Mallory's salmon and sweet potato. "Go ahead," she urged. "I filled up on bread It was heavenly." She nodded for coffee and mixed a bottle of formula.

Then the program moved quickly. It seemed the special guests all had other similar occasions they needed to get to. They presented Roger with a key to the city for his vision and investment. And after, that, David was the one who received all the attention! The person from the City Planner's office presented him with a prestigious award for his buildings and landscape architecture, then jokingly said he could get a job in the city of Houston any time; he could probably replace him. He stated that his office and other agencies in city hall received calls nearly every day,

417

from people who wanted to similarly revitalize their properties! Mallory sat weeping with happiness. If David had indeed been blackballed by architectural firms and the building industry, his talent and hard work were proving that when God is on your side, no one can oppose for long!

Chapter 33: AMELIA

"Hey, Dad, everything okay?" David's dad didn't usually call them late.

"Yes, Son, I figured with the banquet's just ending, that I wouldn't be waking y'all up. Congratulations, Son. I've known about the awards and honors for several days, and I've been so excited, I've been afraid I'd spill the beans. Did you kind of suspect something was up?"

"No, Sir. I didn't have a clue. The Chandler facility does look like an entirely different place! Great subcontractors really took the plan and ran with it. I just felt awful for discovering it and influencing Sanders to buy it. I couldn't really tell it was such a rat hole. I'm relieved it turned out okay."

John laughed. "It turned out better than okay; didn't it? Didn't Sanders have another nice check for you? For more of a finder's fee? Your finding that business, David, has absolutely rocketed Roger from small potato to major player. Well, small potatoes, being relative to what's happened for him in the last year. Uh, David?"

"Yeah Dad, what?"

"I called to congratulate you, but also to apologize."

"For what, Dad"?

"I don't know where to start, David. I guess for always selling you short; for not seeing the potential. I mean, I saw potential. But still, last summer when you married Mallory-"

David laughed. "You definitely thought she got the 'short end of the stick'. I think so, too, Dad! She's incredible!"

"Yes, she is. I agree with that. You two are an amazing couple. How's my little granddaughter?"

David laughed, trying to control sudden emotions. "She's fine, Dad. She's so perfect! Every time I look at her now, well, I can see now why you were always in such a panic about everything I did. She's so sweet, and I'm already praying she'll never be hurt, and that she'll turn out okay for the Lord!"

John laughed, too, trying not to sound totally triumphant. "Yeah, David, you spent your entire teen years telling me to relax, and then making sure I couldn't."

"I'm sorry, Dad. Tell Mom, too. I'm sending you more pictures."

⚔ ⚔

Erik entered the Federal lockup with a few questions for Saxon, who not surprisingly, was un cooperative.

"I can sit here all day." Erik crossed his arms in a leisurely fashion.

"Make yourself comfortable. I'm here until my trial, thanks to you. I'm gonna beat your trumped-up case, and then I'm gonna sue you for everything you've got!"

"I'm pretty sure you have to await your trial in here because you were attempting to flee. You forfeited the comforts of home, yourself. I'm gonna get some more coffee. Don't go anywhere." He grinned gleefully.

⚔ ⚔

Colonel Ahmir listened to his reprimand He left the government building with the severe warning to limit his investigating to within the borders of Turkey, herself. The neighboring nations didn't appreciate his sleuthing. Still, he wasn't too worried about further repercussions, as long as he didn't try it again. His helping to locate a sophisticated smuggling pipeline on Turkey's eastern border, and his facilitating business agreements for some of the bazaar merchants stood him in good stead. Still, he needed to be extremely cautious in sharing his new information with Erik Bransom.

⚔ ⚔

Erik returned, munching on a donut, to the interrogation room where Saxon waited. He sipped cautiously at hot coffee.

420

The millionaire criminal tried not to resent the privilege the agent relished in front of him. "No wonder you have heart trouble, Agent."

Erik met the mocking eyes, mocking back with a startled gesture. "You know, you're right." He dropped the donut into the trash. "Excuse me a minute, again, would you, please?"

When he reentered, he waved an attractive sandwich. "Turkey Reuben on rye. Thanks for reminding me. Bad habits can be hard to break." He chomped into it, chewing slowly. M-m-m, that's good."

"Did you want something from me?"

"Nah, I just came to see how you're gettin' along in here. They treating you okay?"

Saxon shifted and Bransom sensed the temperature rising.

"What do you hear from Junior? He enjoying incarceration?"

"Okay, that's it. I want my attorney."

"Yeah, I'm sure. I think he's in Abu Dhabi playing golf. I'll be done here before any of them can make it. You're kind of isolated in here, ya know?"

"Well, like I said, Bransom. I'm going to be acquitted, and then I'm coming after you. You have ruined my life! My wife is leaving me!"

"I've ruined your life! Well, isn't that too bad? What do you think you've done for the lives of these kids you've forced into slavery? To their parents, and all the family members? The pain you continue to inflict with pushing a hedonistic lifestyle and your web sites!"

Saxon studied his nails, nails which seemed to be manicured, despite incarceration. "That's your opinion. I simply help provide what people want. But I appreciate your friend, Hanson; he's my get out of jail card."

"Oh yeah? He got one for Junior, too?" Erik was trying to process the meaning of the guy's claim without seeming to be hit.

"You made a really big mistake targeting my son!"

Erik took another bite, moaning with pleasure at the deliciousness. "Excuse me; I didn't target Junior. He left evidence all over the desert when he was spying on Jennifer and Mallory for you. You set him up for trouble. I'm pretty sure Hanson has been careful of what he's put on his site. The last thing he wants is to help guys like you avoid trial and conviction. But if, and it's a big IF! You should get off on all the smuggling, human trafficking, attempted murder, and murder charges, you still face the tax evasion! In America, that seems to be the unpardonable sin!. Kind of a sad indictment of our values, but hey, if it puts you in jail for a long time-"

"Well, you can relax now about your wife's daughter. She was far more valuable the first time. She's gotten kind of old, married, had a kid. That puts too much mileage on the merchandise; you know?"

Erik grinned broadly. "Yeah, I know what ya mean!"

He exited smoothly, giving orders for Saxon to receive no preferential treatment. He was serious. If he couldn't stop the manicures and gourmet diet in here, he could get him transferred and get his funds cut off. Wife leaving him; hunh? She might make for an interesting interview. And the parting shot about Mallory~ If that was supposed to unnerve him, or make him back off her security, it wouldn't happen. 'More valuable the first time'! So, it <u>was</u> all interconnected! The grabbing Mallory on the Turkish border when she was seventeen? Wasn't just a few local thugs? Very interesting!

He called Colonel Ahmir once he gained the privacy of the bureau vehicle.

"Hello, this is Colonel Ahmir."

"Yeah, hey Colonel; we've all been thinking about you. When are you going to be able to come back to see us"?

"Ah, sadly, I have used up all of my holiday leave, Agent Bransom. I should very much like to see all of you again. I went, just recently for holiday in the Balkans; very beautiful, but not as much as Turkey! Or your beautiful United States of America."

Oh so you holidayed with your family. I'll bet everyone's growing up. I've never seen the Balkans. Can you send me some of your holiday pictures? I'll send you a picture of Mallory's baby. Maybe some of us can come back to Turkey. We enjoyed everything immensely. With such a large and wonderful place, we barely scratched the surface!"

"Oh, yes, we always like very much, rich American tourists and business people!"

⚐ ⚐

Spring raced into summer time, with seemingly more speed than Nascar racers. Mallory continued to follow sports, but her one-time enthusiasm seemed dampened. "I don't want to become bitter and disillusioned with life; and it was fun going to California with you," she assured David. "Most of the time I'd just as soon have her little songs playing. I still keep up with the stats and stuff. It makes for good conversation."

David nodded agreement. "I think I have things ready so we can be gone. Then, next week we have another trip to Houston."

She nodded. "And then, a couple of weeks later, DC. Are we going to the Ranch at all, in between?"

He nodded. "I want to. I'm trying to figure out a way to get on the airplane with both of our violins, a diaper bag, your handbag, and my attaché case as carry ons."

She nodded. Flying commercial presented difficulties. She always kept her jewelry with her in the cabin, but often, her cute designer clothing got stolen from checked luggage. And now they had Amelia, with her baby seat, stroller, and other paraphernalia people had tried to warn them about.

⊰ ⊱

Erik and Suzanne returned from Turkey with Turkish Delight, souvenirs, and information about the 'Orphanage'. Ahmir's detective work in getting the information had landed him in legal difficulties that the Turkish Embassy had needed to involve itself with, to keep him from going to jail. Like it made headlines! As a result, the Turk's hands were basically tied for pursuing anything further. And Turkey didn't have any freedom of information acts! Still, Ahmir was interested in developments, shocked by Saxon's words about Mallory to the American agent.

"What would have led him to say such a thing? It basically had no bearing on his case or what you had discussed with him."

Erik shrugged. "I don't know; I guess I was needling him, and he decided to get me back! If you can get them off-balance, they nearly always spill something. He's been at this racket for a long time; but he hasn't actually done the 'dirty work'. And, he's never been in jail. Felons who have been interrogated a lot, get wise to our methods; although, as you know, they still slip up. 'Out of the abundance of the heart, the mouth speaketh', as the Bible states"!

"And Hanson, has he really created a problem for the prosecution?" The colonel's voice turned anxious.

"Well, that's subject to speculation. Hanson has never mentioned names, but he has fired people up about this problem of missing kids. Which, hello! We should be fired up about that, with or without his web site. Oberson's attorney is trying to make a case with one of the judges, that Hanson's firing people up, means there can be no impartial jury. That the whole topic's too hot, and just his being accused of the crimes will put his head in the noose."

"Hunh"? The Turkish military man was puzzled by the American legal system. They worried way too much about the fairness of their trials, anyway.

Bransom always left contacts with the Turkish colonel, thankful for the American System, despite its shortcomings and loopholes.

⚓ ⚓

The Denver morning sparkled with dew, but bright sunshine was evaporating it quickly. Mallory carried their Bibles, her handbag and diaper bag and David carried the baby. She was adorable, again, dressed like both her mother and her dolly. Their instruments were at the church, left after the previous evening's rehearsal. David pushed the button for the elevator and they crossed the deserted lobby to air conditioned vehicles.

"People will be disappointed that Nick isn't here," David observed.

"Well, I'm glad they got a chance to go to Hawaii for a couple of weeks. Maybe if people want to hear him, they can buy our new CD."

David nodded. He thought it was extremely good. Entitled: *Our Collection*, it featured a variety. It included instrumental solos, vocal solos, and different groupings. If someone didn't enjoy piano enough to listen to an entire piano album, Mallory's solo of *We Shall See Jesus*, was definitely stirring. Diana sang a vocal solo that none of them had performed before, with Mallory accompanying on piano and featuring Daniel and Cassandra on violin: *I'll Wish I Had Given Him More*. David and Mallory's duet, *It's a Miracle*, was requested every place they went. They did a cute rendition, too, of the fun song, *One More Night With the Frogs*.

"You okay?" David's eyes met hers as they arrived early at the church.

Her eyes sparkled with tears. "I'm nervous about leaving her in the nursery, even with Janice working her security."

His gaze met hers. "Yeah, and she's not away from us enough to be used to strangers. I'm afraid she's really going to cry. I don't want to spoil her, but I don't want her to be miserable either."

"I know, or create misery for the nursery workers."

424

He laughed. "Spoken like a seasoned nursery worker. Daniel and Diana's security are going to be all over the grounds and hallways, too. Let's pray for it to be okay."

They relinquished a jovial baby to a kindly worker and she didn't seem to know when they left. The mini-concert was well-received, followed by a great sermon from the pastor. Over lunch, Daniel asked David and Mallory if they were going to have a chance to see the Sparrow's Nest for themselves.

"Well, that's a good idea, but we're hoping for a nap. Our flight's scheduled for Houston in the morning." David's tone was regretful. "Not good planning on our part for our itinerary. We trust Jack and Estelle, absolutely, but I should really have eyeballs on how things are going, for myself." His gaze met Mallory's. "What do you think about changing our flight?"

"Sounds good to me"! She always loved more time with the Faulkner family, and maybe she could spot a Diamond or two.

⚔ ⚔

Psalm 119:53 Horror hath taken hold upon me because of the wicked that forsake thy law.

Erik studied his outline. Dietrich, Oberson, Saxon, O'Shaughnessy, Brothers Malovich, Rpbertson, Warrington. There were players he was not aware of, and he couldn't necessarily figure out the hierarchy of the ones he was aware of. Ahmir's hard-won intel supported what he already supposed, but~ He tapped a pencil and got up to refill his coffee. 'Okay, Warrington was a talker, try revisiting him! Interview Saxon's soon-to-be-ex. Revisit the news footage of Dietrich and his party-boat friends. Re-examine all of Jennifer's artwork related to the cases. Try talking to her again, and Missy Hanson!' He sighed. Shannon O'Shaughnessy still knew more than he was willing to admit. Okay, so he was far from a dead end.

⚔ ⚔

Houston was hotter than ever; old asphalt was spongy, and the buildings David was consulting about looked like if they sank into the black goo, it would do the world a favor. "Wow! This place makes the *Chandler* property

425

seem like it was heavenly. I think there's only so much I can do. Without a wrecking ball or stick of dynamite"!

"Yeah"! Mallory was usually positive and upbeat, but she had grabbed his arm as she leaned forward to take in the dismal scene. "You know what? Maybe you should call the guy and~"

"Well, I'd be tempted except that Dale and all the other contractors I hired for *Chandler*, really need more work."

Mallory's cool green eyes swept around again. "Okay! Looks like lots of work, with a capital W. What if more jobs come your way, that would be easier, and you're mired down here?"

He laughed. "Remember your Bible story about taking risks?"

She sighed. "Yeah, what about it"?

⊱ ⊰

Not trusting the agents in the LA office to glean information from Warrington, Erik flew in to conduct his own interview. In light of the gruesomeness found on his boat, the suspect had been denied bail and was in a secure Federal location.

"How's Jennifer?" came the surgeon's eager inquiry. "Does she ever say anything about me? I saved her life a couple of times; does she know that?"

Bransom took his time settling into place with his notebook and coffee. This was too good to be true, and he wanted to reel this story in gradually.

"Really, well, hey, would you like to have her come visit you?"

Warrington's face hardened. "What's the catch?"

Bransom leaned back, shrugging nonchalantly. "Hey, no catch. It probably wouldn't work anyway. I doubt if she ever wants to see you again."

"She would! She's married to that no-good beach bum."

Erik shrugged. "Whatever. I'm pretty sure however paltry his net worth is, it's a lot more than you've got."

Warrington shrugged. "Don't forget, Agent, I still have my brain and my education. You know what they say: 'They can't take that away from you.'!"

Branosm scoffed. "A lot of good any of that did you! You've come to an inglorious end. What roses are you thinkin' you can grow from your ash heap?"

426

"The hands of a skilled surgeon are always in demand!"

"So I understand! To both the good guys and the bad guys! But I'm thinkin' you've run out of options and opportunities."

"My attorneys are filing to have the evidence on the sailboat thrown out, due to the inflammatory~"

"Which attorneys? The perjured ones facing jail time and disbarment? Or are there some new ones I should look into? Your medical reputation and their legal ones certainly give the professions a black eye. I'm pretty sure I plan to slam all your so-called legal counsel into the slammer, too. They've been complicit in this entire mess! And~you're never going to share your so-called research! With anyone"!

"It's very valuable!"

Erik vaulted upwards across the table separating them, pounding his fist resoundingly. "Valuable! You haven't discovered any fountain of youth with your poisons and potions. All your elderly victims just looked a lot worse for your wear! You're nothing but a phony quack!"

Warrington shrugged. "Their deaths were your fault!"

"Really"! Erik's face registered exaggerated amazement! "For my trying to be a good guy, I'm being accused of a lot of serious stuff. Saxon's blaming me for ruining his life, and you're trying to blame me because a few more of your victims perished."

"They died because of you," Warrington smirked.

"When we first locked you up, you could have mentioned that you had a boat-load of victims who would die of dehydration. I'm pretty sure your abducting them, experimenting with them, continuing to hold them against their will, places guilt squarely where it belongs! We're done!"

⊣ ⊢

"Well, look at this! Son, do you always travel with your whole family? Little 'ball and chain' doesn't let ya outta her sight?"

David regarded the burly guy framed in the nondescript doorway of the run down office complex. "David Anderson, my wife, Mallory. You must be Axle Delaney? Derek said you're the man for me to report to. Can we come in?" David had extended his hand, but the beefy supervisor was standing there like a Neanderthal. It was hot standing there sinking into the melting asphalt. Maybe Mallory was right; she usually was. "I'm sorry,

Sir. It was my understanding that y'all were expecting us. If there's been a misunderstanding, maybe we can reschedule~?"

"Only misunderstanding was we thought you was coming alone. We got a Motel 6 room ready for you."

"Well, it's early enough that you can cancel that reservation without being charged. Our company can take care of our accommodations. I can't make any recommendations to Derek if I can't get in to look the place over."

Surly, Axle stepped aside. Cockroaches were everywhere, on walls, desks, the customer counter; and distasteful material that made the *Chandler* property seem mild, covered the walls. The difference was that Roger Sanders had taken possession of that company, and he didn't want that kind of garbage. Here, David wasn't in charge of things; just advising.

His eyes met Mallory's apologetically. "Here, why don't you sit here in front of the air conditioner? This shouldn't take me very long." He set Amelia's carrier on the desk.

"That there's my desk," Axle cautioned.

David's voice took a hard edge. "Don't worry about it, Axle, my man. You aren't going to be sitting there, because you're going to be showing me around. She has a nicer desk than this, so not to worry. Okay, what are we looking at?"

Mallory glanced around her anxiously as David and the manager clomped out. The air conditioner next to her clattered noisily; other than that, it didn't seem to be doing much. There were five or six people around, but they seemed resentful of her presence. She pulled her phone free and made several calls for issues needing her attention. Forty minutes. She was hoping David wouldn't be much longer. Amelia, her hair clinging to her head in damp ringlets was beginning to squirm, waking up. The chance of a good place to change her diaper seemed slim. Mallory unfastened the harness, pulling her into her arms. "M-m-m, Mommy's little Amelia! Daddy's working right now."

⊣ ⊢

John Anderson drove around Murfreesboro and out into the county. It was cheering to him as he took note of the signs and banners cropping up on fences and mailboxes proclaiming that Christians resided there. What a great idea. Sometimes, you could get the pity party going like Elijah's: that you're the only one left who believes in God and the Bible. Waylon's idea and a very good one! But Waylon would be a lost-in-the-sauce under-employed country hick, if not for Mallory's vision. A vision of what her classmate could be, even after she realized the severity of his dyslexia and how far behind he was academically because of it.

⚓ ⚓

Tired of sitting there scattering the roaches away, she rose to pace. It seemed as if, in this all-guy business, that there was no ladies' room. A narrow hallway brought her to a couple of steps downward and she entered the murky blackness of another area. Gathering her bag, the diaper bag, and the baby, she made her way back there. No ventilation from doors or windows created a truly musty and dismal space. At least, here, she was free of the threatening and filthy language. She removed the safety on her pistol. She had a strategic advantage that if anyone threatened from the narrow corridor, she could pick them off. A disgustingly dirty break room with more obscenity on the walls seemed to be the only thing down there. Maybe it was slightly cooler. She spread paper towels and then Amelia's little changing pad on the table and did a diaper change, then checked her phone. The little scattered buildings shouldn't be taking David this long; she was beginning to worry.

David had cringed at getting into Axle's truck with him to go view their other site. He hadn't been aware that there was another one. He could see now, why Derek had directed him to the better looking place. He was feeling pretty confident that there was nothing he could accomplish here to gain more attention and admiration of the City Fathers. He looked at his watch, worrying about Mallory and the baby. She had her cell phone and her gun, but still~ He walked through the last two buildings; there was water damage everywhere, from leaking roof to flood waters coming in. He couldn't imagine the mold, or what the roofs of all the aged buildings looked like.

"Well, what do you think?" Axle's question struck him odd. He was supposed to report back to Derek.

"I'm not sure. Like maybe, if one more hurricane would make a direct hit here, you could at least get a little insurance money out of the deal!" He shouldn't have said it, but it was too late to recall the words.

"Man, you gotta help us! If we can't keep the doors open; we all need our jobs real bad~"

"Hey, I'll do what I can."

Houston's codes were far from demanding, but he felt like this business was on the verge of being condemned, even at that.

"I'll make some drawings and talk to Derek and some of the local contractors I know. I have to get back and get my wife and daughter!"

"Ya shouldn't have brought her; then we could stop for a little refreshment."

He shrugged. "She's my best friend and has been for a long time. I wouldn't care to go drinking with you were she not along. Can you drive any faster than twenty-five?"

⚜

Mallory measured formula into a bottle, and shook it vigorously. She checked her watch again, growing more concerned for her husband. With the bottle gone, she made her way back to the main area. To her surprise, the employees were gone and the doors were locked. At least, now she could use the rest room; definitely not the best.

⚜

Terror snatched at David as Axle pulled up in front of the main sales office.

"See, it's all locked for the day. Everybody left hours ago. I've been on time and a half. Maybe your wife called a taxi or went out with one of the guys."

David checked his phone. No texts or missed calls. Mallory would have tried not to bother him while he was looking over the job, but still~ He called Hopkins. "Okay, Darrell, we're ready to be picked up. Have you heard from anyone?"

Silence as the head of Mallory's security tried to make sense of the casually phrased, but ominous question. "Heard from anyone? Like, do you mean Mallory? Oh, don't tell me~"

430

⚔ ⚔

Daniel Faulkner, grim-faced, met Erik as he deplaned.

Fear gripped the agent! "Mallory"? He could barely word the question as Saxon's words echoed through his brain. 'Mileage' or not, Mallory was a beautiful and high-value target. He turned on his phone. As a Federal Agent, he could have left it on during his flight; now he wished desperately that he had exercised that option. A communication from David indicating he was under duress, followed by a lengthy voice-mail. "They were in Houston?"

"Yeah, that's what Darrell said. We transfer to Terminal B to depart for Houston immediately. We need to hurry! Leave your luggage."

⚔ ⚔

"Lord, please help us." Giving up on comforting her distraught infant, Mallory began crying with her. The bottles of water were used up, nothing to mix with the last few grains of formula. No more diapers! David knew all that! "Lord, please let him be okay. Please fix my phone!" As she spoke, she remembered the business phones. Except that her phone numbers were stored in her malfunctioning one. The only number she knew was Diana's and she didn't want to scare her to death! She gazed at her watch in the gloom of an exit sign. She could give it another hour. Then, she would call 911 and the police could come rescue her from the burglar-barred building As brazen as the roaches had seemed all day, she felt like the darkness rolled out the welcome mat to them. David would never leave them in a mess like this unless~ She should call the police; if something was wrong with him, her hesitation might really make rescue come too late for him. Still, she hesitated. If it was just a judgment lapse, she wanted to help cover for him. People still sometimes seemed determined to be 'down on him'. She paced and waited, but nothing was soothing Amelia.

⚔ ⚔

David was still afraid to push Axle too hard. "Look, just call everyone who was working here this afternoon and ask them if they know where

431

she went! Please! You did threaten her to me, earlier, if you recall. If you have her someplace~"

"Look, call where you're staying. She's probably~"

"Yeah, good idea! And you call your guys who were here all afternoon!" David got out of the truck, relieved for freedom from Axle, his buddies, and their strong-arm tactics. He punched the number for the hotel and requested the front desk to ring the suite; no answer! Still nothing from her cell! That was what scared him the most! Her phone didn't seem to be functioning at all. Even the deep black night brought no relief from the heat. What a nightmare! He fought tears, panic, and nausea! "Okay, unlock the place!" For the first time since his ordeal had begun, he pulled out his pistol.

"Geeze, man you're crazy!"

"Whatever! Open this door!"

"Hey, I can't! It's locked down with a timer! Employees were coming back at night and taking things, so they had some security company rig the locks!"

David stared in disbelief, feeling totally helpless! Like Mallory would be just fine! Sitting patiently in a locked down, roach-infested building in the dark, long after everyone else had left! Still~

"Mallory, Malllllorrry! Baby, are you in there?"

He pressed his ear against the bars, hoping for some response! He tensed! "My baby's in there! I can hear her crying!"

⚔ ⚔

Daniel checked messages as he and Erik dashed toward a waiting FBI car at George Bush, International; then let out a cry somewhere between relief and outrage! "A message from David! "They're fine! Back in their suite"!

Reaching the car, Erik sagged with relief, giving Daniel cause to worry about him.

"You okay?"

"Yeah, I'm fine! Just give me a chance to get ahold of myself."

"Okay, Erik! Don't! We still have plenty to do!" The hard edge on Faulkner's voice made Erik get control of his ragged emotions.

⚔ ⚔

Showered, and finally starting to feel a little cooled off, David rocked his distraught daughter. His immediate reaction had been to go straight to an Emergency Room, but Mallory simply wanted to get to the hotel, clean up, be together, just the three of them. Tears rolled down his face! That had seemed like a stellar idea to him. Now Mallory was in the shower and he had given Amelia a bath at the wet bar. It concerned him that she refused the bottle. His phone kept lighting up with calls from everyone who had heard about an 'episode'. He didn't even know what to say! Especially with his dad! But when caller ID indicated Erik Bransom, he figured he'd better talk.

"Hello, Erik!" His voice betrayed the tension he still felt. Beyond that, he didn't know what to say.

"Hi David! I'm with Faulkner. We're in the lobby. Can we come up?"

"Yeah, sure"! He gave the suite number; then gave Mallory the heads up. Rather than pulling on a robe, she got dressed. "Order more room service. They'll be hungry, too, and I'm starved."

A tap at their door, and Faulkner and Bransom's appearance coincided with the room service delivery. David was relieved for the distraction of signing, tipping, mentioning another food order, even doing it all with a screaming baby in his arms.

Mallory appeared; she wasn't sure what to say to the two men, either. 'Sorry! Guess we made a colossal error in judgment?' She was exhausted, emotional, fighting more tears, and hungry. David put the baby into her arms.

"We were just going to eat," he opened. "We ordered more when you called. Y'all probably haven't eaten either. Sit down."

"Why don't you let me try feeding her while y'all eat?" Daniel suggested.

"'t's okay. We got it!" David didn't mean to come across quite so defensive.

Faulkner wasn't one to be put off, already moving purposefully toward Mallory. "Come on, Mallory. Give me a shot at it, please?"

Erik thought Faulkner should stand down! Everybody was too emotionally overwrought already. He watched the scene unfold like it was slow-motion. Mallory trying to go with David's opinion, and Faulkner making grabs at the baby girl anyway. What they managed to do was to bring a tremendous burp forth, followed by a ripple of laughter from

Mallory. It was just cute. A surprised look on the miniature features, and the crying stopped. "That should help her feel better."

"Exactly, see I knew what she needed," Daniel crowed. "You guys pray for the food, and I'll feed her."

"Okay, I know you kids need some sleep," Erik spoke as they finished the plates of food. "I was flying home from California with my phone off. When I landed, I got you duress signal." He directed his gaze at David. "Then the long voice mail was part of a crazy conversation about these guys not wanting you to notify the powers-that-be about the true picture?"

David nodded. "It had already taken so long. When I left Mallory in that office, I thought I was gonna stroll around the structures on that property! Forty-five minutes, maximum. It's really a pretty long story~"

Erik leaned back, determined. "Then hit the high points for me, Cowboy!"

"Well, there was a second property. Hard to believe, but it was worse than the original place. The main reason I agreed to look it over, to begin with, was because this guy, Derek, begged me. And the contractor who oversaw the *Chandler* remodel needs more work."

"So they knew their whole place was a dump, and that the conglomerate in Germany, who owns them, has been kept in the dark about what's really happening." Daniel knew that much and he was livid.

"And they got bent out of joint with you when you couldn't just pull your little genie out of your bottle and fix their world!" Erik's further assessment.

"Yeah, hey, I should have done more homework. Like Derek, he led me to believe he was the go-to man. But then I found out they were a subsidiary, foreign owned, and the management didn't even know I was coming to consult. So, I figured, 'Dumb, David, there goes the consulting fee. I'm not even authorized to be here.' So, I'm trying to extricate myself, but they're not letting it go that easy. They want me to do something to save their necks, save this company, save their jobs! I felt for them. I'm pretty sure both sites have been condemned, and I'm supposed to get them up to code without any cost so the German owners never find out! Or else"!

"When did they turn threatening?"

David sighed. "When I didn't want to go drinking with them! I don't think they planned things to develop the way they did. They're just desperate."

"Well, planned or not, they're all being booked into jail. Maybe pre-meditation or the absence thereof will help them at sentencing." Erik's voice was cold.

He turned his attention to Mallory "What about you all that time?"

She shrugged. "Well, it's like David said. He didn't think it would be long. When he first left, I made a few calls; which my phone wasn't working very well, then. I had to keep shaking it. I mean, I have like a tire around it, so it bounces instead of breaking. But I think the drops have shaken something loose. Since Amelia was born, I always have my hands so full! And David always helps me with her and with all her stuff. I'm more convinced than ever that there's no evolution to help species adapt-or mothers would have more than two hands. Or maybe the 'pouch' idea shouldn't have 'evolved' away. Anyway, I said all that, to say this. I think I've ruined my phone. And another place where I went wrong was thinking I'd be fine, since I had my phone and gun. It's so easy to start misplacing trust and confidence. I never thought of praying, until I was out of formula, and it was completely dark. I mean I was worried about David, and I thought the same thing. He has a phone and a gun. I didn't mean by that, that we don't still need God! I got a good reminder."

Faulkner was frazzled. "Look, yeah, that's a great lesson, but you've had that phone for a long time. Get an upgrade. If it gets damaged, get it replaced!"

"Yes Sir." A subdued Mallory fought tears at the rebuke.

Chapter 34: ADMINISTRATION

"Do you think all those guys really got arrested?" Rather than getting ready for bed, Mallory was applying cosmetics.

"Well, we can hope."

She nodded. "I'm so glad you're okay! I was really worried! What they did was ill-advised–"

Her beautiful eyes met his. Eyes that were wide awake.

He laughed. "What are you thinking about? Or should I ask?"

She blew out a breath slowly. "We should go down and bail them out. Call Darrell and have him meet us in the SUV in half hour."

He was suddenly game. Life with her was an adventure. "But if we get in trouble, will you tell them this was your idea?"

She laughed. "Sure, but they won't believe me."

He agreed ruefully. "They'll think you're covering me for another dumb stunt."

She grew serious. "But, it isn't a dumb stunt. What they did–I'm not making light of it–"

He nodded. "Desperation, born out of this scary economy. I assume you have a plan for helping their grim situation, but I'm sorry, you have a quicker mind than I have. It looks to me like there's no answer."

She concentrated on mascara before responding. "Where do you think those guys are being held? Who do we need to call? I've never sprung any jailbirds before."

He shrugged. "What? You think I'm more familiar with the system? Should I call Erik?"

"Good grief, no!"

Darrell Hopkins regarded the young couple shrewdly. They seemed no worse for the wear, following their earlier escapade. He surveyed the surroundings carefully as they clicked the baby carrier into place and got in on either side of the baby. "Where are we going this time of night?"

"The main downtown police station"! Mallory's voice was charged with extra authority. She knew what time it was, and he worked for her!

"Did you notice," she asked David as they entered the freeway, "that behind the property we were focused on, there were trees and lawn and flowers?

David shook his head. "I guess not. I was focused on the problems I was seeing."

"That's what I thought. It's a big old church plant, and it's for sale."

"Okay, so what's the deal? Are there Diamonds on it?" He liked to tease, one of the things she loved about him.

"In a sense," she responded smoothly. "The facilities of the *South Houston Machine Company* are basically beyond repair? Right?"

"That's my opinion. Dale told me he wouldn't know where to start unless I could come up with something brilliant. It needs to be razed and rebuilt from scratch. I doubt this German company would care to deal with a hit like that."

"Right! But we can buy the church plant, and retrofit it; that will leave a base of operations, so the company doesn't have to close completely while they rebuild. I'm thinking of one of Gabe's excuses when we met with him last. Do you remember?"

"I remember. Their business was backlogged because some of their equipment needed parts, specially engineered by a machinist. I guess, judging by that, that good machinists stay pretty busy. So, if companies are waiting in line for machined parts, why isn't this place doing dynamic business?"

"The only oversight they have is in Germany; and the people here are expending all their energies into hiding their plight from the parent company."

"Well, you're right. So we bail these guys out, and buy this church for them to use for a while but the parent company's still thousands of miles away. How does that fix the problem?"

"We need to start another company; a management company. We can oversee this and return it to profitability. We can place all of our properties under it. I'm thinking *D&M Management Corporation*. I'll call

Kerry and have him research the name and get things rolling. Have you been impressed with Matt Morrison? Why don't you see if your contractor can look over the church in the morning? If he thinks it's feasible, we can make an offer. Then, we just need to get in contact with whoever has the say in Germany."

He laughed. "Yeah, that's all. Mallory, we don't know anything about machine shops."

She shrugged. "Maybe not, but we do know that no one likes to be greeted by cock roaches instead of smiling people. David, these guys we're bailing out of jail, know the nuts and bolts. We didn't know anything about cattle, either, and because of Abe and his store of knowledge, they're thriving."

Within a couple of hours, the Andersons were seated in an all-night restaurant with the guys they had freed on bond. A few family members who had showed up to post bail were included in the meal.

To their astonishment, David outlined the plan.

"Well, you make it sound all right, and it's nice you thought about us. But Zeke Helmstead won't go for it. He's really a tough guy!" Derek's tone was morose.

"You guys are so on the bottom, that up is the only direction you can go. When the stockholders get wind of what a truly failing company this is; they'll demand some type of change!"

"Yeah, to shut us down"!

"Well, then that would be the best news for us," David countered. "Because then we could buy the whole thing at a steep discount! We'll do that, too. Not only for your sakes, but it wouldn't hurt us, either. I think they'll want to hold on, especially when we convince them how quickly we can restore profitability, even in the face of the decaying buildings."

⚞ ⚟

Erik rolled over, surveying the alarm clock. He was too keyed up to sleep. Many more questions he needed to ask David and Mallory, but David had kind of shooed him and Faulkner away. He sat up and tried reading his Bible. At last he showered and started the coffee brewing. He might as well go find out what the HPD had learned from the detainees.

The desk sergeant seemed alarmed at his inquiry. "They didn't really have federal charges, did they?"

Erik frowned. "Kidnapping's a federal offense the last I checked."

That made her extra nervous. "Well, we understood that a 'heated discussion got a little out of hand'. David Anderson, the alleged victim of the kidnapping, said he didn't want to press charges; he and his wife arranged bail."

"They did what? When? And you just turned them loose?'

"Proper bail was met. I followed our procedures."

"I'm sure. How could you be sure they didn't get them sprung to retaliate against them?"

"What? The cute couple with the little baby? That didn't seem to be their logic, although I'm not sure what was."

"Were they properly interrogated? Did any of them make any statements?"

She shrugged indifferently. "Nah; they were a bunch of guys in the holding cell, scared to death. We didn't get around to the thumb screws before they got released." As she spoke, she wondered if the agent before her had any grasp of police work in the real world.

"What they did was wrong," Erik affirmed.

"Yeah, and they'll have to hire counsel and defend themselves against the charges." She smiled suddenly. "I hear what you're saying. Those men were desperate, and they'd already crossed a threshold. It could've ended up bad."

"But your hands are full with the ones that did end up bad. I get that! Thank you, Ma'am, have a good evenin', or mornin', or whatever time it is."

⚔ ⚔

"Oh-oh, we're busted." Mallory's eyes sparkled with mischief as she caught David's attention.

They both watched as the hostess on duty showed Erik to a nearby table.

He noticed them as he took the proffered place.

"Hi, Erik, are you out looking for us?" Mallory's guilty voice.

He pulled a chair up by them. "Well, not really, because you're all safely asleep in your nice hotel suite. Now, if you were out roaming the streets of Houston in the middle of the night–" He shook his head in mock disgust.

"Well, when David ran you and Daniel out and told you we were tired, he was speaking for himself. I was kind of keyed up. All these ideas were just bursting!"

Erik turned an unused coffee mug up, and indicated to the server. "Bursting with ideas to? Save this company and keep these guys' jobs?" He guessed he was glad for a reprieve for a few guys; but this wasn't one isolated case in Houston, Texas. It was a symptom to him, of deep unrest, teetering on panic, nationwide. Maybe he should have stayed in his room, reading his Bible and praying.

"Yes, Sir! She has good ideas," David defended.

"I'm sure. Well, I couldn't sleep either. I'm getting a bite to eat and heading for the airport."

"Erik, we're really sorry–"

"Yeah, y'all didn't do anything wrong. We have a few new things to tweak now. It's a learning curve. Try to get some sleep sometime."

☰ ☲

Harold Schmidt had spent ten restless hours on a flight from Frankfurt, Germany to Houston, Texas. Unbelievable what he had heard. He was arriving for damage assessment and control. His early arrival at the *South Houston Machine Company* struck him with fresh panic. He thought everything was well in hand here. Now his employees had assaulted and kidnapped David Anderson, someone they had brought in as a consultant. Schmidt hadn't even approved bringing in a consultant from the outside. The Conglomerate was more than adequately staffed for any and all issues.

He sank back into the cooled interior of the Mercedes, conferring gloomily with his assistant.

Seven AM, the doors should be releasing, and staff should be arriving on scene. He was appalled at the appearance of the place; the photos he routinely received were deceptive. An SUV pulled in and crossed the asphalt toward another property. Then a couple of nondescript cars rolled in for business as usual at the company.

The decrepit exterior of the buildings weren't adequate warning for what Schmidt beheld as he stepped through the door!

☰ ☲

Dale and David together walked around the exteriors of the church buildings. Things looked pretty good. Kind of aging, but kept up decently. From what David could tell, the church didn't seem to still be in use at all. Maybe they could take immediate possession. They needed to.

"Hello, Sirs; Good mornin'"!

They turned to take in an older lady, small in stature, with a huge smile.

"Good morning," David greeted. "My name's David; my friend, Dale! We think we're interested in this piece of property, but we were looking around a little before we called the number on the sign. I hope we didn't alarm you."

Her smile broadened more. "Honey, if you saw what I see in this neighborhood, you'd know that you're not alarmin' in the least! I'm Margaret; I live across the way over yonder; kind of help keep an eye on things. Why are you lookin' at land here? You ain't lookin' to put in no honky-tonks?"

David smiled. "Oh, no Ma'am! It looks as if the church no longer meets here. Did it close down?"

"No, it's still goin'; moved to a better area. Not that this neighborhood's bad."

David laughed, aware that she didn't want to scuttle a possible deal. "Well, the area's industrial, and that's what we are. No honky-tonks, I promise."

"We thought this would sell easier. Maybe another church would buy it."

David nodded. If the church was like most, they needed the money from the empty facility.

By ten o'clock, they had signed a contract to obtain the church complex, and modular buildings were appearing on the parking lot. Derek rushed to meet David. "We got trouble. Schmidt flew all night from Frankfurt and got here this morning. He's in a tizzy. Are-are you suing us"?

"Well, maybe that's something you should consider next time, before you use strong arm tactics on people. The thing is, if I were suing, I wouldn't sue you because you don't have anything."

"I got a nice truck!"

"Who are you kidding? The finance company has a nice truck, and they let you drive it. I'd sue your company because they have insurance, they'd settle, and your company would be unhappy with you. No, we're not suing. Where's Schmidt now? Mallory's been trying to contact him at his office. We need to talk to him."

David turned his attention to Dale. "So, with the roaches in mind; what's salvageable?"

The guy met his gaze steadily. "With the roaches in mind, nothing! They infest everywhere. Refrigerator linings; they're all inside the copy machines and everything. Houston is the cockroach capital of the world. But those guys weren't even trying to keep ahead of them."

David nodded. "Okay, let's call an exterminator; a real pro. Have them spray down these new modulars before we do anything with them. The parking lot, the whole acreage! He can advise us from there."

"Okay, Axle, here's what I need you to do. Call some office supply stores and get some prices on four mid-size desks and chairs. Good stuff, but not fancy. Try to get the best combination of reasonable prices and quick delivery. You know, chairs for the desks, but also for customers across the desks."

"Yes, Sir, I can do that!" He was relieved for something to do, and also for someone to take charge.

Janice Collins arrived on shift for security, presenting Mallory with a new cell phone.

"Awesome, Janice, you're the greatest!" She sank onto the shady steps of the main church sanctuary, lowering Amelia's carrier down next to her, shooing mosquitoes.

She waved to Margaret, who continued to monitor all of their activity from her yard across a narrow street. The little lady scurried over in response to the friendly gesture. "I'm Mallory; this is Amelia," Mallory greeted warmly. "We already signed a contract, and they're setting up a closing at the title company for next week."

Margaret's bright eyes revealed that she was already in the loop.

"What I was wondering, Margaret, since I know we've already qualified as buyers, is if we could deposit earnest money, or pay for a lease, to take immediate possession of this property. I mean, we won't make any structural changes, whatsoever, until the deal is done; but if we could get the utilities going and start using it right away, it would help us immensely."

Mallory could tell the neighbor lady was processing the request. Margaret felt sorry for the beautiful girl and her baby out in the heat; her own home seemed much too humble to offer as a respite.

"I don't know why they couldn't work out somethin' quicker. Could I use your phone and save my legs from walkin' back and forth to use the telephone?"

-੨ ੩-

Daniel Faulkner went from the Tulsa airport to *GeoHy*, calling Diana again as soon as he reached his inner office.

"Did you get any rest at all?" she questioned.

He laughed. "Yeah, I guess more than anyone else did. Erik couldn't sleep, so he got right back up and went to the PD to question the guys that got arrested. David and Mallory had already bailed them all out of jail and were eating breakfast at three AM with all of them. Erik showed up at the same restaurant for a bite on the way to the airport. Said that they acted like a couple of guilty school kids. They haven't been to bed yet; they're forming a new Management Corporation and they're attacking that company with a fervor that makes me tired just thinking about it!"

"Wow!" was Diana's response. "Well, who was watching the baby? They aren't still dragging her around with them from pillar to post, are they? She needs a schedule, and-"

Daniel cut in with a laugh. "Well, I like the way we operate, and that we're in agreement about how we parent. Honey, we need to remember, that they're not us. They don't have to be 'us' to be okay. I'm pretty impressed with them."

"Well, wasn't David foolish? To just leave Mallory and the baby there"?

"Well, he wasn't really in light of how he perceived the situation. The thing that blows my mind is that Mallory's phone just totally stopped functioning when she needed it most. She was saying something that she shouldn't trust her phone and not God. I guess it just floors me every time I'm hit in the face again, with how much the devil would love to extinguish her light for the Lord. And, if he's after her that dramatically, he is us, too. Why did you quit making those sweaters with the sharks? They were a good reminder for me."

-੨ ੩-

443

David emerged back into blazing sunlight. The heat and atmosphere were still oppressive, but the infested building gave him the willies. He needed to talk to Mallory further about her experience. He was still amazed that she wasn't madder at him than all get out! Whatever that meant!

The office furniture delivery truck appeared, and he directed unloading into the new temporary buildings. He was relieved. They still smelled heavily of bug spray, but the exterminator had assured him the fumes wouldn't hurt the baby. Humming air conditioners seemed to be making a difference. At least a place a little fit for human habitation. He glanced around for Mallory and panicked when he couldn't see her. She answered her new phone immediately.

"Hey, where'd you go? I panicked when I couldn't see you."

"Sorry," she apologized. "I'm on another call I've been holding on. I'll call right back."

No chance to argue, and he turned his attention to another large commercial truck; a fencing company. A guy hopped out of the passenger seat. "We're on the clock here. You got permits?"

David was shocked. Evidently Mallory was keeping busy; maybe she had the cart before the horse, with the workers on site without permits, but she was right that when this place was up and running, it would be a target for malfeasance. He laughed easily. "We're so busy, that my wife and I aren't having much time to communicate. We need fencing around the property ASAP. I don't mind paying for your time, since we kind of created a snafu." He pulled out a fifty. "Would it work for you guys to go eat lunch on me, while I get the permits in order?"

The other man's response was good-natured in turn. "Sure, we'll check back in an hour and a half. If I know city hall, you won't have any kind of permit by then. But we can unload all this stuff, if you'll have security to keep it from walkin' off."

David slapped the door of the truck as it swung shut. "Sounds like a good plan. A couple more things for me to address"!

Mallory called back as the truck geared up past him.

"Hey, who were you talking to?"

"Okay, you are not going to believe, but I managed to lease the church plant for two hundred dollars until we close on it next week. I've been on the phone with the utility companies. We can't start tearing out or retrofitting at all until the place is actually ours. And, there's a bit of a roach problem here, too. Margaret told me that the pastor and congregation were always aggressive with the problem, but with the machine shop not fighting the bug battle, it made it worse. The bug man's here now fumigating us."

He laughed. "You've been busy. That's great. I'll come over for you; the temporary buildings now have furniture and air conditioning. The fencing guys were here, but I have to go get permits lined up. Is Collins staying on top of you?"

"She is. I have plenty of calls I want to make."

"Word of David's new project was actually already the buzz. People in the building permit office moved into high gear. "Good luck; you'll need it. Give us a call when you're ready for an inspection."

He waved the paper jauntily as he exited. "Will do"!

❦

Delia O'Shaughnessy finished her daily 'to do list' and straightened her office to perfection.

"Shay, did I hear you come in?"

He appeared at the top of the staircase. "Yes, Ma'am, it's good to be home. I was going to say 'hello', but I could tell you were on the phone. How's my beautiful grandmother? You look gorgeous in that color. I was starting to unpack, but if it's time for tea, I'll finish later."

Delia regarded him wonderingly. It was miraculous, really, the way he was in her life, looking after her, helping take over a family business that she had at one time, figured was going to die with her. He was incredibly handsome, and it looked to her like he had grown yet taller, and was more filled out, manly and muscular.

"I cancelled tea. I was hoping that your flight would arrive on time. What do you think about going out somewhere for a steak? The Patterson deal just funded, and I feel like celebrating. Finish your unpacking first."

"How was Emma?" Delia's eyes twinkled as she inquired.

Seated across a white tablecloth, Shay met her bright, inquisitive gaze. "She's fabulous. She sends you her love. Shannon's okay, too. David and Jeff are giving him pointers on remodeling projects. I'm pretty sure building stuff isn't his calling, but he hasn't grasped that yet. He finally made a statement to Bransom about some of the stuff he knew. He's relieved about finally doing it."

Delia's eyes clouded. "That's good. I think he'll be safer since he talked than when people were afraid he might."

Shay shrugged. "Yes'm, I hope so. So, the Patterson deal! Tell me about all the details!" His changing to a better subject felt awkward, but she rose valiantly to his effort.

"Yes, Shay. It's amazing. Lawrence approved our end of it last week; he thought it was a sweet deal. A lot of work for you though, overseeing the mills! A lot of traveling"!

"Well, I enjoy traveling, and most of the time, I can take Emma with me."

"Well, that sounds great, and it's not my business about how you're planning a family~"

He laughed. "Well, yes, Ma'am. Especially since we aren't even married yet! David and Mallory are doing everything together and keeping Amelia right with them. I mean, they nearly had things get ugly, but they're okay now."

Cutting into a crab cake with a small fork, she looked up sharply. "What did that mean, Shay? Where were they, and what do you mean, 'things nearly got ugly'?"

He dipped a spoonful of chowder. "Well, they were in Houston~"

"Oh, I never did like that place! Bugs everywhere, even in the supposedly better establishments. Winters are long here, but at least it kills off some of the vermin. Try the crab cake; it's excellent, Shay."

She was right. He continued the narrative.

"Okay, backing up, David did such an outstanding job with the *Chandler* properties for Roger, that Roger paid him a whole bunch more money. Also, his work garnered the attention of some of the big-wigs in Houston's City Planner's office."

"Ah, and whenever you get accolades like that, you also get attention you wish you didn't"

"Well, sort of. I mean David wanted it to bring more Houston jobs because he likes the contractor down there. He and his men always need more jobs. What he didn't know was that this bunch of clowns was owned by a huge German Company that's pretty much clueless about what's really happening in Houston, TX. So, they're desperate to get their run down mess updated to code to keep from being shut down. I guess when David told them there was no way, even if they had money to throw at it~"

"What, Shay?" Delia's features were the picture of concern.

"Well, they had taken David to another set of buildings thirty minutes away. He had left Mallory and Amelia in kind of a rat-hole, thinking he'd

446

be right back. Well, he kept insisting he needed to get back, and they should let the corporation that owns them handle the problems. Well, they kept insisting he could surely do something! Then they wanted him to go drinking with them. He said, 'no', again and they started threatening him and carrying on."

"Where was their security?"

"Uh, good question. I guess they told Darrell they'd call him to come back for them when they were done. Usually David considers himself Mallory's security. Anyway, for some reason, Mallory's cell phone died on her completely. It's a long story, but now they're working hard to fix the place up and form a Management Corporation, offering to oversee operations where the ownership is separated by distance."

"Oh my goodness, Shay! What is this world coming to? I know it makes me sound old, but I can remember when people didn't act that way! I read a verse about that this morning."

Proverbs 14:34 Righteousness exalteth a nation: but sin is a reproach to any people.

⊣ ⊢

On returning, David became involved with the immense fencing project. The foreman on the job, also partner in the company, was clearing the plans with David. The architect in David preferred better planning than to have the company show up on site, saying they were already charging for their time, demanding an answer off the top of his head, what he wanted done. So, getting the permits, yeah~ But Mallory was really pushing when she didn't know anything about stuff. Maybe she felt like making mistakes was better than doing nothing; he wasn't sure. Another delivery truck appeared and she waved them toward the church to unload.

He strode over. "What's this coming now?"

"Office systems. We can't bring in the computers or anything from the old buildings. Sam is sending someone tomorrow to get the files off the old stuff. We need to keep this company open for business; isn't that the idea?"

He scratched his head. "Well, yeah, I guess it is. I mean, if we're bringing in expensive new electronics and equipment, we need the fence in place. I wasn't ready for these fence guys, Mallory. I'd like a minute to draw a master plan; maybe even an hour or two. I don't even have a survey to determine where the boundary lines are."

She frowned slightly. "I didn't hire any fencing company, David. Maybe Dale did. I agree it's a priority, even if we have to move parts of it as we get farther into the project. But, while you're considering the master plan, can I ask you something?"

"Sure!" He realized that the strain of the previous day, no sleep, and the frenzy of the current job was making him short-tempered. He followed her out the side door of the main church building.

"Since this is going to be one melded property, I was thinking it would be better to place the main access, the driveway and the gates around here."

"Why? We'll have to pour concrete to make a new drive. Let's keep it where it is."

"Okay, here me out, please."

"Okay, I'm sorry. I'm listening. At least it's cooler here."

She laughed. All right, thank you! Look, this is only a block from that main intersection. It's controlled with turning lanes and turning arrows, and everything. The present entrance, with the median strip, forces customers to go up three long blocks before they can make a u turn and get back around. And traffic moves fast. There isn't a deceleration and turning lane for right hand turns. I just think it's something to consider. And it looks prettier and more inviting."

"I'm not positive drillers and miners care a lot about the aesthetics, but you're right about the sheer logistics, too. Are you hungry?"

She nodded. "I am. Food's actually on the way. Give it fifteen minutes and a caterer's coming with barbecue!"

His eyes sparkled with renewed energy. "Mallory Anderson, you are truly amazing! Hope you ordered lots!"

She laughed. "Why would you wonder?"

⊰ ⊱

Wednesday dawned hot and humid, actually chasing a way a night which had also been-hot and humid!

David was unsure how to respond when Jeff rolled on-site followed by a couple of other pickup trucks with more help on site.

"I know you're trying to give these Houston guys as much work as possible, but I also know you're in a time crunch to do everything at once. Don't worry. Waylon and Luke are both keeping the lid on stuff at the Ranch. Whatever you need us to do; we can tear down, help on the fence, order stuff, be gophers."

David nodded. "Okay, get some of your guys uncrating those new tables and set up a bunch right on the parking lot. Sam and some FBI tech people are getting ready to go through the old computers."

How 'bout setting up in the shade instead"? Jeff looked longingly at the trees and lawn on the new piece of land.

"Well, that would be okay, but we're trying to contain a cockroach problem. This is the cockroach capital of the world, and you're standing at the epicenter. They'll skitter everywhere when we bring out the electronics. Got a couple of guys ready with exterminating equipmen."!

David's jaw dropped with awe as another truck barreled onto the lot." The driver hopped down, gazing at his manifest and the surroundings quizzically. "Is this where the weddin' is?"

Mallory approached, pushing Amelia in her stroller. "Hello," she greeted. "I'm Mallory. I didn't actually say 'wedding', I think I used the term, 'event'. I believe the financial arrangements are taken care of?"

He nodded. "Okay, so this is actually to get set up in the church yard? That makes more sense."

She laughed. "We're crazy people. Don't try to make sense of what we're doing. I actually want the pavilion set up right about here. Yes, sir, on the asphalt. Delivery trucks can still get in and out. This is perfect. Of course we want the air conditioner up and running as quickly *as possible." She turned her gaze toward David. "These guys are providing chairs with the rental; can we wait and set the tables up in here? In the mean-time, Luke, could you take a couple of the camp crew to the discount store? I have a list. Ice chests and ice, fans, light bulbs, cleaning supplies, toilet paper; to name a few~get lots of snacks, too! Cookies, and chips and dip! Just grab a big assortment. And lots of it! We're going to have a big work force and guests in and out throughout the day."

David scowled. "What are you waiting for? Use a Ranch check."

Chapter 35:   ACCOMPLISHMENTS

Harold Schmidt directed his driver past the *South Houston Machine Company* once again. Furious with Derek Harland for having deceived him about the true depth of the crisis *South Houston Machine* was in, he was trying to do the same thing with his superiors. He guessed he could sympathize now with their panic.

David was aware each time the 'Benz' appeared. Derek had informed him that the car belonged to the company, and Schmidt was keeping an eye on the beehive of activity. David was busy helping with the fence. Without having a copy of the survey on site, surely it would be okay as long as it ringed the asphalt. David conferred with the expert, explaining Mallory's plan to move the entryway around onto the cross-street.

"That's a great idea! How did you think of that? I'm just so locked into where the driveway is, that I never would have considered-"

"I hear ya. Actually, my wife thought of it. The new property presents more options, and it can alleviate some of the traffic problems and difficulties for customer access. I have to admit I thought that she had hired y'all before I was quite ready."

The fencing contractor laughed. "No, it was Dale. With the economy tanked, people steal everything worse than ever. His insurance company has helped him take a couple of heavy hits on supplies he has had delivered to different sites. Now he always erects fences, lighting, and security cameras before he gets the first nail delivered."

That made sense. David felt a sense of awe that the only thing ever stolen from the Arkansas property was a couple of cords of firewood.

With the tables ready in the air-conditioned pavilion, David led the machine company employees in hauling the electronics. As he feared, the disgusting bugs swarmed at the disturbance. He couldn't stand them, tensing against the revulsion. He couldn't drop the stuff before files could be recovered. He had actually considered wearing industrial hazmat gear, but he was too hot for that. Fortunately, with everyone helping, he only needed to make the one trip. He grabbed the canister and directed the hose full force at the offensive legion.

As the Mercedes approached once more, he waved it down. The tastefully turned out German executive and the smooth car intimidated, but David moved forward anyway, extending his hand as he introduced himself. "Welcome to mayhem."

"Au contraire"! The businessman laughed at his own attempt at the French phrase. "I beg to differ with you. If it seems chaotic, I am amazed at both your progress and your brilliant planning!"

"Uh, thank you, Sir." David was pleased at the compliment, but nothing looked to him like it was progressing or brilliant."

"Anything that seems brilliant was my wife's idea, I'm sure. We have been trying to get in touch with you. We may be a little presumptuous-"

The stoic guy shrugged noncommittally. "I would not say 'presumptuous', but I must confess I do not understand why, especially in light of the way things developed. You have good grounds for a law suit; you owe these men nothing, who threatened you and your family with harm."

"Well, actually, we do have a method to our madness. I need to get in a couple more intensive hours; then my wife and I are going to get presentable to close on that other property. We need it yesterday, and the church that's selling it needs the money last year! Would you be able to join us for dinner at seven? We're staying at the Intercontinental by the Galleria. Its restaurant is great!"

"I shall see you at seven o'clock."

Mallory was busy! Between caring for Amelia and making plans and ordering goods, her time flew past. She placed a call to her mom.

"Mallory are you okay? Erik just now filled me in on-"

"Yeah, Mom; we're great! I have a project I'm calling you for your expertise on! I need some new landscaping put in."

"Well, yes, Honey, but it goes in last so all the workers and heavy equipment and stuff-"

"I know that, Mom. And some may get damaged and need replacement, but I want to make things look as pretty and groomed as possible, even in the interim. Like the church had actually bought out other properties in the neighborhood, planning to expand. Then, they ended up just relocating. We have a couple of city blocks that are kind of separate from the main church complex. I want to create a park for the neighborhood. With flowers, and grass, and paths, and trees, and flowers, and shrubs!. And a fountain that looks pretty, but that kids can play in. I don't know where to start."

"Awesome! I'm on my way. Roger's always after me to get down there and check on things at *Chandler*; the thought never appeals to me. But with you guys and Erik down there, and a big gardening project, I'm on my way. I'll rent a car so I can get to *Chandler* and around to the lawn and garden stores. Tell Amelia Grandma's on the way. She can help me plant flowers!"

"She heard you, Mom. She can hardly wait." Mallory felt oddly emotional.

⚜ ⚜

Back for a quick break in Dallas, David and Mallory celebrated their first year of marriage. His eyes met hers across china and linens. "I love you Mallory! You're more my dream-girl than ever! We've had quite the eventful year!" At home, he presented her with a small paper bag of candy he had sought for everywhere!

She laughed. "You found all my favorites!"

He nodded. "I try! The wax pop bottle set was the toughest! Here, put on the jewelry and I'll send a picture to Faulkner! He doesn't think I treat you good enough!"

Eyes alight she played along, posing with the candy necklace and bracelet.

She presented him with a nice acoustic guitar. He tuned it and sang to her and Amelia.

The Way You Look Tonight and, *Daddy's Little Girl*!

⚜ ⚜

Details with the German conglomerate pretty much consigned their failing Houston operation to the hands of *D&M Management Corporation*. Given carte blanch, David and Mallory tackled the offensive materials issue

452

and set up training sessions. They gave the talks on personal excellence, and expecting full effort and focus in exchange for a reworked benefits package. New computers were for business purposes only! They meant it, and followed up on the edict.

The old buildings were razed and the huddle of church structures updated and remodeled to serve new purposes. A new, lighted sign stretched skyward, and business from advertising and the newly energized sales department picked up dramatically.

Mallory's park progressed gorgeously. With the standing trees, new palms, shrubs and plants, the space drew people immediately. David's crews set cute benches into concrete and created asphalt bike paths and a basketball court. The fountain was an immediate hit, and brightly colored ceramic planters spilled every hue of flower. Elegant, old-fashioned street lamps provided illumination, and charming hand-painted signs illustrated Bible verses. One pictured sheep and a staff, stating: *I am the good Shepherd.* Another located beside one of the light posts proclaimed: *Jesus, the light of the* world! Beside the playground: *Jesus loves the little children!* HPD kept an eye on things to prevent the park's being taken over by gangs and the unsavory section of society. Still, Mallory was negotiating with Roger Sanders about Mac, the head of security at the *Chandler Chemical Company.*

"Come on, Roger, she wheedled. He has abilities you aren't using! Set him free, and he'll be able to be more helpful to you, and lots of other people, too."

"What do you mean by that? Aren't you trying to hire him away from me?"

Mallory laughed. "Would if I could, without making you mad at me. No, here are David's and my thoughts. We should set him up as his own security corporation! He can earn more with less tax liability~"

"Okay, I'm following you now. He hires and trains additional security personnel and we contract with him for them. How's that different than the cops-for-hire of similar security companies?"

"Well, he'll be newer and smaller, hungry and more hands-on over his organization. If he succeeds in a great way, in twenty years, he may have a bloated, inefficient organization of inadequate and under trained clowns."

"Okay; good point. Give me time to think about it! And talk to Mac; I'm not sure he's hankering for the headaches of becoming a corporation."

"Well, he'd be in a great position in the marketplace. I hate to say it, but the need for corporate security is going to get worse and not better. He could train his own security people, but he could offer outside training, too~! Either one of us would make money backing him. The possibilities are endless."

⚑ ⚐

Mallory glanced at caller ID as she pushed the button to accept a call. From Rhonna! "Hello, Rhonna! Hey, you doing okay? We've been so busy the past month I've barely hit the Dallas office."

Silence, rather than a response!

"Rhonna, are you okay?"

"Yes Ma'am, Mallory. I'm fine! I think I might have made this big mistake, and you said~" Her words trailed off in her struggle to speak.

"Yes, Rhonna, I did! I meant it, too! How soon can you give Jim notice and come back?"

"He is now defunct! Taking all the earnings for himself. None of us got our last checks; creditors are mad! I already filled out my paperwork in triplicate to come back. I~I~"

"Awesome news! I mean, not about Jim and his company. I'm sorry for that. Can you start back tomorrow? Who all didn't get paid? Any good people we can use? If anyone wants to apply, encourage them. If you're impressed, send their info to me pronto! Maybe we can work out some cash advances, or something. Welcome back. Get to work!"

Rhonna smiled, relieved, as her phone went dark.

⚑ ⚐

"You're not going to believe this," David's voice.

Mallory laughed. "Try me! Then, I have news for you!"

"Okay, I'll go first. We went to shoot a few baskets, and I noticed someone put a Buddha in our park. It has some smoking incense and a few oranges that look like they've had a hard life!"

"You have got to be kidding me! You threw it all away, right?"

"No, I wasn't sure what to do. What's your news?"

"My news is that Rhonna's back, and she has a bead on some other potential employees. David, go throw that garbage away; just throw it in

454

the dumpster. Although we've turned it into a space for public use, it's still our private property.

"Great news about Rhonna," He responded. "You're right about the trash. Anything people leave behind is litter."

"I think so; if someone wants to worship Buddha, they can buy their own property and set up Buddhas there. We're not establishing an 'All roads lead to heaven' mentality at our place. One of the things bringing God's judgment on ancient Israel, was that the wicked kings began bringing false deities and idols into the temple at Jerusalem. God hates idols!"

⊣ ⊢

"You needed something, Mother?" The question came tinged with sarcastic disdain.

Lilly's eyes shot sparks. "Or I wouldn't have sent for you, Michael." She tapped a picture. "Try to make it clean this time."

"I always do."

"Hmmmph! Boston? Agent Bransom still references that fiasco nearly every time I see him."

"I'll take care of Agent Bransom!"

Lilly's voice rose. "You'll do as I say"

The handsome man shrugged nonchalantly. "I've never had the pleasure of visiting Boston. I think our sworn enemies took out Oscar Malovich. Hence, the sloppiness! Do you mind if I smoke?" He lit up, not waiting for permission.

Lilly squinted through the haze. "Ah-h-h, Malovich; you are thinking that because he used that route to smuggle Mallory, he gave the route away! A route through which Iran was smuggling quite a bit of material for her nuclear aspirations"!

He nodded, pinching a piece of tobacco from the end of his tongue. "My assumption is that they framed the Egyptian on the Harvard Campus to point suspicion at Israel for the entire operation. Malovich is no big loss, either way. Nor the Egyptian student! Does anyone care beside Bransom?"

"Be careful, Michael."

"And this assignment? Is for Israel, her economy and Diamond industry?"

Lilly's gaze didn't falter. "Always! Why would you question?"

⊰ ⊱

Mallory tickled her freshly bathed baby, relishing the giggling response. "M-mmm, love you Sugar-bunchies!" She smoothed on lotion. "Why are you growing so big so fast? Where's Mommie's little baby girl?"

David appeared. "Hey, I heard that! The proper question is 'What happened to Daddy's little baby girl?' Say, da-da." He tickled the baby's chin. "Da-da"!

Her response was a big smile.

"Ah, she always saves her biggest smiles for you!"

David slid his arm around Mallory's waist and kissed her. "Maybe, but she loves her momma!"

"I think I hear the chow bell. I'm hungry; I'll hurry and finish dressing her."

⊰ ⊱

"Look; there's David's truck!" Jeremiah's voice rang with enthusiasm.

"Yes, I saw them pull in about an hour ago," Daniel answered. "I'm dying to see them, too; but I hated to barge over the second they arrived."

"Maybe they'll eat supper in the chow hall. They like to spend time with the men and see how the operation's going," Alexandra added.

"I can't wait to see Amelia. She gets cuter every day, judging by the pictures Mallory sends me." Diana moved to the back porch.

"Honey~"

She laughed at her husband's concern. "Come on out and sit with me. It's easier to spy on them from out here!"

⊰ ⊱

Caramel Du Boise paused long enough to check her electronics for updates. David and Mallory's baby was cuter than a button; Rhonna Abbott seemed to be returning to *DiaMo*; and what she was really searching for, Amon was loving his work with the *Patrick O'Shaughnessy Foundation* in two African nations. She regarded his smiling picture for long moments. Her heart had been torn apart for months, since she had put him in contact with Mallory and Dr. Kenneth Wilson. Her hopes were that Amon could get a taste of the trials ministering in third-world countries and come back, more eager to form a medical partnership with her in Hope, Arkansas. In that instant, rather than changing his heart, God changed hers. Tears filled her eyes with the relief of surrender.

⊨ ⊨

"Okay, they're heading down to the chow hall," Alexandra announced. "But now, Ryan needs a diaper~"

"You guys go on," Diana reached for her youngest. "Surely they won't evaporate away before I can change him and get down there!"

After the hubbub of greetings and settling babies, filling plates and drinks, and asking the blessing, everyone began to talk at once.

"Rhonna's coming back, and she might bring some good people with her."

"That's good," Diana responded. "She's cute as everything; I thought she treated you kind of badly."

"Well, those kids are so young, and they're feeling their way in the world. I'll be glad to get her back."

"Yeah," David spoke slowly. "She's an awesome worker; but I've been thinking, maybe we should talk to Jim. You know; find out what happened? I kind of researched him when Rhonna first started talking to him~"

"Oh-ho-ho-ho!" Mallory caught on quickly. "Duh, Mallory, we're looking for in-trouble and under-performing companies for D&M. You are absolutely right. Maybe he got caught in a cash crunch. With banking tightened up the way it has~"

"I guess I'll try calling him in the morning." David opened a jar of baby food and began spooning it to a hungry baby girl.

"She's adorable! A little Mallory made over!" Diana's lilting voice.

"Well, I was hoping her hair wouldn't be red, but I think she's really sweet."

They all laughed at her words.

"Hey, Mallory, did anyone tell you that I've been called to preach?" Jeremiah's transitioning the conversation was far from smooth.

"That makes me so happy, Jeremiah. I can't say I'm surprised at all!"

"You aren't?" Diana's voice showed her amazement. "Of course, we're thrilled, but we can't say we saw it coming."

"Yeah? And what about Alexandra"? Mallory decided she might as well seize the moment.

"What about her?" Daniel's expression was totally blank, then, creased with concern. He didn't want this to be about Tommy Haynes.

"Well, she's nearly a senior and she can start on some college classes. What does she want to study?"

Diana's blue eyes widened expressively. "Nursing! All the Prescott girls study nursing."

David tried to shoot Mallory a warning look. At which, she usually proceeded, or clammed up, according to his cautions. But not this time!

"Well, um, she's not a Prescott girl. She's a Faulkner! I'm glad you studied nursing and that you're so good at it! I owe my life to your pulling me out of some crunches."

"Yes, you see? Nursing skills are vital—"

An amazed Daniel held his hand up, silencing his surprised mate. "Whoa, Honey. You're right; your skills are vital. You've save my life before, too. But we want our kids to follow the Lord's will for their lives."

Diana nodded. "Once she gets her nursing degree—"

David wiped Amelia's mouth, and pulled her free of the high chair. "Mallory, we better go—"

"Here, let me hold her." Daniel stretched out his hands. "Don't rush off. We care a lot about what y'all think. Diana?"

Diana fought tears. "You both admitted that nursing saved your lives!"

Mallory nodded. "Because it's true! But, because you're a nurse and a good one, doesn't mean that Alexandra—"

"Well, she wouldn't have to work in nursing—"

"I'll get a cobbler and we can have dessert up at the house. Meeting to reconvene in fifteen"! David scrambled to gather the cobbler and his family.

"Are you mad at me?" Mallory could hardly bear anyone to be upset with her, let alone David.

"No, I guess it's a can of worms that needed opening. I just didn't want to play out our drama in front of everyone down there."

Mallory changed Amelia into her pj's, fed her a bottle, changed her diaper, and had her sleeping soundly—with no further word from the Faulkners.

"You were right. I shouldn't have pressed it."

"Well, I think I was wrong, and you were right. They're like my mom and dad. My parents really loved me a lot, but, they wouldn't listen to me, and I wouldn't listen to them. I mean, Alexandra could do worse stuff than not being a nurse. I didn't know Diana was that rigid about it"!

"Yeah, I don't know if 'rigid' is the right word. She just always assumed, I guess. Now she's kind of shocked, almost like it's an affront to her persona as a nurse. Diana's kind of right; it comes in handy having a medical expert that knows what to do in crisis. But, everyone can't be that."

David nodded. "That's one of your strengths; being able to see both sides of an issue. I don't think they're mad at you for bringing things to a head. They may just be having a family talk, the three of them. I don't think Daniel had an idea Diana was that determined about the nursing."

Mallie's phone buzzed with a text from Diana: *Is it too late for us to come for that cobbler?*

Mallory texted back: *No, come on. We're just starting coffee!*

⊣ ⊢

Harold Schmidt turned in an itemized list of expenses from renovation and modernization of the *South Houston Machine Company* to the comptroller in the German main office. "This is the main part. I'm certain a few more expenses will drift in."

The comptroller squinted at Schmidt quizzically. "I'm not certain how you came out of this so well. It seems that it could have easily gone the other direction."

The executive nodded almost imperceptibly as he exited. Yes, he was well aware of that! Very well aware! He was impressed with the young couple who had no desire to sue, and showed such a work ethic. An ethic they were demanding of the employees at the machine company. If their profits matched their forecast, Schmidt hoped to recommend many of their initiatives throughout the entire operation. Yes, he had come back from the brink of disaster very well, indeed!

⊣ ⊢

Daniel, Diana, and Alexandra all seemed to have been crying. Jeremiah and Cassandra helped with their younger siblings while participating in the meeting.

"I just still think that once she has the training, she'll be glad~" Diana, woebegone, hadn't given up her cherished notion.

"Okay, Honey, we've been over that!"

Mallory poured coffee and glasses of milk while David scooped ice cream atop the still warm blackberry cobbler.

"Okay, back to the business at hand!" David took control of the meeting as he settled into a chair at the kitchen table. "First of all, Jeremiah~ I hardly said anything to you about your being called to preach. I'm really glad for you! But that's a subject that's hard for me to deal with, because my Dad still hasn't given up on making me into a pastor. There's just nothing about pasturing or preaching that appeals to me. Just like nothing about nursing appeals to Alexandra. I'm glad for all the preachers and nurses that there are, but~"

Diana's hands shook as she fumbled with her coffee. "Well, I, um, I just always thought~"

"I could tell you did, Mom, and I kind of tried to drop little hints. I don't like hospitals and blood, and stuff."

"Well, you get used to it, and it's just this skill set~"

"Diana! We get that!" Mallory's eyes snapped. "Stop acting like it's so personal. She respects you as a medical professional, to no end! We all do! We keep telling you that! But she's not you, and she doesn't want to study nursing!"

Diana bridled in response. "Well, in this whole evening of trying to tell us what she doesn't want, she hasn't spoken a word about what she does want to do. She could still take the nursing prerequisites while she's deciding~"

"Well, you haven't really given her a chance."

Diana addressed their first-born. "Well, what, Alexandra? The design business?"

"No, Mom. I mean I like that, and I like the business experience it gives me. It's better than nursing."

Daniel filled with sudden dread. Evidently, he didn't know his own family. His eldest daughter, seemingly happy and submissive, suddenly filled with her own ideas! He fought panic! Fearing her answer, he forced a smile and asked the loaded question. "Okay, if you don't want to be a nurse, we get that, Al; but what do you want to pursue?"

She burst into tears. "You really don't know?"

He gazed helplessly toward David who shrugged.

"Okay, Mallory, you're the one who started us down this path!" Daniel strove for levity "Do you know the answer to the mystery question?"

She met his gaze levelly. "I think so. I think she wants to be a Geologist and work at *GeoHy*"!

Chapter 36: AFTERWORD

Mallory gently tucked their sleeping daughter into her bed at the Ranch. "Look how long she is," her words a soft whisper to David.

He moved nearer, circling her waist with his arms. "Yeah, everybody's got it right about how fast they grow! She gets cuter every day, too! And more fun! Look! It's starting to snow! I can't wait for Christmas!"

The baby squirmed, and Mallie put her finger to David's lips. They crept softly to the master suite where a fire beckoned cozily.

He drew her close and searched the depths of eyes made greener by the Spruce-tone of her Alpaca jacket. "It's been another sensational year! In every way! I have a special gift ordered for you!"

Her lovely features changed from laughter to soberness.

"I have a gift order in for you, too! But delivery will take a while! It's a special order!"